NAYTHORN BLACKMANE UNICORN

AND

HIS ANIMAL BAND

Book 2

G. D. Hanson

This is the second part of Blackmane Unicorns, a story that takes three more parts to tell.

Briarburr Blackmane and the Unicorn Hold

Naythorn Blackmane Unicorn and His Animal Band

Naythorn Blackmane Unicorn and the Gift of the Winged Horse

Naythorn Blackmane Unicorn and the Seventh Prince

Naythorn Blackmane Unicorn and the Ghost Wolf

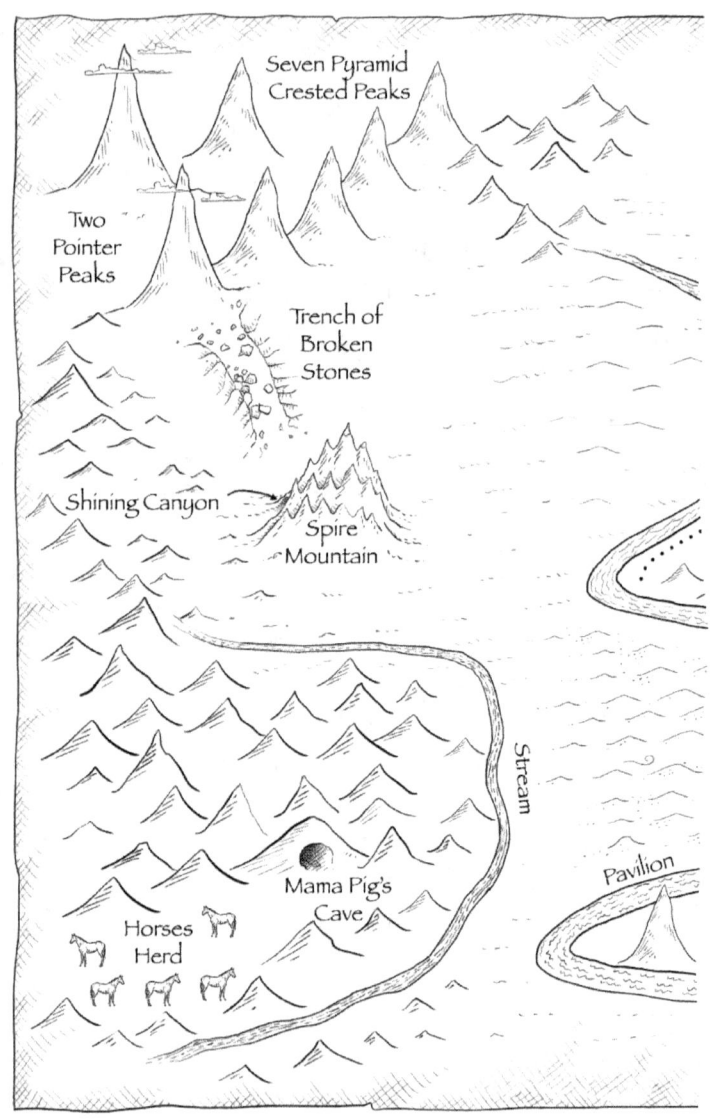

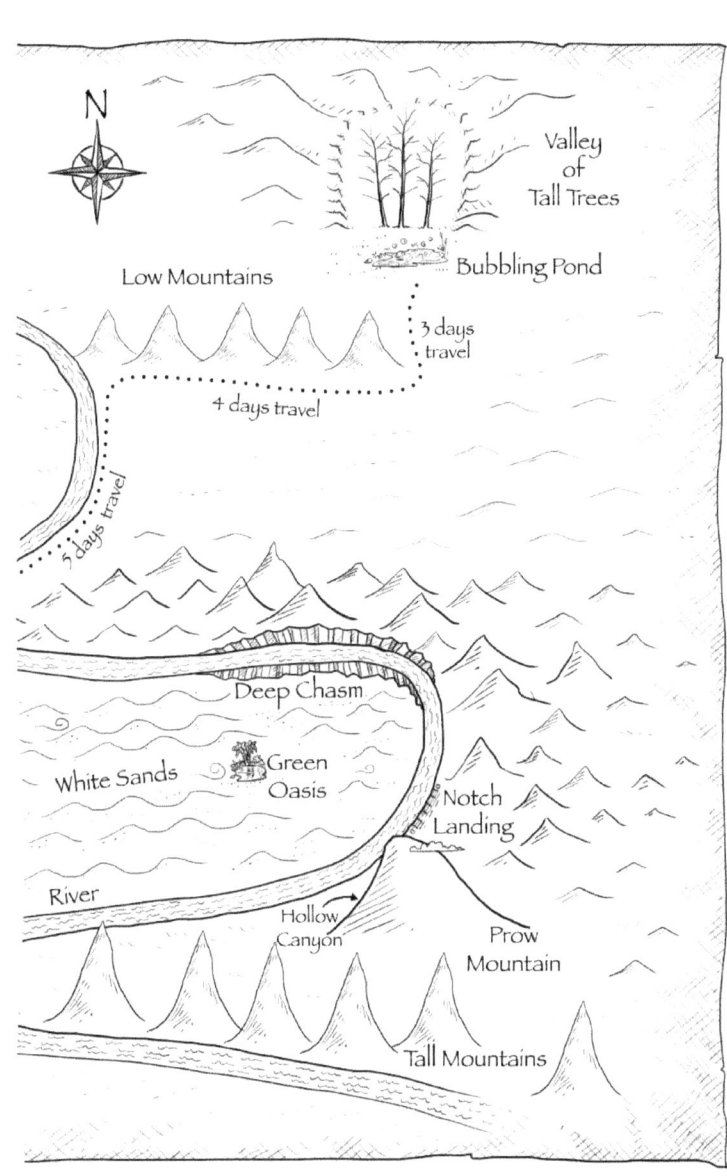

hidden in a secret pavilion

Psalms (Authorized KJV)

CHAPTER 1

OUT FROM WITTANOR HOLD

"Five against one is *not fair!*"

"It is not up to you, *Naaay...thorrnn!* I am bigger! I can make you play bite-tag!"

"Why should I?" objected the blackmaned unicorn shaking back-and-forth his head. "So that the arrogant Hoovefort and his four followers can all bite me at the same time? Only the unicorn who is it, has the right to bite! No! Today I will not give in to Hoovefort the bully. If no other unicorn will stand up for me, I will stand up for myself. I do not care if I get in trouble. Anyway, here in the unicorn hold I am *always* in trouble."

After eighteen moons of biting-tag punishment, the year-and-a-half-old Naythorn had become agile at dodging and blocking other young unicorns, and biting them back so they ouched loudly and became *it*. But this afternoon's odds of five against one were decidedly against him.

"You see that, Vor," neighed Hoovefort to the biggest of the four unicorns with him, "the freak unicorn with the black mane thinks he can neigh *nay* to me."

Five unicorn stallions began to walk towards Naythorn. But instead of running away like he had always done at the start of the *Bite Naythorn* game, the blackmane suddenly charged at Hoovefort. Butting a shoulder into his chest, Naythorn knocked the astonished bully onto his side. The blackmane next wheeled hips into the belly of Vor, making the stallion to lose his balance and topple over. When Naythorn jumped threatening hooves at the three unicorns with Hoovefort and Vor, they quickly retreated from the blackmaned unicorn whose eyes this day glared a look particularly fierce.

Back on his feet Hoovefort charged at Naythorn. The blackmane feinted left, instead moved right, and whirled front hooves into a shoulder of the skidding Hoovefort. The bully could not prevent himself from once more toppling onto his side.

"You hurt me! It was unfair to attack me and Vor without warning! Next time you will not catch me off guard! I will teach you your place! You are nothing more than... a freak unicorn!" That neighed, Hoovefort and Vor limped after three young unicorns no longer inspired by the game of *Everyone Bites Naythorn*.

In the distance Naythorn saw his sire shake reprovingly his head at him. At that, the young unicorn reared up sullen at the day.

"*Nyeerhaargruhgruhh!* I do not care if my sire is again upset with me," neighed the blackmane boxing a foreleg at a stealthy shadow. "It is enough that for the first time I was not *forced* to be the victim of bullying games. My sides and shoulders are not even that sore, and Hoovefort will not tomorrow bother me."

The blackmane kicked at a flowering thorn bush that he wished was his sire, and asked himself why Cabalblade could not stand up for his offspring. But the year-and-a-halfling knew the answer to that question. Every time Cabalblade saw his colt's black mane, the big stallion was reminded that he had sired *a misfit*. What made it worse for his sire was that the one and only strangely colored horse in the unicorn hold, was his one and only colt.

As the afternoon sun traveled slowly westward the restive young stallion wanted to go off somewhere, anywhere away from the hold of the unicorn herd, to cool his hide. On a quarrelsome day in the life of a young misfit unicorn, the forbidden side of the barrier forest beckoned.

For an almost full-grown unicorn, or for that matter for a unicorn of any age, Wittanor Hold was a very safe place. But because Naythorn had the ingrained habit of saying *no* amidst a herd of horned horses that reflexively said *yes*, for him the peace and security of Wittanor had become... numbingly and boringly restrictive.

It was said that an occasional black panther was the only predator that dared to enter the unicorn hold. But in all his eighteen moons Naythorn had only once seen a panther. The easy life in Wittanor provided so few challenges, that according to his sire even the unicorn guard stallions had become lackadaisical in duty.

The blackmane had been many times told that powerful unicorn magic rippled invisible waves into the spiritual ocean of life. And that the existence of unicorns made a little more noble, albeit in some unknowable way, the lives of animal persons near and far. How much nobler, Naythorn had never been told. The blackmane held the opinion that it was too easy for unicorns to relax in the protected hold, where with little thought they pertained to something favored and good.

Beyond the straight-poled barrier trees that grew on the inland side of Wittanor Hold, flowed the Alone River... that was so named because it was the only river that unicorns knew about. Naythorn was convinced that other rivers had to flow back-and-forth across lands and places far beyond Wittanor. Of course, unicorns other than himself did not care to know where meandered other rivers. The Alone River, the limiting edge of Wittanor, as well signified the limit and cessation of unicorn curiosity.

The maverick unicorn had many times thought to himself that just like the Alone River, he was also destined to lead a life solitary and apart. But if because of his black mane he was to be set apart, and in the midst of a herd of magical unicorn horses be made to feel alone, he might just as well on this day have all by himself an adventure... beyond the confines of the unicorn hold. After all, by ably defending himself against five young unicorn stallions he had earned the right to have some fun. Unfortunately, the rebellious and adventuresome Blackmane had been fifty times informed that the lands beyond the Alone River were places of trouble and discord. Actually, that one and same instruction had been invoked by his sire Cabalblade more like one hundred times.

As Naythorn contemplated skirting around inviolate unicorn precepts, his mind presented a fleeting image of his deceased mare scolding him for daring to think of escape beyond the limits of Wittanor Hold. Still, Naythorn missed his mare. It was not fair that barely three moons after he was born, his dam had died.

He was sure that upon first nuzzling her little foal's shockingly black mane, his mare had concluded that her colt was born with a wild streak in him. The look of her foal's black mane went against the sheen of his mare's pure white coat. For a respected mare of a stately clan whose every member wore a hide displaying nothing but the color white, to bring a blackmaned foal into the world was very inconvenient. His black markings were simply... *untoward.* In that regard it did not help that predatory panthers possessed as well black colored hides. Not just his mare, but all the unicorn mares wondered from what unfortunate circumstance had come Naythorn's strange black markings.

Naythorn had learned to tolerate his cousins, their cousins, and their cousins' cousins making fun of him. It hurt far more that upon noticing his mane, his mare had presumed to see rebellious thoughts lurking behind her foal's eyes.

"Nothing in life is fair," lamented Naythorn shaking his mane. "For most unicorns life turns out too nice. For me, life stays ever and always... difficult." The horned horses that overheard his grumbling paid not one bite of attention to Naythorn's complaint.

Cabalblade, Elianor, Aneilee

When tussles broke out among the colts, as had once more just happened, the unicorn matriarch Elianor and the unicorn high escort Aneilee looked at once to see... *where was Naythorn.* In their minds the blackmane that stood a hoof taller than any other colt his age, was most likely to be the culprit found in the middle of the problem of the day. Naythorn was sure that unlike his departed mare, Aneilee could really read behind his eyes. Today she did not take the time to try.

Accompanied by the matriarch and high escort, Cabalblade trotted toward Naythorn. Observing the nervous demeanors of his sire, Elianor, and Aneilee made Naythorn wonder if the rumor was true that the white herd of unicorns would be forced to change their comfortable way of life.

"I suppose my recalcitrant colt was too busy scrapping to look in on his grandsire," neighed Cabalblade crossly.

"Wrong! I *did* look in on him! This morning I found Grandsire to be in a dismal mood." Having been unfairly reproved for not doing something he had in fact done, the hard-angled young unicorn kicked and fussed to let his sire know the true extent of his discontent.

"Leave him be," whinnied the matriarch nudging Cabalblade. "We are today too busy to worry about your bothersome colt."

"Elianor is right. We cannot today waste time bothering about Naythorn," seconded the high escort Aneilee.

"No... more... biting-tag!" Cabalblade grew more cross as he added, "I do not now have time to scold my colt for something bad he happens to be thinking, or planning to do. Just go away... anywhere away! And do not return until the sky darkens our meadow!"

That... was precisely the instruction that Naythorn wanted to hear from his sire. After jumping about, Naythorn broke into a gallop. He neighed laughingly as he ran off with tail held high. At this moment he did not care that because of some magical accident his mane was jet black, with an annoying rooster tail-like puff of hair cropping up at his withers. If the strange colored mane was for him not punishment enough, some strands of his long tail were definitely unwhite. To top it all, the black speckles of his spiraled horn were unreconciled to the ivory's underlay of whiteness. As he put more distance between himself and the white herd, Naythorn did not care in the least that the strange black markings of his mane, tail, and horn made him an oddity, a young stallion to be made fun of by white hided unicorn colts.

He used to count how many times he was each day bullied. If the count summed to ten or less, Naythorn counted himself lucky. He could not begin to number the myriad kick fights he had lost to older and bigger colts during the first eighteen moons of his life.

It seemed that wherever he went he heard young unicorns neigh sarcastically, "There goes *NayayayayyyTHORNY!*"

"*NayyySAYER* today finds himself in another bad mood!"

"Look at the bugs crawling on *BlackMANGY's* hide!"

From bitter experience Naythorn had learned that name-calling hurt deeply. He would not do that. He promised himself that he would not now, or ever, be a bully.

As he galloped the image of his failing grandsire flashed into his mind. According to the very old stallion the great magic bestowed on Wittanor had an unhappy influence on out of place things. And the big colt's coloring was, very possibly, the only wrongly placed thing to be found in any part of the unicorn hold.

Grandsire Cabalbard had more than once neighed that because his grandcolt's sad color was based on a future reason, no one could know why Naythorn's mane had turned out black. And moreover, by virtue of that unusual coloration his life would somehow come to be different from other unicorn colts.

When Naythorn realized that he was all by himself, his front legs punched up over his head and his back legs kicked out for joy. Having left behind reclining foals, yearlings at play, and unicorn mares grazing in two's and three's, he would neigh *nay* to the idea of suffocating unicorn herdness.

Naythorn angled through shallow waves so that no one could track to where had proceeded his hooves. Leaving the sea waves behind, Naythorn turned his head toward the clustered branches of lush green trees.

He could scarcely believe it. For the first time in his life he was... *completely on his own!* He was for sure certain that this day would become a great adventure. As he ran fast through the trees he did not even mind an occasional branch slapping his soft nose.

After making sure that no guard stallion was found nearby, Naythorn splashed hooves into the Alone River. Panting deep breaths as he climbed up the far bank he muttered, *"Nyerrrghh!* I am three times better at running than swimming."

With his escape from Wittanor made good, he ran full out. After three thousand running paces Naythorn found himself beset by arroyos that cut every which way.

The rough-cut ground before him splayed out in a profusion of gnarled and scrubby trees with twisted trunks.

Wolves

Ahead of him something fierce... was happening. Naythorn debated how smart it was for a magically born and bred unicorn to be curious about an altercation taking place in a far arroyo that was not his affair. He quickly decided that an opportunity presented, and that in order to learn useful things about new places it was better for him to be more curious, than not enough curious.

It took more than five hundred big running breaths to locate the spot of the loud yawling. A not full-grown bear, perhaps like himself eighteen moons old, was surrounded by one small wolf wearing a dingy yellow hide, four bigger wolves, and a gray coat leader half again as large as any of the other wolves in his pack. The bear was cornered within a rocky indent no more than twenty horse-hips wide, which to the bear gave no exit.

Naythorn concluded that the kill was only a small matter of wolf time. With a modicum of patience, and his sire said that wolves on the hunt possessed much more than a modicum of patience, the bear would be ground down. Big hard-biting teeth would methodically cut and slash the bear's hide the same way a beaver grinds apart a sapling tree.

To wolf minds the existence of one less bear presented a major benefit to hungry lupine stomachs, a welcome boost to hunter pride, and no meaningful loss to the animal person world. Though not completely full-grown, this bear was big enough for the wolves to tell stories about him as... *all grown.* Only nasty wolves would dare to attack a bear this big. To Naythorn these wolves, and especially their leader, looked to be exceptionally mean.

The bear was cornered with no other bears to render help, and nowhere to escape. While the odds in this fight were entirely on the side of the wolves, Naythorn noticed that the bear had extra fight in his spirit. Reflecting on the scene playing out before him, with six wolves against one bear, Naythorn knew it would be a fight to the death. The bear's dreadful chances in this fight did not sit well with the blackmaned unicorn's own painfully acquired sense of fairness, learned the hard way from too many bullying matches of bite-tag. A fair match of combat would have no more than four wolves arrayed against this particular bear.

Naythorn told himself that before doing something he would later regret, he should think practically. After all, this fight was not about him. The unicorn code instructed that only if they remained apart from the world of other animal persons, could their horn magic be preserved. The precept of non-involvement and non-friendship applied just the same to hungry wolves, as it did to beavers. Still, the blackmane abhorred the idea of one-sided slaughter.

To say *yes* to a fight that was not his to begin with, would go against what he had always been taught. But to say *no* to the plight of a cornered young bear went against the spirit of the misfit unicorn. The blackmane wondered how selfish it was to stay true to himself the contrary, blackmaned, naysayer. Naythorn decided. To himself he would say *yes*. On this day six mean wolves were not to destroy a young bear.

Like an actor self-aware of his movements on a stage, Naythorn walked slowly, pausing every other step to tear at blades of grass. The unicorn moved with confidence, as if his hooves owned the small boxed-in spot of land. Puzzled at the appearance of the unicorn, six wolves halted their orchestrated attack. Not comprehending the unicorn's intentions regarding a bear fight in which they were physically, emotionally, and in every way completely invested... the wolves stepped back.

The black bear's instinctive response to Naythorn's entrance was to himself advance toward the position of the strange horse person. Bear paws reached to feel the texture of the blackmane's horn that had begun to glow softly blue. His curiosity satisfied, what mattered to bear logic was that the intruder was not a seventh wolf. The bear sat on hind haunches and yawped loudly. Should the fight resume, the lupines would have to confront the bear while looking askance at the interloper unicorn.

Blackmane made no gesture acknowledging wolf presence. He surmised that to the wolves his horn looked to be a punishing weapon.

Without being told, Naythorn knew that wolf logic taught that horses were herd animals that ran away from peril and did not voluntarily, much less needlessly, approach danger. For that, it was to be expected that wolf sensibility interpreted Naythorn's nonchalant presence as outrageously arrogant.

After snarling at the sight of a unicorn and bear stacked together before them, six wolves slunk back and then melted into the shadows of boulders.

As if he had seemingly not marked the retreat of the wolf pack, the blackmane continued to graze. But Naythorn had noticed that the jowls of the grayback leader were scarred, his sides bore slash marks that wolf hair could not mask, and his eyes had an evil shine that the unicorn had not before imagined to exist in any animal person. Clearly the biggest wolf, a veteran of many vicious kills, now hated him.

But so what if he had made an enemy of the huge grayback wolf? If he could at the same time take on Hoovefort and Vor, he could handle six wolves. And, at that, upon his return to the unicorn herd he would never again come upon the unusually large and deeply scarred wolf. Still, Naythorn told himself that he would relish kicking hooves at the hatred emanating from out the big wolf's eyes.

Observing the seated bear take on a relaxed demeanor, Naythorn decided the six wolves were gone... well away. Clearly wolf intelligence instructed that it was better to consent to a humiliating retreat, than to lose a bone-breaking battle against unicorn hooves and horn.

Pulling at the odd clump of grass, the blackmane began to walk in the direction that led back to Wittanor Hold. Out of the corner of his eye Naythorn saw that the bear was following.

A Second Time Wolves

Twilight deepened as the blackmane slowly picked his way through the many twists and turns that obstacled his return to the hold. In his rush to gallop fast away from the Alone River, he had not paid careful attention to the route he had taken. He came to a place with three possible ways to proceed. As Naythorn looked back-and-forth from one arroyo to another, the bear slipped past and headed into the leftmost draw. The bear swung his head back at Naythorn, shook it twice, and through low tree branches plunged ahead. It was as if instead of being a bear, he was the equine that needed to get back to his herd of unicorns.

Walking side by side, a black bear and a black marked unicorn reached a brook that shimmered invitingly in the moonlight. The unicorn and bear drank deeply. A sudden *whamp, brump, crash* made Naythorn jump forelegs. A big razorback hog smashed through the brush bordering the other side of the brook, and slid to a dead stop at stream's edge. Two razorback eyes squinted in astonishment at the horned horse and bear.

More smacking and thumping sounded. One, two, three, four little wild hogs plopped against their mother's rump and tumbled about her sides. With no more pause, all five razorbacks plunged into the stream and waded directly toward Naythorn and the bear.

The reason for their flight became evident. The wolf pack led by Mean-eyes had decided for ham supper to replace bear steak. The quick-thinking razorback sow decided her best chance to save four little ones that could not outrun wolves, was to get her litter protectively close to the unicorn and bear. One big wild sow and four piglets piled between where passively stood the horned horse and the bear.

From across the stream, wolves came to glare at Naythorn. Five razorbacks, a bear, and a unicorn stared back. In the short expanse of time between declining sun and rising moon, losing out on both bear steak and tender ham made not one, but two egregious humiliations suffered by the wolf pack. Teamed together in strength on the opposite side of the stream from the wolves, the blackmane and the bear did not much care how upset were become the lupine predators.

Wolf anger gave way to venting. The howling, jumping about, and ground-pawing of the big gray wolf showed he regarded the imposition of a unicorn into his predatory affairs... to be outrageously unfair. Naythorn guessed that his protective presence violated the rules of wolf craft. After all, from the moment they were born, pack wolves were called to be fierce four-legged hunters afraid of no animal person.

Standing on the bank of the stream, the blackmane and the bear were now less penned in than when they faced the wolves in the boxed arroyo. The horned horse, bear, and five wild boars outnumbered by one the wolves. The strange group could freely walk or swim away from the wolves as if nothing had happened, and from Naythorn's perspective precious little had actually happened. As into the stream he led six animals in a direct path toward the wolf pack, for a second time at the passage of Naythorn's hooves, wolves vanished.

It suddenly hit Naythorn that he had broken the sundown curfew set by his sire. Already in trouble with

Cabalblade for tardiness, Naythorn decided he had nothing more to lose by taking the time to enjoy an evening stroll through trees and shrubs. The blackmane noticed that the four wild piglings had no problem keeping pace with their mama sow, an ambling bear, and a walking horse. And it was *fun* to watch the piglings play at grabbing sticks with their snouts. Their rescue made safe, somehow it would not do for the unicorn or the bear, to so soon abandon the wild boar family.

The blackmane's thoughts turned in a new direction. How would he explain to his sire, and to Elianor, why his return had been until middle night delayed? He hoped that at least Aneilee *would not* become apprised of his tardiness. The eyes of the high escort penetrated too deeply, and saw too much. But because the unicorn guards were most vigilant after the fall of darkness, his return in middle night would assuredly be noticed and brought to the high escort's immediate attention.

To the young stallion's mind a solution occurred. It would be more convenient to not arrive back at the unicorn hold until the next day's sun was burning hot, horned horses were busy napping, and the vigilance of the unicorn guard horses was relaxed. Just as no guard stallion had observed his departure from the hold, perhaps none would detect his re-entrance.

Naythorn cautioned himself that it would not be smart to report that the return from his forbidden tour was delayed because he had happened to help a bear and a family of wild boars to survive attacks from mean wolves. He once again wondered if offending some bloody wolves could really contradict the precept of unicorn neutrality and aloofness from animal affairs. As far as the blackmane could tell, the wolves really had no redeeming virtues of kindness or helpfulness. Still, having good motives had seldom before helped Naythorn win an argument with his sire Cabalblade, with the matriarch Elianor, or with the high escort Aneilee.

Naythorn recalled that whatever the occasion of misbehaving colts, he was always the one presumed to be guilty, and then nipped several times on his behind. And the bites of the unicorn matriarch really hurt. Naythorn shook his mane as he next remembered how the high escort's scolding neighs hurt even more than the matriarch's bites. During the remainder of night darkness Naythorn relished the idea of being nothing more, nor less, than a young stallion roaming wonderfully free under the subtle light of friendly stars.

The Grayback Draws Blood

Night came and went without presenting notions of heaviness behind the blackmane's eyes. By midmorning the leaves, shrubs, and flowers had brightened with colors luxuriant.

Seven animal persons filed out of the forest to stand on the bank of the river that boundaried the unicorn hold. Naythorn there found something strange, something totally unexpected. He had never before, not even once, observed wolves moving about on the far bank of the Alone River where he now stood. But right in front of him Mean-eyes and five more wolves were feasting at the great expense of waterfowl. Cunning wolves had recognized that on this morning unicorn magic had failed to hold sway over *both* banks of the Alone River.

Long counting on protective unicorn magic, the waterfowl had grown careless in regard to hiding well their nests. Parent ducks and geese fluttered about in panic as they did their best to protect eggs and hatchlings. More often than not the fowl feigning a broken wing to distract a wolf ended up forfeiting his or her own feathers.

"*Nyrruuuhhuhhuhh!* This is all wrong! How are so many wolves found on the doorstep of our unicorn hold? Where are the big guard unicorns that protect both banks of the river?" The blackmane's blood began to boil. Without asking himself one question more, Naythorn knew he must send the feasting wolves low-tailing away from the Alone River boundary of the unicorn hold.

Close to where stood the unicorn, one big and one small waterfowl had managed to dodge the ill-consequences of the huge gray wolf's sharp teeth. As they fluttered about with wings dragging, half-hopping and half-flying, the two waterfowl feigned to be convincingly wounded.

This time the unicorn with the black mane would teach Mean-eyes a harsh lesson. In a few running paces Naythorn reached and bowled over the big wolf. Undeterred, Mean-eyes quickly brought himself up on all fours, lunged at the stallion, and sank teeth into the thigh of a hind leg. The wolf drew unicorn blood.

The pain he felt made the horned horse fight even

harder, and in that regard the blackmane had a lot of experience in the tricks of bite-tag. The stallion turned, lowered his head, and snapped his horn back to grab at wolf belly. The body of the wolf leader was launched into the river.

The scampering and fluttering duck and goose saw their best, and perhaps only hope to survive was to get behind the horned horse. That they did.

Whirling hind hooves, the blackmaned unicorn dispatched a second wolf into the river. With quickness that surprised even himself, the stallion's horn pinned down a third wolf as powerful front hooves cracked lupine ribs.

The other wolves found it had become their time of decision. The three concluded that even attacking together, they were no match for the horned horse. Three unharmed wolves turned and fled along the river bank. None of the three looked back to see whether the remainder of their pack had survived the stallion's wrath.

For the hurt of his wound Naythorn had not cried tears. Upon delicately touching his horn to his gashed leg, blue light sparked healing magic. While his leg began to mend, the unicorn rested. By the time Naythorn found he could again walk on the leg that had suffered wound, the position of the sun in the sky was where it had been the day before when Naythorn escaped Wittanor.

When he again directed himself toward the hold of the unicorns, the blackmane cared little that he was noticeably limping.

CHAPTER 2

PLANK BARGES

N aythorn was both perplexed and disturbed about what had undone the magic that had always protected the Alone River boundary of the unicorn hold. Somehow, in some way, Wittanor felt to be all wrong.

As he crossed the Alone River for only the second time in his life, the blackmane swam slowly. Having nowhere else to go the bear, five razorbacks, one duck, and one goose followed the unicorn into the river.

After shaking water off his hide and climbing up the river bank, the blackmane's limp was forgotten. Unicorn hooves shot fast through trees. Naythorn disappeared so quickly that the goose and duck wondered if just like them, the horned horse could make himself to fly.

Emerging from Wittanor's forest, the blackmane was stunned. Across the length and breadth of the hold's great meadow not a mare, foal, yearling, or stallion was standing, grazing, or sunning. Nor was a single unicorn present to make fun of his wrongly colored mane.

From out on the wide water came flashes of reflected sunlight. Squinting his eyes to see further, Naythorn made out unicorns bobbing up and down upon platforms apparently made of tree planks. Here and there a horned horse reared up on hind legs. Positioned on the corners of the floating planks, the blackmane saw what could only be men persons holding shiny metal shields. Why... were men on tree boats freighting unicorns into diminishing skies?

When the boats began to pivot about, Naythorn glimpsed many long poles dipping and pushing together in rhythm. As unicorns continued to nervously rear up legs, enormous sheets colored white, orange, and green lifted to fill with wind. Found apart from the departing white herd that he had dwelled among since his birth, Naythorn grew distraught.

"The same way that I separated wolves from their prey, men persons now steal my unicorn herd *away from me!* Wait! I see him! My sire stands alone on the closest vessel of the plank fleet!" So that his sire might notice him, Naythorn reared high and waved front hooves. In immediate answer his sire jumped front hooves skyward.

"He saw me! My sire was looking for me!" For the time taken by each reciprocated jump, from his sire Naythorn became a little more separated. Duty bound to obey the code of unquestioned obedience to the matriarch and high escort, his sire could not change the path of his vessel to redirect journey back to his colt.

Naythorn had the thought that wherever Elianor and Aneilee were taking the white herd, it had to be somewhere very far away. He reasoned that at this momentous time of departure from Wittanor Hold, the abandonment of a year-and-a-halfling mattered little to the leaders of the white herd. The matriarch and high escort had more important things on their minds than to be concerned for the whereabouts of the misfit blackmane.

As he watched the life he had known since he was a little foal sail away on great plank rafts, Naythorn froze his stance. Everything had for him changed. When the fleet of vessels carrying unicorns melted into a delicate mist caressing a far line of water, the unicorn with the untoward mane found himself to be... *forsaken.*

Abandoned

Naythorn reassured himself that his sire had not deliberately deserted him. In spite of the black markings he wore, his color and dark disposition had always been at least... tolerated by his sire.

For his responsible leadership of the company of guard stallions, Cabalblade had earned the admiration of the entire unicorn herd. However, the respect Naythorn showed to his sire absented outward displays of affection or love. On the other hoof, the young unicorn with the contrary mane had often neighed his love and affection to his grandsire. When stung by his sire's anger for something he had done, or hardly done at all, Cabalbard would try to calm his blackmaned grandcolt's resentful mood.

"The sire I respect, and the grandsire I love, travel far away and are never to return," muttered Naythorn. Upon thinking that thought, Naythorn learned that his eyes could shed real tears. Even so, Naythorn cried more inside his heart than from out his eyes. Sitting down rear haunches, the blackmane lowered his head between propped up front legs. His thoughts tumbled one upon another.

"Who were those gold-chested men? Why did they

come to take away the unicorn herd? Why did the matriarch consent to leave Wittanor Hold, and risk dangerous travel over the immense water? And what is now to become of the blackmaned unicorn's life story?" Finding no answers to his questions, Naythorn slumped more his head. All he for certain knew was that because the matriarch had not waited for his return to the hold, he had been left forever behind.

"If he were here and now wearing my hooves, what would my sire do next?" inquired Naythorn of himself. When the answer came to him, the blackmane slowly nodded his head. "Yes. My sire would persevere. No matter how badly went the day, permission to give up and quit is not found in the blood that flows through the strong chest and flanks of my sire."

Ending a time of self-pity, Naythorn jerked up his head and neighed loud for no unicorn to hear, "I will search every corner of the unicorn hold for clues of what happened to the white herd. Perhaps the human persons left something behind." He forced a wry smile as he added, "The entire herd of unicorns will miss having me... to pick on."

Raising up on all fours, Naythorn was surprised to find gathered behind him the eight animals he had collected on that morning and the previous afternoon. The serious expressions on hog, bear, duck, and goose faces showed they sensed that inside the unicorn's heart something had turned wrong.

Naythorn straightened his back and raised high his head. He had to summon hardness of heart. He smiled wanly, for by unkind neighs and bites he had many times before been taught *the hardness lesson.*

Looking once more about, Naythorn noted eight unkempt animal persons craning necks to see what would next do the extraordinary horned horse that had intervened to rescue them from a pack of very ferocious wolves.

An Honest Demise

Naythorn's gaze lingered on the straight-faced cliffs, where halfway below their crest gushed out a wide eye of water. The curtain of falling water obscured the entrance of a stable that ran deep into a cavern. Naythorn would go to the place where his infirm grandsire had long lain.

Until his mind started to play tricks on him, Grandsire Cabalbard was said to be the wisest unicorn in the herd. He was the stallion that best remembered stories from the long ago unicorn past. Perhaps in the place where the infirm Cabalbard had for so long reposed, some token of a message was purposefully left behind. At least the comforting scent of his grandsire's hide, would there still reside.

After entering the cave stable, Naythorn paused to let his eyes adjust to semi-darkness. His ears alerted. Had he heard his name whispered? The year-and-a-halfling made his way deeper inside the cliff. This time he was sure. From somewhere ahead he had heard a weak voice gasp *Nayyythorrrnnn...*

"Not just me, my grandsire was also left behind!"

Naythorn nuzzled warmly the cheeks of the sprawled Cabalbard. After all that had that day taken place, the simple fact that each was not entirely and completely alone, brightened the eyes of a young blackmaned stallion and his grandsire.

"So my disappeared grandcolt is returned to the unicorn hold."

"Tell me what happened to Wittanor?" neighed Naythorn plopping down on his belly. "Why did unicorns leave, and where have they gone? And since I was born a rightful member of the white herd, why did they not wait for me to go with them? You look exhausted, Grandsire." Naythorn noticed something more; there was no shine to Cabalbard's hide.

"*Nyeerrcughcugh,*" coughed noisily the very old unicorn. "I would not leave the home I had known since my first memories, and I would not leave you. Besides, my old bones are too frail to undertake a voyage to a distant and unknown place. *Nyeerrcughcugh...* this, dear colt, is what to both of us happened. A prophecy I thought was impossible for me to ever see fulfilled, at last came true.

"A long-ago vision of a great matriarch unicorn, an ancestor of ours named Aneighlee, was over long generations passed down from sire to colt. Our ancestor foresaw that after a thousand years of peace and protection in Wittanor, men with chests gleaming golden would save our herd from three deaths... one from a cloud, one from the mountain, and one from the sea. Today's arrival of Phoenician barges proved that those thousand years have now come and gone.

The prophecy foretells that after the ground beneath our hooves begins to move back-and-forth, our guardian mountain will explode to rain down a cloud of poison dust upon the unicorn hold. Next, a wall of hot rock will wash over our hold. Finally, a towering sea will crash through Wittanor." The very old unicorn saw that his grandcolt did not understand his neighs.

"Naythorn, the important part is that the prophetic rescue happened. The gold-chested men put down walkways for unicorns to mount onto their vessels. Under the direction of the unicorn guard stallions, clan by unicorn clan the white herd boarded five barges and placed themselves at the command of the sailors. Each barge is now formed into a battalion of more than one hundred unicorns and two hundred sailors. The Phoenicians call each of their five-masted barges with square sails, a brig. The entire fleet of five vessels is called a sea brigade."

"Grandsire, you liked being a military unicorn. It was you that reestablished the company of unicorn guards."

"After nearly a thousand years of peace, the white herd had grown too relaxed and too lazy. When others said we unicorns had nothing to fear, I would have none of that. I recruited and organized a company of thirty unicorn guard stallions and divided that company into three platoons, each with two squads. Every third day the ten unicorns in a platoon had the responsibility of making sure Wittanor Hold remained safe and secure. During that day and that night, two squads of five stallions rotated duty... but all that is now ended.

"This morning I decided that I would be the one unicorn not component to a brigade of sea barges. My plan was to hobble my way to the place of the unicorn dead, and there expire. But upon learning that you had not climbed onto a barge, I could not decide to so quickly die. I knew that now, more than ever, you would need the blessing that only I was left to give. Besides, someone had to tell you to flee the unicorn hold and save your hide, before everything in the way of an exploding and collapsing mountain and a rushing sea came to be destroyed."

"Why could not Elianor wait for me to return to Wittanor?"

"Danger to the white herd was too close at hoof. The sailors would not delay the evacuation of unicorns. But I will tell you, Naythorn, that your sire was desperate for you to rejoin your clan of unicorns. He galloped everywhere about looking for you... but in Wittanor his blackmaned colt was nowhere to be found."

"My sire told me yesterday to go anywhere away. So I did."

"Cabalblade was the last unicorn to board the last barge. Beside himself with worry, your sire hated that you were left behind.

"By one thing only was I comforted. Amidst all the excitement and confusion of the white herd's departure, a truth was to me revealed. Of a sudden I knew that your very first absence from Wittanor, particularly on this day, was so unusual that it had to be for an important reason... a purpose extraordinary.

"Naythorn, in my entire life this is my first and only prophecy. Your life story will one day come to reunite a divided and lost unicorn herd. When two separate paths come together, my grandcolt will change the destiny of the white herd."

"How do you know this thing, Grandsire?"

"Because when the Phoenician Admiral read from a scroll that described travel toward the fixed star," Cabalbard managed a small smile, "I finally understood the mystery that had forever puzzled me. On this very morning I realized that should the spirals of your horn be unrolled in one long strip, like a piece of unraveled bark, the seven black markings on your horn would represent the pattern that points to the fixed star. The future journey of my grandcolt, is by the stars *marked*.

"*Nyeerrcughcugh*... it makes me glad to imagine how you will become so grown in magic that you will change the lives of eight clans of unicorns."

"When I complained about my appearance, you always told me the color of my mane mattered less than what lay heart-hidden underneath my hide. I want my heart to grow big enough to fulfill your prophecy."

"Do you remember what I said when you would come to me feeling hurt and abused? I told you to... *guard your heart*. I die content to know that your heart remains pure."

"Like you, does my sire think that one day I am going to be a helper to the unicorn herd?"

"Not exactly, no. After your unpermissioned disappearance yesterday, your sire still thinks that you are undisciplined..."

"My sire calls me unobedient, unhumble, unserious, and unpleasant."

"Calbalbard neighed that your being left behind was punishment exact for your disobedience. Of course your sire wanted you to carry on after him, to someday lead the unicorn guard stallions. As for me, I often told your sire that your curiosity and independence showed a heart earnest for, and about, *life.*"

"My heart beats strong to be free." The grandcolt's ears laid back. "Someone enters the stable!"

Two Makers of Weapons

"My memory, Naythorn, is not what it used to be. I knew there was something else I had to tell you. The approaching footsteps belong to Master Hammerclaw and his apprentice blacksmith Lucars. From the one clan of unicorns still found in Phoenicia, the two received the magical gift of the uniform animal speech."

The men came to where lay Cabalbard, sat down on the ground, and crossed their legs. Showing deference to the old unicorn, the men did not speak until spoken to.

"The same as for you, my perfect grandcolt, these are the first men persons I have seen up close. Left behind by the barge brigade with orders to find the blue gold that Phoenician blacksmiths fashion into magic swords and shields, they now prepare for long and difficult travel.

"Time became too short. *Nyeeerrcuhcuh.* Finding themselves very busy, Elianor and Aneilee left it up to me to tell these two men where to find the hidden place of blue gold that is kept apart from the greed and avarice of human persons. Based on my instructions, Lucars scratched out a map of where to find *Shining Canyon,* and its deposit of blue gold. I hope these two can make sense of the clues I recalled from the very old saga; clues that have been neighed down from one unicorn generation to another."

Lucars unrolled a scroll marked to be a map. Seeing that, the blackmane motioned his horn in little circles as if it were being unrolled like the scroll. In response Cabalbard nodded knowingly at Naythorn.

"Although I once committed the long oral story to memory, most of the saga is now to me gone," neighed Cabalbard to the two blacksmiths. "I do recall that the blue gold lies in a canyon within a notable and unique mountain that stands in the direction of the fixed star. Within that mountain is a big structure with stone columns that men called a pavilion palace. *No, wait!* About that I am not sure. I might be confusing the pavilion mountain with another. Still, I feel that I have forgotten a necessary instruction that I should recount. It had something to do with... *clue stones.* In fact, now that I think about it, there may be more than one special stone that marks the place of blue gold."

"But Grandsire, rocks of all sizes and shapes are everywhere to be found."

"Master Cabalbard," spoke the older man with a dark complexion, and big bunches of arm muscles that flexed in hard angles. "Thank you again for sharing the clues from the unicorn saga. Your instructions tell us that we have as many as two hundred leagues of northward travel before finding... *special stones...* and the canyon of blue gold. So then, from you there is no more instruction?"

"I am sorry, Master Hammerclaw, but my mind has grown too feeble to remember all the things that I once knew. May you fare well in your quest for the blue gold."

While he listened and did not speak, the youth rerolled the scroll. Naythorn thought that the eyes of Lucars were rooted in an open and unselfish part of his heart. Something about the younger man's eyes reminded Naythorn, of himself.

"I and Lucars must now go." The older man with big arms hand-saluted the old unicorn. Upon seeing the youth bend down to hug Cabalbard's neck, Naythorn wished that he had a human person friend to show him such a gesture of affection.

The two men rechecked the packing of their weapons, tools, food stuffs, and a few personal items. Each item had a unique place of transport on a shoulder, waist, or belt. What would have amounted to a light load on Naythorn's back freighted far heavier on the backs of Hammerclaw and Lucars. As they turned to leave, the two blacksmiths nodded heads slightly at Naythorn.

The blackmane thought that human person magic that brought immense barges across a far sea at the critical time for rescue of the white herd, must be very powerful. The two men had barely acknowledged his presence. But thinking about it, Blackmane asked himself why they should trust him. No rule-breaking young unicorn was supposed to have been left behind by the barges. To the two men that had before seen only pure white unicorns, his black markings surely seemed out of place.

"The Phoenician sailors arrived here beset by a hard disposition," neighed Cabalbard guessing at Naythorn's thoughts. "During a long sea journey undertaken for the purpose of unicorn rescue, many of their number perished in foul storms." Cabalbard's eyes brightened. "Did you know, Naythorn, that men persons have names for the four directions?" The old unicorn stallion shook his head forward and neighed, "That direction is called... *east.*" He shook his tail and added, "That direction is... *west.*" With movements of his head the old horse identified north and south. "Remember, Naythorn, that a horned horse is never too old to learn something new."

The demeanor of Cabalbard darkened. He rested his jaw on the ground.

"What troubles you, Grandsire?"

"I worry that the instructions I gave for finding the blue gold may not be of much help to the two men. All that I really remember from the old unicorn saga is that the canyon that shines of blue gold lies quite far to the north."

The old unicorn struggled to raise himself on all fours. That accomplished, leaning against Naythorn he began to hobble toward the bright light that shone at the entrance to the vast cavern.

"*Nyeeerrcuhcuh.* Tell me again why unicorn magic holds importance for human persons."

"Grandsire, I do not think that unicorn magic can so much matter."

"Brought an impossible distance over far and dangerous seas, Phoenician sailors would disagree with what you just neighed. Without being drawn by our magic, how could they have found Wittanor, right before its destruction was to happen? Those sailors know that unicorn magic provides hope and protection to hearts filled with good will. For that reason, the seamen made great sacrifices to rescue our herd of unicorns.

"Did you know that when hearts unfeeling of unicorn magic darken toward the heavens, jealousy and rapacity cause evil things to transpire? Our magic is a medicine that cleanses the heart of envy and the lust for power." Lacking strength to walk and whinny at the same time, the old unicorn swayed unsteadily on his hooves.

"The cave entrance is close, Grandsire."

"After battles and wars are ended, our magic helps innocence and love to be regained." Cabalbard looked closely at his grandcolt and added, "You do know that because this is my last day, I only neigh about... *important things.*"

Accompanied by his grandcolt, a very old unicorn emerged from the cave stable intent on surveying the distant mists into which Phoenician barges had vanished. Cabalbard found that he and Naythorn were not alone. A bear, a duck, a goose, and five razorbacks waited in welcome.

"What... is this strange group of animal persons doing here?"

"Last night and this morning I decided that these animals would not be either wolf supper or wolf breakfast."

"So they look to my grandcolt as their... protector? Hmph, friendship between unicorns and common animal persons is something I have never before seen. Actually, our code forbids it. How can a magical unicorn feel responsibility to protect lowly animals with lives of paltry value?"

"I feel kindly toward this frayed looking group of animal persons. From the moment in the arroyos when I stumbled upon the big wolf leading his pack, I despised his mean eyes and bullying manner. It became my purpose to deny that wolf his plunder."

"Strange... this is strange... you interfered..."

Right then the ground shook so hard that it seemed to roll. Thereafter the lapping sound of waves breaking onto the beach was overwhelmed by loud and menacing sounds come from the top of the volcano looming behind Wittanor.

To keep from falling, the old unicorn again pressed his side against Naythorn while he neighed, "We have little time. I must bless you before Wittanor is forever gone."

"Grandsire! The sunlight... err... seems to be making the roots of your mane to blacken!"

"At last you learn the truth about your grandsire." Cabalbard lowered his head to not look Naythorn in the eyes.

"A long time ago, after I stopped growing taller, my mane began to color black. Upon first noticing it I fled into the far darkness of the cave stable. Ashamed to be different, for seven suns I stayed hidden from other unicorn horses.

"When from the depths of the cave I emerged half-starved, my despair changed to joy. Quarantine in darkness had dimmed my black coloration. From that I learned that without the warmth and burn of the sun, my coat would continue white. To preserve my black secret, I lived my days in cave isolation. Now that I consider, I cannot even remember the last time that my hide felt the warmth of the sun. Imagine my pain, Naythorn, as I daily lived a lie. The punishment for my lie... was by the night sentenced."

"It is all right, Grandsire. Your secret will with me be safe." The colt could not refrain from adding, "*Nyeerrumhrrum*... so I am not the first blackmaned unicorn. Just knowing that makes your confession become to me a blessing."

"I feel a weight lifted from my withers," answered Cabalbard with a few tears moistening his eyes. "Although I lived my life afraid, I can no longer afford to fear."

"You were the champion sentry of the night guard. You were a brave stallion that protected the herd of unicorns."

"Because I did my duty under moon glow and starlight, I was doubly brave on night patrol. But no, Naythorn, with myself I made a... *bad bargain*. I should not have run away from my destiny. Unlike me, my grandcolt will to himself stay true. The stuff that forms your heart is greater than the bits of black color in your mane, horn, and tail. It will fall to you to untarnish the loss of honor that came from your grandsire's cowardice." The old unicorn smiled large, but strangely crooked.

"Now, let us see what this old frame can give to my grandcolt. Because for the first time in my long life I am made to be an honest unicorn, what I can give to you is become worth more. Since my grandcolt also shares the coloring of my mane, the blessing I give... will be indeed special."

"Grandsire, I ask you to do even more. Kindly bestow magic on my new companions that are intent on following me. If they possessed magic I could talk to them, and they to me. The gift of their conversation would lessen my loneliness."

"*Nyeeerrcuhcuh!* That is the most *outlandish* petition I have ever heard! If this request came from anyone other than my grandcolt, to whom because of my long deception I am indebted, I would limp away neighing laughter. And mind you a hard laugh would today be very painful to my chest." Cabalbard shook his head back-and-forth, and then shook it more slowly up and down.

"Are you certain about your strange request? This outrageous thing, to give speech to ordinary animal persons, will take strength of which I have little to spare. The magic I give to them will diminish the blessing that remains to you."

"I *am* sure of it, Grandsire."

"I always knew that human persons, like Hammerclaw and Lucars, could be given the gift of the uniform animal language. I had never thought that a pig, duck, goose, or bear could master the art of talking intelligently. Imagine my having a conversation with a... *wild boar.* What could I have to say to a pig? I cannot imagine what a pig would have to say to me.

"*Nyeeerrcuhcuh.* All right my colt. We will see what next happens. Mind you, I will try my best to make this work. Watch now an old and spent unicorn do something not sensible. But... I do recall a danger. The touch of a unicorn horn can concentrate the evil resident in a perverse heart."

"I know that the heart of the mean-eyed wolf that bit my leg is wicked, but the hearts of my animal companions are not."

"So *that* is why I detected you to have a slight limp. Beware, Naythorn. For tasting your blood that mean wolf became even more perverse."

The old unicorn stepped close to a duck, goose, bear, and five razorbacks. Because they instinctively sensed that something important was about to happen, Naythorn's eight animal companions froze in place. Cabalbard bent his head and touched long moments his horn to the forehead of the mama sow. Afraid to move, the big razorback sow waited patiently for whatever next was to happen. It took some time, but Cabalbard's horn finally began to spark and glow blue.

Neither the sow nor the old unicorn was prepared for what came next. As if her head had been struck by a weighty stone, the big sow fell to her knees and rolled over unconscious. No matter, the old unicorn touched his horn to each of the remaining seven animals that accompanied Naythorn. Following the example of the sow, when touched by Cabalbard's horn each animal collapsed. The task accomplished, the grandsire also crumpled down and to himself became oblivious. A very old unicorn and eight animal persons lay dumbly sprawled on the ground.

"Grandsire! Do not die! Not here! Before dying you must enter the place of the unicorn dead where your ancestors await you. I can escort you, but there I cannot enter." Stirring himself, Cabalbard motioned his horn at reawakened groggy and disoriented animal persons.

"My magic, Naythorn, is given. There is no telling how this will turn out. I will hope to believe that this most silly blessing, in all of unicorn history mind you, may lead to something good. Who can say? Perhaps what I just did for a platoon of animal persons will become a gift uniquely profound.

"Possessing first a black mane it is I, and not you, that should have borne the scorn of pure white unicorns. For that deceit I am not worthy to enter the place of the unicorn dead. I will right here die. And Naythorn, you must right away leave. Take for your guide the direction of the fixed star.

"I wanted to do more for the two men. Had I the strength, *nyeeerrcuhcuh*, I would have gladly led Hammerclaw and Lucars onward. It is too bad that my life this way ends. Soon my hooves will no longer tread the ground. I can only hope that my spirit will come to race across the clouds, and will join from above my grandcolt's travel toward the fixed star."

To Live a Life Unrebukeable

Cabalbard bent up his head. Upon touching each other, two unicorn horns began to glow a deep shade of blue. Naythorn felt brilliant light, fused with energy intense, engulf and make to shake his horse body.

"Grandsire, you... you gave me your blessing!"

No answer came. Instead the old unicorn's head slumped to the ground. When the young stallion nudged his grandsire, the nostrils of the old horned horse once more started softly to blow. Cabalbard reopened his eyes.

"Your sire was proud that men persons came to our rescue. They crossed the great sea in barges. That you rescued a platoon of poor animal persons is a sign of your... kindness. On your horn are specks... a pattern of stars. Not Naythorn, I was to myself the *nayyy... sayer.* Of my own destiny... I was unwelcome." Touching again his horn to Naythorn's, the old unicorn finished his blessing. "My grandcolt will live a life... *unrebukeable.*" Cabalbard's muzzle dropped a last time to earth. The old unicorn had finally found a lasting peace that was honest.

After stretching his white cheeked head and black neck, the goose looked curiously at the duck. It was as if the bigger of the two waterfowl had had a thought to occur. The goose chugged a wing to the duck's brown feathered chest, scampered a few steps as done by geese to gain speed, and left the ground flapping wings in the direction of the Alone River. The duck followed after.

"The goose and duck go to investigate to where have gone the wolves," groinked the razorback sow to the bear.

"I hope, Mrs. Sow, that they find the wolves to be *long gone.*" No one noticed that a razorback pig had communicated, for the first time ever, with words understood and answered by a bear.

The shaking of the mountain worsened, making it past time to depart Wittanor. Naythorn led the way northward along the beach. Turning back, he saw framed in the distance the silent and still body of his grandsire. In the last moments of his very last day,

Cabalbard had sacrificed his remaining strength to give his grandcolt a blessing, and to make a bear, five wild hogs, and two waterfowl to converse with Naythorn. With one another, the motley group of animal persons could now share true friendship.

Before a thousand paces were traveled by the unicorn, the duck and goose fluttered down with the news that fleeing the wrath of the mountain, wolves ran northward on the banks of the Alone River.

Rearing high, Naythorn waved a final farewell to the body of his grandsire now shrouded in the semidarkness of falling night. The blackmane would no more commune with the old unicorn that had never laughed at him, never unkindly kicked him, and never bit his mane as a mocking reminder of its black color. Rearing hooves once more, Naythorn bade a last farewell to his whole world.

As if triggered by the waving of the blackmane's forelegs, the top of the tall conically shaped guardian mountain exploded. An enormous plume of gas and dust blew high, and then settled eastward to rain down on Wittanor. Naythorn had the thought that it was somehow fitting that his grandsire had not entered the place of the unicorn dead. By volcanic debris Cabalbard's body would be given burial in the meadow where he had once played as an innocent and carefree colt, with mane still colored white.

Naythorn left Wittanor forever behind. Close after him followed a platoon comprised of eight new companions.

The entourage led by Naythorn had traveled only a

thousand more horse paces when there occurred... an unimaginable explosion. Bursting out of its side, an overwhelming avalanche of red molten stone flowed toward the place no longer the hold of the white herd.

CHAPTER 3

Very Own Names

L eft behind was a panoramic vista of clouds of ash and streams of fiery rock spilling from out the top and chest of the mountain. After traveling some five thousand more paces along the beach, Naythorn hearkened to a growing chorus of insistent squeals to the effect that four small boarlings... were exhausted. The banks of a convenient brook dissecting the beach came to provide a spot for rest and refreshment with grass for Naythorn, berries for the bear, grubs for the razorbacks, and minnows for the duck and goose.

Quickly become adept at understanding words spoken in the uniform animal tongue, four boarlings utilized their new vocabulary to tease each other. Grown tired of the teasing, the sow ordered her offspring to sit down in front of her.

"Now behave yourselves! For my piglets I have a serious question. *Besides* his magic horn, what did grandsire Cabalbard have that you do not?"

"Big hooves."

"A long tail."

"A mane."

Not one of these answers from her three biggest offspring satisfied the porcine matron. She turned to the littlest and shyest of her litter, and waited for his response. A small boarling paw slowly extended upward.

"Yes?"

"Mama, I have feet, a tail, and a thin mane that sticks straight up. Other than his horn, the only thing truly different between me and the grandsire horse is that he... *had a name.*"

"Why does my littlest piglet not have a name?"

"Because my pretty sow has not given me one."

"My four little boarlings are right now going to get... *very own names!* When I tell you to do something, or scold you for something you did wrong, or even when I note your smartness you will know exactly who I am talking to or about." That grunted, the big sow walked over to a girl piglet that compared to the other three, was very neat and organized in her habits.

"Because you are the most practical of my boarlings, from this day on your name is... Practicia."

One name given, the sow swung her big head to fix eyes on her other daughter pigling and groinked, "You ford streams fast, and of my four piglets your snout is the best at digging roots. I will call you... Roothyford. Once in a while I may call you Roothy. But that will be well-intentioned, for Roothy is a delicate name. Despite your strong snout, you are also my most sensitive piglet."

The sow next fronted her problem boarling whose thoughts very often turned mischievous. "With your constant funning you like to *ham it up.* You are also the biggest of my litter, but of course it is an exaggeration to suggest that you weigh a ton. However, that said the name... Hamilton will work well enough for you. I hope the formal and weighty name you now carry will someday give recognition to a big razorback boar grown more serious about life."

"You, a very smart piglet, are too shy," grunted the sow as she sat her square haunches in front of the littlest of her offspring. "Let me see now." As she thought on, the big razorback sow swung her head up and down. "Yes, that is it. Although I wish you had more confidence, you are well-suited by the name... Timidthy."

The sow flexed her shoulders and took on a serious and consequential air. "Because I am a black hided razorback sow, with big upper and lower tusks and a tree-hard neck that can thwack when you deserve a spanking, you four piglets are to call me... Mrs. Razorthwacker." The sow softened her tone to add, "However, when the day goes well and you see that I wear a gentle mood, I am to be called Mama Pig or even Mrs. Sow."

Not stopping then or there, the porcine matron stepped over to the duck and goose.

"Bird animal persons also need names. Does the goose have any ideas for an appropriate name for his great black bill, white scarfed cheeks, and grand pile of multicolored feathers?"

When without answering the excited goose repeatedly cricked and straightened his long black neck, the duck interrupted, "My webbed feet can kick furiously!" The sow turned her head to more closely inspect the duck.

"My, my! Such big webbed feet on a water bird that

sports a yellow bill and green head. This duck is not afraid to say what is on his mind. It strikes me that when he gets bored our duck likes to use his big webbed feet to stir things up." The sow's eyes lit up as she added, "The name of this duck is to be... Webstir. You are the web footed stirrer-upper."

"*Qvackk, qrrackk, qrraaaaackk!*" bothered the quacks of a now perfectly contented duck.

"Now back to you, Master Goose," groinked the sow.

"Although bigger than Webstir, I cannot move my wings as fast as he does. Hronkk! But there is one thing I do very well. When wolves chase me I can act convincingly injured, even when I am not one bit hurt. Faking one way and swerving the other, because of my quickness I can run wolves in circles until they get dizzy."

"During the wolf chase you whirled and jumped like nothing my eyes ever before saw," responded the sow. "Your feet and wings pop as fast as sparks sizzle from Naythorn's horn. And, your deeply hued and brightly toned feathers display a sparkly pattern. So then, the goose with the white crescent that sashes across his tail, long black neck, black beak, and white cheeks will ever onward answer to the name... Featherspark!"

Rather than looking up like the goose had done, because of his large size the black bear sat peering down at the sow.

"I can guess that you, Master Bear, do not know what it means to be afraid," began Mrs. Razorthwacker craning upward her neck. "*Ggrruunkh!* I wish I myself could learn to not ever be fearful. Tall as a sapling tree, your heart is as durable as a tree trunk. I shall name you... Treestandbear."

"Mrs. Sow, because that name is a mouthful I would answer to Tristanbear, which sounds almost exactly the same, and is a less formal way of saying my name."

"*Do not* protest the name that I gave you!" exclaimed the sow shaking back-and-forth her head. "Descriptive of your strength, Treestandbear best fits you."

"*Yaaarwwaall!*" wuffed the bear. "Although it sounds a bit unwieldy, I do thank Mrs. Razorthwacker for bestowing upon me my very own name."

The possession of a unique name made the duck, goose, bear, and the five members of the razorback family to feel special. All the animals including Naythorn, even though he was not given a name because he already had one, held heads high as they turned to again follow along the beach.

"My short life has taught me one thing," wuffed the bear ambling at the rear of the animal platoon. "Every gift brings with it a cost. Not one bear will share a fishing spot without receiving something in return. I wonder what will be my cost for the name gift of Treestandbear."

Because no animal knew how to answer the bear's question, no animal did. The porcine matron was not even sure the bear was aware that other animal persons had heard him talking, as if only to himself.

As he trotted onward Timidthy wondered if charity also brought cost to the gift-givers. If that were so, the boarling hoped the future payment charged to the blackmane for his gifts of rescue, and the petitioned uniform animal speech, would not be hurtfully costly to Naythorn.

Journey Begun

Noticing a heavier roll to the waves lapping the beach, Naythorn was reminded of his grandsire's warning about a massive surge of water. So when he came upon a new stream, the unicorn decided it was prudent to follow inland the brook.

As they trotted along Hamilton busied himself finding sticks to carry in his mouth, and Practicia busied herself grabbing sticks from out her brother pig's snout.

"Hamilton!" scolded the practical girl boarling. "Yes, now that you have your own name you *know* who you are. It will not do for my biggest brother to choke on a huge stick lodged in his throat!"

Naythorn turned back, saw it, and froze. For perhaps the first time in his life the blackmane could not move or neigh. Then the razorbacks, bear, duck, and goose saw it and heard it. Toward the hold they had left behind, barreled a giant wave so large that it washed over the tops of palm trees lining the beach of Wittanor. When the wave had spent its energy, the receding water swept big trees back into the ocean.

"I am very sorry that the unicorn hold is... no longer to be found," grunted the sow.

"All traces of the magic white herd, my sire and grandsire, and the meadows that we colts played on are now forever gone from the place once called Wittanor."

The followed path came to intersect another. Deciding he liked the direction of the new path, Naythorn changed course. "This way takes us in the direction of the fixed star that my grandsire talked about." Some two thousand paces later the blackmane neighed, "Since we are made safe, let us look for a place to rest."

With no permission asked or given, Featherspark flighted up. He soon returned and informed Naythorn where could be found a lush glen with a welcoming cleft in a rock wall. Soon enough, members of the animal band positioned their sides and bellies on the floor of the cleft. Very soon after, they all found themselves asleep. But Timidthy did not stay asleep. Awaking, he crawled quietly to the front of the cleft carved into the rock, sat on rear haunches, and surveyed the meadow so as to detect the movement of any passing wolf. Stirring from his sleep, Naythorn joined the shy boarling.

"With you standing guard, Timidthy, my magic sense tells me that we will this night rest safe and sound." At the side of the little wild pig Naythorn sprawled down and became once more asleep.

A still seated and wide-awake Timidthy wondered how many of the stars he saw above had been given names. He next wondered who it was that had given the stars their very own names.

Ragged Bison and Lonely Cattle

When birds began to warble melodies about rebirth, of a sudden new light appeared. The look of the meadow took form. On the other side of the stream walked two big animals toward the middle of the glen.

Gathered quietly together in the opening of the rock cleft, the band watched a bison bull and a cattle bull begin to graze side by side. As more light permeated the air, Naythorn and his companions saw that the hair coats covering the big bovine bodies had been deeply scarred by what could only have been teeth, or teeth and horns. The bison's hide was notable for its many clumps of torn and puffed hair.

Finished with breakfasts of grass the two bulls ambled away from each other, turned, pawed the ground, and then proceeded to run directly into and onto each other's heads. From the force of the collision both beasts fell to their knees. Shaking heads, the bovines raised themselves to again stand. A second time they moved away from each other, turned about, pawed earth, ran to gain speed, and once more knocked heads. Each new collision bounced their large bodies down, and forced them to pause longer and longer to collect their wits before once more charging at each other.

For his paunchy belly, the white faced and brown hided cattle weighed heavier. His strategy was to charge at his opponent with his head very low to the ground.

Because the black-haired bison was taller, and relative to his height leaner than the cattle, the bison's tactical maneuver differed. Right before making contact the bison bucked upward his front legs so that he could leverage downward momentum to crash into his opponent.

In spite of respective advantages of height, weight, and strategy, in the struggle of great clashing heads it soon became evident that neither the cattle nor the bison would prevail. The unicorn could foretell that the winner in this contest, if there was a winner, would be so beaten and bruised that there would be no victory to celebrate. No matter which bovine outlasted the other, the fray would end in two-sided defeat.

Naythorn splashed across the brook, and with his teeth began to pull grass in the direction of the fracas.

"That is strange. What is the blackmane doing?" inquired the sow.

"I before saw Naythorn slowly mix himself into a scene of battle," replied Treestandbear. "His method is to walk and graze in the direction of the conflict, and then before you know it he is in command of the field of battle."

"Technically speaking, rather than a field of battle it is a *meadow of battle*," chimed in Practicia.

"I hope he convinces the idiot bison and the dullard cattle to rest and recuperate," commented the sow.

"I do not want Naythorn to get hurt by either the bison or the cattle," groinked the sensitive Roothyford.

"He will not be hurt," assured Timidthy. "Naythorn is just going to say... *nay.*"

Committed to their desperate match of bovine supremacy, the cattle and the bison were little impressed with the entrance of the intruder. They found Naythorn's decision to nonchalantly graze at the edge of their fight to be utterly disrespectful. No matter. The bovines huffed, snorted, ran, smashed heads, and banged even harder against each other's skulls. The collision this time was so bruising that both beasts dropped to their knees and found themselves temporarily unable to regain their hooves. Bent down on their knees each bull tried to remember what exactly he was doing, and why he was doing whatever it was that now occupied his time and rendered so much bodily hurt.

Moving between two bovines still on their knees, the unicorn deftly touched his horn to the cattle's broad forehead. Blue sparks sizzled, and both horns of the cattle began to glow. The big body of the cattle untensed and his large mostly white face broke into a relaxed smile. Mrs. Razorthwacker imagined that compared to a slamming head smash against the bison, the tap of the unicorn horn was like feeling a warm and gentle rain to fall upon the dullard cattle's forehead. At the touch of Naythorn's horn to a second bovine head, the horns of the idiot bison glowed.

Two great bovines struggled to regain their hooves. Placing himself as a sideways barrier between the head-crashers, Naythorn neighed, "Now, be so kind as to tell me why you two are so intent on destroying each other."

"That foul smelling bison wants to graze in my pasture!" mrawed the cattle without realizing that he had for the first time in his life understood words neighed by a horned horse. "He should go find his own place to eat grass!"

"This meadow was all mine before that blasted cattle trespassed to steal *my* grass!" responded the provoked bison.

While the two big beasts huffed, pawed the ground, and shook heads it began to dawn on them that something strange was happening.

"I hear you to... *talk to me*," mraooed the cattle glaring at the bison.

"And I hear you to *talk back to me*," brayed the bison

with his eyes widening in astonishment.

Two big bovine faces turned to look in wonderment at Naythorn.

"*Nyeeerryeesss!* To each of you large-headed geniuses my magic horn gave a present. When I touched you, I willed that you would be given the ability to understand the words spoken by other animals that were also touched by my horn. Now you can tell me about the dispute that led two rough-cut old bulls to so much hate each other."

"*Qvackk!*" Webstir fluttered down to plant webbed feet on the broad back of the cattle. "A very smart sow just referred to you as a *dullard!* As for me, I think you are moreso a *dunderhead!*"

"Do you... really think that?" responded the cattle who did not seem to be offended for having been called either derogatory term. "I will admit that I am not very smart. To be honest, I was not precisely motivated by a dispute over meadow ownership. I just *felt* like having a good fight today. The bison happened along to oblige my wish."

"And as for me," added the bison, "I was bored stiff. I needed the big oaf cattle to insert some excitement into my dreary and useless life."

"I am coming to the conclusion that this cattle and this bison are not what they seem," neighed Naythorn. "I think that down deep both of you bovines are animal persons of good sentiment. Just tell me how the lives of two big strong bulls became so boring that they now have nothing better to do than to thrash each other. You do consider that your quarrel does not even pertain to the same race of bovines?"

"I do not like to hear myself admit this," mraooed the cattle, "but when the young bulls took from me my herd of cows, I was disgracefully sent into exile. I lost my one purpose in life, to be needed by my cows. I *really* miss them."

"Humph! That very circumstance happened also to me. When young bison bulls drove me off, I found that without bison cows to watch over and care for, my existence had no purpose."

"Since for practical purposes both of you bulls are now retired," answered Naythorn, "why not eat your fill, take long naps, and... worry about nothing at all?"

"That, I tried," answered the cattle. "But having been most of my life a boss bull, I found that it was boringly impossible for me to just stop leading. Protecting cows is for me instinctive. Sometimes I feel that I want to just lie down, quit sucking in breath, and let wolves and lions quarrel over my carcass."

"Do you *really* feel that way, Cattle? I myself have also thought about just giving up."

"Yes, Bison, I *most certainly* do feel that way."

"It is too bad that there is no way for you two bovines to experience new adventures," neighed Naythorn baiting the bovines.

The bison looked right, left, up at the sky, down at the ground, and finally looked Naythorn in the eyes as he brayed, "Now that for the first time in my life I can talk words, I feel rejuvenated. I would be ready for a new..."

"Tell me, horse with a horn..." interrupted the cattle.

"My name is Naythorn."

"Well Naythorn, unlike the duck perched on my back I do not think you want to be a nuisance to me. What precisely are you and your companions up to?"

After motioning with his head for the wild boars, goose, and bear to join him, the blackmane turned to the bovines and neighed, "Have you time enough to spare to listen to a rather long story?"

Two huge bovine heads nodded *yes*.

Naythorn recounted how after he had rescued his companions from wolves, witnessed the death of his grandsire, and saw his home poisoned and destroyed by an exploding mountain and a great wave that pounded out from the sea, he had set off accompanied by his new friends to find his disappeared herd of all-white unicorns.

"I *would*... like to see new lands," came a spontaneous admission from the cattle.

"That would be an adventure of... *real* discovery," added the bison.

"What can a displaced old cattle and an unofficially retired bison offer in return for membership in my platoon?"

"I have learned a lot from bad experiences that proved costly and difficult, and left deep scars on my black hide. I know, as well, that the cattle has learned from painful things that happened to him. Benefiting from what we bovines have the hard way learned, we could help defend you and your friends through the long journey ahead."

"Maybe you do not know this, Naythorn, but you

need us to go with you," mraooed the cattle. "Two pairs of bovine horns and four pairs of bovine hooves can well-protect razorbacks, a pesky duck with a green head, a black-billed goose with a long-neck, and an imposing but not fully grown bear."

"Because formality of address fits two great bovines, I will call you Sir Cattle, and you Master Bison. Now then, I cannot believe that I had not thought of all that you say. I have already made enemies of several dangerous wolves, one of which is particularly fearsome. The idea that Sir Cattle and Master Bison suggest, is astute and shrewd. Upon finding myself in a future fray I will not only call upon your strength, I will also rely upon the wisdom gained from your many experiences. Some battles are won by strength in numbers, or by great valor. For strategic thinking and maneuvering, other battles come not to be fought at all.

"The problem with you two butting heads all day is that for the cattle to win, the bison has to lose. The problem with a win for the bison is that the cattle must lose. I cannot promise that joined to me you will never face defeat or disaster. But I can promise that as fellow helpers on my sojourn we will win together, and if we lose, it will also be together. So, in conclusion, to a splendid Sir Cattle and an imposing Master Bison I declare welcome to my unique band of animal persons."

"What are your..." The sow caught herself, "Uh, sorry, I forgot that you do not possess names. Well that will never do!"

"I repeat that for the natural gravity of their personalities, I think of them as Sir Cattle and Master

Bison," interjected the blackmane.

"But they each must have a personal name. Possessing very own names will make them to be an even more special Sir Cattle and Master Bison." Waiting to see what interesting and unique names would be invented by the sow, Naythorn's face broke into a smile.

"Sir Cattle, when you fight you move athletically and with measured gait," gruffed the sow. "You also weigh a ton."

"How much is a ton?" inquired the cattle.

"A ton is five times more than what I weigh, and of course, I weigh more than I should. As I was just saying, given your elegant presence and the impressive girth of your belly, you deserve a formal and weighty name that combines well to your striking physical circumstances. Hmm. You shall be known as... Taurington."

After sounding out the three syllables of his name, the cattle was in agreement. "That name does fit me." In response, the mother pig nodded approvingly at the newly named cattle.

"Now, Master Bison, I could not help but see that you are adept at bucking. You also merit a formal name that bespeaks your strength. So, you are to be called... Buckmight."

"From this day on I am to be referred to as the mighty Buckmight!" bellowed the bison bucking up front hooves.

"Those are two very fine names!" squealed Roothyford.

"Those are far better names than the one you gave to the bear," added Hamilton.

Most of the animals in the band went to sleep that night in the safety of the rock indent. Not caring to seem too familiar and forward with their new companions, Taurington and Buckmight slept outside and apart.

The next morning the razorback family feasted on nuts, big starchy roots, and best of all juicy grubs. Naythorn, Taurington, and Buckmight ate grass and more grass. Webstir and Featherspark paddled the nearby brook in search of big water bugs to devour. After finishing all the berries he could find, Treestandbear graduated to eating fish. He would paw a fish onto the bank, devour it mostly whole, and for that accomplishment look particularly pleased with himself.

CHAPTER 4

TAURINGTON AND BUCKMIGHT IN THE LEAD

Journey renewed in the direction of the fixed star. By early afternoon Naythorn could not help but notice that the bovines were furtively doing their best to nudge ahead of him and take the lead. By late afternoon the blackmaned unicorn found himself, along with the bear, walking directly behind the cattle. Behind the bison plodded the five razorbacks. When not perched upon the wide back of Taurington, the two waterfowl took turns scouting from above.

Naythorn did not like *not* being in the lead. Still, the unicorn knew that possessing a lifelong tradition of walking in front of the cows they protected, the cattle and the bison could not suppress their ingrained instincts to lead. The unicorn reluctantly resigned himself to the fact that just as Buckmight and Taurington had before led in one direction or another their bovine herds, the two bulls would be resolutely marching at the front of his band of animal persons.

When wind, rain, and white bolts of light brought turmoil to an evening sky, the band took refuge under a protective granite overhang.

"In a violent storm it comforts to take cover with friends," allowed Treestandbear. The sleeping pattern that night changed as Taurington and Buckmight moved to rest beside the other band animals. Still, the two bovines slept outermost.

Naythorn decided that his *strange platoon,* as his grandsire would view it, consisting of himself and now ten additional animal persons... had come to enjoy surprising unity. He thought that until he overheard a half asleep Taurington mutter to Buckmight that he did not relish the idea of sleeping next to a snoring bear that had sharp teeth and ate big pieces of fish steak for breakfast, lunch, and dinner. Naythorn next overheard the bison mumble something about bears being notoriously unpredictable, with at times terribly nasty moods.

The unicorn grew pensive. The bear was the only member of his band that had big teeth exactly suited to puncture flesh and tear at meat. The unicorn recalled that upon first meeting each other, when the bear had reached to grasp his horn, he had felt something to flow back from the bear's heart. When they had been briefly by magic connected, Blackmane had come to know that Treestandbear was selfless, steadfast, and loyal.

"The bear will soon become your staunch friend," neighed Naythorn nuzzling Taurington awake. "Tristanbear's unwillingness to give in to fear, or to accept retreat, will someday bring rescue to our platoon."

The cattle nodded his head in agreement, through big nostrils expelled a huge huff of breath, and with surprising promptness was once again asleep.

As travel toward the fixed star progressed day after day, Naythorn noted with satisfaction that the bear was the only member of the band that did not mind being pecked at by a pesky duck, or fussed at by razorback piglings.

"What, Bear, is wrong with you?" inquired Hamilton. "If you do not quit growing so fast, you will grow right out of your own skin!"

Stars Uncountable

The trail followed by the bovines led into a rock formation that made animal persons, from biggest to smallest, to stop and stare. Slender sand-hued rocks speared upward in the form of impressive pillars. The spires, that tapered little as they grew tall, rose ten times higher than Treestandbear standing upright on hind legs.

"Mama," inquired Timidthy, "who exactly chiseled apart these rock columns, and stood them so high on end? I think it not possible that a *very* strong wind blew them upright."

"I cannot answer that question. But if I had to guess, I would say that it was someone very powerful that had as well an eye for beauty."

The band entered next a big basin whose far part was crowded by shallow lakes graced by becalmed surfaces. After one day of leisurely travel through pleasantly flat lands, the band came to the first lake. Naythorn wanted to maintain travel in the direction of the fixed star, and not detour around the lake that to the east and west spread long.

The blackmane made a command decision. With his teeth, Naythorn grabbed the scruff of boarling necks and one after another hoisted the litter onto the broad back of the white-faced cattle. With the piglets so situated, the band walked carefully across one lake, and then waded across succeeding shallow lakes that narrowed at their waists to facilitate passage. When the basin was at last traversed, the band made camp amidst large boulders strewn about the top of an imposingly high ridge.

Timidthy observed that the huge boulders adjacent to the camp site did not fit a ridge covered elsewhere with a thick stand of trees. And he was sure a wind could not have blown so many big rocks to the top of a place so high. However, the boarling did not feel confident that his mother could solve the puzzle of the misplaced boulders.

Noticing that the most quiet boarling seemed perplexed, the unicorn came up with a question to distract the inquisitive Timidthy.

"Since our platoon is now camped high up on this ridge, are tonight's stars hung closer to us than were hung last night the stars?"

"The stars *should* look bigger the closer we are to them, but about that I really cannot tell. What is more, I cannot imagine a way to measure how close or far away from us, are the stars. All I can say is that this night we admire a heaven with more stars than anyone can count."

That night four boarlings, that by the light of each new day seemed to have grown a little bigger, took it upon themselves to perform sentry duty. Taking the first watch the brother boarlings circuited again and again the circumference of the camp. While the boarlings napped, their two sisters marched the next watch.

While that night thankful for boarling sentry duty, Naythorn was also confident that the pack of the huge grayback wolf could not have found out and followed the difficult trail his band had taken. Even though they were now a group of eleven big and small animal persons, their trail would have vanished each time they splashed through the middle of a lake.

"A unicorn would lose footing climbing upward the jagged peaks that back against that far away river," neighed Naythorn the next morning. "When we reach the river we will follow it westward until there is an opening into mountains that again takes us toward the fixed star."

The big bovines began to pick downward a trail in the direction of the far-off river. Members of the band were impressed with the unrelenting determination of the two bulls to lead onward through treacherous terrain.

Hamilton dropped the smooth stone carried in his mouth to ask his mother if she thought that the far river had more twists and turns than her curly tail. Because she was determined to concentrate so as to not ungraciously stumble and fall head over heels, Mrs. Sow at first ignored the comment. Hamilton persisted, "Mama, it is not polite to not answer my question. Now I ask again, is your tail curlier than the far river?"

"*Foosh!*" came the brusque response from the sow. Hamilton decided that the word used by his mama sow had something to do with the idea of... *nonsense.*

Bear Negotiates

The animal band reached a welcoming canyon with a tributary stream flowing toward the river where led the two bulls. In the pleasant canyon the animal band began to feast on tubers, berries, nuts, grass, and of course fish for Treestandbear.

Breaking through shrubs and branches on the other side of the stream, fifteen mostly adult bears made a ruckus. The growling bears stepped into the creek, all the while flailing arms in a threatening manner. The bears would not willingly permit intruders to appropriate food from their prize kitchen.

Approaching the bank of the stream, Buckmight and Taurington started pawing the ground and harrumphing great breaths in warning that they would fight hard to defend the platoon they led. In fact, both bulls looked to welcome a purposeful fight against real enemies, and not against each other. Dashing between the big bovines, Treestandbear galloped toward and then into the stream. Gaining the position of the angry bears he began sniffing at each one, and was in turn sniffed back.

The clan of hostile bears stepped back to their side of the stream, where they began to chase the new bear in play. Then Treestandbear began to chase the other bears in reverse play. It was next decided to sit and converse in bear talk. After all their exertion and conversation, it became time for every bear to enjoy a nap. Treestandbear yawned, roused himself, and ambled back toward the now bored and impatient members of Naythorn's band.

"You are free to pass whenever you choose. I told my distant bear relatives that the blackmane had done me the great favor to escort me here so that I could spend a vacation with my uncles in their beautiful and plenteous home by this stream. I only stretched a little... the truth."

"Did you inform your new bear friends how with my help you escaped savage wolves?"

"Strangely enough, that topic did not come up," wuffed a grinning Treestandbear. "Anyway, they would not have believed that I could not by myself handle a pack of only six wolves."

"But the grayback wolf was extra large."

"Be that as it may, I did mention how these bears were known as the boldest and bravest to be anywhere found. You know, Naythorn, that it is always good to compliment bears more senior than oneself. I explained that I had always wanted to meet and get to know them, and not just to hear second-paw stories about their many victories in battle. For their part, they were impressed that a bear only fifteen moons old could be grown so big. Come to think of it, since I first felt the touch of your horn, I do seem to be growing rather..."

"Only fifteen? When I first met you I took you for eighteen moons old."

"Our situation could have become tricky. These particular bears, Naythorn, are not to be trifled with. In a battle against these bears some of us would surely have come to harm. I did not want to happen a needless battle, especially one not against the vicious enemy wolves that are our true adversaries." Although Treestandbear had never before had so much to say at one time, he was not done yawling,

"Captain, on the day we met you saved my hide from being torn apart. That was for me a day of awful battle. To make this a day of peace, I must remain here. I gave my word to my uncles."

"Because you were the first animal person that I rescued, the bond between us is special. For me the loss of your company is like separation from a piece of myself."

"Compared to the loss you suffered at the sudden departure of the herd of unicorns, my taking leave from your band is but a small thing. Taurington, Buckmight, and the rest of your band will remain ever loyal to you. Besides, I think that someday our friendship will renew. When that day arrives, I will witness more of your magic. I have the idea that you will do even more wondrous things."

With a big bear smile relaxing his face, Treestandbear wuffed to the close by cattle and bison, "You two bovines before worried about the sharpness of my teeth. Today I showed you that my head contains more than just big teeth." That stated, Treestandbear was off to rejoin the river bears.

"*Qvackk! Qvackk!*" nuisanced Webstir feathering with his wings the head of the loping bear. "Next time I will catch a bigger fish than Treestandbear!" That was the duck's way of saying farewell to the bear with whom he had relished fishing in streams.

"Since the green-head duck's luck at fishing has been so bad for so long, it has to take a turn for the better," replied the bear in farewell.

"I am glad that here no blood was shed," groinked

the most sensitive piglet to her mama.

"About that only Taurington and Buckmight are disappointed," grunted Mrs. Razorthwacker smiling back at Roothyford.

The consequence of the peace that day achieved by Treestandbear was that Naythorn's platoon suffered only one loss, the departure of a staunch-hearted bear.

CHAPTER 5

THE SECRET PLACE

Although the razorback sow found the mountains beyond the westward flowing river majestic to behold, her piglets tired of what they took to be endlessly uninteresting patterns of trees, rocks, crags, and impossibly looking climbs. Out of boredom Hamilton began to fuss.

"He wanted to be called Tristanbear! Had my mama sow given our bear a more suitable name, he would yet be here with us, and I would still have a bear to play with!"

"Foosh! I will have my Hamilton know that Treestandbear is a proper formal name for a young bear."

"What does *Tree... Stan... Bear...* even mean? Now since the middle part, *Stan,* is a proper name you should have called him *Treestanley.*"

"Errm, Mama," joined in Timidthy, "Bear's name would have been more understandable had you picked *Treestaunchly.* Remember that when you named him you said he was a staunch and stalwart bear."

Overhearing the ribbing of the sow's naming skills, the unicorn interjected, *"Nyeeerrhaha!* Were I to become a less serious horse, Mrs. Razorthwacker would change my name from Naythorn to *Playthorn.*"

"If Naythorn's black and white colors someday meld together into one," joined in Roothyford, "my mama would call him *Graythorn*." The girl boarling turned to her sister, "Your turn to play at names!"

"I am not prone to exaggerate. But if I did stretch the truth, just like our brother Hamilton invariably does, then my mama would have to change my name from Practicia to *Ficticia*."

Since Hamilton had been mentioned by his sister, he decided it was his turn to continue the round of humor. "If just like Taurington and Buckmight, Naythorn had two horns on his head, my mama would call him *Natehorns*."

"If I quit neighing *nay*, and were to instead develop a more positive and supportive personality, Mrs. Sow would call me *Yaythorn*." Naythorn nudged the bison.

"If as I grow old my hide changes from black to white, Mrs. Sow will rename me *Buckwhite*, and I will no longer be known as Buckmight."

The cattle studied closely the smile directed at him by his bovine friend. At that, Taurington felt he had to accept the challenge of the naming game. "Err, since I am such a great soldier bull, Mrs. Sow should right now change my name from Taurington to *Warrington*."

"If the cattle's girth gets any larger," teased Hamilton, "our mama sow will change his name from Taurington to *TauringTONS!*"

"Enough teasing!" grumphed the sow. "Next time I will do better at giving names. And I promise to recall our bear not as Treestandbear, but as Tristanbear." So out of a boarling's boredom was born a game of nicknames. The departed stalwart friend, whose presence everyone missed, was to be ever after remembered as Tristanbear.

The band reached a place where the chain of mountains no longer loomed defensively upward. At that place of entrance into mountains, the river that the bovines followed veered correspondingly hard to the right. In agreement with the changed resolve of the river, the cattle and bison turned to lead again in the direction of the fixed star. The ground on which walked the hooves, paws, and webbed feet of the band animals was high above the river. Cuts through the high river bank ended in a deep chasm where the current flowed fast.

As the two bulls led onward, encroaching clouds came to shade the sky in pinks and oranges. Soon enough cliff walls rose to tower over the band. Bovines, razorbacks, water birds, and a unicorn craned necks to stare upward in wonderment at rock contours and dispositions calling to mind bears, lions, and eagles with their features framed delicate by the interplay of softening light and darkening shadow.

The next morning the stone architecture gradually settled lower. In an open place between two high hills the band paused to stare eastward at an enormous solitary rock, more pillar of stone than mountain. With one side contoured into three massive steps, the monolith soared upward as if to present the bottom rungs of a ladder scaling the sky. Had there been fourth, fifth, and sixth steps, they would have swept away from sight to become washed in clouds.

At last the river gorge opened to a wide valley with mountains on all sides. The bovines found that the river they followed shifted eastward in quest of a far mountain face, that angled in presentation like the prow of a giant rock ship. On the valley side of the river that flowed toward the place of first morning, sand and thin soils nurtured grass, small trees, and intertwining shrubs. On the other side of the river, hills piled upward in quest of distant peaks.

Since the river they had for many days followed had revealed much character, Buckmight and Taurington decided that a more full reconnaissance of the fast moving stream was called for.

The mountain toward which the bovines directed, that reminded of a ship, looked to be impenetrable. It was not possible for the river to invade its sheerness. Somewhere before the set of the prow-shaped mountain the river would require new juncture toward the fixed star. More than once the cattle and bison assured each other that from behind a solid rock mountain no danger could present.

Deciding to be doubly safe, Naythorn neighed for Featherspark and Webstir to make sure the impressive rock face of the looming mountain presented no hidden places of ambush. Upon being given a scout mission that made uniquely important their wings, the green-head duck and long-neck goose quickly obliged Naythorn's request.

Two sets of wings gained the mountain whose terminus called to mind the nose of a great stone ship. The water birds saw that up close all seemed exactly as it looked from afar. Except for possessing two conspicuously wide notches that were placed one above the other, the rock face was a continuous wall... and that was all. Having completed from top to bottom their inspection of the mountain's face, Webstir and Featherspark paused momentarily before wheeling their wings in return to the animal band; right then the duck heard something.

"Was that a neigh?" Without waiting for his feathered friend to answer, Webstir renewed flight toward the cliff. Because the goose knew that Webstir's tiny feather-covered ears were particularly sensitive to identifying the location from where came sounds, Featherspark followed after his friend.

"I *was* right!" exclaimed the duck. "It *was* the neigh of a horse!" The glancing of duck and goose eyes confirmed to each other that both had heard something more; the kind of growls made by wolves. But how could horse and wolf sounds issue from behind a solid wall of rock?

Following the faint sounds, the waterfowl came to an enormous evergreen tree with its trunk split down the middle. Cleaved in two, the tree should have died. But its stubborn needles managed to grow sufficiently abundant to hide a folded entranceway into the stone wall. If not from the vantage point of a bird on wing, only very close inspection would have revealed the well-hidden passageway.

Featherspark decided that scout duty required a more close inspection. To his surprise the goose found that as the fold penetrated into the rock cliff it narrowed to become, of all unexpected things, *a tunnel.* Someone had chiseled through rock to complete the progress of the natural indent. To the consternation of the now trailing Webstir, the goose flew right into the tunnel.

"*Qvvaaackkk!* What if the tunnel dead-ends?" His complaint voiced, on slower wing the duck followed after his friend.

Featherspark felt his wings current a fresh breeze. The draft of air meant the tunnel had an open exit. A large clearing rimmed by scattered trees soon presented to the goose. On the left side of the hollow place contained within the mountain were set half fallen columns made of huge carved stones that had once lifted high. To the right of the crumbling edifice a majestic tower climbed upward in three steps. Featherspark recognized that the thick spire was a miniature of the far-off step mountain whose vista had impressed the band before they entered the wide valley.

From within the crumbled structure came the terrified whinnies of a horse and the snarling growls of wolves. With Webstir trailing close behind, Featherspark flew over the place of half collapsed columns. At the far end of the fallen structure, a filly kicked with all her strength to counter the slashing attacks of wolves.

CHAPTER 6

BLOOD MAGIC

Four wings beat fast return flight to Naythorn. A short of breath Featherspark began his report, "*Hronnkk...* there is a hidden passage... and tunnel through the cliff that leads to... a lost and forgotten ruin bigger than..."

"*Qvackk!* It is huge!" interrupted Webstir.

"And the place of crumbling rock columns has close by a tall..."

"Tower!" interrupted once more the duck. "And next to it is a pool!"

Naythorn jumped hooves in surprise. "That must be a great thing to..."

"There is more!" qvackked Webstir. "*Wolves!*"

"Mean ones!" hronkked Featherspark. "They have cornered a young filly horse... to kill her!"

"Fly fast like storm wind and count the wolves in the fight," neighed the blackmane to the goose. "How big is the tunnel?"

"One horse body high and three horse bodies wide," replied Featherspark as he sped away.

"Webstir, take me to the tunnel!" neighed Naythorn. Bovines and razorbacks charged after a galloping Naythorn. As he ran, Timidthy could not help but wonder how high stood the stone tower.

Winded from his new personal record for winged velocity, the returned goose gasped for breath while hronkking to Naythorn, "The filly will not... long survive... the teeth of eight wolves."

While Naythorn ran faster than the bovines had ever before seen him to run, the big bellied Taurington did his best to not fall too far behind the bison. The horned horse vaulted into the river. After fifty swimming breaths the unicorn climbed up the opposite bank, whereupon Webstir guided Naythorn behind the split tree that hid the fold entrancing the cliff.

Rescue

Passing through the tunnel, Naythorn rushed headlong into the structure of crumbling stone columns. Sliding and twisting, Naythorn's clattering hooves ungripped; he fell on his side. His ungainly fall was fortuitously cushioned by the ribs of two astonished wolves. After kicking legs to get his frame aright, the blackmane propelled himself onto the raised platform. With hooves and horn the unicorn turned to defend the desperate filly.

After being momentarily distracted by the sounds of Buckmight careening full-speed through the crumbling hall, Naythorn turned back his head to see a small wolf with hide mottled yellow spring out of the crumbling stones littering the floor behind the dais. The filly lowered her neck so that the wolf missed his aim for her jugular, whereupon the lupine pawed along the length of her mane. Wolf teeth set deep into the filly's withers.

The unicorn swung himself about, jabbed his horn, and jerked upward his head. Clung by his teeth to the filly's back, the small wolf tumbled heels over head. When in a following blur of movement a big gray-coat leapt from out of the shadows, wolf teeth again tore at the filly's back flesh. Both sides of the filly's withers now bore deep wounds.

At the same time that the Blackmane's hooves elevated to stomp downward, the big wolf sprang off the filly and lunged upward. Moving faster than the unicorn, the grayback wolf sank incisors into the base of Naythorn's neck. The blackmane had never so intensely felt pain. To make things doubly worse for Naythorn, the yellow wolf returned to sink teeth into a unicorn leg.

It was Buckmight to the rescue. As if he weighed no more than a very agile small dog, big bison horns deftly swatted the grayback wolf off Naythorn's neck. Before the bison's horns convinced him to do so, the yellow wolf wisely decided to ungrip Naythorn's leg. Taurington joined the fray. Thrashing about long horns, the cattle bowled two brown wolves into the crumbled rocks of spent columns.

The overwhelming advantage held by eight wolves against a young filly, had vanished. Led by the grayback and the yellowhide, six wolves sped out the fallen columns of the great hall to vanish into the tunnel. Where they had fallen, the bodies of two wolves remained still and unbreathing.

Fleeing wolves encountered razorbacks. An all-out fight in the constricted space of the tunnel would have badly bloodied both sides. But with little fight left in them, the wolves slipped through and around the sow and the plucky boarlings set about her. Circling high up,

Webstir saw six wolves run out of the folded rock passage and vanish into thick riverbank reeds.

Upon reaching the scene of the fierce and bloody fight, the sow saw the gasping Buckmight standing resolutely next to the sprawled unicorn. Drawing close, the sow flinched at the blood washing out of Naythorn's torn neck. She had the fleeting thought that the red blood leaked with a silver sheen that reminded of sparkling stars.

When her eyes marked the horribly gashed back of the roan colored filly lying next to Naythorn, Mrs. Razorthwacker recoiled in shock. The breath of the filly rasped thin and faltering. The deep cuts in the filly's back were spilling out her very life. The matron hog gasped again with horror as she realized that the filly's hide was not a reddish color. Her dark brown coat was everywhere stained with her own red blood.

It was fortunate that Practicia was the first boarling to arrive at the dais, for amidst the carnage the practical piglet right away understood what must be done. "Naythorn! Naythorn! Help her now... or she will *die!*"

Practicia's command, that the unicorn save the filly, penetrated through the searing pain of the blackmane's body and the confusion of his mind. Raising his head, Naythorn saw what he had to do. With the head and shoulders of Buckmight serving as a crutch, the unicorn stepped to where lay the filly.

Right then a miracle happened that the bison, the cattle, the waterfowl, and the wild boars would never, ever, forget. When the stallion bent to touch with his horn the filly's withers, the blue glow of all-encompassing hope penetrated into the filly's wounds, and magic blood spilling from the blackmane's torn neck sluiced into the deep lacerations on her back.

Naythorn's legs gave way; his head slumped down to rest against the side of the fallen filly. Having lost too much blood, the unicorn relinquished touch with himself, with the filly he had fought and bled for, and with the members of his platoon.

Costly Victory, Recovery, and Rest

Roothyford buried wet eyes into Naythorn's mane. Amidst her tears she turned to the animal person she thought to be the wisest in the whole world and asked, "Is he going... to *die?*"

"No, little Roothy," the sow would be confident. "His horn still tinges the blue light of hope. And because his grandsire said his path would come to unite the herd of unicorns, Naythorn cannot today die. While he sleeps, the precious healing carried in his remaining blood will begin to mend his body."

"Buckmight, Taurington," grunted next the sow, "make sure that all the wolves are truly gone from this place." After gravely nodding heads, the cattle and bison went off in opposite directions to scout within and without the crumbled ruins.

The sow next ordered her four boarlings to stand guard at the sides of the intertwined filly and the unicorn. Those instructions given, the razorback sow went to look for something that would hold water. With her teeth she grabbed a still serviceable pottery bowl and dipped it into a pool graced with two old and worn stone statues. After haltingly carrying in her mouth the half-filled water bowl, Mrs. Razorthwacker wet her nose to gently cleanse horse and unicorn wounds. That done, the sow sat down her bottom and feelingly hoped for healing to take place.

Buckmight found the white clay he was looking for. He called to the boarlings that with each passing day became a little less piglet and a little more grown and responsible hog, and explained that a bison in need of healing would lie down and roll in a special kind of clay. Since Naythorn and the filly could not stand and walk to the deposit of white clay he had found, would the little razorbacks be so intelligent as to figure out a way to move healing clay to where lay the wounded unicorn and horse?

At once and all together, three boarlings turned to look at Timidthy. The smallest piglet sat down his rump to think on the issue. When no solution right away presented, Timidthy got up and began to walk in a little circle that as he continued to walk grew to be a bigger little circle. The boarling stopped in midstep.

"We piglings have front paws to scrape clay with, and teeth to grasp hold of things. So then, with our teeth we will grab two of the flat metal pieces that litter the floor about us, carry them to the deposit found by Buckmight, and push clay onto them. Two of us will partner our teeth to grasp a clay laden metal plate and carry it to where lay the filly and the unicorn. In a way that heals the most and best, our mama sow will nose the clay onto horse body wounds."

"That solution just may be a little bit better than mine," groinked Hamilton. "I was going to propose carrying the clay in our mouths."

"Yuck! A mouthful of clay would choke me!" exclaimed Roothyford.

The sister boarlings soon had their metal plate mounded with white clay. Not long after the plate of Timidthy and Hamilton was heaped with clay. Stepping one piglet's left front foot with the right front foot of the other, the two teams spilled very little as they transported the clay.

"You have clay to doctor with," groinked Practicia pawing at her mother's face.

The sow expertly snouted and patted the clay into and onto gashed horse and unicorn flesh. Thinking to herself that she was indeed raising a bright litter, the big razorback sow all the while worked with a heart-hidden smile.

Pounding winds washed in wetness the night. Having established the right snoring rhythm, an exhausted sow ignored the inclement weather. Of course the duck and goose found their drenched feathers to be perfectly acceptable.

"The night is warm enough, so why is my big brother shivering?" muttered Practicia noticing the trembling of Hamilton nestled close to his mama sow's belly.

"I get scared of the dark, especially in this creepy old pavilion. I much prefer sunlight. Mama should have named me not Hamilton, but Hamilsun."

"I cannot believe that my big and strong boarling brother is afraid... *of anything.*"

"While I am the bigger boarling, Timidthy is braver than me."

Night changed to day, and day changed back to night. Naythorn finally stirred.

"Your neck must heal, and that will take more time," counseled the sow. "Lie quiet and do not worry yourself for the filly. She will soon be galloping under sunny skies." Upon receipt of the good news, Naythorn lapsed back into rest insensible.

On the following morning the dutiful Practicia once more busied herself monitoring the breathing and slumber of the two equines. Roothyford hoped to believe that while Naythorn and the filly slept, they did not suffer greatly from their horribly deep cuts. While Timidthy wondered how great must be the magic and pureness of unicorn blood to heal the filly's wounds gashed so deeply, Hamilton did his best to behave himself for an entire morning.

On the third day after the *Battle of the Lost Pavilion* Naythorn was awakened by a soft nose nuzzling his eyes. The unicorn lifted his head to see the face of the filly, with eyes wonderfully tender.

"I find that on this new morning my gallant unicorn feels better."

As if needing to rid his brain of spider webs, the still reclining unicorn shook his head in a small circular motion. Naythorn had not smiled, for he could not make his face to manage that. Instead he whispered, "You are to become whole and strong again... I was burdened with the fear that I had arrived too late to save you from wolf violence."

"Thinking that you were the biggest wolf of all, I was at first frightened at your loud approach. Just imagine how your arrival must have scared the mean wolves that were about to devour me for their supper. Until your flying hooves crashed into them, I was about to lose all life."

"It seems that we are both to well-heal," responded the blackmane upon noticing the crusts of white clay layering his wounds. "Now, can you steady me while I stand up on all fours?" Naythorn slowly made himself erect. Supported by the filly he walked little steps toward the statued pool where he drank many small sips. Looking about, the horse with a horn said the first thing that came to his mind, "So my grandsire's old story is true; a pavilion was once made. How long has this old pavilion been to the world lost?"

"I shall *again* run very fast, Naythorn. I know your name, for I have now heard it mentioned often by Mrs. Pig. After you have rested more, you will tell me who you really are and where you came from, for I never before met a unicorn. Oh, and yes thank you for the wondrous uniform animal language given to me by your miraculous horn and blood."

For the first time since he had been savagely attacked by wolves, Naythorn found himself able to smile. Because he had had the self-confidence and courage to enter a fight destined to save a filly, a new and wonderful friendship was to begin.

CHAPTER 7

THE PRECIOUS FILLY

Mrs. Razorthwacker began to notice that when the girl horse with a starry white flash on her forehead was near, the animals in the band became like sunflowers that followed the course of her sunny disposition.

The filly's walk was smooth and rhythmic, her mane bounced with softness, and her eyes were as deep to look into as a night sky. Upon being spoken to, she returned undivided attention to the animal person addressing her. At that moment, the one she was neighing to felt to be the most important animal person in the world.

"The filly is a... *horse princess!*" groinked Roothyford to Practicia.

"Of that I cannot be certain. But I do know that her charm makes her to be truly special." Both wild boar sisters were captivated with the filly's elegant bearing and manners. Hamilton appreciated the spontaneity of the filly's laughter, and Timidthy was sure that the filly did not have an unkind bone in her body.

Thinking that the filly's bright disposition combined perfectly with her light-stepped gracefulness, the sow named the filly Rayalas, which meant *Light on Wings.* The filly thanked the sow for giving her one of the prettiest names in the world. Band members agreed that the name fit perfectly a filly most lovely.

Rayalas would know details of how the unicorn and his band had come to find the secret pavilion. Seated on hind haunches, Naythorn informed the filly that the adventure started with the rescue of a bear, a family of razorbacks, a duck, and a goose. Rayalas laughed at the story of how Naythorn prevented two bovines from breaking apart each others' heads. Of course Naythorn wanted to know more about the filly.

"Hidden in the mountains beyond this valley is a lake with water so clear that I can see all the way down to its bottom. One day after swimming across the lake, I was so full of energy that I decided to go exploring. That afternoon I found myself outside this hidden canyon. I noticed that a very big tree had split in two. My heart *jumped* when through the middle of the split trunk I glimpsed a passage that folded into the face of the canyon wall.

"Because my character is too curious, I simply had to investigate where led the passage. Imagine my surprise when I found this mountain to be... *hollow!* After exploring the crumbled walls of the pavilion, I was distracted by a tuneful noise that came from the pool with two statues. Drawn to the pleasant whistling, I reclined and listened intently to the musical sounds. I did not intend to fall asleep, but when I did, I dreamt that I became the pool's winged horse statue made new and come to life. Only try as I might, I could not in my dream make the other horse statue with the broken horn, to wake up."

Hearing about the dream, all the band members turned heads to look closely at the statues in the pool. They saw that the still recognizable sculptures of a unicorn with a broken horn, and a horse with part of her wings still intact, looked in opposite directions.

"I was awakened from my nap by a different sound that scared me all the way through. It was the growling of... *wolves!* Then you came," Rayalas turned to look intently at Naythorn, "and saved me with your strength and courage, and healed me with the power of your horn and the magic of your blood. Because I like to neigh a lot, I am so happy you gave me the ability to understand exactly what bovines, razorbacks, and water birds say to me." After pausing to shake her mane, the neighs of the filly again turned serious, "But I have noticed something strange. When I crane back my neck I see that underneath the closed wounds on my withers are bumps... *of something.*"

"So long as the unicorn is pure of heart, the magic cure of his horn and blood is supposed to work perfectly," reflected the blackmane. "And I think that your hide looks beautifully healthy. Still, Rayalas, something may have gone wrong with the healing I imparted to you." Naythorn shook his head, "Could my heart not be pure? Straying beyond the unicorn hold and then rescuing a bear, five wild boars, and two waterfowl broke lots of unicorn rules. I had hoped that by helping unfortunate animal persons to escape the cunning of mean wolves, I had made up for leaving without permission the unicorn hold."

"Captain Naythorn is a wondrous unicorn," grunted

the razorback sow. "Never fear, Rayalas, his healing power will make you good as new."

Become troubled about the purity of his spirit, Naythorn would walk and ponder. Wanting Naythorn to feel not alone, Rayalas followed after.

"I did not know that Captain Naythorn was so *sensitive* a unicorn," neighed the filly softly to herself.

Animal Person Soldiers

The band's favorite resting spot was next to the statued pool. While listening to the sound of falling water, Timidthy one day offered, "Some of the wolves in the pavilion were from the pack that Naythorn fought on the bank of the Alone River."

"So then, it was us they were following," responded the cattle.

"When we water birds spied them in the hollow mountain," qvackked Webstir, "they were come very close to our band."

"Since there are everywhere plentiful game animals to hunt," continued Taurington, "why would that pack of wolves need to pursue after us?"

"The wolf pack followed us, moved ahead to find a place of ambush, came across the trail of the filly, and followed her into the pavilion canyon," responded Buckmight. "They left off their hunt for us in order to make a meal of Rayalas. That makes these mean wolves to be very determined... and very devious. And the way the yellow wolf fought makes me think he is even more devious than the large grayback leader."

"The yellow wolf certainly has more brains than the goose that with me flies," needled the green-head duck.

"The yellow wolf is twice as smart as you two water birds put together," That said, the bigger of the boarling brothers immediately set off to race through the crumbling columns of the pavilion, all the while dodging the sharp pecks of duck and goose bills.

Timidthy, who had begun to grow a puff of hairs under his chin that showed he was maturing in pig age, began to pace back-and-forth. Upon returning to the animal persons gathered at the pool he plumped down his behind, tilted his head, and shared his thoughts.

"In their first encounter with Naythorn these particular wolves that abhor goodness, encountered the purity of unicorn magic. It may be that oppositional things, like dry soil and rain, attract each other. If that is so, the purity of Naythorn's magic draws this pack of mean wolves to follow after our band.

"The enormous grayback has twice swallowed Naythorn's magical blood. The yellow wolf has now also tasted the blackmane's blood. They both have felt the magic of the touch, or rather the cut of his horn. Thirsting for more unicorn magic they will follow us on and on. We have to think of more and better ways to protect our band."

"Who would have thought that a less than half grown razorback, like my Timidthy, could have a mind that thinks full grown?" Having grunted that, the smile of the proud sow faded. "I brag about the smartness of my boarlings, but I am a mother wild boar that feels responsible for more than my four offspring. I feel called upon to care for each member of Naythorn's band," she nodded at the bovines, "even if you are bigger or older than..."

"Humph!" interrupted Taurington. "Although I am much bigger and older than Mrs. Pig, being joined to this band makes me feel like a *stripling bull!*"

"That pack of wolves has become very dangerous for us to contend with," asserted Naythorn. "For that, on this journey we must protect one another. Soldier persons like the blacksmith and his helper that now search for the canyon of blue gold, defend well each other."

"While we march forward, we each must keep careful watch so that we are not surprised in an ambush," mrawed Taurington. "Without waiting to be asked by Naythorn, the duck and the goose can circle above us to make sure no wolves are close by."

"When on the move, we all need to keep track of one another, and watch out for each other," added Buckmight.

The animal persons traveling with Naythorn felt to be not only needed by one another, but to be as well important to each other. Everyone in the blackmane's band believed they were becoming a true platoon of animal soldier persons.

Rayalas Reunited

Webstir flapped down with news that a band of horses was fast approaching the canyon of the lost pavilion. Upon hearing that, Rayalas bolted. In no time at all she had run out the tunnel, swum the river, and galloped into the plain. In greeting their filly, her horse brothers and her mare whinnied and jumped for joy.

Rayalas had grown up playing chase with her

brothers; this day the chase was special. The horse brothers and their sister ran circles, bucked, and kicked out until they tired and it became time to stand restfully still.

"We had looked everywhere without finding a trace of our missing filly," neighed the mare. "The last place for us to search was where the river curved against the high mountain with a sheer rock face. *Nyerrrhunh!* What are those lumps growing on my filly's withers?"

"My brand new name is Rayalas. The only way I can explain everything that has happened to me... is if you come through the canyon wall and meet my new friends."

Having carefully marked where he had seen his sister emerge like magic from behind the canyon wall, the youngest stallion brother led the way toward the folded passage in the cliff.

Because the smell of an animal person tells not only where an animal has been and what the animal has eaten, but also how is made the animal's character, every stallion brother proceeded to smell each and every animal person gathered with Naythorn. Of course the horse brothers showed most interest in the unicorn.

So that razorbacks, water birds, and bovines understood everything the horses neighed, and vice versa, Naythorn's horn sparked the head of each visiting equine.

The filly recounted how in order to get apart from horse brothers that had not stopped teasing and bothering her, even after the morning *tag* and *bite* games had ended, she swam across the favorite lake of the mountain horses and then went away exploring.

"After running hard and long I came to this sheer mountain where my curiosity was piqued by the split tree. Upon investigating close-up, I discovered the hidden opening into the rock cliff. So, of course, I ran through the tunnel and found this secret canyon. Unfortunately, eight ferocious and vicious wolves followed me here.

"I fled to the raised rock platform at the far end of the crumbled pavilion, and kicked back the wolves for as long as I could. The grayback was the largest wolf I had ever seen. Had Naythorn not arrived when he did, and brought the cattle and the bison with him, I would not have survived. Unicorn magic brought me escape from certain death, and then healed the terrible cuts made to my back."

"Between mountain horses and wolves there has been a long honored truce," neighed the oldest brother of Rayalas. "Does the wolf attack on Rayalas mean our horse herd is now in danger? If that is so, I worry about the safety of new colts and slower-afoot old mares."

Upon the rise of a new sun it became time for the mare and brothers of Rayalas to depart. Naythorn accompanied them through the tunnel and across the river. There he joined the brothers of Rayalas in athletic horse play. When his heart began to pound and his chest began to hurt, Naythorn quit the games. Soon enough the blackmane watched Rayalas and her horse family gallop away. He was envious of horses united together and running free, and he would very much miss the filly. But what his body most needed, was *rest*.

The excitement of the horse visit, neighing too much animated horse conversation, and participating too soon in strenuous horse playfulness had left him exhausted.

Resting later beside the pavilion pool, Naythorn made his mind to dwell on the many little things that he and Rayalas had done together. He recalled each of their conversations, each time they had grazed together, and each time they had stood touchingly close to each other. The unicorn counted more than twenty memories of Rayalas that were distinct, vivid, and comforting for him to recall.

Naythorn began to wonder if everyone missed the filly the same way that he missed having her at his side. In answer to his question, he heard Webstir qvackk a rhyme.

Her beautiful hide is free of fleas
She is the most fun animal person to tease
Because Rayalas galloped away at dawn
I shake my tail and tuck my head down

Fluttering his wings and laughing at his rhyme, Webstir fell over backwards. Even the departure of the filly that had treated him so nicely could not make the duck descend into moodiness.

Although the blackmane had never enjoyed friendship with the colts and fillies in the unicorn herd, he had to admit that as a herd animal he still missed the unicorns that teased and bullied him. Now, the one filly that had ever liked him was to him gone away. The unicorn wished he had neighed more compliments to the filly while she had been near. Naythorn decided that even for a magical unicorn half of life amounted to the hard things of loneliness and heart loss.

CHAPTER 8

ISLANDS AND A DANGEROUS STRAIT

"We are well put to sea," observed Admiral Zoumar motioning arms toward his fleet of five barges. "I will have the high escort Aneilee and the matriarch Elianor to know that I have always been proud to wear armor forged with the blue gold that was brought to our land with the help of long ago unicorns. So long as Phoenician soldiers are honest and true, and our army respects others choosing to live in peace, blue gold magic protects my country.

"Because my king believed the prophecy that came from the unicorn horses that still dwell in our land, it became my duty to bring rescue to the hold of the unicorns before the mountain fell upon you, and the divination was fulfilled.

"The ascendant column of black smoke, the river of burning rock, and the enormous wave all proclaim that Wittanor is no more," neighed Aneilee. "Because the prophecy that golden-clad persons would a second time arrive at our shore is now fulfilled, the destiny of the white herd now rests with you and your skilled mariners."

"The unicorn presence on these barges, the largest

ever built in Phoenicia, is now become recompense for my sailors that on this voyage were to the sea lost. You see, Aneilee, I began this voyage with eight great vessels... and now only five remain." That said, the admiral brushed something from his eyes.

"I am terribly sorry for the loss of your vessels and brave sailors," consoled the high escort. "Your rescue, Admiral Zoumar, signifies a debt that the white herd can never repay."

"Whatever the cost, it had to be borne. Knowing that unicorn magic and blue gold are intrinsically intertwined, I also knew that without the survival of horned horses my armor would lose its enchantment.

"Ermm, I *need* both you and Elianor to trust my captains. When attacked or blown hard by a foul wind, the high escort and the matriarch must be obedient to the commands I give. My officers and sailors will shed their blood to protect you. That reminds me of a question I have for both of you. Can the magic that rests in your horns be brought to bear upon even the sea and the air?"

"Yes it can, Admiral," replied Elianor without hesitation.

"When the hearts of the sage unicorns are united, our magic is very strong," added Aneilee. "And if I might ask, Admiral, what of the two blacksmiths?"

"As you recall, Hammerclaw and his young apprentice travel apart in search of the canyon of blue gold. Because during the last thousand years our army has grown in number, we cannot return from this far journey without an additional supply of the magic gold.

When the unicorns are brought to a place of permanence, and our barges are no longer in your need, we will reunite with Hammerclaw and Lucars.

"Aneilee and Elianor, I am convinced that all things piece together. Separate journeys to transport the unicorn herd to a new land, and to search out the blue gold, will for my sailors conclude at the northern place of our landing."

Island Hopping and Magic Mist

From out of emerald waters appeared a distant island. With thick hands gripping long oars, the Phoenician mariners propelled five immense barges to anchor off a white sand beach. Mist descended off shore so that the barges came to be set before a surrounding bank of thick fog. After sailors filed off barges to form a line of sentries facing a verdant forest, unicorns splashed ashore. Overjoyed to again feel solid ground beneath their hooves, unicorns exercised leg muscles, played, grazed, and drank from a clear flowing stream.

"So it is unicorn magic that brings this concealment," said Zoumar joining the matriarch on the beach. "I say, Elianor, it would have been handy to have made your acquaintance years ago. Finding myself many times before in the thick of battle, and badly outnumbered by enemy forces, I would have cried tears of thanks for the presentation of such a saving mist."

"Admiral, it is the pleasure of unicorn sages to provide the protection of misty camouflage."

After men and unicorns reboarded barges the following morning, with surprising suddenness the mist lifted. Two nights later unicorns found themselves at rest on another island.

"Solid footing on dry land suits us," neighed Elianor to the admiral. "I commend you for bringing us to a place with such delicious beach grass."

"My hope is that on each new island where my barges drop anchor, we continue to eat heartily and bask in precious anonymity. Unicorn hooves will again tomorrow practice the art of grasping firm hold to swaying deck planks."

A Brave Maiden

"Two islands and a strait!"

Observing closely where pointed the flagship lookout, the admiral made a decision, "We sail the strait!"

"Sir," neighed the high escort, "unicorn magic is not enough powerful to shroud both island shores in mist."

"A detour around one of these islands would require much precious time. Do not worry, Dame Aneilee, my men will be on high readiness." The force of a powerful compelling current soon made it impossible for Phoenician barges to change course.

It was not long before the high escort stomped front hooves and neighed, "Admiral, I sense great evil. On these islands there is bloodshed, subjugation, and violence. One tribe of human persons oppresses another."

"As the current now has us in tow," answered Zoumar, "we must pass on through the strait." He barked an order, "Raise the red flag!" Warning flags on five barges began to bat in the wind.

"Warrior canoes approach from the north island!"

shouted the lookout perched on the main mast of the admiral's barge. Natives with luxuriantly feathered headdresses paddled more than one hundred large war canoes toward the lead barges in the fleet.

"Unicorns to the middle! Form with shields a protective wall around the horned horses!" commanded the admiral.

"Ahead whirlpools!" shouted the lookout.

Admiral Zoumar realized that the warriors launched their attack, when they did, because they knew that the barges would become caught in whirling currents that made it impossible to speed away from their canoes.

As the war canoes drew ever closer, arrow points came to cut the flesh of both sailors and the huddled unicorns they protected. Aneilee neighed for the unicorn sage stallions on the flagship barge to join to her. Crossed unicorn horns raised an invisible shield that dulled the penetration of arrows raining down on mariners and unicorns. However, as the barge rotated about in the whirlpool, the one-sided shield went with it. The concentration of unicorn sage stallions could not fast enough move the magic shield from one side of the barge to the other.

While standing with Mariano, the youngest youth on board the lead barge and as well the youngest in the entire Phoenician expedition, movement directed the eyes of both Elianor and the boy toward the island opposite from where launched the war canoes. With a knife in her hand a native maiden ran across the beach, threw herself into the waves, and let the current help propel her toward the war canoes. Elianor instantly understood the maiden's purpose. The knife was intended to penetrate the hull of a canoe, cause it to sink, and so compel the warriors carried in the canoe to abandon the fight.

Mariano grasped as well the maiden's intention. Clutching a dagger in his waist belt, the youth threw himself into the water and swam toward war canoes.

Elianor shook her head, hesitated, summoned more courage, and jumped over the deck rail. She caught up with Mariano and neighed, "*Climb on me!*" With her mount the unicorn swam toward the big canoe in the lead of the native attack. With quick movements of her horn, Elianor deflected spears flung at her and the youth.

Upon drawing close to the canoe Mariano planted his feet on the unicorn's back, and pushed off into the water. His knife tore through the canoe's bottom. Thrusting herself half out of the water, Elianor grappled front legs over the side of the damaged canoe, whereupon warriors rolled into the sea.

Turning her head, Elianor saw the island maiden thrust her knife into the hull of the closest war canoe. At that instant a war hammer landed a blow to the side of the maiden's head. Into churning water the knife-maiden disappeared.

"Mariano, the maiden sinks down!" neighed Elianor. "*Save her!*"

A bleeding half drowned body was soon brought to the surface. With Mariano again mounted on her back, and the wounded maiden cradled in his arms, Elianor swam back to the flagship.

Following the example of the native girl, Mariano, and Elianor, without a command being issued stallions dove into the sea. Phoenician sailors armed with knives followed after them. Grabbing hold of manes, sailors swung themselves onto the backs of unicorns. One war canoe after another was scuttled by knives, horns, or hooves. Only a few undamaged war canoes found their way back to the north island.

Zoumar had won battles against ten thousand enemy soldiers. For one reason he still felt elated by the fleet's victory over the many war canoes. Without being issued orders to do so, sailors and unicorns had together swum at the enemy. The victory reassured him that when beset by danger, his men would think fast. More than that, with the aid of mighty unicorn horses his sailors would fight better than by themselves alone.

The admiral mused to himself that a problem he had long worried about, how to unify the men and unicorns on his barges to fight as one, would not present a difficult challenge. Still, Zoumar was disappointed that the victory was gained not because of his own prescience and superiority at command. He had issued the reckless order to enter the dangerous strait. He should have waited to study more the currents. When confronted by the combination of war canoes and whirling currents, the captain of the fleet had worried more about protecting the integrity of his barges than destroying the enemy. He had relied too little on the strength and magic of unicorn steeds. The youthful Mariano had reacted faster than his admiral.

The South Island

With the scuttling of the north island's war canoes, Zoumar decided he could safely land barges on the wide beach of the island gracing the southern side of the strait. By defeating the war canoes of one island, friendship could be gained with the natives of the other. After all, it was from the southern island that the maiden had so bravely run into the sea to rip open the bottom of a war canoe. Set on solid soil, wounded men and bleeding unicorns could more quickly heal.

Twisting out of the current, five barges purchased land. Judging by the enthusiastic shouts of natives lining the beach in welcome, the admiral surmised that the sailors and unicorn horses would be treated as heroes that had on this day vanquished a much hated enemy.

Taking time that evening to walk along the shore with Elianor and the heroic island girl, the admiral focused his gaze on a crop planted in rows bearing a fruit of multicolored kernels hanging from stalks.

"The fruit is a wonderful tasting grain that we call *maize*," informed the island girl whose name was Alexzana.

"Sir, have Alexzana, whose head I sparked to both heal and to speak the uniform animal tongue, petition the islanders to provide us maize to restore strength to the unicorns that swam hard this day in battle."

CHAPTER 9

THE FILLY AND THE BAND

While Phoenician barges freighted unicorns upon the high sea, Naythorn's platoon readied to leave the secret pavilion. Wanting to be certain the band's departure would not be beset by ferocious wolves, a cautious blackmane sent one afternoon the two waterfowl to scout up and down the length and breadth of the valley. Naythorn decided to also reconnoiter.

Standing on a high place the blackmane calculated that travel to the range of northern mountains would require three or four suns. He observed that intermittent patches of white sand extended across the length and breadth of the great valley.

Upon closer inspection, Naythorn noticed in the distance a large dark spot highlighted by surrounding white sand. He decided the patch of deep color was an oasis where midway on a journey across the valley, his band could find water to drink.

Naythorn moved to the bluffs above the river that flowed before the prow shaped mountain. If his platoon followed the course of the river in order to arrive at the mountain range set to the north, they would avoid traveling across areas of white sand. The less direct river route would take longer, but at least the river would provide plentiful water for a unicorn, bison, cattle, and razorbacks to drink. And of course the duck and goose would be in their element.

Naythorn arched higher his neck; something had caught his attention. At the base of the northern mountains wisps of black clouds were rising into the sky. He had never before seen so many columns of thin dark clouds rise at once from the ground. Naythorn told himself not to worry; there was little need for him to believe that the strange elongated black clouds represented danger. Still, he found himself worrying.

He began to feel dizzy. He had that day walked and trotted far. His body was letting him know that it still had not fully recovered from deep wounds made by wolf teeth. The unicorn decided that recovery sometimes had three phases: immediate healing, a setback, and final healing. Pausing from time to time to pull at grass, Naythorn slowly made his way back to Prow Mountain. Arriving there, he lay down to rest.

Awaking in the fading twilight of evening, he thought he was still dreaming. But, it was not a dream. The bright eyes of Rayalas were really looking down at him. Naythorn had never before noticed that the filly possessed such a delicate muzzle. In two shakes of a razorback's tail the blackmane brought himself to stand on all fours.

"*Nyeerryyaahh!* Rayalas, I am... *so pleased* that you came back!" Two muzzles rubbed in affectionate greeting. "How is it that the filly is returned to me?"

"I disturbed your rest, and for that I apologize. I have much to neigh to you. But because it is late and I today

have traveled far, our talk will best wait until morning."
Two happy hearts nestled close.

Rayalas

The next morning smiling bovines, water birds, and razorbacks sat rumps down about Rayalas and Naythorn.

"Upon returning to my horse herd I shared my story of how I found the secret pavilion, was attacked by wolves, and was saved by a blackmaned unicorn and his band of loyal friends. I was made to tell and retell that story five times." After smiling at those gathered around her the filly continued, "Of course my stallion brothers noticed that I was not happy to leave behind the valiant blackmaned unicorn that had saved my life.

"Unfortunately, a very serious problem has arisen. The day after I rejoined the herd of mountain horses a forgetful old mare wandered off, just like she had done many times before. This time she did not return. What was left of her carcass was found three thousand paces from the meadow where grazed our herd. She had been killed and devoured by wolves. Including mine, that makes two recent wolf attacks.

"Because our herd had enjoyed a long truce with wolves, this news was startling to my sire. He is the stallion in charge of protecting our herd. Then, a second thing happened. Across the valley we saw strange black columns of clouds begin to rise upward.

"Since my stallion brothers know that the blackmane is experienced in military matters, they decided it would be well to learn what you know about the wolf attacks and the mysterious clouds, which could possibly be related. My dear Naythorn, you cannot yet depart this place. My horse brothers bring my sire, and my roan-coat uncle horse, to meet you by the river at midday."

"I wish, Rayalas, that when I was a unicorn colt I had come to know horses without horns."

"And, there is something more. The horses in my herd now treat me differently. The big mares used to smile at me and call me *little fox*. You see, I was very quick on my hooves. Instead of teasing and laughing with me, the mares now avoid me. My sire neighs that I am now treated differently because I have lumps, of something, growing on my back. The mares do not trust a filly that looks different." The tone of the filly's voice softened, "Naythorn, your magic saved my life and healed my wounds. I know you did not give me... *a disease.*"

"Who you are as a horse, Rayalas, is unchanged by the wounds you bear from wolves," responded the blackmane. "You are a beautiful filly that is courageous and honest."

"None of the mares have ever seen a magic horse. Maybe they also think I talk too much about the blackmaned unicorn that rescued me. *Nyerrheheh!* Maybe they think horns will sprout out of the two bumps on my back. That would make all the old mares to laugh at me. But at least then no wolf would again dare to jump upon my back." That said Rayalas whinnied a giggle. Of course the polite bull, bison, waterfowl, and wild pigs joined to laugh with the filly.

"If you are still the same horse on the inside, how does it matter if your outside appearance is different?"

groinked Roothyford. "Why, just look at our noble Captain. Although his mane is black, I know that Naythorn is more noble than completely white unicorns."

"Since I know that the mares in my herd are confused and afraid, I should not complain to be treated this way. They cannot comprehend the arrival of a magic unicorn, a platoon of big and small animal persons, wolf attacks, and my back growing bumps."

"Foosh! Animal life in our band is all about change," interjected an animated sow. "Just look how we razorbacks are doing things we never before did. Two by two my piglings march guard duty, and carry healing clay on metal plates. I, a mama wild boar, had the temerity to order two big bovines to secure the pavilion. And of course Buckmight and Taurington had to learn to quit fighting each other, and instead to work together as a team of bison and cattle. Just imagine that our two large-bodied bovines have actually come to like each other." At that comment the cattle and bison began to cough and clear their throats.

"Buckmight is not such a bad fellow," mrawed Taurington. "I will grant that for a bison he is very tall and very strong. But, Mrs. Sow, I would hesitate to describe our relations as exactly... friendship."

"Do you not mind that my horse body is *changed?*" asked Rayalas looking in turn at each animal person gathered about her.

"Why on earth would that matter?" answered Timidthy. "We members of Naythorn's platoon are each and everyone different from the rest of the animal world. We talk to each other, think big ideas, cooperate hoof and paw with each other, and led by a blackmaned unicorn travel all in one direction."

"I am glad that is the way Timidthy feels about me. Would it be agreeable to the captain of this animal band if I inform my brothers that I return not with them to the horse herd? You see, I want to join your band and become a fellow helper in the quest of the blackmane."

Naythorn felt his heart to jump. Wanting to make Rayalas feel important not just to himself, but to everyone about him, Naythorn spoke in a whinny that he wanted to sound very serious and grown up. "Because each member of my animal band has to me become invaluable, I want my companions to take part in a decision that is important for all of us." Naythorn turned to the bovines, "Do the cattle and bison agree to welcome Rayalas to our platoon?"

"Rayalas runs very fast!" blurted Practicia before the bovines could answer.

"She is the prettiest filly that I will *ever see!*" chimed in Roothyford.

"Except for me, she smiles more than any of us... *grhungk, grhungkk,*" chuckled Hamilton.

The band members looked at Timidthy and waited for him to agree with his three siblings. But the boarling sat down on his rear quarters, tilted his head, and covered his eyes with a paw as if he were a rabbit too timid to say anything.

"If not the filly," interjected Taurington, "who else would tail-swish pesky flies off my back... without me even asking for that to be done?"

"Who else on the take-off for a gallop jumps up her front legs just like I do?" brayed Buckmight.

"Hronkk! I like to ride on her back!" added the goose.

"Rayalas is the only unwinged animal person that knows how to play chase with me!" exclaimed Webster.

"Not so, Duck," responded a miffed Hamilton. "When you and I frolic at chase, I play the game twice as good as you do."

Naythorn looked to Timidthy and neighed, "Little boar, you did say that you did not mind that her body had changed. I want us to make our decisions with one voice." The band waited anxiously for the boarling to voice his opinion.

"Sometimes my head cautions me to peel away more layers to see how a root really smells or tastes. So when I paw at the hide of Rayalas, I uncover two things. First, some of the mares may think that our band is the reason that the wolves have suddenly turned dangerous. If that is so, the lumps on her back are not the real reason the old mares will not talk to her. The mares think Rayalas was contaminated by spending too many suns in the questionable company of a strange band of animal persons of all kinds and sorts. In the eyes of the mares, the reputation of Rayalas was besmirched by her ties to us. If she joins to us her reputation will, unfortunately, suffer more.

"My second reason to think long on this decision is that we are by vicious wolves still hunted. Our lives are dangerously lived. If the filly joins our band her life will, just like ours, become fraught with peril. Rayalas has to think this through carefully. If she joins to us she must accept that wolves may someday again cut and tear her. As for me, everyone must already know that there is no other animal person I could want more to become a member of Naythorn's band... than Rayalas."

"Thank you, Timidthy. But, I still want to join Naythorn's band."

"Well, Naythorn?" mraooed Taurington.

"Do you promise to protect and defend our fellowship of animal persons?"

Finding it more eloquent to gesture than to neigh, the filly eagerly shook her head *yes*.

"Young lady horse, as of this breath I now take," Naythorn breathed in deeply, "I pronounce you to be the brand new member of my animal platoon. Congratulations to Rayalas for finding this special group of bovines, razorback pigs, and water birds to be much to her liking."

Farewell to Horse Brothers

When the sun waxed high her brothers, along with their sire and a big roan uncle stallion, arrived at the river meeting place. Naythorn touched his horn to the sire and the uncle horse, and so imparted to them the uniform animal tongue.

"Is not Rayalas a sleek filly?" neighed the black coat sire of Rayalas that like Naythorn stood tall. "Your horn is even longer than I thought it would be. I trust all is well with the tall bison and big cattle standing behind you."

"You see for yourselves that Master Bison and Sir Cattle are formidable protectors of those in my platoon. Their valor helped me to save Rayalas from despicable wolves."

"Speaking of wolves, they now congregate into larger packs," neighed the roan coat uncle of Rayalas shaking his impressive golden mane. "They have become so bold as to attack old mares that make the mistake of straying from our horse herd. Before their character changed, we had with wolves lived in peace." The uncle stallion pawed the ground with his front left hoof as he added, "The columns of cloud smoke we see at the far end of the valley are spaced too regularly to be accidental. They can only signify the presence of warriors. We have little experience with human persons, but we know they will not willingly share with us this place."

"In order to conquer this valley, the warriors burn it," neighed the sire of Rayalas. "They first destroy what they will make theirs."

"On the day that I forever left behind the hold of the unicorns, I met two human persons," neighed Naythorn. "Those warriors had clever minds, sharp weapons, strong arms, and they were good hearted. While they were peaceful, other men are dangerous and cruel. I too fear the cloud smoke rising at the far rim of the valley. I had before thought to take my animal band in the direction where rises the cloud smoke.

"Sire of Rayalas, change is coming that neither horses or a blackmaned unicorn can stop. My grandsire warned me that the hearts of men too quickly become deceitful. When that happens, unicorn magic helps to restore goodness... but the unicorn herd is now departed from this land. To lessen our vulnerability and better defend one another, I and the members of my platoon are

G. D. Hanson

learning where to position ourselves as we travel, or do battle. Just like my band, the horse herd will need to exercise vigilance to not become ambushed or entrapped. Like us, you must prepare. I fear that wolves and warriors will someday force your horse herd to depart this valley."

"Naythorn, you just neighed what I suppose I already knew," answered the sire of Rayalas. "I had to make certain that through flawed thinking I did not cause unwanted tumult for my herd. It will not be easy for old mares and stallions to consider leaving the only place they have ever known."

"I have something to share," neighed the filly nodding several times her head. "My sire, brother colts, and my uncle horse all know that I was before the happiest filly in the herd. I now find myself to be changed, except that my heart remains the same.

"Where the fixed star leads, go I with Naythorn. Because the mares no longer want me in their presence, my decision is best for our herd. You do not lose your filly, your little fox. Know that my heart will ever beat with yours. Tell my mare that I will be watching and waiting for her, even if that someday future reunion lasts only for a day. I know that some good thing will come from this big change in my life."

Shaking their manes, the brother horses looked crestfallen. Still, no brother colt tried to dissuade his sister filly.

"Never forget that I would do *anything* for you," neighed the sire as he pressed his forehead to the cheek of his filly. "I will tell my mare that with his every breath the blackmaned unicorn will protect you."

"That, I *will* do. And I will also make sure that your filly eats the tastiest shoots of grass."

"Although I hate to lose my niece," neighed the roan uncle stallion, "it is fitting that she goes with the horned horse that rescued her from cruel wolves. Keep her safe, Naythorn, and be wary of men persons."

"I am one year older than Rayalas," neighed a brother stallion. "And I am envious to think of the new places she will come to see."

"I am the next youngest after Rayalas," offered another brother stallion. "For my part, I am glad that my sister filly is to begin a great adventure."

"I am going to dearly miss my sire and brothers. I will also miss much my uncle horse. May you stay ever safe."

"Your sire and your stallion brothers are strong, fleet, and smart," responded Naythorn. "Do not worry for them, or for yourself. You now have me to do the worrying for you. When my blood entered your wounds you became part of me. You are become... *my heart.*"

Nothing remained to be said. After nuzzling their filly's head and mane in fond farewell the sire, brother stallions, and uncle of Rayalas galloped away. The unicorn with a black mane, and the brown filly with a lovely white marking on her forehead, would together travel on a star guided journey.

Naythorn and Rayalas turned heads toward the tall rock face of Prow Mountain. Upon their arrival the filly was given a rousing greeting.

"I notice the intimacy shared in the small gestures

made between the unicorn and the filly," groinked Roothyford to her sister.

"Seeing our captain and Rayalas so content with each other," responded Practicia, "makes me think that for the special filly that he has found, Naythorn would not now trade the entire herd of unicorns lost to him."

While slept a still recovering Naythorn, the filly lay awake recalling each thing that the razorbacks, waterfowl, and bovines had that day said to her. She then whispered each word that Naythorn had that day neighed to her, and placed the unicorn's words in a hidden corner of her heart.

CHAPTER 10

TRAPPED

Following the departure of the sire, uncle, and brother stallions the members of Naythorn's platoon now grown larger by one ate, rested, and played with celebratory light-heartedness. Everyone felt that the filly's enlistment to the band of Naythorn boded well for the future.

The next morning Rayalas noticed that the lump on her back had swelled larger than the day before, making it awkward for her to run. She looked back at the lump, or bump, or whatever it should be called, shook her head back-and-forth and shuddered at the awful memory of wolf incisors tearing into her flesh.

Noticing her worry, Timidthy consoled, "Your painful memory of attacking wolves will soon be vanished into forever exile."

"I will be only too happy to leave behind my memories of the secret pavilion," responded Rayalas. "And I do like that my favorite razorback boarling is always positive."

"Since you say that, I will tomorrow try to look even more on the bright side of things," groinked Timidthy.

The following morning Rayalas reposed long and late. That being the case, Naythorn decided that departure from the hollow mountain could wait one more day. After all, the crumbling pavilion palace was still the most imposing home any of the band animal persons had ever known.

That afternoon Webstir and Featherspark took to the sky to see if wolves were moving. The news they brought back was troubling.

"The thin columns of smoke, that now spread across the entire width of the valley, are come closer to Prow Mountain," hronkked Featherspark to Naythorn and others in his band.

"And this time we flew directly above the fires," added the duck.

"To force animals into the open, warriors set flame to brush and pieces of dead wood," continued the goose. "Flighted animals are hunted down with long spears, and thin short sticks that they make to fly far into the..."

"*Qvackk!*" nuisanced Webstir. "The sticks that were shot skyward at us are called *arrows!* Of course I moved my wings too quickly to let an arrow penetrate my little..."

"Human persons act like they are related to the wolves," interrupted the goose. "No animal is safe from their weapons and..."

"Their cunning," interjected Webstir.

"So had our band left the secret pavilion yesterday to resume our journey, or the day before," brayed Buckmight, "we would have been trapped before the wall of fire."

"Well, that makes me feel better that we delayed and here rested longer," mraooed Taurington. "I do not want to end my days being hunted down in a circle of fire."

"If by the warriors we are here found out," continued

Buckmight, "we will be cut off with no means of escape." The bison smiled wryly at the duck and goose as he added, "As you two can see, Taurington and I wear no wings with which to fly out of this hidden place. And unfortunately for those of us not in possession of wings, the place where we and the horses forded the river to here enter can also be crossed by warriors."

"*Ghhrrunngkk!* As sure as the nose on my head is a big one," snuffled the sow, "the warriors will find their way across the river. Once on this side of the river they will explore the cliffs from one end to the other, and so happen upon the folded entrance."

"I disagree," offered a grinning Hamilton. "My mama's nose is perfectly normal sized. But because my sow is right about everything else she says, the entranceway to this canyon will surely be found out."

"We can for now prevent the passage of warriors through the tunnel," brayed Buckmight. "But sooner or later their sharp pointed spears and arrows would take their toll on us, our defense of the tunnel would be thrown back, and then it would be ended for all of us."

"All I know," hronkked Featherspark, "is that for making so many fires, they are too many warriors for us to fight head-on in battle."

Since no one could come up with a plan of escape that would outmaneuver the warrior tribe, the platoon bedded down for the night in a grassy area by the statued pool. Resting touchingly close to one another made each band member feel more safe. It was fervently hoped that some member of Naythorn's platoon would dream a revelation of how to safely depart the hollow mountain.

At first light the band members stirred themselves awake to find Naythorn pacing up and down the rock strewn center aisle of the pavilion.

"Drink with me at the pool, Buckmight," solicited Taurington. After satisfying his thirst the cattle placed himself in a like position to the statue of the unicorn and mraooed, "I just noticed that the statue of the horned horse gazes directly at the tunnel entrance."

Buckmight turned himself in the opposite direction to assume a like position to the pool's statue of the winged horse. "Hmph! I now notice that the statue of the winged horse points at the sheet of falling water. What can be the reason, Taurington, for two side by side stone statues to look in opposite directions?"

"With you two bovines jabbering over there, I cannot concentrate on identifying our means of escape!" exclaimed an irritated Naythorn. Neither Taurington nor Buckmight had before seen the blackmane to become with anyone impatient.

"We were only struck by a moment of curiosity," responded Taurington.

The band, including an unsettled Naythorn, gathered around the bovines. Timidthy cocked his head sideways as if listening to hear what the stone statues should say to each other. The boarling butted his nose against the sow to get her attention, "Mama, do you hear a whistling sound?"

"Now that you mention it... I do hear a faint and delicate sound."

Hamilton jumped over the ledge of the pool and

landed with as big a splash as he could make. He proceeded to wade through water as high as his neck. In imitation of his boarling brother, each step was taken with his head cocked sideways. All eyes watched Hamilton as he waded past the statues of the unicorn and winged horse and then proceeded to the stone wall of the tower, with its thin cascade of water, that formed the closed side of the pool.

"You surely must hear it, Hamilton!" exclaimed Rayalas. "It is the melody I heard the first time I entered the pavilion. On that terrible day that music lulled me asleep."

"The whistling comes from out of the falling water!" responded the boarling pointing a paw.

"Here... we see a pool with two old statues... and my brother boarling," groinked Timidthy as he thought out loud. "We hear whistled music coming from... somewhere close to the falling water. The eyes of the statue with the half broken horn look... toward the tunnel door. The other statue with one broken wing folded at her side, and the other stretching over the back of the unicorn, looks toward the falling..."

"The two statues must have once been very beautiful to see," interrupted Roothyford with her front paws gripping the ledge of the pool.

"Master Bison," continued Timidthy, "I say that you were right to ask why the two statues were placed in the positions in which we see them. Not just one, but both statues could have been made to look toward the tunnel that provides entrance into this hidden place. Or, both statues could have been set to look at the tower from where falls the sheet of water. They both could just as well have directed their gaze at the closeby pavilion palace. Someone long ago decided to make the heads of the two statues look in opposite directions. The question is... why?"

"When with heads raised high my cows huddled close together, the way I now see the two statues, they were fearful," observed Taurington.

"*That is it!*" brayed Buckmight. "The unicorn is wary of what comes through the tunnel. But why is the winged filly not staring at the tunnel entrance along with the..."

"I just noticed," interrupted Practicia, "that both ears of the winged horse point in the direction she is looking, as if they are alerting to... *something.* Perhaps the ears of the winged horse are focused on the whistling that we hear that comes from behind the falling water."

"The bent joints of the horse statue's wings also point at the same thing her ears point to," observed Roothyford.

"So the horn of the unicorn statue points to where danger approaches," added Timidthy. "And the ears and wings of the statue of the winged horse alert to... *I have it!* Her ears identify the place of rescue! Our escape from the hollow mountain has to do with finding from where come the whistling sounds. The alerted ears of the winged statue, and the musical sounds the statue hears, point us to where is found a means of escape from this hidden canyon."

"I do not understand how something so long past sculpted from stone can show a present means of escape," grumbled Naythorn shaking his mane. "My head is getting dizzy." As if he needed to think on something else, the unicorn turned to look keenly at the goose.

In response to the penetrating look of the unicorn, the water bird pecked at Webstir.

"*Qrraaeekouchh!* That hurt!"

"Naythorn wants you and me to go scout!" That hronkked, the goose lifted off with Webstir in tow.

"Because the advance of the warrior fires makes all of us nervous," mrawed the cattle reassuringly to Naythorn, "it is a good idea to have the water birds check on what is now taking place outside Prow Mountain."

After Buckmight ahemmed once, and again once more, everyone turned to hear what he had to bray.

"We just saw that the duck and goose have an alternative exit from this hidden place. The waterfowl can not only leave through the tunnel, they can fly up over the side of the canyon. The men persons that built this pavilion and pool were, undoubtedly, smart. But men persons cannot fly like birds. Sir Cattle, do you not find it curious that the builders, who were ten times smarter than you or I, did not fashion a second way to depart this hidden enclave?"

"Put that way, I would have to agree with you," responded Taurington. "The builders would not have taken so much time to erect the wondrous pavilion palace only to make this canyon into a trap with only one exit that can be blocked shut by a small enemy force." Taurington's big jowls broke into a sly smile,

"However, Master Bison, I must correct one thing you said. The builders were not ten, but only *five times* smarter than me."

"On the broad plain outside the pavilion the chances of boarlings out-running either the fire warriors, or our wolf enemies, are not good," offered Mrs. Pig. "Our best hope is to solve the riddle of the ancient builders... a riddle that has something to do with this pool and its statues."

"Think on it, Captain," continued Timidthy. "How likely is it for a real live unicorn and a real live horse to be standing here right now, at the same time that we are staring at two statues that correspond so closely to you and Rayalas?"

"I do not have wings."

"Rayalas," answered the sow, "both your name and your heart possess wings."

Naythorn looked down at Timidthy and neighed the word *"Pro...phe...cy,"* that because it was pronounced so seriously made all the difference to his band members.

"A long time ago men were visited by magic visions," continued Naythorn. "For that matter, perhaps they still are. A man must have dreamt that one day in the far future we, or animal persons closely resembling us, would be found standing right here. Because they did not know when that future day would arrive, they fashioned the statues of stone to last a long, long, time. They can only have meant for the statues to point a way for us to escape from danger."

"Mrraaughhh... that is something..."

Buckmight finished what he thought the cattle was

going to say, "Fantastic!"

"I was going to say that that is something... hard for me to believe," responded Taurington.

When Timidthy began to nervously wiggle his rump, all eyes turned toward the smaller boarling.

"During the dry season, from a big storage cistern inside the high tower a thin sheet of water discharges into the pool. Because the pool does not overflow its sides, we can surmise that an equal amount of overflow runs from the pool into the base of the tower. That small amount of pool overflow could trickle away anywhere below us. But what happens in the rainy season when for days at a time the heavens stay wet? The cistern is not large enough to hold all the rainy season water that runs off the mountain into the top of the tower. That means that a lot of extra water has to overflow out the spired tower through... a *big tunnel*. Captain, we must find where flows the extra water that currents down during the rainy season. The overflow channel... is our emergency escape route."

The returned fowl alighted. In order to make his report appear both more profound and more official, Webstir saluted Naythorn with both wing tips.

"Captain, we have..."

"Something important to report!" interrupted Featherspark saluting also with both wings. In spite of his band's dire situation, Naythorn could not help but smile at the bird salutes. Try as they might to stay serious, the two water birds could not help but also smile pridefully at their officiality.

"We counted them each one," qvackked Webstir,

"because we knew you would ask how many there..."

"Thirty warrior persons approach our..." hronkked Featherspark.

"I counted thirty-three!" interrupted Webstir.

"Where we cross the river six wolves..." continued Goose.

"Scout in front of the fierce..." interrupted again Webstir.

It became the turn for Naythorn to interrupt, "Among those six wolves did you notice if one is a very big grayback and another is yellow and small?"

"How could you know that?" blurted Webstir. "The big gray wolf is three times the size of the little yellow..."

"More like four times bigger!" interjected the goose.

"Webstir, the two wolves that clawed and bit the back of Rayalas were a big grayback and a small yellow hair. They know well this hidden place. For tasting my blood, magic now runs through their bodies. Soon the war party they lead will enter the tunnel. We cannot permit warriors and wolves to rush out of the tunnel into this hollow..."

"*Hronnk!*" interrupted the goose. "Because the enemy army extends across the whole valley, more warriors will come to follow the wolves that now approach us."

"The warriors know it was magic that made the one wolf triply large and the other to wear a hide uniquely yellow," brayed the bison. "We can expect that warriors that hold the white bison to be sacred, for I myself have seen that warriors will not harm a white bison, will willingly follow two wolves magically transformed in size and color."

"Until we find the overflow channel we must block and hold secure the pavilion side of the tunnel," neighed the blackmane. "Who will help Mama Pig and Timidthy to find the door to the hidden escape route? Who will join with me to defend the tunnel?"

"I go with Naythorn," answered immediately Rayalas.

"I go also with Naythorn," groinked Hamilton. Practicia and Roothyford moved to stand beside Naythorn, Hamilton, and Rayalas.

"While Bison and I want to fight," mrawed Taurington, "Mrs. Razorthwacker will need heft and big shoulders to open up the door, for there must be some manner of rock door that enters the tower." The bovines moved to stand beside the sow and Timidthy.

"As quickly as they can the sow, Timidthy, and the bovines will discover the second way to depart the pavilion canyon," neighed the blackmane. "While you two water birds scout from high above, take care to not be noticed by the warrior persons."

When wolf smell wafted on a sprite of contrary breeze, Hamilton alerted. The unicorn bent his knee and raised his right hoof up once, then twice. When his hoof touched the floor a third time Naythorn and Rayalas charged into the tunnel. Positioned between the unicorn and the filly, three razorback boarlings bolted forward.

Horse and razorback bodies filled the tunnel, blocked the penetration of light, and constricted wolf defensive movement. Caught flat-footed by the sudden clash of big and small bodies upon them, six wolves were sent tumbling backwards.

The following warriors had not the time to throw

spears before fleeing wolves, a unicorn, a horse, and three razorbacks crashed into them. Equine heads, shoulders, and a unicorn horn knocked warriors down. Razorback teeth clamped onto warrior legs and ankles. Stumbling and dragging one another, warriors scurried out of the tunnel they had just entered. Naythorn, Rayalas, and three boarlings peered out from the folded cliff entrance to see wolves and warriors in retreat across the river.

"On this day it was them or us," neighed Naythorn. "In order to purchase valuable time we had to fight not only wolves, but for the first time warriors. There was no other way for us to survive. When the warrior persons return, they will move slowly through the tunnel with shields positioned to protect themselves, and spears extended to pierce a horse's chest."

Naythorn, Rayalas, and three boarlings picked their way back across a tunnel floor littered with spears, war hammers, and broken shields. By the statued pool awaited them a surprise.

CHAPTER 11

CAVERN, CAUSEWAY, CARVINGS

When he saw that all but the hips of Buckmight and Taurington had disappeared into the screen of falling water, Naythorn's heart skipped a beat. Squeezing between the two bovines, Timidthy and the mama pig emerged out of the descendent sheet of water.

"Naythorn, when I and my smallest boarling investigated the crack below the rock panel where discharges the pool overflow, we found small troughs containing round rocks. Just imagine that the heavy rock slab was built to roll! So, of course, bovine heads pushed open the stone door."

"Guess what else!" continued Timidthy. "The music Rayalas heard comes from flute holes carved into the door! When the water tunnel carries a breeze that blows just right, the notes sound perfect."

"Here lies our escape!" brayed exultantly Buckmight after the bovines backed themselves out of the hidden doorway.

"That means that I will have twice *not perished* in this hollow canyon," neighed Rayalas.

"Webstir, you and I will find where leads the water channel," instructed Featherspark. "Since you are smaller and more agile, I order you to go first." The two birds pedaled sideways and backwards to slow travel down a stairwayed current. From the water passage Featherspark soon re-emerged.

"It is a lot easier to float down the watery rock staircase, that has too many steps, than to swim back up," hronkked the out of breath goose. "Webstir is still exploring to see where it ends. It is dark down there!"

"My horn will light the way as we follow after the duck," neighed the blackmane. Featherspark led the through the doorway; Taurington came last. Finding that the door rolled easier shut than it had opened, the cattle felt proud that he knew to close the stone door without being told to do so.

Leave-taking happened too fast for the secret pavilion to be given a proper farewell. With the exception of Rayalas, the entire band had come to feel comfortable in the hidden canyon. After all, the crumbling pavilion palace still possessed the most beautiful half columns the platoon members would ever come to see, and perhaps never, ever, return to see.

When heavily armed warriors later entered the hidden canyon of the secret pavilion, a stone door set behind a curtain of water spilling into a statued pool, would go unnoticed. The painted warriors would not take the time to contemplate, not like Timidthy had often done, the grace of the pavilion's crumbling columns and the architectural elegance of the three-step tower. The warriors would not stop to consider the immense size of giant legs required to climb up the three steps of the tower's exterior façade that could be imagined to be a skyward ladder.

Cavern

Stepping carefully down a descendent path, Hamilton would look on the bright side, "For so long I craned up my head at the high stone columns, that my neck was about to lock in that position, and then I could not ever again have rooted out acorns with my snout. I would have *starved* to death!"

"You joke, Hamilton, because deep down you are afraid of the pressing darkness," chided Practicia.

"I would be afraid, if Naythorn's horn quit glowing blue *light... light... light... light,*" responded the boarling.

"Stop funning!" fussed the sow at Hamilton for groinking echoes off dark walls. "If you do not pay attention to the water rushing fast through your paws, you are going to tumble down these steps!"

"It occurs to me," mrawed the cattle, "that above us warriors are now yelling threats of vengeance against a vanished unicorn and his platoon."

"They better not notice the stone door you closed shut!" responded the mama sow.

Naythorn had hoped that he and his band of animals would know a peaceful trek toward the unmoving star. The journey had instead become perilous, and the dark cavern heightened a foreboding sense that something ominous was about to take place.

Amidst the gloom of semidarkness an unwelcome thought occurred to the blackmane. Something told him that before completed, the quest to reunite himself with his unicorn herd would exact a costly price. For the first time the unicorn had the thought that he might not live to an old age where he told stories of how in the ancient secret pavilion he and his friends rescued the filly

Rayalas from mean-eyed wolves, and escaped the hollow mountain through a secret door. Deciding he had other things to think about, the unicorn shook worry from off his mane.

When the downward stairwell finally came to an end, a very large cavern presented with a roof higher than once were the columns of the pavilion palace. From somewhere ahead came the sound of falling water.

Catching a whiff of something acrid, Naythorn paced rightward across a smooth rock floor and came to a cavern wall. There he smelled an invisible liquid seeping through crevices in the rock. Because he had inhaled that same smell once before while fleeing the smoke and fire of an exploding mountain, an idea struck him. Perhaps it was risky, but their situation was anyway covered from top to bottom with troublesome measures of danger. As he scratched the point of his horn along a crevice, sparks flew. A subtle lattice of flames began to finger along the cave wall. Following cracks in the stone, the fire traced out until it stopped... at a waterfall that looked to be twenty horse paces high. As he imagined the astonishment of long ago miners upon finding that the overflow passage opened into a natural cavern complete with a waterfall, the blackmane's long face relaxed into a smile.

Wide as the length of a horse's back, the flow of falling water plummeted into a little lake that extended across the middle of the cavern floor. As he drew close to the ponded water Naythorn saw something, *amazing*. A stone viaduct, or causeway, two horse bodies wide traversed the width of the small lake. At the end of the causeway Naythorn saw one... two... three large doorways. Without understanding from where came the thought, Naythorn was struck with the idea that only one of the doorways conducted safe passage out of the cavern.

"I will cross to make sure the causeway is safe."

"No, our captain is not expendable," responded Taurington. "Once the weightiest member of the band, that being me, is safely across the viaduct only then does Naythorn follow me."

"No, Sir Cattle, this time it will be my sister and I who walk first," groinked Roothyford. As they wiggled their hind quarters along the course of the raised causeway, the girl boarlings knew that all attention was focused upon them. For that, pig feet slowed and began to step with style.

Deciding it would be fun to copy the elegant promenade of the razorback sisters, the water birds exaggerated the swing of their feathered tails as they web-footed after the two boarlings.

Reading Hamilton's mind, Timidthy informed his brother that were he to copy the wiggling walk of their pigling sisters and the water birds, he would be shoved into the lake. For the second time in a row, Taurington came last.

The Door that Leads to the River

The causeway ended at a rock floor set before the three openings in the cavern wall. Upon closer inspection, each doorway measured two horse bodies wide and one horse body tall. Into each doorway channeled overflow that spilled from out the lake.

"Each of these three openings reminds me of the tunnel entrance into the lost pavilion," grunted the mama pig.

"Instead of three, I would prefer that there was only one doorway for us to follow out of this cavern," added Buckmight. "But we can presume that all of this water eventually ends up in the river."

"But why make three doorways when we only need one passage to depart the cavern?" inquired Rayalas.

"Maybe we should penetrate a little distance into each doorway and look around for clues," qvackked Webstir.

"Do you remember the water we saw gushing out of the cliffs below and beyond the folded entrance to the pavilion?" inquired Featherspark of his feathered friend.

"*Qvackk...* yes, we saw two big and fast flowing eyes of water."

"Exactly!" responded the goose. "Two big torrents of water spew out of the cliffs and crash down to the river bank. If pigs or bovines get caught in one of those torrents, they will have bodies broken on the rocks below."

"I get your point," answered the duck. "Two of the three door openings lead to water torrents. Only one doorway obliges safe exit."

"*Hronkk!* Exactly! We explore the two false exits at our peril!"

"But... since water flows into all three doorways, how come only two water torrents exit the cliffs above the river?"

"*Hronkk!* That is obvious, Webstir. Water flowing

into the safe tunnel somewhere rejoins the water carried by one of the unsafe tunnels."

Naythorn jumped up hooves to motion at something that surprised him, "Above the doorway openings are... *carvings!*"

"I see them too!" seconded Rayalas. "They were etched into the rock mantels of the doorways by the human persons that built the secret pavilion." The filly stepped close to the left doorway and peered at the carvings, "Why, this is a carving of a... winged horse."

"I think this is a carving of... *stars,*" mrawed Taurington moving to inspect the carving above the right doorway.

"Above the middle door is chiseled nothing less than the form of a unicorn," brayed Buckmight.

"The placement of the carvings provides clues to identify which doorway supplies safe departure from this cavern," observed Naythorn. "The clever builders made three doorways so that villains, or villains in pursuit of the innocent, might be fooled into selecting the wrong tunnel to leave out of this cavern. Those who take the dead-end tunnels may perish in a pit, drown in a torrent, or collapse in bad air that inflames like the air escaping from the burning crevices. If we can know which tunnel provides safe passage, we will reach the river. We cannot afford to decide wrongly."

"Humph! So the door mantels provide clues," mraooed Taurington. "Naythorn is valiant... beyond that he is a very nice animal person. Because of the blackmane's many unmatched qualities, I think the previous inhabitants of the pavilion meant for us to follow the middle tunnel with the magical unicorn carved above it."

"*Nyreeeuuugghh...* I do not feel well," complained Rayalas. "I cannot right now go onward." The winged filly grimaced from a sharp pain and neighed, "I go across the lake to rest alone for a while. Do not worry, I will be fine. Just give me a little time by myself to recover."

After brushing her head against Naythorn's neck Rayalas walked onto the stone causeway. She looked back. "Since it is my turn to do sentry duty, tonight I will stand guard on the other side of the viaduct. The exercise will do me well and help me to recover."

"Feel better soon," encouraged the sow.

The ever thoughtful Buckmight glanced at his bovine friend and brayed, "The warriors above us, that still have no idea that we are here below, continue to present a danger. We cannot afford to neglect the opportunity our present hiddenness provides. While the filly rests, you and I will do well to think more on which door to choose."

"Because it fell to me to close the slab door at the statued pool, my neck is sorer than yours, which of course will slow my thinking process," answered the cattle.

"For you, Sir Cattle, that is really not a big problem," interjected Hamilton who could not ignore an opportunity to tease. "Slowing your thinking only reduces your smartness to the same slow plodding speed of Bison's thought process."

"Hamilton is wrong," chided Practicia. "Both Sir

Cattle and Master Bison are *extra* smart. When my boarling brother is scared by the dark, his humor becomes unfunny."

"My big boarling brother should be *nice* to the bovines," added Roothyford.

"My two sisters *always* pick on me," moped Hamilton.

"Outside this cavern the heavens unfurl a blanket of stars," brayed Buckmight dismissing the boarling's attempt at humor. "After a good night's sleep our door choice will be made more clear."

The duck and goose soon nestled against each other. Practicia and Roothyford made sure that they rested on the opposite side of the sow from their brother Hamilton. The cattle and bison reclined back-to-back. Naythorn set down in front of the left door with the carving of the winged horse in its mantel.

Hearing the faint steps of Rayalas marching guard on the far side of the little lake, the band was reassured that all would be well. Soon the only sound registering with the animal band was the gurgle of water into three cave doorways that transformed into the notes of a subtle lullaby.

Sparkling dust shimmered onto Naythorn's horn. In a dream seemingly without end, he flew above the crowns of the tall trees that once edged Wittanor Hold, and then stretched his wings to touch puffy clouds. He awoke mumbling sleepily to himself that it was wonderful to fly just like Featherspark and Webstir. After yawning and shaking his head the unicorn was surprised to see that his body did not possess wings.

Since no one else was stirring he muttered, "While they sleep a while longer, I will check on Rayalas. The poor filly is still healing and regaining her strength."

So as to not wake his companions, the unicorn stepped lightly as he crossed the causeway to the other side of the lake. He looked right and then left. Rayalas was not to be found on either side of him. His eyes widened as he began to cross the cavern floor in the direction of the stairwell. On the lower steps of the stairs a dark bulk sprawled in an ungainly fashion. If it was the filly, her middle body seemed too large and out of proportion to her neck and head.

"Rayalas... Rayalas... is that you? Are you all right?" The blackmane heard sobbing.

"*Nyeerraghnhnhnn!* I am unmade! Like this you cannot see me. Go away Naythorn... leave me behind."

With reluctance the unicorn stopped his hooves. "Darling Rayalas, do not cry. Tell me what happened. You must know that my heart will always beat with yours. I could *never* leave you, and it would break my heart if you left me behind."

CHAPTER 12

RAYALAS CHANGED

"Rayalas... what to you has *happened?* Rayalas...?"

"I am a filly... *broken.* I dreamt, once more, that I could not awaken the pool's crumbling statue of the unicorn. Then my dream burst painfully out of my back. When my back sprouted open, I collapsed sprawling down. Now I cannot make my legs to stand. I was too ashamed to neigh to you for help. Besides, when I needed you most you were... apart from me fast asleep."

"The strife felt in your body is in my debt only. Whatever your back has become is owed to the blood I spilled into your wounds. I am sorry that I could not control the magic that to you flowed from my... all I wanted was to save your life. I should last night have stayed with you."

Now but a few paces from the filly, Naythorn caught his breath. In the soft light emanating from his horn he saw that, by itself, her back *was moving!*

Scrambling to the filly's side Naythorn pressed his nose against her back, "What... how... you have grown *feathers!*"

"*Nyeerrwaaggwha,*" the filly began to cry, "it happened at middle night. When my back exploded out in feathers it was as if... *nyeerrwaaggwha...* I was once more by wolf teeth torn deeply. While my legs will not move, my back moves uncontrollably on its own. When my wings broke through, what to my hide happened? I do not want feathers sticking out of my back unless... *they make a filly to fly.*"

The soft part of Naythorn's muzzle rubbed back-and-forth the patch of white star on the filly's forehead.

"After the fight in the pavilion both your body and mine felt the pain you are now feeling. We both survived that awful pain. While this is a hard change for the still growing body of my filly to bear, you will soon transform into something marvelous. My blood that spilled into the wounds of your back made to happen a miracle. Your new wings will make you... *to fly!* Darling Rayalas, you will soon be more beautiful and inspiring than ever before."

The internal time-keeping of bovines, razorbacks, and waterfowl told them morning had come.

"This cattle is hungry! It is time to get the band moving! Where is Naythorn? I say, Bison, why has not Rayalas returned from her overnight guard duty?"

"We would know, Sir Cattle, if something had gone wrong. Thankfully, all is quiet."

"The unicorn and the filly would never desert us," grunkked the mama sow. "Naythorn is not the misfit that the other unicorns made him out to be; he is instead a most loyal unicorn. And of course Rayalas is loyal to Naythorn, and to us. Both will soon be back."

Once again Mrs. Razorthwacker was more right than even she herself knew. The sow turned her head. In the dim light of the burn still emanating from fissures in the cave wall, she saw a unicorn and a filly walking side by side. That was exactly what the razorbacks, bovines, and water birds were waiting and hoping to see.

As Naythorn and Rayalas approached the end of the viaduct the unicorn's horn seemed to glow... *happily*. Buckmight, who for a bison was quite sensitive, thought to himself that the unicorn's horn was glowing as soft as the new light of dawn that now shone somewhere above them.

"Look, Goose!" exclaimed the abruptly flighted Webstir as he jigged up and down hovering in the air. "Rayalas is dragging... *wings!* And just like ours they are one on each side of her!"

"*Hronkk!* Except for a big splotch of black feathers underneath, her wings are white. Rayalas has grown big pelican wings!" This time neither waterfowl had exaggerated.

Buckmight stared long at the approaching filly whose clumped wings dragged feather tips along the ledged floor.

"What is the bison thinking," inquired Taurington.

"If it were not for the wolves attacking Rayalas, we would never have found the hidden canyon. Had Rayalas not tarried in the secret pavilion, we would not have found the tower's hidden door, and we might now be somewhere far away completely surrounded by wolves and fierce warriors. Delaying our travel for the filly's wings to present themselves, has brought to us a notable benefit."

While curious band members delicately nosed at her feathers, Rayalas neighed a sudden thought, "From all other horses I will ever after be... *different*."

After gathering as best she could her wings close to her sides, Rayalas began to rest. Naythorn's blood, that had before planted the seeds of the filly's new wings, began to renew her strength. From this day onward the band would embrace both a unicorn and a winged horse.

When the next day the internal timing of animal person bodies once again signaled the dawning of new morning, the band once more stirred awake.

"*Groin...heherrm.*" Timidthy politely cleared his throat as he shuffled toward Naythorn standing before the wall of the three doors. The boarling was so naturally shy that he never opened his mouth, not even to clear his throat, unless it was to let others know that he had something worthwhile to be heard.

"Errm, Naythorn, do you notice anything unique in the pattern of the stars that are carved above the rightmost entrance?"

"No, Timidthy, the star pattern is to me strange and unreadable."

"That is what I expected your answer to be. Each night, both of us look closely at the stars in the sky. Is not it strange that neither you nor I recognize a pattern to the carved stars?" After pausing a suitable lapse of time to mark thoughtful reflection, Timidthy continued, "A carving of a unicorn portrays a big and unique animal person. All we have to see is the one and only horn to know it represents a unicorn. A carving of big wings on a horse is also easily identified. So to my mind two carvings are perfectly clear, and one is perfectly obscure.

But I ask you, why would not the third carving also have been made clear and prominent?"

"Because a carving of stars is made of small cuts into stone," replied the blackmane.

"Exactly right, Naythorn. What if some of the small-cut stars in the mantel piece of the right door are not visible to us? In this long forsaken and dusty cavern the cuts forming little stars might be easy to overlook." Timidthy stopped talking, but continued to crane his neck upward. Remaining band members, except for the filly that remained fast asleep, joined to look with curiosity at the stars nicked into the rightmost door mantel. Judging from their blank stares, it seemed that not one of them knew what to look for. All they knew was that Timidthy thought that there was something more to be seen.

"Featherspark," solicited Timidthy, "could you with the tips of your wings kindly brush the engraving of stars?" Not one, but two waterfowl fluttered up and started dusting. The black neck goose employed his wings, and the green neck duck used his tail. It immediately became a contest to see whether the goose or the duck could whisk through more dust. The layers of cave dust the waterfowl removed represented many human lifetimes, come and gone, with no house cleaning taking place in the cavern.

As if he were choking to death from the dust that his feathers had raised, Webstir began to cough in an exaggerated manner. "I not only need an apron to keep the dust out of my feathers, I need a kerchief to cover my bill!" To register disapproval of Webstir's clowning at a serious moment like this, Featherspark gave his bird friend a webbed kick. The cloud of dust began to settle. Instead of only a few, many big and small stars were now to be seen.

Rearing up on hind legs, Naythorn scratched the tip of his horn to a side of the star carvings. On both sides of the star pattern the cavern wall ignited into crevice flame.

"Look there! Three of the star centers are sparkly stones!" exclaimed Roothyford. "I myself am partial to the green colored gem."

"If I am not mistaken," mrawed Taurington, "the two pointers of the ladle star cluster are bejeweled, and the third and last in the line of bejeweled stars represents the fixed star that we follow. Other stars, that we at night see clustered about the fixed star, are also carved into the door ledge."

"Except for one, the stars in the heaven change position as time passes," responded Buckmight. "Many, many lifetimes ago human persons carved these stars to be in exactly the position we now see them in the night sky. There must be a purpose for the stars cut in stone so long ago, to show exactly where they now glow at night above us. I think that the long ago builders of the pavilion knew that the unicorn hold would one day come no more to be. More than that, they must have known precisely when the mountain would explode over Wittanor."

"Grandsire Cabalbard said that Wittanor Hold would last a thousand years," added Naythorn. "But in the unchanging lushness of the unicorn hold, horned horses scarcely knew when one year changed into another. No unicorn knew how long ago Wittanor came to be the home of the white herd. This formation of carved stars proves for certain that a thousand years have passed since Wittanor was made to be the hold of the unicorns.

"Cabalbard said the blackmane's sojourn had to do with the fixed star, and so that star has been our captain's guiding light," brayed Buckmight. "This cave is dark like the night. In the darkness where we now stand a bejeweled star was placed to again guide us onward. With both a unicorn and a winged filly now in our band, we have no reason to select the unicorn doorway over the winged horse doorway. If we cannot choose one, we cannot choose the other. Thank you, Timidthy, for helping us to see that the door with the starry mantel is the one we need to enter."

"So soon as Rayalas is again made strong," neighed Naythorn, "we will press ahead through this rightmost door."

Upon awaking, the filly noticed exceptionally broad smiles that told her the puzzle of the three doorways had been solved. Gaining her hooves she found that for the very first time her wings moved not as they wanted to flutter, but as she wanted them to flutter.

"Naythorn, even if I am not ready to gallop or to fly, from out of this place I am eager to walk."

"*That* is the happiest news!" exclaimed the blackmane.

"Marching out of this grassless cavern will make my stomach to be my... most happy part!" mrawed Taurington shaking his noticeably diminished belly.

The Right Door Taken

"As I crossed the causeway it felt like my paws were stepping upon thick snowflakes made of dust," groinked Practicia to Timidthy as behind Naythorn's brightly glowing horn the boarlings entered the right doorway. "That made me, and of course my sister as well, to imagine that we walked very stylishly on a soft carpet. You noticed that your two sisters left paw prints in the long undisturbed dust. That gave you the clue that dust obscured some of the stars in the carved ledge above the right door. So here is my question. Do you think the paw prints we left on the causeway will long remain undisturbed?"

"Without a doubt, sister."

Practicia's broad smile let her brother know she thought it was clever of him to have been so logical in deciphering clues having to do with floor dust and stardust. Her smile came to be shared by Hamilton and Roothy. To Timidthy there occurred the thought that his siblings held him in growing esteem. And to the smallest boarling that meant... *a great deal.*

Water from the cavern lake that overflowed into the rightmost doorway tunnel had cut deeply and smoothly the rock floor of the passage. The birds bobbed up and down as they paddled hard to slow their progress.

"Do not swim too far ahead of us!" admonished Naythorn. "I need our two water birds to stay with us."

It was not long until the blackmane came to a room that had not one but two exits, with water flowing along the floor of each one.

"You go one way, Webstir, and you go the other, Featherspark. Scout separately ahead to see which path we are to follow." The two birds promptly complied with Naythorn's order.

Soon returned, Featherspark hronkked that the left passage he had followed had narrowed such that a horse could not squeeze through tunnel walls. When Webstir did not return, Naythorn decided that the duck must have found the safe exit from the cavern. The unicorn led into the passage that the duck had taken.

As the angle of descent increased, the flow of water quickened. Naythorn lost sure-footedness, slipped, and found himself seated on a water slide that careened left and right as it shot downward. Where the water slide curved hard, Naythorn kicked out to not bang against a wall. The unicorn splashed into a big pool of whirling water. The light glowing from his horn made the pool luminescent. Feeling himself pulled down Naythorn kicked hard to keep his head above water; he soon crawled onto a rock ledge. Above him the blackmane saw Taurington kick himself out and away from the curved part of the water slide. The cattle splashed hugely down.

"Over here!" neighed Naythorn.

"Over here, Rayalas!" yelled in unison Naythorn and Taurington.

The limbs of the last boarling to slide down were less athletically coordinated than those possessed by his siblings. When Timidthy hit the big curve in the water slide he bounced, tumbled head over heels, and back-flopped into the pool. Hog breath had been knocked out of him. Fortunately Featherspark grabbed hold his tail to retrieve him.

Having had enough of water channels, water slides, and pools the band members breathed a collective sigh of relief that the passage leading away from the whirl pool... was dry. Although smallish, it still fit the girth of Taurington. Although lowish, the tunnel ceiling still fit the height of Buckmight who had grown markedly taller since being touched by the blackmane's horn.

Naythorn noticed that sharp angle-cuts had been chiseled into the tunnel wall. Because human persons would not expend such effort to no purpose, the unicorn decided that was a good sign. His nose caught a wisp of breeze scenting of fresh earth. As they too felt and smelled fresh air, murmurs of satisfaction were heard among the animal platoon. Daylight identified ahead. The band had at last found the long sought opening to the above-ground world.

Satisfied that the fresh air carried no odor of warrior or wolf, the unicorn emerged into sunlight to find himself high above the Pavilion River. Upon the landing where he stood, narrow and intermittent rock strips stretched across the length of the notch. Among and between the layered slivers of rock, grass and wild flowers grew as high as his belly. Past the far end of the landing set closest to the pavilion, two torrents of water gushed out.

Naythorn noticed something whish out and wash down. He peered over the edge of the landing to see Webstir bob to the surface of the river. The duck took flight and soon his feathers were dripping water onto Naythorn's back.

"You just survived a water torrent that crashes down

upon rocks!" exclaimed Naythorn craning back his horse neck. "I could not find anywhere a tougher duck to be a member of my platoon."

"*Qvackk!* I fell into a wonderful whirlpool of water. Because I relaxed too much, the siphon torrent got the best of me, and I was sucked down. Although I tried and tried, I could not make headway against the torrent. I finally gave up and let the torrent carry me onward and outward. Lucky for me, the rocks at the end of my fall were coated by a protective cushion of churning water. *Qrrveeckk...* although undignified, my fall was surely exciting."

"I commend you, Webstir, for finding how the water in the third doorway tunnel joined into one of the two gushing torrents," responded Naythorn.

The Notch Landing

The unicorn's chest heaved a big sigh of relief. Having avoided and escaped the warriors entering into Prow Mountain, he was now much closer to the river bank on the valley side... where he wanted to be. All that remained was to negotiate a route down the cliff and then swim across the river.

Featherspark flighted back to inform Naythorn that the only path down to the river had been hewn for human hands and feet. The alternative to climbing down was to jump, but the river was a long way down. Even worse, its rock-strewn bank jutted ten paces out from the base of the cliff. If a jump landed onto rocks, bones would break and an animal person would be crippled. The blackmane decided that while worrying would not help their situation, a time-out might clear their heads.

"The grass and flowers look to be *excellent,*" neighed Naythorn.

Mama Pig led her boarlings toward humid ground where roots, insects, and grubs were sure to be plentiful. Webstir decided a long nap was the needed thing to mend feathers scraggled and tussled from his fall into the river. Before suppering, the goose took flight again to scout for the presence of nearby wolves.

While the bison and cattle grazed on one side of the landing, Naythorn and Rayalas grazed together on the other side. Her stomach full, Rayalas was soon fast asleep. The band had food and water, and for the present felt safe. Nightfall found the entire band clustered about Rayalas.

Everyone was the next morning awakened by a filly who found herself to be in an exuberant mood. Rayalas felt bouncy; her legs would not stop jumping. She was like a newborn colt that could not anywhere walk, but everywhere had to run. She not only trotted and galloped in short bursts, she fluttered movement. Her wings had awakened not as useless attachments to her back, but as much a part of her body as her legs.

The filly tumbled the sow onto her side. Managing to get her muzzle under Hamilton's stomach, she lifted him off his legs so that he fell chortling onto his back. She bumped Taurington with her hips, but could not unplant the big cattle's hooves from the ground. Undaunted, she used her wings to propel herself over the cattle so that she could with her hooves kick down at his back.

"You see, Master Bison, that wings born in magic grow magically fast," mraooed Taurington.

The bison noticed that Naythorn was the only animal person Rayalas did not tease or bother. For some reason the flying horse dared not with the unicorn stallion, to act silly. For his part the blackmane felt proud of the filly's playfulness that made everyone to smile. He saw that the more Rayalas tried to fly, the more she almost flew.

Again Wolves

When from somewhere above came the sounds of growling, eyes turned upward to where movement was glimpsed. Hugging tightly the face of the cliff, lupine bodies slunk closer to the notch and Naythorn's platoon. The razorbacks instinctively moved against the edge of the cliff wall so that wolves could not drop down upon unprotected porcine backs. The goose and duck took to the air. As the two bovines did not much fear wolves falling on their tough hides, Buckmight, and Taurington stood their ground.

Naythorn motioned the wild boars to re-enter the mouth of the tunnel. With the boarlings protected within the tunnel opening, and the larger band animals standing close by, the members of Naythorn's band needed a plan of defense.

Taurington wanted everyone to jump into the river. The sow objected that she would not be able to jump out far enough to gain the water. She and her four offspring would surely crash onto the rocky riverbank. Timidthy most wanted to know how wolves had come to so soon discover that the band was resting on this very isolated landing. The boarling opined that something must be giving away the band's location to wolf persons. Rayalas neighed that her every muscle felt an incredibly strong urge to fly in defense of the band. Having before felt proud for procuring safe exit from the cavern, finding wolves now moving steadily closer, weighed down the unicorn's spirit.

"Am I tough enough to lead another fight against wolves?" neighed the blackmane more to himself than to those gathered with him. "Why do wolves risk their lives in relentless pursuit of a lone unicorn and his platoon? For a blackmaned unicorn cornered on a notch landing, life is... *not fair.*" The situation of Naythorn and his platoon members looked to become even more unfair.

When the bison charged at the first wolf that made entrance to the notch, the unfortunate lupine was sent flying into the river gorge. Taurington joined Buckmight's charge at six more wolves that one after another dropped down onto the notch. Because the wolves proved expert at biting, dodging, jumping, and darting, the bovines soon found their horns full of trouble. Positioning themselves to protect the razorback family, the unicorn and the winged filly fought off a second phalanx of wolves.

With three wolves simultaneously attacking his legs, Buckmight was in the worst fix. When a fourth wolf leaped onto his back, the bison bucked high to dislodge the attacker. The bison's rear hooves landed down on the outermost edge of the notch floor. Losing his footing, Buckmight began to slip off the landing. Naythorn rushed to grab with his teeth one of the bovine's horns. Unfortunately the grip of Naythorn's teeth could not stop the big bison from slipping more.

The bison's body began to totter backwards toward the deep gorge of the river. Clawing and biting at the bison's legs and back, the wolves paid scant notice to the fact that clung to a skidding bison, their position was also precarious.

Buckmight's hooves ungrasped. Startled by the awful realization that his body was about to be crushed on riverbank rocks, the bison's eyes flared large. Then happened an extraordinary thing that neither Buckmight, nor any member of Naythorn's band, would ever forget.

CHAPTER 13

FLIGHT

At the instant that Buckmight's body began to topple, beating furiously her wings Rayalas jumped off the cliff. The filly plummeted straight down. One breath before her body was to crash into the profusion of rocks littering the river bank the winged filly found herself... *flying!*

She bent flight upward in a collision course with the falling bulk of Buckmight. Her neck and shoulders banged against the big body. The shove from Rayalas propelled the bison out, over, and then into the river. When he realized that he had not landed on the crushing rocks of the riverbank, but had instead fallen into a refreshing current of water, Buckmight's eyes enlarged even more with astonishment.

Naythorn, razorbacks, Taurington, and even wolves stretched necks over the edge of the notch to watch the wonder of a horse in flight. Friends and foes together watched Rayalas graze the ripples of the river with her hooves, and then beat wings upward to land gracefully on the notch landing. The filly had become a big and quick horsebird in flight.

Without neighing a word she moved to where stood Hamilton at the edge of the notch, jumped forward with head lowered, and batted the boarling off the side of the ledge. The sow and her two daughter piglings were astonished to hear Hamilton groink laughter as he fell downward. He had guessed what was to happen next, and about what Hamilton thought to know, he was right.

Rayalas dove under Hamilton so that his paws clamped onto her back. She carried him over the water and then swerved hard so that the boarling tumbled unceremoniously into the river.

As he swam safe and sound toward the opposite shore, Hamilton could not stop squealing with glee. He, a wild boar, had unimaginably flown on the back of a winged filly! To a free-spirited boarling there occurred the idea that he was the very first hog to ever fly.

Staring down at the river, Practicia's curiosity had left her vulnerable. With menacing wolves encircling, and with no other alternative of escape, Practicia jumped off the notch. Clawing air with her paws the girl pigling gained the flying filly's back and was carried down and out to splash into the river. After two more winged trips all four boarlings were safely descended from the notch. From the far river bank squeals of boarling encouragement directed at the mama sow.

With more wolves dropping onto the ledge, the sow decided that jumping onto the back of Rayalas was her only means of escape. Mrs. Razorthwacker also knew that her belly was a heavy weight to be carried by the filly's new wings. No matter, the flying horse caught the sow in midair and descended rather faster than before. Into the river the matron razorback landed a big pig belly flop.

Taurington took a running jump. With a shoulder push from Rayalas that came in mid-fall, the cattle was propelled beyond the rocky river bank to be dunked unhurt into the current.

The last band member still positioned on the notch landing wheeled about, accelerated his hooves, and jumped high into the air. With no help from the following shoulders and wings of Rayalas, the blackmane plummeted safely into the river.

"Over here!" Speaking the same two words at the same time, the hovering Featherspark and Webstir pointed wings at the best spot for unicorn hooves to climb onto the far river bank.

No matter how big the lupine, the jump to the river was beyond the reach of wolf legs. Growling and howling, the wolves that could so do clawed their way back up to the higher of the two notch landings, where in a foul mood they glared down at the animal band put safely on the other side of the river.

"All is well, Naythorn" hronkked Featherspark returned from a scout. Stretching high his neck he held up wing feathers in the sign of a *V* to signify that on their side of the river no wolves were found near. Every animal person in the band of the blackmane was grateful to be alive, unbroken, and huddled together at rest.

CHAPTER 14

TWO WOLVES AT TWILIGHT

"See the brightly colored feathers of the goose bobbing on the river by the camp of the blackmane?" yipped the small yellow wolf seated on rear haunches upon the higher notch landing. "He is the unicorn's main scout."

"*Grrrraaaaoouu,*" responded the big gray haired wolf, "while I am stranded on the wrong side of the river, two wretched bird scouts play in the water. I still cannot believe you let the blackmane to escape me."

The small wolf motioned a paw as he counted, "One... two... four... six... nine wolves with life crushed from out their bodies lie on the notch landing and river bank rocks. Seven more unfortunate wolves with bodies broken, cry piteously on the notch. They should be shoved off the landing, and so dispatched from their misery."

"*Grrrraaaawwww... no!* Let their suffering serve as a lesson to other wolves. Under my command the cost of failure is pain and torment."

"*Yrruuff! Yggruuff! Yraarruuff!*" At their general's comment, wolves gathered about him voiced cruel agreement. In the army of the big gray wolf no sympathy would be given to a gravely wounded brother, cousin, or friend.

"Might you have something you want to confess to me?" grrrd the fierce grayback.

"*Yrrruullpp,*" the yellow wolf lieutenant slumped himself smaller. "I am heartily ashamed... that I failed to prepare a plan to fight on both sides of the river. But not even the wolf general could have foreseen that the filly's unnatural new wings would provide a means of escape for the unicorn's band.

"I still do not know how, after so much punishment from wolf teeth, she was brought back from a certain death. When we came within one bite of killing the filly in the hidden canyon, she did not possess wings. The magic of the blackmane's horn and blood is even more powerful than I had previously imagined. Do you acknowledge, great cousin that I could not have been prepared for the transformation of the filly into a flying horse?"

"I do not tolerate sloppiness. You, small fry, had better not fail me again." Although he invariably made fun of his lieutenant wolf's unusually small frame, the big wolf commander also knew it was not muscles or frame that made the yellow wolf valuable to him. The puny wolf's usefulness came from the ideas that presented from his oversized brain.

"To defeat the blackmane my cousin wolf needs a bigger wolf army."

"Do not concern yourself about the recruitment of more wolf privates. Refusal on that count brings crippling or death to the cowardly wolf that does not comply with my command to enlist."

"The unicorn's band is very close to us," yipped the

small mottled wolf changing the subject. "Yet because of the cliffs and river that separate them from us, they are beyond our grasp." The face of the lieutenant wolf relaxed as he added, "Seeing them so close reminds of how *Good* attracts *Evil*."

"You better not be insinuating that the unicorn is good, and that I am evil."

"Well, my vengeful and violent cousin, I confess that sometimes it does seem that way to me."

Raising a paw to strike, the big wolf glared down at his lieutenant. With one blow the wolf commander could then and there end his small cousin's life. The grayback lowered back to ground the threatening paw. Instead of punish, he would this time rebuke.

"My yellow runt cousin is... *dead wrong*. I thought you were smarter than to say something so outrageous to me. By stepping between me and my prey, the freakish-colored unicorn broke all laws of nature. The blackmane took first from my grasp the young bear. From my clutches the unicorn next stole five wild pigs, a duck, and a goose. A cattle and bison aided the blackmane in the theft of the filly. That makes every one of the animals with the unicorn, from the big bison to the little duck, the unnatural and evil ones that have outlived their destiny.

"Now pay attention and learn something... you miserable excuse for a wolf. I and my loyal wolf soldiers are doing the job we were born to do. It is my task, a responsibility I take very seriously, to kill weaker animal persons. By doing what I was made to do I obey the rules of nature. The unicorn does not. That makes me a good wolf and the blackmane an evil unicorn. *Grrrrrraawwwr...* you got that straight yellow cob?"

"*Yipe, yipe.* With my master's logic I cannot... am not able to argue," answered softly the yellow wolf. He lowered his head to the ground in a sign of abject obedience. "But cousin, your war of revenge has become very costly. We today lost too many wolves, and we still did not stop the horned horse."

"This is for your insolence!" growled the grayback backhanding a large paw to the face of the yellow wolf. "Think of something worthwhile to say to me so that I will not have to again cuff your face." The yellow wolf sidled two steps away from his big cousin before next speaking.

"Your wolf soldiers need time to rest, recover, and replenish bellies. On empty stomachs wolves do not fight well."

"All right! I will for seven suns delay my pursuit, but I refuse to delay my scouts. I do not quit until the blackmane is no more. When you and I again meet, my yellow wolf lieutenant had better come prepared with a flawless battle plan for the next action of my war against the blackmaned unicorn. Now that I think about it, since the filly was made magical, her meat will be very tender and tasty."

"But the unicorn is still your greatest foe. As I yelped before, it was his magic blood that authored the miracle of a horse to grow wings. And, of course you know it was the taste of unicorn blood that made you to grow enormous."

"*Grarrhaha!* I am at that much grown." The big wolf

stood and stretched. "I go to conscript more wolves for the next fight. Get to work on a new plan of ambush. Remember that if your new strategy does not give me the unicorn, you will feel my wrath. Even for a blood relative my anger is harsh and difficult to placate." The conversation ended, the still fit and whole wolves seated about the two leaders left to hunt rabbit and deer.

Unable to reconcile himself to the failure of the day's battle, the eyes of the yellow wolf remained fixated upon the band of the blackmaned unicorn. The small cousin wolf worried that if his next plan of battle did not succeed, the consequence for him would be nothing less than calamitous. However, as the mood of the yellow wolf lightened he began to wonder why the taste of unicorn blood made his cousin to grow bigger and meaner, and himself to only smarten and yellow more.

On the Far Side of the River

"We were completely surrounded on the notch, and badly outnumbered," brayed the bison to his half asleep bovine friend. "We had no place to escape or flee. Do you grasp how close we came to losing the *Battle of Notch Landing,* and so losing our lives?"

"Err... our survival is a miracle engraved with the name Rayalas," responded Taurington shaking drowsiness from his eyes.

"Nor you, Taurington, nor I have ever seen anything to compare with the feats of rescue she today performed. Her winged prowess, so soon after sprouting feathers, is a singular accomplishment that leaves me absolutely amazed. Today she was our warrior princess horse."

When past middle night the mother pig awoke, she moved to watch over the slumber of a filly exhausted from hard transport. Mrs. Razorthwacker observed that while the unmoving head of Rayalas flew dreams through night stars, the twitching of growing feathers was the only movement her body made. The razorback sow watched long to grow miraculous feathers.

CHAPTER 15

APART

At daybreak Naythorn's platoon broke camp and left forever behind the *Battle of Notch Landing*. In early afternoon the cattle and bison turned to follow a path into river bluffs. Soon band members were contentedly grazing tall grass, harvesting nuts, digging succulent roots, and eating whatever else presented. At day's end the band members came together to develop a plan for future travel.

"Just like the warriors that now depart this valley in movement to the south, we must leave behind the valley of Prow Mountain," began Naythorn. "Following the Pavilion River with plentiful water to drink, we travel toward the fixed star. However, the wolves know that we are by this river to be found.

"A second course that cuts across this big valley toward the line of far northern mountains, would be harder for the wolves to anticipate. Duck and Goose confirm that there exists an oasis where we can take respite. Because the big grayback wolf does not relent, whichever route we take must be fast traveled."

"Piglings do not very fast move," grunted the sow. "If the big swift animals slow down so that we wild boars can keep up, I fear the whole band will be placed at risk."

"Perhaps we can invent a plan that fosters trickery, and so confuses fast traveling wolves," offered Timidthy building on his sow's comment.

Every member of the band grasped that a perplexing problem was at hand. Not knowing what next to say, they did what to them came natural, and sought slumber. Somnolent minds did not, however, stop thinking about the complex and disparate problems involved in moving quickly and far a band made up of big and not so big animal persons.

Revived by a time of rest, and as well by more food put in their bellies, the band reassembled late the next morning to come up with a solution to the problem presented by little pigs slower afoot than a unicorn, winged filly, and bovines. Webstir's right wing had come up limp, which further complicated the discussion.

"No! My wing is *not* sored from my tumble down the torrent of water! It is sored because a dull fish, as big as Mrs. Razorthwacker, rammed headlong into my wing!"

"It surely was a dull fish... but one the size of an overgrown minnow," chided Featherspark.

After smiling at the water birds for their gifts of exaggeration, Buckmight brayed, "Because magic is by our captain possessed, he is the one to decide which path we will follow."

"You must know, Naythorn, that sooner or later the grayback will have to be dealt with," interjected Taurington pawing dirt. "Maybe we should pick a spot to fight his army, and at that time and place defeat all the wolves... or succumb together with our dignity intact."

"Sir Cattle, the more I think about how to keep us one and all safe, the more frustrated I am with wolves that do not permit us free passage out of this broad valley. The grayback wolf hates me so much that... *his thinking* has become deranged."

"Since Naythorn raised the issue, I wonder how exactly *thinks* a wolf," brayed Buckmight.

"They are very shrewd," responded Taurington. "Wolves surround a cattle herd, scare the cows to make them run wildly, and in the confusion pick off defenseless calves made unluckily separated."

"Can you believe that arrogant wolves wrongly think they are smarter than a razorback boar?" grunted Hamilton.

"A devious wolf knows not to show interest in a flying duck," qvackked Webstir. "So he deceives a duck into believing he has left, patiently waits for the duck to land and settle, and then springs upon the nested duck."

"You, all of you, are right," answered the bison. "Remembering that wolves are smart strategists, patient, deceptive, and overconfident should help us to make them think they know where we are, when we are not there at all."

"I see what you are getting at," mrawed Taurington. "However being physically strong, I am not accustomed to being deceptive in my thinking."

"None of us are devious by nature," neighed Rayalas. "But if we put our heads together, before nightfall we can think of a way to outsmart overconfident wolves."

When four wild boar siblings adjourned to sit with their sow, who wore a grave demeanor, their discussion grew lengthy.

"But that is too dangerous," groinked Roothyford. "We cannot weaken ourselves by splitting up our platoon. Like separated calves, the wolves would then pick off one little group of us at a time."

"But the plan thought out by our boarling brothers provides an element of evasive trickery that favors us," responded Practicia.

"Tell me again how this plan works," grunted the mama pig.

"*Grunkhahaa!* Because I am far more eloquent than my brother Timidthy, this time I will explain the plan."

"You are definitely ten times more a talker than is brother Timidthy," answered Practicia.

In imitation of his brother, Hamilton tilted his head quizzically, held up a paw, and groinked, "First, we send the smaller band members toward the mountains where rests at night the sun. Once arrived safely there, we razorbacks and the water birds find a place to hide for a few following suns.

"Second, the band's big and fast animals continue to move along the river. Lusting for Naythorn's magic blood, the wolves will of course decide to follow the trail of the big animals.

"Third, somewhere along the river route the speedy Naythorn, Rayalas, Taurington, and Buckmight lose the wolves.

"Fourth, the two halves of our platoon rejoin at the oasis found in the middle of this sandy valley."

"Again, how exactly do I and my four boarlings travel fast enough to the western mountains to elude the wolves?" responded Mama Pig.

"Because Rayalas is to fly each wild boar to the new hiding place," answered Hamilton, "there will be no pig foot prints for the wolves to follow. Wolves cannot track a flying horse at night. We will hide quietly in a cave until it is safe to move along the base of the western mountain range, and thereafter move to the oasis. Since Webstir's wing is sore, we will rely on the eyes and wings of the goose to help keep us safe."

"So for the purpose of deception we divide and make ourselves look weak, in order to once again reunite in strength," replied the sow. "Well, we will soon see what the big animal persons think of my boarlings' complicated plan. Who knows, if this plan confuses your mother sow, it might do the same to the wolves."

The Band Divides in Two

The plan devised by Hamilton and Timidthy was presented to all the band animals. After many questions were asked and answered, and the plan was finally by all understood, the strategy was accepted.

That same evening Rayalas knelt for Timidthy and Hamilton to jump onto her back. A filly's back is nothing if not strong, and Rayalas knew her back would not bend under the weight of both boarling brothers. Featherspark flew escort. It took many thousands of flying horse breaths to travel all the way across the valley and arrive at the base of the western mountains. The keen eyes of Rayalas soon identified a suitable hideout. Before the night ended, five razorbacks and a duck had hitch-hiked on the wings of a flying filly to become newly situated in a cave favored by a small nearby stream, whose banks offered roots and berries to eat. The cave as well offered a vantage point for detecting movement in the constricted ravine.

After two days in hiding the animals became infected with what Timidthy called *cave-fever*. When Featherspark accused Webstir of only pretending to have a lame wing, the duck began to energetically nip at the goose. To readjust the duck's attitude, the bigger waterfowl sat on the smaller. Noisy water bird disharmony spread to infect Roothyford, who found she could not abide the sight of her sister pig.

The razorback sow got stern with Roothyford, and for that matter, with everyone else. Webstir, Featherspark, Roothy, and Practicia were made to sit in separate corners of the cave. For good measure the sow made her other two boarlings to sit very quietly one on each side of her.

On the third morning in the cave Mrs. Razorthwacker sent Featherspark scouting.

"Excellent!" hronkked the white-cheeked goose fluffing his feathers. "I can finally get away from the pesky duck!" Featherspark returned having sighted only one wolf, and that one at a considerable distance from the ravine leading to their cave.

On the fourth morning the scout goose returned with the news that the deeply scarred black wolf he had sighted on the previous day, was now at the entrance to their ravine. Seven pairs of pig, duck, and goose eyes were soon peering out of the cave to detect any movement of wolf legs. It did not take long for a black wolf to be spotted stepping slowly and stealthily up the ravine. The sow, her boarlings, the duck, and the goose moved deeper into the shadows of the cave.

"I once before saw those scars on a black hide," grunted the always observant Practicia. "In the tunnel Rayalas batted that wolf into warriors wanting to entrance Prow Mountain."

"So it is a lone wolf sent out to find us," observed Timidthy. "He will soon catch our scent. Since we are too many for one wolf to handle he will depart, only to later return with wolf reinforcements. Now found nowhere near, Rayalas cannot carry us away from here. It is too late to make a run for it, and we dare not let the wolf report our presence to other wolves."

"I will be the decoy," offered bravely Practicia. "If the lone wolf sees our big mother sow, he will run away from a fight. When he sees just one little girl pig, me, he will give in to his nature and chase me. I will lead him here to the rest of you." The razorbacks, duck, and goose crawled and waddled back to the cave opening.

"Even if he was ordered not to do so, the wolf will not be able to resist his nature. He *will* pursue me. Fall upon him twenty pig lengths before the cave entrance, otherwise it will go very badly for me."

As Practicia disappeared into tall grass, Mrs. Razorthwacker, Hamilton, Timidthy, and Roothyford readied themselves to attack the wolf.

Thinking that he could have volunteered to play his broken wing trick on the wolf, Webstir whispered to his feathered friend, "I cannot pretend that my wing is broken, because it already *is* broken. Hah! And since wolves prefer pig meat, it is best that we waterfowl sit out this fight."

A ruckus of pigling squealing began. Along with the pounding of pig and wolf paws over scrubby rocky ground, sticks were heard to break.

The big predator clamped teeth onto a leg of Practicia. An instant later a razorback sow sank her teeth into a back wolf leg. Too late the wolf realized that his headlong rush to enjoy tender ham for lunch had left him exposed and vulnerable. Before the wolf could fight off the sow, Hamilton and Roothyford grabbed front legs and immobilized the snarling lupine. Showing no fear, Timidthy sank teeth into wolf throat. Trembling with the excitement of a life and death struggle, five razorbacks came to stare at the dead wolf whose blood came to stain deeply the ground.

As a token of his animus toward the animal kind that had killed his family, Webstir hissed at the body and bit at its fur. Batting Webstir away from the dead wolf Featherspark hronkked, "Calm yourself. This wolf will no more devour ducklings or goslings."

"I was not brave enough to unfeelingly end the life of the wolf," groinked Hamilton.

"Someone had to," replied Practicia.

From inside the cave came the sounds of shoved stones. Upon investigating, pigs and water birds found Timidthy snouting aside rocks and dirt to make a depression destined to become a wolf grave. The sow returned to the wolf, grabbed a back leg in her teeth, and by herself dragged the body into the cave. After four boarlings had made deeper the grave, the sow snouted the black wolf into the hole. Pig snouts pushed dirt and rocks to cover an inert body.

"Because it was the first time I had done such damage to a fellow creature," reflected Timidthy, "I was feeling guilty. But I decided, rather quickly, that I do not possess the luxury of time for regret or shame. It does not matter if the lupine happened upon us by accident, or not. Wolf pursuit of us will continue relentless. When the black wolf does not return, his clever wolf brothers will follow where he scouted, and the scent of the dead wolf's trail will lead to this ravine. Whether or not wolves smell the spilt wolf blood, or discover the buried carcass, makes little difference. The chance that we will be found by wolves is now far greater than it was two suns ago."

"*Qvackk!* We have to get away from here! I must make my sore wing to fly!"

The mama pig reminded that in the case of their discovery, instructions were to move north along the base of the mountain chain. At the fall of darkness seven members of the blackmane's band departed their cozy cave, now become wolf cemetery.

Before the topmost tip of morning sun brought slivered light to the valley stretching long and wide before Prow Mountain, razorbacks and waterfowl had journeyed fifteen thousand pig paces in the direction of the fixed star. By the time the full round of the sun became visible, five wild boars and two water birds were hidden in tall reeds.

As the razorbacks and waterfowl traveled more through the succeeding night, they clung to willows and rushes bordering the stream they again followed. The dawn of the following morning found them asleep in a bed of rushes with bodies half covered in puddled water. Late that afternoon the waterfowl quit humming duck and goose songs. Noticing their sudden silence, Practicia peered through tall reeds to see a tawny brown wolf trotting on the bank of the stream. The wolf had come from the same direction the razorbacks and birds had traveled. Practicia nudged awake her mother. Following the example of the sow, four boarlings submerged their bodies with only pig noses, from time to time poking up for air.

Webstir thought it funny to see five hogs, like ducks diving to catch minnows, holding their breath under water. Peeking out of the water, the always curious Webstir saw that after pausing to sniff in all directions, the tawny wolf moved past the hidden pigs, duck, and goose.

Featherspark was sent to spy out the location of the oasis and determine how best to travel toward it. Claiming to be now fully recovered from his battle with the huge dull fish, Webstir had wanted to go with his friend. But Practicia pointed out that because it was unusual to see a duck and goose flying together, maybe the wolves would be smart enough to follow such a disparate flighted pair. When Webstir remained unconvinced, Practicia repeated twice the saying, *"Better to be safer than sorrier."*

Upon his return to the reeds the glide of Featherspark's wings scarcely sounded. No one would have thought that a goose had landed in a bed of reeds to rejoin a duck and a family of extra smart razorback pigs. The goose brought the welcome news that the green oasis was not so far away, had not been burned by the warriors, had more palm trees than a goose could count, and as well possessed a pond of water fed by a spring. Featherspark noted that on the route to the oasis he had seen not a single wolf. Under cover of night the half band set off for the oasis.

When the next morning the odd troop of animals entered a patch of true desert, Hamilton became inspired. Mounting a sand dune, he threw himself down in a belly slide. His idea spread. Even the razorback sow decided to participate in the fun. Practicia finally cautioned that her sow and siblings needed to conserve body water for the remainder of the journey to the oasis.

Hamilton next organized the boarlings and waterfowl to march two by two in formation. Practicia had to admit that her brother was uncommonly good at calling *march... two... three... four... march... two...* When the waddling Webstir and Featherspark fell too far behind, they fluttered wings to rejoin the marching boarlings.

Insisting she march at the front as the squad sergeant, the sow joined in. However the matron razorback had difficulty making her longer legs stay in step with the shorter legs of Hamilton calling cadence. For that transgression she was demoted to pig private, and made to march behind the two waterfowl at the rear.

Upon achieving the oasis the seven marchers unanimously decided that the pond interested them. "Victory over the white sand monster!" groinked an exuberant Roothyford splashing water indiscriminately.

"I now feel more confident about our piggly abilities," reflected a subdued Hamilton to Timidthy. "We thought up a plan, traveled to a hideout on the far side of the valley, won a battle against a ferocious black wolf, marched in military formation, and arrived on schedule at our planned rendezvous... and all without the loss of one razorback or water bird."

"We two boarlings have become real grown up soldiers," responded Timidthy. Both boarlings chuckled at themselves for being so small, yet thinking themselves so big.

"Foosh! I want quiet... *now!*" exclaimed Mrs. Razorthwacker upon the fall of night. Immediately, for that matter *too* immediately, came sounds of snoring. The sow could only hope that the widely disparate and unique snoring sounds emanating from four piglings and two waterfowl were real, and not pretend. She muttered, "Since the snores sound at least half real... I will be content to leave it at that."

The next morning Featherspark had something to get off his fluffy chest.

"On the bank of the Alone River wicked wolves took from me my goslings and mate. Now I have come to possess an extraordinary new family. When by herself she lured the wolf into an ambush, Practicia taught me courage. Timidthy every day teaches me to think as hard as a goose can. Hamilton and Roothy are always nice to me, even when I pester them with my sharp bill. And Mama Pig lets me know that in her eyes, even I am important." Wingtips flecked teardrops from off white feathered cheeks.

In response to the testimonial, five razorbacks bowed gracefully to Featherspark... and then to Webstir.

"I had no clue that a goose head contained sentiments so deep," qvackked the duck.

"While my mind is not so large as a pig's, my eyes see things that make to throb my heart."

Naythorn, Rayalas, Taurington, and Buckmight

Following northward the Pavilion River, Naythorn took the lead. When river banks compressed movement, the unicorn entered the river and swam panting hard until he found a new place that hooves could stand on.

On the second day of northward travel the blackmane veered away from the river. Following the instructions of his sky scout Rayalas, the unicorn led into the chain of mountains towering upward on the sunrise side of the Pavilion River. Before entering the course of a creek or stream, Naythorn became expert at doubling back on his trail. After three days traversing high mountain meadows a unicorn, winged filly, and two bovines descended in a wide return sweep to the river.

It became the turn of the two bovines to lead the way into the dry basin before Prow Mountain, where the one who suffered most from thirst was Taurington. With every step traveled under a hot sun the cattle felt his big belly to shrink. His only thought was to not let Buckmight see him falter and fall behind.

Naythorn and the three biggest members of his platoon arrived at the oasis dizzy with thirst. As they drank from the pond set amidst thick palms, the razorback family and the two waterfowl emerged from shady brush. There followed a joyous animal reunion with head butts, and affectionate nudges made by many different kinds and sizes of noses and bird bills.

Mama Pig warned that drinking too much water too quickly can do harm to large overheated bellies. Not for the first time Taurington, Buckmight, Rayalas, and Naythorn obeyed the razorback sow.

"I am no longer as fat and jolly as I was when we first met," complained Taurington to the family of razorbacks as he settled down to rest. "These last days of hard travel cost me a quarter of my girth."

"You were not so jolly when upon our first meeting your sole intent was to destroy the head of Buckmight," responded Practicia. "Sir Cattle, even with your diminished paunch you must still be one of the largest bovines in the whole wide world." With his big face breaking into a grin, the cattle found himself to be asleep.

Overhearing the banter of Practicia and Taurington, the sow was glad that her *new* family had grown to include equines, bovines, and water birds. Happy to be reunited with their big-framed friends, the four piglings counted it a privilege to that night march the perimeter.

While on guard duty Timidthy had the thought that the magical dimensions of the blackmane, whose blood gave wings to a filly, must be unique to the kind of unicorn that he was. If he was right about that, the boarling was sure that other unicorns would possess their own unique magical gifts to display to the world.

Unicorn magic had made animals to talk, minds to

enlarge, and fellowship to abound. The days absent from one or the other part of their band had convinced big and not so big animal persons that they needed to commune together while they traveled. Apart from each other, they were only half complete. The members of Naythorn's platoon had come to not only rely on each other for protection, but to *love* each other.

CHAPTER 16

A GIRL, DOLPHINS, AND A VERDANT ISLAND

Phoenician barges left behind the southern of the two islands separated by treacherous currents and whirlpools. Fair winds billowed sails northward.

Having triumphed over many canoes filled with warriors, the performance of sailors and horned horses in the *Battle of the Island Strait* gave confidence that Zoumar's voyage of the unicorns would ultimately achieve its appointed end.

"Because I still feel loss for the blackmaned unicorn left behind at Wittanor," neighed Elianor to the admiral, "I wish you had not consented to take with us the thirteen year old orphan girl. Like the blackmane who is now alone, she will ever more be separated from her tribe."

"But, Elianor, she would not take *no* for an answer. I remind you of her astonishing dream which foretold the arrival of barges laden with unicorns. It was because of her dream that she swam with a knife and showed how enemy canoes could be sunk. She quickened the resolve of sailors and unicorns to attack war canoes. Her ability to communicate with other native islanders, to be yet encountered, could help us avoid future battles. And upon receiving the gift of the uniform animal language,

Alexzana immediately spoke it perfectly."

"Hundreds of dolphins!" shouted the lookout from his high perch. Zoumar soon found his barges to be escorted by the largest number of dolphins he had ever seen. Like his sailors, the admiral believed a dolphin escort was a propitious sign.

When a squall passed in front of the fleet, a perfectly formed rainbow framed by patches of clouds and threads of blue sky took stance. A dolphin escort and a rainbow foretold a day of clean sailing toward their destination, wherever and whenever that landing should be found.

On the fourth morning after departure from Alexzana's island, the admiral directed his pilot to lead to the nearest land providing secure anchorage and plentiful grass. A substantial *L*-shaped island was sighted. When the barges turned toward the island the dolphin escort promptly swam away, as if their work had been accomplished.

A scouting party was sent to climb the mountain dominating the island. Upon the party's return it was reported that the island was everywhere incredibly green. Unicorns began to neigh that on this beautiful island they could with permanency remain. When notice of this reached her ears, the high escort was not pleased.

"Regarding this troublesome matter," insisted Elianor, "our unicorns must hear and listen to the neighs of the high escort."

Mares and stallions came to stand in assembly.

"Unicorns do not like to travel, much less travel over

water," began Aneilee. "A horned horse will every time prefer the security and fixity of a place where things do not change, and each new day looks and feels the same as the day before. But when on one past day our hold was destroyed, everything changed. A fleet of barges magically appeared to provide rescue, and we have now learned to travel on the sea and fight against war canoes.

"I had before thought that the one purpose of our journey was to find a new hold. But something else has now to me been revealed. Before our long journey ends, dissension will come to divide us. When that happens, my firm hope is that unicorn hearts will be re-established, and that new unicorn leaders will be nurtured.

"If the true purpose of our journey is to grow larger our hearts, that can only be accomplished as we learn to surmount difficulties and trials. Only by traveling onward toward the fixed star will we come to understand the new destiny of our magic herd." The heartfelt message of the high escort could not be ignored.

"Your message was received better than I thought it would be," neighed Elianor. "For that the High Escort should now wear a smile."

"I cannot, Elianor. Something inside tells me that our troubles are far from over."

The verdant island was left behind.

Following Dolphin Pilots

A very large body of land came to extend as far as the eye could discern. The admiral and his captains met to decide whether to steer east, or on the other hand to steer west around the promontory that was perchance part of a mainland. No clear signs pointed for them to sail one way or the other.

The young island maiden experienced her second moment of revelation. Without so much as asking permission, Alexzana interrupted Zoumar's meeting with barge captains.

"Admiral, the dolphins *will tell you* which way to go."

Zoumar was upset by the intrusion. First because he did not think a mere girl should get involved in a serious grown-up discussion, and second because he really did not understand what she was trying to say.

"What in blazes? Dolphins do not speak. I doubt that dolphin fishes can ever be made to understand the uniform language, and that is the only way they could tell us... anything!"

"Rather than speak to you, admiral, they will *show you*."

So it happened. Grasping a rail on the admiral's barge the Phoenician youth Mariano yelled, "Look! Dolphins swim toward where sets the sun!"

Zoumar joined the youth to see for himself what the commotion was about. Formed in a tight school, dolphins swam slowly away to the west. All in unison the dolphins rolled onto their sides and motioned with fins for the barges to follow them.

"Can dolphins truly be showing us the best way around this big place of land?" inquired Zoumar.

"Why else, Sir, would they all move in one direction in such an orderly fashion?" responded Mariano.

"It *does* seem that they are trying to influence the

movement of my barges."

"Dolphins are very friendly fish," reassured the youth. "They accompany these barges because they know that Phoenicians and unicorns mean no harm to come to them."

"Sir," interjected the first officer Captain Avalcar, "since these special and unique fish know these seas inside and out, what else can their movement mean... other than that we are to follow them?" The head nods of sailors standing beside the captain indicated that they also believed the dolphins were signaling for the barges to turn westward.

"For the first time in my naval career I give the *fish* order," said the admiral. "Where the dolphins lead, my barges follow."

A few days later, with dolphins still sporting in play beside and in front, the barges rounded the western end of the large land mass and again resumed a northerly direction.

"You know it can be hard for someone in high authority to pay heed to those that are too often taken for granted," confided Zoumar to the unicorn matriarch and Avalcar. "But, sometimes the smartest thing to do in life, is to make oneself listen to small and unusual voices."

"Alexzana weighs about as much as an empty barrel," responded Avalcar, "yet the girl does have important ideas."

"By listening to the small voice of Alexzana our admiral passed an important test of command," observed Elianor, "one that I before failed to heed.

Remember the obstinate colt I told you about that was constantly involved in scraps and problems? I hardly ever took the time to hear his side of the story. Because I now find myself to miss his unique and wrongly-colored presence, I wish that I had before listened better to the blackmane."

"By the way, Admiral," offered Avalcar, "after giving it some thought it occurs to me that a dolphin that comes to the surface to breathe may not be a real fish."

"That is right," agreed Elianor. "Real fish breathe not air, but water."

CHAPTER 17

THE DOLPHIN FRIEND

At first sight each dolphin seemed to look like every other. With more study of them as they swam close to the barge, or jumped out of the water to gracefully curve their bodies down in a dive, one dolphin was observed to be bigger, another thinner, another shorter, and another longer. One dolphin was observed to have a scar on its left side, while another wore a scar on its back. Each dolphin in the pods accompanying the barges was in some way found to be unique.

A dolphin that had a heavier angle to one side of the face often swam next to the admiral's barge. The dolphin would accelerate, dip down below the surface of the water, and jump to soar high in the air. This particular dolphin welcomed the touch of human persons, and wanted as well to hear their talk so that a suitable response could be slapped by its impressive tail.

Belaflor took a keen interest in the friendly and jumpy dolphin with uneven cheeks. All by herself the filly decided that the likable dolphin should have the name Quixsoar. Belaflor next decided that from the sparking given by a special and distinguished unicorn horn, Quixsoar merited the gift of the uniform animal language.

When Elianor reminded that Belaflor's idea went contrary to the unicorn code of apartness, the filly responded that more communication with the dolphin guides would benefit navigation through perilous seas. The matriarch was finally cajoled to get down on her knees and touch the powerful magic of her horn to the nose of a dolphin balanced half out of the water on its tail. Quixsoar immediately realized that she had much to say, and now that she knew *how* to talk in the uniform animal language, she would indeed have her say. Consequently, to each other Quixsoar and Belaflor talked a lot.

The unicorn filly and the dolphin were soon playing a game that they and Alexzana called *the forty-pace race*. Along the length of each railing the deck of the flagship was clear of obstacles. Readying themselves to spring forward, Belaflor and Alexzana would crouch down heads and shoulders. Quixsoar would at the same time stand at the ready with her dolphin body half out of the waves. Together they would count *one... two... three... go!* and spring forward as fast as hooves, feet, or dolphin fins and tail could carry each one. After sprinting forty paces the particular challenge for Belaflor and Alexzana was to stop dead in their tracks.

The athletic and fleet Belaflor could almost always beat the dolphin and the girl, *except* when the filly was unable to stop at the appointed fortieth pace. In that event she would distressingly crash horn, head, and shoulders into a cabin wall. When the filly crashed the finish, and so broke the rules of the race, Quixsoar or Alexzana claimed the victory.

For Admiral Zoumar the sole consolation for the commotion of a unicorn and a young girl racing the length of the deck was that for her age Belaflor was small of stature and weight, and so her falls did no lasting damage to cabin walls. For her part, Alexzana was so athletic and hard bodied that she never hurt herself when she fell or crashed headlong.

Not About Sharks

When not racing or playing with her friends, Quixsoar loved nothing better than to chatter about the wondrous benefits that pertained to dwelling in her sea home. She relished the rush of water over her nose and tail, the thrill of a dive to explore a reef, and the bedazzlement of schools of fish with the most amazing colors and strangely shaped fins and faces.

Quixsoar informed that sharks were violent bullies. To the dolphin's mind, just like giant squid and death whales, sharks were as unintelligent as they were ferocious. Unfortunately for Quixsoar, the lingering presence of so many dolphins often attracted sharks to the barges. Fifty sharks could not by dolphins be fought off. Whenever sharks decided to scrutinize the dolphin business with the barges, the air breathers were forced to retreat from the vessels. Quixsoar somehow knew immediately when the sharks had moved on and it was once more safe to escort her friends on the flagship.

Alexzana became Quixsoar's *most* special friend. With the island girl clutching tightly to her back, the two became wonderfully adept at body surfing the crest of a wave. Sailors knew it was a singular portent of good fortune to have their passage to be guided by an island girl riding the back of a very friendly dolphin.

One afternoon while stroking with an extended hoof the dolphin's belly, the unicorn filly inquired, "Why are you today so quiet?"

"The fish are acting strangely. Schools of fish leave these waters, as if in fright. Fish are like foreigners to me. I cannot tell what fish are able to sense, or understand why they swim like they do. Only I am worried by the sudden change of fish behavior."

"Is it about sharks?"

"I do not think that... it *is* about sharks. It must be that a death whale or some great sea beast is swimming toward these barges. It may be that having sensed unicorn magic, a monster that governs these seas is not content to let your barges pass through these waters without a fight." Quixsoar slapped with her tail for emphasis. "Belaflor, go tell Elianor of the flight of so many fish from these waters. Perhaps the matriarch can feel if the swell of the sea is changing from good to bad."

"I have an important question for you," neighed Elianor come later to talk with the dolphin. "As well as the fish, have sharks also departed these waters?"

"No," answered the dolphin. "Sharks are the only fish that remain. Rather than fear monsters, sharks look for meat to scavenge, especially in a fight of sea creatures that are bigger than they."

CHAPTER 18

DOG WOLVES AND MOUNTAIN SHEEP

Relaxed in soft green finery, oasis palms breezily saluted a new day. After the band's difficult treks across rivers, hills, mountains, and burning sand a cool north wind made the desert oasis seem like a paradise. That is except to Featherspark, who had suffered too much foolery from an annoying duck.

"If you do not right now go scout, my big black beak is going to pull every feather from your tail! At least that way our duck will have a valid excuse to not take to wing!"

Webstir responded that he had finally healed enough to exercise his wings... *at least a little*. But before lifting off in flight Webstir shook his chest, tail, and yellow bill. Then he made a show of stretching one wing after another, strutting back-and-forth, and fluttering about ostentatiously. After soaking up all the attention he could get, the duck launched aloft. Almost immediately Webstir plopped back down, splattered the goose with sand propelled by webbed feet, and for good measure pecked the goose.

"*Qvackk!* Over there! In those boulders! Intruders!" Webstir's ruckus alerted not only Featherspark, but everyone else in the band.

"Webstir must be mistaken," asserted the sow. "We buried the black wolf, and he was the only one that could have known to find us."

"Mama Pig is right," brayed the bison taking to his hooves. "This is simply not possible. No wolf could so quickly have found us here." The big bison snorted once, twice, and thinking enough was enough and that it might be impolite to snort a third time, fell in behind Naythorn. The unicorn and bison separated to block two sides of the rock sprawl. Rayalas flew to the far side of the rocks to ensure that a scout wolf, or wolves, would not escape to alert other wolves. Taurington and the razorbacks joined the surround.

"It is a black wolf!" hronkked Featherspark circling above.

"*Qvackk!* It is two black wolves! But as far as wolves go, they are far from being big ones."

When four wings pointed down to where the wolves had disappeared into the boulders, five wild boars proceeded to corner the intruders.

"These are not real wolves but... *dog wolves!*" gruffed the sow. "And at that, they are not even *big* dog wolves."

Small enough to penetrate into the rock warren, the four piglings forced out the intruders. Two trembling and nearly identical small black dogs emerged with tails between their legs.

"Are not these, Webstir, the fiercest wolves you have ever come upon?" neighed Rayalas with a smile replacing the previously worn frown.

Naythorn approached two dogs that cowered before a horn they were sure would stab them through.

Instead, two dog heads came to feel the penetration of blue-lit magic that raised their front paws off the ground, and made them to feel clean and new inside. Dog fear turned to contentment. With almost no hesitation two reassured dogs were soon answering the blackmane's questions as easily as if they were communicating to each other in dog tongue.

"Who are you, and why are you spying on my platoon?"

"We lived by the creeks and marshes on the sun-sleep side of this big valley," barked the bigger of the two skinny black dogs, and he was only bigger by a little. "We had always lived there with no complaints to make to anyone. Seven or eight suns ago a new kind of wolf, that acted differently from the ordinary lupine, invaded our land. Down to their very bones these new wolves are mean-spirited. For no reason they attacked and captured our pack of dogs. We two, our aunt, and our cousins were snarled at and batted about for information about a blackmaned unicorn," the dog set his eyes on Naythorn, "which *surely* is you." Having barked what he thought was enough the slightly bigger black dog sat down his rump.

"We could not a thing tell the wolves, for we had not seen you," continued the slightly smaller black dog. "Upon escaping the mean wolves, you see we two are very quick afoot, we saw the razorbacks and water birds move off into the whited sands. Since the wild hogs acted like they knew where they were going, we decided to follow them to wherever they were headed." The somewhat smaller dog pawed a shoulder of his brother signaling that it was his turn to continue.

"When the razorbacks came to the oasis, we knew we had followed really smart animals. For who else could have found a green place in the middle of so much sand? We quietly hid in this scramble of rocks during the day, and drank water from the pond at night. We decided that when the hogs finally departed this oasis, we could either stay here or choose to follow them to their next destination. When four very big animals met up with the wild boar family, we two felt to be even more..."

"Bird eaters cannot follow us!" interrupted Webstir. "We make friends only with animals that eat grass and roots!" When Webstir chugged with a wing Featherspark, the goose felt compelled to support his duck friend.

"Captain Naythorn, bird eaters will bring bad luck to our band. Send the two dogs back to where they came from."

"Mrs. Razorthwacker," neighed Rayalas turning to address not Naythorn but the sow, "can you escort our dog prisoners to the edge of these rocks? Four of us are still exhausted from the hard travel of the past suns, and your boarlings can easily guard these doglets, or doglings. Tomorrow our captain will make the right decision regarding two stray dogs."

"Guard them well!" qvackked Webstir wanting to have the last say. "If these doggerels run away, they will lead the wolves back to us!"

The sow turned herself about. Without being told to do so, the two dogs fell in behind her. Marching two by two, with Hamilton calling cadence, the four boarlings formed the rear guard. Rayalas remarked to Buckmight that the skinny dogs did not at all seem to mind their new status as prisoners.

Hamilton, Timidthy, Practicia, and Roothyford found that the two dog prisoners did not act rough and tough, nor did they show any intention of wanting to run away. The two instead seemed to be surprisingly nice doglets, doglings, doggerels or whatever name they should be called. Timidthy reflected that given their fear of the vicious new wolves roving about the sun-sleep marshes and ravines, the behavior of the dogs made complete sense. Quite simply, the two little black dogs had nowhere else to go.

Soon enough the passive twin dogs found themselves to be guarded by only one boarling at a time. At the approach of twilight, as the sun furrowed its brow in preparation for rest, it became Practicia's turn to guard the prisoners. The inquisitive boarling asked the shy dogs one question after another. She concluded that more than anything else the canines were twin... cowards. Born small in size, they had been bullied for as long as they could remember. The parting barks of their mother when she abandoned them, were to the effect that even though the two black puppies were of her own blood, that did not prevent them from being abject and useless. The two strays readily admitted that they were afraid to associate with any dogs other than their aunt and their nicer cousins.

"These pathetic dogs totally lack self-confidence," groinked Practicia to her sister.

"I do not like that they wear a perpetually fearful look," answered Roothy. "And I am annoyed that I cannot finish a conversation... with either one. Both interrupt my words to nervously sniff whatever whirl of air that passes."

"No matter," answered the razorback sow that had overheard her pigling daughters. "I cannot tolerate even a *pathetic* dog."

In the presence of the harmless and decidedly nice dog persons, no boarling had any concern for his or her own safety. Although slightly taller than Timidthy, ever the smallest of the razorback litter, the dog twins were afraid of him. Still, for the sow all dogs were dirty shirkers, and as well opportunists of the worst sort that ate weak and undefended baby animals whenever and wherever they could.

Names Given

The gift of golden sunlight came the next morning wrapped in blue sky and tied with wafting ribbon ends woven of cool breezes. On such a luxuriously gorgeous morning no animal person wanted to do anything but recline lazily and nap uninterruptedly. After days of moving fast to leave wolves far behind, the idea of restfulness remained especially welcome to the considerations of a winged horse, a unicorn, and two bovines.

"It is to be expected that a mother sow will dislike and disdain dogs," observed Naythorn to Mrs. Razorthwacker in late afternoon. "Still I was curious about what names you think would best fit the twin canines. Seeing as how they received a magic touch from my horn and can now talk to us, I think the dogs deserve to be given very own names... before one way or another their little lives are unhappily ended by our wolf enemies."

"I will right now talk to my daughter pigs that know the most about them," responded the sow that liked nothing better than to think up the most suitable names for animal persons. "Among us we will come up with satisfactory names for two little dog cowards."

Practicia and Roothyford set to work on the naming. They decided that because the slightly smaller black dog marked by a flash of chest white that continued between his forelegs, could detect and identify scents and smells better than any animal they had ever known, that he would be called... Trackler. He could even follow the track of a single ant back to the hole in the ground from where the ant had emerged.

The slightly larger dog had no distinguishing characteristics except that he was an unassuming, squalid, black canine. The girl boarlings suggested to their sow that even though it was not a very creative name, that the all-black dog be called... Blackler. With satisfaction the mama pig noted that the two dog names rhymed.

Trackler Proves His Name

Buckmight informed his captain that since evening was approaching, it was time for everyone to discuss and plan for the next stage of travel. Only Roothyford absented herself from the discussion to continue guarding the docile Trackler and Blackler close by the piled rocks.

The session of planning had hardly started when a streaking Blackler tumbled into the midst of the assembly to bang against, and so cause an astonished Mrs. Razorthwacker to lose her balance and topple over. Everyone knew that Blackler feared the razorback sow more than he feared even Buckmight. That fear did not stop him from barking to the sprawled Mama Pig that his twin brother Trackler had become frozen stiff, and could not move.

"*Grrrooaaannk...* so what?" answered the sow dusting off her snout with a paw. "We all know how lazy dogs are. Trackler fell asleep standing upright on his paws, and that is all."

A small voice inside his head told the unicorn that the dog ruckus was about more than a standing dog taking a nap. Naythorn left to see for himself what had happened to Trackler. One by one the other band members followed after their captain.

"Tell me what happened," neighed Naythorn noting fear in the unmoving eyes of Trackler. "I am here to protect you. Do not be afraid of anything." Trackler remained unaccountably unmoving and motionless.

"The dog is scared," groinked Timidthy. "Hmph. Could that be the way Trackler alerts to danger?"

Naythorn heard what sounded like running paws. He turned to see big incisors about to tear into Roothyford, the exposed guard for the one remaining and frozen in place prisoner dog. The unicorn jumped instinctively to intervene his horn between Roothyford and the huge attacking wolf.

Naythorn was a quick, powerful, and athletic

stallion. However he did not this time move fast enough. For that his horn cut empty air. A superb athlete himself, the tawny brown wolf had twisted out of the way of the lunging unicorn. Fearing to see wolf teeth buried in the girl pig's neck, the blackmane turned back to Roothyford. The unicorn instead beheld a trembling and wounded wolf body. Half galloping and half flying, Rayalas had swooped to attack. When Naythorn caused the wolf to swerve to the side, to his shock the wolf found Rayalas had centered on him. The filly's front hooves struck full the wolf's back.

Upon seeing the wolf flop his head in rage and pain, from fear Trackler became unfrozen. Tail tucked between his legs, the dog ran away yelping.

In a half broken wolf, fight remained. Turning his head back from following the escape of the fleeing dog, Naythorn saw launched at him eyes filled with pure hate, sharp clawed paws, and incisors glistening with the wolf's own blood gurgling out his throat. When a second time Rayalas brought hooves down on the unfortunate wolf soldier, his dangerous teeth were closing on Naythorn's neck.

The second blow from the filly's hooves left unmoving the wolf's hind quarters. The wolf's state was similar to Trackler's when he became temporarily frozen by fear. But for the tawny wolf the condition was unchangeably worse. Clawing at dirt and stone, front paws finally succeeded in pulling the wolf back into the hole in the rocks where he had before lain hidden. Wolf eyes reddened with the self-knowledge of final defeat. With insides burst and a spine irreparably damaged and unable to relay brain messages to back legs, during the brief remainder of his existence the broken wolf would know only anguish.

"My heart pounds," neighed Naythorn to Rayalas. "The savage wolf came this close to killing Roothyford, and gravely wounding me. Thanks to you, valiant filly, Roothyford and I still stand."

"*That* was a particularly dangerous wolf," answered Rayalas directing her gaze at the hole where wolf eyes burned red with a mixture of pain and anger.

Taurington decided to disrupt a view of which he had quickly tired. The cattle's horns pushed a big rock to shut the hole containing burning lupine eyes. Seconding the effort of his bovine friend, Buckmight wedged a second big rock to reinforce the placement of the first. Weighing many times more than the paralyzed wolf, the two sealing stones could not by fifty wolves be dislodged.

"The cruelty embedded in a fierce wolf heart fixes now upon black despair," neighed Naythorn upon witnessing the closure of the wolf's tomb.

"You see, my dear Blackmane," neighed Rayalas brushing a wingtip across Naythorn's back, "that I now pay returns on the miracle that gave wings."

"You must know that your flying skills have become *most* impressive. When I am not looking, the winged filly must be practicing flight."

"During our entire circuitous travel to the oasis, the half of the band comprised by the four largest animals had avoided contact with wolves," brayed Buckmight.

"I think it was the wolf that we saw a few suns back

while we hid in reeds," groinked Hamilton.

Once again by wolf spies the blackmane's band had been found out. The unicorn could not imagine how the tawny wolf had tracked a part of his band to an oasis set in the middle of a huge swath of white sand. Naythorn worried that when the wolf intruder did not return, companion wolves would pick up his scent and follow it to the little island of desert green.

Morning came. From Buckmight the tallest member of the band to Webstir the smallest member, Naythorn's platoon drank water, and then drank more water as they readied to leave the oasis.

The bovines trotted fast toward the mountains looming on the north side of the valley before Prow Mountain. Following behind came two small black dogs whose presence no one, not even Mrs. Razorthwacker, bothered to mention. It was not forgotten that Trackler had fortunately alerted to a very dangerous wolf.

When the sun positioned itself high in the sky and its heat began to burn into bovine hides, Buckmight and Taurington spotted a mighty rock casting a welcoming shadow.

"We bovines have decided that after travel in a weary land, a rest in the shade is warranted," informed Buckmight. The bison and cattle were surprised to find a small encampment within the arroyo containing the mighty rock.

Big Horns

Two mountain sheep adorned with extra large and impressively curled horns would disinvite unwanted guests. Heads lowered, the two sheep charged.

Buckmight reared and simultaneously clubbed one front hoof to each sheep head. Before the dizzy sheep knew what had happened to them, Naythorn touched his horn to the bloody spots welted by bison hooves. To their surprise, the mountain sheep soon found themselves able to converse with a horned horse.

"I trust the knocks from bison hooves did not too badly hurt you," offered the blackmane. "You do understand that you left my friend Buckmight no choice other than to defend himself. Now, would you be so kind as to tell me what you are doing in this isolated arroyo."

"This arroyo is our home, for now," answered the bigger of the two sheep. "And right now I am more concerned about a bad headache than answering pointless and thoughtless questions coming from a horned horse."

"My goodness gracious!" snuffled Mrs. Razorthwacker while shaking her head disapprovingly. "A mountain sheep must learn to show manners when addressing a magical unicorn. But, first things first. In order to be a mannerly animal you really must have a name. For example, the name of the goose with deeply hued feathers is... Featherspark.

"Hmph! Well, I do suppose that the brash attitude of this ram might be one thing in his favor. He is certainly rambunctious. He as well likes to puncture things with his horns... even a thing so big as this bison. Hmm, yes. I shall give him the name Rambuncture. Now, Rambuncture, you will need to show some manners when you next address my captain. And... *do not* make me to repeat myself."

The mama pig turned to the smaller in size lady sheep. "You also dared to attack a huge bison. The name that comes to my mind for you is... Ewelissas. That strong sounding name is particularly appropriate for a brave ewe sheep."

With the naming of two mountain sheep completed, Rambuncture began to act more deserving of his civilized name, and Ewelissas quieted and acted more the part of a gentle lady sheep.

The ram turned to Naythorn and explained that he and his mate had removed to the dry wash to stay out of the way of an unusually large number of ill-behaved wolves that were at this time, for who knew what reason, traveling everywhere about and making a great annoyance of themselves.

"With regard to marauding wolves I am of like mind as you," replied the blackmane, "and do not suffer them well. Now, Master Ram, I have a question for you. I know that a river runs before the mountains that loom ahead of us. Are there marked paths that we can follow down to the bank of the river?"

"There is a trail down to the river, but it is unmarked, and next to impossible to follow. That is, unless you were to be led by an expert guide like a mountain sheep."

"To what is owed the impracticality of the path down to the river?"

"It is really quite simple. Although from our vantage point the plain appears to extend smoothly to the mountains, the sudden and surprisingly deep drop of the river chasm is deceptive." The ram nodded his head toward the distance and added, "In fact, that part of the river canyon stands grandiose and incredibly steep. Its nearly vertical rock walls are tricky and dangerous to negotiate."

"Could my platoon disappear, and so find safety within the twists and turns of the river bottom?"

"Wolves know not how to enter that particular part of the river bottom."

"Then, Master Rambuncture, let me propose a deal to you and Ewelissas. If two mountain sheep will be kind enough to conduct us to the river and guide our descent without us falling and tumbling down over ourselves, I and my platoon of loyal companions will in exchange offer to you enduring friendship. Except for your joy of Ewelissas, you will find that the companionship offered by my band of animal friends is uniquely rare."

"My ram has not before had a friend," interjected the lady ram. "His dour personality does not promote that sort of thing. Still, that sounds to me like a fair exchange. But, tell me exactly what kind of animals are you that can talk to other kinds of animals? I have before baahed only to mountain sheep. And now that I can understand all sorts of animal persons, and they as well can understand me, I want to more fully enjoy the art of conversation."

"Ewelissas, the members of this platoon share magic issued by the horn that grows from out my forehead. You do remember that the touch of my horn gave you the gift of uniform animal talk?"

Naythorn went on to explain that he and his animal

friends were escaping from a pack of particularly dangerous wolves led by an extra large grayback, that he needed to find to where had disappeared the white herd of unicorns, and that he and his band followed a path appointed by the fixed star. With the unicorn's explanation, both Rambuncture and his more talkative mate looked to be satisfied.

After a time of rest in the shade of the mighty rock, the band of animals began the last part of their trek to the river. Two mountain sheep with subtle and pale hints of yellow and orange sketched into their coats, and big circled horns that thrusted out their foreheads, walked solemnly in the lead.

Late that afternoon Rambuncture and Ewelissas came to the place permitting descent into the river canyon. The two sheep led downward into rocks, boulders, and sheer drop-offs presenting in all directions. After difficult and arduous passage, by the light of a full moon the band saw the bottomlands of the canyon come to present clearly below them. The trek to the river had a high part now traversed, and a low part still waiting climb-down.

The band rested on a table of rock whose edges plummeted in impressively vertical architecture. No one in the band guessed that the hardest part of their descent awaited them still.

The next morning the band of Naythorn followed two sure-footed mountain sheep down an intricate zigzagging trail. Front legs constantly braked a bull, a bison, and a unicorn from tumbling downward. To amuse themselves, the sure-winged duck and goose did balancing and bouncing acts on the wide back of Taurington.

While short-legged boarlings clambered and pitched as required by the turns and drops of the trail, the razorback sow walked ever watchfully at the front of her brood. The sow's primary concern was that Hamilton and Timidthy, respectively the biggest and the clumsiest of her piglings, should stay always upright on their paws.

Rayalas grew so bored at the sluggish progress downward, that it made her head to hurt. Having finally had enough of the slow trajectory, she jumped into wind currents and wafted on wings. Pretending to keep her friends safe when they were already in a safe enough part of the trail, Rayalas nosed and nudged her companions to jostle against boulders and rock walls. Her wings batted a teetering Taurington to lose his balance and fall inelegantly upon his rear end.

"Come now, Rayalas," mrawed the frustrated cattle, "more than protect, you purposefully *vex* me."

The waterfowl could not resist joining the pestering Rayalas had fostered. They admired that the winged filly flew as athletically balanced as a duck and goose, born with wings already in place.

CHAPTER 19

FEATHERSPARK FLIES AN EXPERIMENT

Rambuncture and Ewelissas at last succeeded in maneuvering the band down to a place on the floor of the gorge where gushed an eye of water to collect into a pool. As the band drank deeply, all was quiet except for the sound of churning water.

"This is too peaceful to last," muttered Timidthy. "Somehow, in some devious and inexplicable way, wolves *always* find us."

"In this very difficult place for *us* to have found," replied Practicia, "you have just put my nerves on edge."

"Sister, it has for me become an ingrained habit to expect that calm precedes the tempest brought by mean wolves."

"Timidthy could be right that something is not as it seems," neighed the filly. "Wolves show up when we least expect them. That these particular wolves seem to know where we are, as soon as we get there, is both inexplicable and disturbing."

"Hmph," brayed Buckmight, "now I am going to have to fret about how our wolf enemies always seem to know our whereabouts."

"I think there is a *magilogical* reason to explain how wolves find us," chimed in Roothyford. "That is where the taste of magic blood elevates the power of wolf logic."

"If after tasting magical unicorn blood, wolves become luckier," added Hamilton, "then our discovery by wolves is something *magicapricious.*"

"It might be *magistitious,*" added Practicia sharing her view of the matter. "That is where magic is rumored or feared to have happened, but whatever did happen has an explanation more ordinary."

After sitting down on his rump and taking on a serious aspect, Timidthy tilted his head and timed the movements of a raised paw to give emphasis to his spoken words. "Maybe... we are... onto something. The very words we each day speak to each other confirm the magical impact of Naythorn's horn touch. By the same logic the two wolves that bit Naythorn, and tasted his blood, must now feel some connection to the blackmane's magic. The huge grayback wolf's relentless pursuit is not normal. But how works that magical connection between Naythorn, our band, and the two wolves? When Webstir, Featherspark, or Rayalas fly over the enormous grayback wolf, do you suppose his mind senses a current of unicorn magic in the wind?"

"All this about mental connections is nothing more than a rumor," grunted the sow that tended to grow impatient when not understanding something.

"In that case, Mama, it is *magistitious,*" clarified Practicia.

"Oh... all right! Maybe the wolves have just been enjoying a long run of good luck, and that is how they find us."

"In that case, Mama, you should call it *magicapricious*," corrected Hamilton.

"Somehow, in a way that we cannot explain, the wolves know where to find us," groinked Practicia bringing the conversation back to the point that both Timidthy and Rayalas had made. "And that supports the idea that a connection exists among everyone touched by Naythorn's magic, to include not only the members of our band, but also the wolves that bit Naythorn and tasted his blood."

"I have wondered about something, that try as I might I cannot explain... that just might provide a small but useful clue," offered Timidthy. After a polite pause the boarling continued, "Let us think back. We might logically presume that a spy wolf noticed our band grazing on the Notch Landing, and so led other wolves to attack us there. By the same logic, the tawny wolf at the oasis could have picked up the trail into the desert left by razorbacks. But, because in the dark of night we wild boars jumped off the wings of Rayalas, exactly at the cave opening where we then hid, no ground trail was left for the black wolf to follow us up the ravine. So, the question that needs to be asked is how could the black wolf that we destroyed and buried, a wolf that we before saw in the hidden pavilion, have guessed that we pigs and waterfowl were hidden in an isolated ravine so far distant from the Pavilion River?"

"Hold on, Timidthy!" exclaimed the bison. "Are you telling us that it was neither acute sense of smell, nor pure chance, that led the lone wolf to locate razorbacks and waterfowl in the cave ravine?"

"That, Master Buckmight, is what I surmise. One odd circumstance is that Featherspark sighted that same black wolf the day before the wolf found our cave hideout. It seems that the wolf somehow grew suspicious that the goose flying above him was a member of Naythorn's band, and so followed toward our ravine the flight of Featherspark. Still, I cannot explain how a wolf could distinguish Featherspark from all the geese that have similar size and feather patterns."

"Since the tawny brown wolf that tracked us to the oasis was probably the same wolf that we saw when we had before hid in reeds," groinked Practicia, "could that wolf also have tracked the flight of Featherspark?"

No member of Naythorn's band could think of how to answer the questions posed by Timidthy and Practicia. The afternoon sneaked away, and the onset of darkness found the subject of conversation had not changed.

"I tire of trying to *imagine* how relentless wolves keep finding us," brayed Buckmight. "I say it is time for us to conduct a little experiment. As Roothyford or Practicia might say, an *imagicking* pretend."

The bison set his gaze on the goose and brayed, "Of our two bird friends you are the bigger one, so we can see your flight the best. Just maybe, as suggested Timidthy, wolves notice something about your flight. So, I have a favor to ask of my fine feathered friend. Wing upriver until you are beyond our sight, wheel about, and when you come upon us pretend we are a group of hungry wolves that want to eat you. Be sure to think and feel whatever you do when you see real wolves. When alerted to danger, maybe your wings make sounds that wolf and dog ears can hear."

"Hah! The black dogs will, like wolves, howl as loud as they can at our goose!" exclaimed Roothyford.

"My wings would refuse to give away anything about us," objected Featherspark crooking several times up and down his long neck. "I would not let my wings to do that. Besides, I have never experimented, and I am not going to start doing that... now!"

"Do be a good sport about it, Goose," cajoled Roothyford. "Just like Trackler freezes stiff when he alerts, perhaps our goose alerts to the presence of wolves in a unique way. We do not want to have the wolves keep showing up of a sudden, like the black one did in the ravine."

Featherspark looked in disbelief at Buckmight and Roothyford, who looked earnestly back at the big water bird sporting distinctive sweeps of white feathers on his cheeks and tail.

"Your test flight could someday mean life or death to us," neighed Naythorn quietly. "Perform the experiment, and let us see if anything is learned. It might help us to explain how the black wolf found you at the ravine, and how the tawny wolf found all of us at the oasis. As mama pig likes to grunt... *nothing ventured, nothing gained.*"

"*Hronnkk...* all right!"

"Phssshh!" the goose scolded a hiss at the dogs. "I will pretend Blackler and Trackler are the wolves that destroyed my family's nest on the bank of the Alone River." That honked, the long-necked goose was skyward gone.

The entire band took to cover. In that regard it was fortunate for the unsmall bovines that close by were found big boulders.

Goose honks came to sound. When Featherspark was still some ways off, Blackler and Trackler jumped out from their hiding place and ran about barking and howling loudly, as though they were real wolves. Thinking the color of their sheep hides looked wolf-like, the tawny coated Rambuncture and Ewelissas bounded about as if they were bigger wolves than Trackler and Blackler. The goose honked make-believe fright, wheeled, and flew fast away.

Faces broke out in broad smiles. They had every one seen sparks of light emit from goose feathers.

"Even before he came close enough to see the dogs, Featherspark began to sparkle," noted Timidthy. "All by themselves his feathers alerted."

Deciding to extract from the experiment any fun that he could, as he in return circled down the goose continued to honk affected fear.

"Goose," barked Trackler, "when I alerted, my body stiffened. When your feathers alerted to our presence, *they sparkled!* Gosh, it would be exciting to feel my dog hair glow when I sensed danger near."

"We now know how the wolves found the pig family and the waterfowl in the cave of the ravine," brayed the bison. "It was the same way they found us on the notch landing and at the desert oasis. Since the wolves are not aware that we have discovered the secret of our goose's wings, perhaps we will someday find a way to benefit from our new knowledge."

Plopping his belly down upon the goose, Hamilton groinked, "I am going to quit calling you Featherspark and instead call you *FeatherSPARKLES!*"

"Our goose must learn to control his feathers so they glow only when he wants them to," instructed Naythorn.

It became Webstir's turn to fly the same experiment. But no matter how much the dogs barked and growled at his approach, the feathers of the green-head duck refused to alert. Webstir began to sulk because unlike Goose, his feathers would not sparkle and glow.

"It is amazing to see the impact of the blackmane's magic on Featherspark," bleated Ewelissas who only scant days before had felt Naythorn's magic penetrate her hard sheep skull. "Of course, from personal experience I know that the unicorn's magic is wonderfully strong."

"For my part," continued Timidthy, "I have decided that every unicorn has at least one unique gift to share with the world."

"The comments of Ewelissas and Timidthy make me think that Naythorn's magic can accomplish even more," neighed Rayalas shifting up and down her head. "So it is now the turn of the blackmane to do me a favor... by experimenting. Stretch your horn to touch the ponded water."

Because the unicorn had never before been asked by anyone to do anything like that, he was not sure if the winged filly was playing a game with him, or if she really had a good reason for making such a novel request. Naythorn looked intently at the filly. She stared back at him.

"Should I be thinking on something as my horn touches the water?"

"Good idea," affirmed Rayalas. "While I hover above the pond, you think about where our wolf enemies might now be moving toward us."

"All right, I will close my eyes, retrace my steps, and concentrate on movement of wolves." The stallion touched his horn tip to water. The force of wind generated by the rapid wing beats of Rayalas caused a mist to form.

In the murky swirl created by the batting wings of Rayalas came to be seen... *shadows of wolves*. The ghostlike figures stopped and stared at a place that the band members recognized. It was the oasis rock pile where behind two big stones lay a lifeless tawny-coat lupine. Wolves had come to the oasis and sniffed out the tomb of their deceased comrade. The wolf shadows began to howl silently in chorus. When Rayalas dropped down to land beside Naythorn, the mist shadows melted into the pond.

"Naythorn's magic is even *greater* than we knew!" squealed Roothyford.

"We have now discovered a way to find where travel our wolf enemies," added Bison.

The Animal Column

"The magic shadows showed that the hateful wolf legion does not stop their pursuit of us," grunted Mrs. Razorthwacker. "We cannot make peace with them. We cannot long hide from them. All we can do, is from them flee." With her eyes welling up in tears, the hardness of the struggle against mean wolves momentarily overcame the razorback sow.

"You are not to worry, Mama," groinked Practicia. "We will think of some way to outsmart our enemies. After all, this band is made up of strong and staunch animals that think and talk very intelligently."

Roothyford drew next to the smaller of her two brothers and nudged his head up, for when he was most thoughtful Timidthy's head hung low.

"If he is right now not asleep, I say that my brother is thinking on something."

"I am... at that. Who, sister, would you say is stronger: the enemy wolves or the platoon of animal persons that our captain leads?"

"The wolves are very many, and we are few."

"Well then, when Practicia groinked that we can outsmart the wolves, I recalled how she and Hamilton like to wrestle. Since from that they get ideas on how to best shove down and trip each other, their play betters them at martial arts. So, even our games and funning can matter a lot to our self preservation.

"*Grrrooinkk!* Let us do something the wolf legion does not expect, something no band of animals has ever before done. Let us make of ourselves to be... an *organized* platoon. Each of us can be positioned and matched where we can fight the best. Military discipline can make us to fight twice as strong as our numbers."

To signal that he had something to say, Taurington shifted his great bulk from one shoulder to another. "As I have expressed before, I like to walk ahead."

"If Naythorn and I follow behind Taurington, and position the razorbacks between us, wolves will then find it very difficult to assault the pigs from our front or sides," offered Rayalas. "And with a mountain sheep on each side, Buckmight can follow behind the pig family to close out the diamond formation."

"But I get to rotate one day's march behind, and the next day's march in front," brayed the bison. "Taurington does not get to have *all* the enjoyment of leading."

The two mountain sheep liked the idea of being a rear guard with the flexibility to turn around and head-butt wolves, without worrying that the pigs and the big animals in front of them should get in their way. The goose and duck declared they would alternate winged scout missions with relaxed times of webbed feet planted upon the backs of the bovines. The bison suggested that Blackler and Trackler be assigned as roving forward and lateral scouts, instructed to stay close to each other and away from danger.

"Me and my brother dog are better at smelling out danger, than we are at attacking big wolves," barked Blackler. "Count on Trackler and me to have the two best smellers in this whole land!"

"So long as we stay in formation and remain ready and alert we can joke, play, and even wrestle a little," offered Hamilton.

"I will work extra hard on my feather-glow problem," hronkked the goose. "Very soon I will *not* sparkle when I do not *want* to sparkle."

Neighs, mooorahs, grooinks, quacks, honks, barks, and baahs broke out. Although the animal persons in Naythorn's platoon knew they had far to go in their quest to find the white herd that had sailed away on Phoenician barges, with a disciplined plan of march in place the members of Naythorn's band felt confident of eventual success.

CHAPTER 20

THE BATTLE OF TALL TREES

Grown by two mountain sheep and two dogs to number fifteen, Naythorn's band followed westward the river gorge. Seemingly without stopping, Blackler and Trackler ran a perimeter on the band's front and sides that rotated perfectly with the progress of the platoon of animal friends.

One particular canine behavior brought smiles to the blackmane. Upon their periodic returns to the band, when they could get away with it the small canines much enjoyed nipping the legs and sides of the bovines. The entertainment of biting, nipping, and dodging about allowed the small black dogs to temporarily forget that at heart they were both great cowards.

As high canyon walls melted downward, the gorge yawned wider and wider. Changing into a back-and-forth pattern, the curves of the river reclined more lazily. However, after two days of slow travel in the river canyon, the blackmane grew impatient. While the time-consuming path along the river drew the band more and more in the direction of the evening sun, he very much wanted to resume travel in the direction of the fixed star.

The water birds and winged filly were sent skyward to find the best way to change northward the band's direction. Watching their departure, Naythorn was captivated by the sight of his three winged friends speeding away in a chevron formation with Rayalas at the point.

The unicorn was sure that the two waterfowl, and the filly that was beginning to hint at being more bird than horse, would bring back valuable information regarding the fortuitous location of rivers, mountains, and plains. In late afternoon the whoosh of big wings got everyone's immediate attention. Naythorn was proud to see that Rayalas landed with even more grace than the duck and goose.

"We *finally* found the best route toward the fixed star," neighed Rayalas.

"*Qvackk!* That is not all we..."

"*Hronkk!* There are lots of big..."

Webstir interrupted back, "Trees taller than you have ever seen! And there is..."

"A pond that bubbles!" finished the goose for his friend.

"Tomorrow we will come to a stream that descends from the direction of the fixed star," neighed Rayalas. "We follow five days northward that stream until we come to a low chain of mountains. There, a long canyon opens in the direction of sun-birth. After four days we will reach the end of that long canyon, and turn to travel three more days across a dry plateau toward the fixed star. We will then and there find ourselves in trees, that as Duck says, grow very tall. At the entrance to the tall trees is found a pond that gushes up."

A Plea and a Request

"Walk with me," brayed Buckmight to the ram. "Now this is just a suggestion but on such a nice morning as this, for the benefit of the rest of us, could not Rambuncture wear a smile?" When first acquainted, the bison had thought the ram was moody. Now that the mountain sheep was better known, Buckmight found him to be a true pessimist.

"You are altogether forgetting everything that can right now... go wrong," responded the ram.

"And on such a splendid day as this, tell me what *can* go wrong?"

"Well for one thing, we *could* be ambushed by wolves."

"Do you not think, Master Ram, that this part of the river bottom is rather too flat for that? This plain lacks the cover needed for wolves to carry out a surprise attack on big animals like us."

"Well then, we are now probably... *lost.*"

"Well, at that," Buckmight began to play along, "with all these stones cluttering my way I suppose that it will be difficult for me not to break a leg today."

"And what if the river water we drink is bad, and it kills a mountain sheep *or* a big bison?"

"And, an attack by one hundred war eagles would be next to impossible to counter," added Buckmight.

The ram paused his walk, turned, and playfully butted Buckmight's shoulder as he baahed, "But, I will admit that right now I feel quite safe walking beside this big and tall bison with sharp horns." Hearing that, Buckmight smiled on the outside, while the ram smiled only on the inside.

On the same day that Buckmight failed to persuade a mountain sheep to be more positive, it was not the ram but Naythorn that felt uneasy as the band made camp. About what worried him, he could not say. Perhaps it was a premonition of something bad that was soon to happen. Maybe it was nothing at all. Still, he decided he would take a precautionary measure. The unicorn neighed for the filly to walk with him.

"We may someday come to be separated in battle. If that happens, Rayalas, will you do something for me?"

The filly nodded her head.

"Hammerclaw and Lucars, the two Phoenicians I told you about, now search for a place my grandsire called Shining Canyon. Cabalbard said that it is a real place with magical blue gold. I think of it as a haven from strife, a place where you and I could be happy together. I do not ever want to lose you."

"Naythorn, if we should ever to one another become lost, my wings shall find Shining Canyon, and there I will wait for you. I also am curious to see the canyon that shines of magic gold." She brushed the neck of Naythorn with a wing. "Maybe we ought to lose a small battle, so that you and I have a perfectly good excuse to find each other in that beautiful canyon."

"When you joke with me, Rayalas, it does my heart good."

"I will tonight dream of my Naythorn and me walking side by side in the canyon of blue gold."

Bubbling Pond and Tall Trees

Having for five days followed the northward flowing stream the band turned hooves, feet, and paws toward where the sun each day found renewal. Just as Rayalas had said would happen, on the fourth day of eastward travel canyon walls collapsed down, and the land transformed into a wide basin. The bovines changed northward their course.

On the morning of the third day of travel toward the fixed star a dark and unmoving shadow loomed in the distance. By midafternoon, the shadow lightened to a green color. Before the sun decided to take rest, the members of Naythorn's band could make out individual trees standing mighty and majestic. The excitement that pulsed through the band was contagious. So much so that even Rambuncture, who had grown up and lived entirely in desert lands and rocky canyons, could hardly wait to walk beneath trees so tall.

Just as Featherspark and Rayalas had said, where the tall trees began a big pool of water bubbled with excitement churning its surface. Only the very center of the pond proved deep enough for an evening swim. The fall of darkness found every member of Naythorn's platoon relaxing in the bubbling pond.

Grown curious about the water sources for the lush valley, Rayalas the next morning investigated. As she flew the winged filly had the thought that the far cliffs were trembling. Upon close inspection, she discovered that the movement she had seen came from delicate sheets of water screening out between layers of high canyon walls. Rocky indents and caves accounted for the deeper colors that hinted behind the subtle flows of falling water.

The filly decided that the water-curtained caves

presented places suitable for defense. She as well observed that the water washing down the cliffs fed a stream that nurtured tree growth. In advance of the pool of bubbling water, the stream quite surprisingly disappeared under ground. Naythorn and his friends soon found themselves listening closely to Rayalas tell of sheets of cascading water, hidden caves, and a vanishing stream.

The bubbling pond provided a welcome diversion. The band bathed, drank, splashed, rolled about, and played water tag. Times of play invariably grew into times of laze. Finding himself in a place of tall trees and bubbling water, Naythorn felt himself to be at peace with his world.

Albarochk

"Wolves are upon us!" yelped Blacker crashing into the band's camp. "They come fast and they are very, very, many!"

"That cannot be!" exclaimed the mother pig. "They cannot have found us, *not here!*"

"It can be, Mama," answered Timidthy. "The idea of our destruction consumes the wicked grayback."

"The wolf villain's scouts are everywhere!" baahed Rambuncture.

"Flight through the valley's thick trees cannot be well-negotiated," neighed Naythorn, "especially by bulky bodied bovines with huge horns that snag on branches. If we flee rather than fight, big and small band members will surely come to be separated, and to wolf attack be made more vulnerable."

"We cannot fight with trees at our back that are

conducive to wolf penetration," grunked Mama Pig.

Hearing that, the bison and cattle each moved to defend opposite corners of the knoll before the bubbling pond. The mountain sheep, dogs, and razorbacks arrayed themselves on each side of Naythorn, who placed himself at the center of the defensive line. Rayalas would move where needed to reinforce the line.

The blackmane crashed hooves into the too-eager wolf leading the first charge. There was no doubt that Naythorn would be the foremost target of lupine hatred.

In this their first battle as members of the unicorn's band, the sheep that each weighed almost as much as Mama Pig, butted wolves with surprising violence. Their curled horns suited perfectly to slam back wolf bodies, and the points of their horns punctured lupine hides with devastating effect.

As she bit and thwacked wolves, the sow marshaled her four halflings to fight as a coordinated squad of razorbacks. Showing uncharacteristic courage, the two quick dogs dashed everywhere about in defense of Naythorn's line.

For Rayalas the wolf soldiers had no answer. Her wings gave her the lift to jump up fast and then crash down shocking hooves. Precise organization, unrelenting discipline, and raw courage kept Naythorn's platoon in a fight in which they were vastly outnumbered.

A howled command gave pause to the attack. Keeping his shoulders level as he walked with a certain élan, from out of the ranks of wolf soldiers emerged the big mean-eyed grayback. The stately walk of the outsized wolf commander did not befit his dirty, matted, and scarred appearance.

Since the day that Tristanbear was by Naythorn rescued, the wolf general had more than tripled in size and his teeth had come to set differently. At an unseemly angle the great wolf's incisors protruded savagely from out his jaws.

"The grayback wolf has become... *a monster!*" groinked Roothyford moving protectively close to her sow.

Though it was only midafternoon, haunting sunlight burned cloud edges and painted in fragile hues of reds and purples the sky above the tall trees. The strange look of the heavens heightened the drama of the wolf leader's warning.

"*Grraarrooooo!* I am Albarochk, the ferocious wolf general whose name bespeaks destruction and desolation. Surrender the unicorn to my invincible army... and I will have my wolves to spare a few pathetic pigs, sheep, cows, dogs, and ducks. The meaningless lives of the lesser animals in the blackmane's band can perish far removed from this place. For all I care, the winged horse can fly far away.

"The unicorn with the black mane is not only an abomination to the white herd of unicorns, but also to the established order of the animal world. The blackmane's treachery requires that on this day just recompense be paid. Tonight my teeth will gnaw the last magic horn left in this land, and my belly will be sated by the flesh of the deceitful unicorn. The blackmane will no more to me be insolent! *Yowrrrkkkhehaha!*"

For the first time ever a unicorn, horse, pigs, big-horned sheep, bovines, and waterfowl had heard a wolf to laugh. Upon hearing the cruel pitch of the wolf laughter, Roothyford cringed and squealed, "That laughter is all... *wrong!* Laughter should not commend a cruel-hearted purpose."

"Any animal with a half kind heart would despise laughter that foretells evil punishment," grunted the mama pig in agreement. The sow and her sensitive girl pigling hoped to not on a second occasion hear what passed for mirth from the throat of Albarochk.

"Give up the blackmane... *now!*" insisted the monster wolf.

"Wolf numbers grow," brayed Buckmight joining the unicorn. "The wolves are too many and we are too few. Before the sun sets they will triumph over our weakening state and sure diminishment."

"I am afraid that about that, you are right. With neither protection nor place of exit, we find ourselves roundabout blocked. If the wolves push us into the bubbling pond, they will overwhelm us. To better defend ourselves, we have need of rock walls or a box canyon. But unfortunately, our band cannot from here escape."

"Naythorn, since we are both agreed that our position cannot hold, I am going to suggest a tactical maneuver designed to transform the battle while preserving your platoon. A lone unicorn can crash through the wall of wolves, and flee across the desert toward the sun-sleep."

"But I cannot in the middle of a bloody battle...

abandon my friends."

"*Grarroouuu!* My patience will not long persist! Give me the blackmane, and save his friends!"

"Hear me out, Captain. If you flee, what will the wolves do? The giant grayback wolf said it himself. He does not care two shakes of his evil tail for my old hide, or for the hide of an old cattle, a few pigs, sheep, or dogs. Albarochk's sole pursuit is to gift himself the magic of your blood. If you break out of this place, and I know that you still have left in you the strength and stamina to spring free, every big wolf will aspire to achieve personal triumph over the blackmaned unicorn. Three of every four wolves will pursue after you." Buckmight paused to let his words sink in.

"Only smaller and slower wolves, that cannot begin to match your speed and strength, would stay behind to here fight. Taurington, Rayalas, and I would then have the advantage. Against the remaining wolves we could even retreat into the waters of the bubbling spring. Small wolves cannot fight well in water up to their necks. So, the odds of battle would here change to favor us. Naythorn, if you flee and take the big wolves after you, both you and your band will survive." The bison nodded his head slowly up and down for emphasis. To all that the bison had brayed, the blackmane remained silent.

"We that here remain will next find safety in the caves sheeted by falling water. In the following moon you can return to us and regain your band. Or, during the next moon we will find a way to meet up with our blackmane. My captain, you must lead the battle away from your band. Take Albarochk with you. Outrun the monster general and his nasty wolf soldiers."

"The wolves are more nimble, but in a race into flat lands the length of my horse strides will separate me from..."

"*Grawrrrarrr!*" Albarochk interrupted the unicorn. "Give me at once the horned horse, and so spare the lives of his platoon!"

Ignoring Albarochk's command, Naythorn took the time to think on. Without finding water to drink, he would not survive long flight through dry lands. But even if he were to perish from thirst, against the small wolves that remained behind his friends would triumph and live on.

"Bison, if I were to do as the grayback commands, and give myself up to him, the giant wolf would anyway break his promise. He would not let you and the rest of our band to go free. The only chance for me, and for my platoon, is to do as you say. I race into the dry lands." The blackmane's exhausted look changed into what for the unicorn was an unusually mischievous smile.

"From that look on your face," muttered Buckmight, "it is obvious that our captain has of late spent too much time in the company of Hamilton."

"The wolf general offers a cruel treaty that because his wolves are too many, too big, and too strong I am forced to accept," neighed loudly the unicorn. "But before I surrender, I will say farewell to my friends that Albarochk has promised not to harm. When my farewells are done I, the fierce blackmane, will walk over the giant grayback. Errmm... *walk over to him.*"

After howling triumphantly the monster wolf sat his rear quarters. Leering, and wearing sniggering smiles, the wall of growling wolves sank down to rest on behinds and bellies. Seated in the midst of his wolf battalion, Albarochk would receive the unicorn's self-sacrifice.

With loud neighs, so that even the wolves heard, to each platoon member the unicorn said *farewell*. What the wolves did not see was that as Naythorn neighed his goodbyes an eye winked twice at Buckmight, twice at Taurington, and twice at the razorbacks, mountain sheep, dogs, and waterfowl.

When Naythorn lastly approached Rayalas his gaze fixed upward at the sky. The unicorn neighed in a voice that carried well, "Remember, Rayalas, the shining place where we will soon be reunited. Do not ever give up hope. I there will find you."

"Could it be that we will all reunite somewhere up in the stars?" inquired the sow of her little ones. Not even Buckmight knew what was meant by the unicorn's comment about a future reunion in a shining place.

To the dismay of Roothyford, the unicorn's final words to Rayalas made the huge grayback wolf to laugh a second time.

"*Grrawwrrkhaharr!* Wherever takes place the next reunion of the blackmane, it will be under my authority and command." The paws of the very sensitive girl pigling were not large enough to stop her ears from hearing a third time the frightening laugh of the hideous wolf.

The unicorn straightened his back, lifted his black-flecked tail, and with the majesty befitting a strong unicorn stallion walked away from the friendship and valor of his platoon of loyal animal soldiers toward a wall of bloodthirsty wolves. As they watched their blackmaned captain walk toward sure and certain death, Roothyford and Practicia began to bawl pigling tears. Emotion swept over a cattle that bent a knee and bowed his head to Naythorn.

Not able to overlook Naythorn's winks, Hamilton decided that something was not as it appeared to be. He grunted, winked at Timidthy, and then nudged his brother. Timidthy immediately caught the gist of what his brother was thinking. Both began to feign loud groinks of despair. They were immediately joined by the bison's loud and despairing brays. Taurington decided to follow suit, and began to woefully mrawoo. In short order all the members of the band were heard voicing loud, and in some cases raucous and discordant lament. Wolves joined in with their own cacophony of savage yelps and howls.

Not minding the clamorous discord sounding all about him, through stacked files of snapping and howling wolves Naythorn walked a gauntlet. Hardened wolf soldiers had to admit that the unicorn possessed inspiring battlefield presence. The blackmane drew to within four paces of a smug Albarochk seated with straightened forelegs. In a bow to his enemy, Naythorn bent his knee and neck.

"So far, so good," whispered Buckmight to himself. Standing only thirty paces distant, the bison noted that the relaxed Albarochk was overjoyed at the surrender of his hated enemy.

It happened with the suddenness of a thunderclap. Instead of finishing his bow of submission and sacrifice, Naythorn charged head down. The horn of the unicorn tore into the left shoulder of the astonished grayback. Unicorn hooves slammed into and bowled over the body of the barbarous grayback wolf.

For a long instant no wolf soldier could fathom what wolf eyes had just seen to happen. Adding to the confusion the members of Naythorn's platoon brayed, mraaughed, neighed, grunted, qvackked, baahed, and yapped as loud as they could.

Untouched by wolf soldiers, the blackmane was soon one hundred paces beyond the wolf phalanx. The horned horse shot downhill, crossed the stream that outletted the bubbling pond, and raced into a wide and desolate plain. The band reformed to once again defend themselves.

More than anything, Rayalas wanted to help her captain flee from the great wolf. However, she realized that Naythorn needed her slashing hooves to defend pigs, bovines, sheep, dogs, and waterfowl. The flighted filly whirled about and kicked down hard at wolves launched anew at her companions.

Running all but over each other, big wolves streaked after the fleeing unicorn. Wolf fighters were enraged that their fearless leader, the most crafty and cold-hearted wolf of all, had just suffered awful wound. Worse than that, by the horn of his arch enemy Albarochk had been dealt stinging humiliation. But wolf soldiers were of one thing proud. Hobbling on three legs, close behind them loped their formidable general in pursuit of the blackmaned unicorn.

Chase across Flat Lands

For the success of his scrapping flight through Albarochk and the wolf ranks, Naythorn felt elated. More from his lifted spirit than from the wetness of the stream he had splashed across, his chest felt clean and new.

The unicorn stopped to look back longingly at his friends. He saw Buckmight, Taurington, and Rayalas mete out harsh punishment to the most aggressive of the lesser wolves that surrounded them. The unicorn next took note of big wolves plunging into the stream in pursuit of him. Among them Naythorn glimpsed Albarochk. Because his left front paw dangled useless as he ran, the grayback's other three limbs performed extra service.

Counting himself very fortunate to have passed through so many vicious wolves, the blackmane wondered a new thought. Did an invisible protector hover above to guard and shield him? Naythorn decided he liked the idea of having a sky guardian, someone like Rayalas with wings to keep him from harm. He next remembered that his dying grandsire had expressed the desire to accompany from above his grandcolt's journey toward the fixed star.

Renewing gallop, the hooves of the blackmane settled on a path between the place of sun descent and where soon would be seen the fixed star. Behind him the wolves spread out in a wide line. The unicorn would not be permitted to double back and so rejoin his friends.

Since the wolves knew that their more compact bodies withstood thirst better than a big-bodied horse with legs built for bursts of speed, the wolf hunt became one of resolved patience. The wolves quickened pace as the unicorn did. To whatever gait the unicorn chose for his gallop, the fierce lupines adapted.

For the severity of his wound the grayback wolf was forced to slow his pace and fall back. When the time should come that the blackmaned unicorn was cornered, Albarochk would attend to the kill. Every wolf soldier understood that their leader insisted the kill be a trophy for the wolf general alone. The unicorn's blood would bestow its magic, all and entire, for the benefit of the monster grayback.

Before nightfall the blackmane came upon a dry river bed. Stopping to paw dirt, he was rewarded by a trickle of water. After digging more hoof shovels he drank the small puddle of water that had formed. In an attempt to surround their quarry, a few wolves moved to his front side. More water was gulped down the throat of the horned horse.

The unicorn jumped up and at the same time kicked with rear hooves the chest of a wolf launched at his rear quarters. His horn pierced the neck of another wolf. Two destroyed wolf bodies lay shuddering on the sand. Confident of his strength and size, the blackmane crashed through the thin line of four wolves that had interposed themselves.

Behind him the unicorn heard growling and snapping as wolves individually tried to possess a spot of water dug by unicorn hooves. Naythorn imagined the snarling wolves drinking as much sand as they did water. Leaving behind the dry creek bed, Naythorn fixated his gaze on the shadowy outline of a butte to the north and west of where he ran.

CHAPTER 21

SOLITARY JOURNEY

As his hooves pounded deep into flat lands Naythorn had ample opportunity... *to think.* Only a few moons back he had been a naive and inexperienced unicorn yearling sheltered from all danger and harm. The safe, boring, and yes, dissatisfied life that he had before led was unobservant of and unconnected to animal persons unlike himself. Grown bigger and more muscled he was now the leader, and protector, of a disparate and motley band of animal persons. The unicorn with the black mane was making his story to be all his own. His future victories, and even defeats, would be laid to his charge only.

The discipline of his sire and the love of his grandsire were now distant memories of a life that on one errant day came to be irrevocably changed. Still, even now, his past life mattered much to him. The cruel games of bite-tag in Wittanor Hold had hardened his frame and spirit. The development of his rebellious streak had made him gritty. To himself he admitted that in spite of the life-and-death danger he now confronted, he did not dislike his status as the hated enemy of ferocious wolves. Naythorn Blackmane was now important enough to have been made the great enemy of the implacable Albarochk.

Slowing his trot, he came to a new realization. Before his story could be ended either he would have to kill the giant wolf, or be himself destroyed. Albarochk would not have them both to live on. The huge grayback and Naythorn could not agree, ever, on terms for a truce. Either the insatiable hatred of Albarochk would finally triumph, or the great wolf's body would someday be trampled lifeless by a blackmaned unicorn.

Naythorn's thoughts shifted to practical things. He needed to think ahead, carefully. For the unicorn to survive the dangerous and solitary journey he was now traveling a plan had to be prepared that would chart forward movement, anticipate wolf ambush, and play well his strengths against wolf arrogance. So long as he could decipher wolf strategy, some way would arise to take advantage of his knowledge of the enemy.

The observant unicorn studied the tactical advantages of ravines, cliffs, and boulders, and as well imagined where might be found Shining Canyon. His grandsire Cabalbard had said that the magic gold was deposited within a canyon somewhere in this part of this wide land. Naythorn assured himself that the wondrous hidden place would offer sanctuary to a unicorn in flight from a battalion of wolf soldiers. He asked himself how a horned horse could find a canyon purposely hidden so as not to be found.

The blackmane's thoughts turned to Rayalas. He felt compellingly drawn to the winged filly that was yet an enigma to him. In his eyes, Rayalas had become a horsebird more beautiful than the brilliantly colored scarlet and blue parrots that had once dwelled in the dense forest of the unicorn hold. The fact that Rayalas liked him, made her different from the fillies in Wittanor. Because of the outlandishness of his black mane, not one filly in the unicorn hold had looked at him twice.

When he first came to know her, after she had healed from wolf wounds, her joy of life charmed him. But it seemed that as her wings feathered more long, her nature had become more serious. Naythorn next wondered how many scars the *Battle of Tall Trees* had seared into the lovely filly's heart. He longed for her to be running next to him.

When the light of new day came to define the forms of distant mountains, the unicorn decided that perhaps from atop a high place he could catch a glimpse of where lay the magic canyon. Naythorn selected a mountain whose sides appeared rather squared, and whose crest tipped in shape triangular. The proportions of the mountain's peak hinted somehow unnatural. Suddenly his heart felt stronger. The formation of a plan, albeit a modest one, had energized his chest. From that mountain height maybe he would even see a shadow in the far sky resembling the shape of the winged horse.

Not able to match the speed proffered by the unicorn's newly gained hope, the wolves fell back. Angling into a dry river bed the unicorn further separated himself from the wolf pack. The blackmane next sought obstructions to remove himself from the line of eyesight of trailing wolves, while from them his hooves pounded steadily away. A strong crosswind whirled sand and dirt making it more difficult to follow a horse track deliberately designed for concealment.

Naythorn imagined that the wolves following him could not stop themselves from believing their prey dimwitted. The stallion smiled at the thought that arrogant wolves found every prey animal to be unintelligent. Naythorn next imagined his pursuers arguing heatedly about which way the horned horse had fled. The biggest wolves were not necessarily the keenest trackers, but in a battle of lupine wills, size and strength would end-out persuasive.

Forceful shafts of desert wind shot tumbleweeds across his path. Caught in a dust storm, the unicorn thought it odd that he was not concerned about losing his bearings. He soon realized that he was unafraid because in the midst of the wind gale he somehow always knew his position in relation to the pyramid crested peak that beckoned him onward.

Approaching his destination the stallion moved to the mountain's south side that was thankfully shielded from the forceful wind, and began to climb upward. The path he took crossed open areas that following wolves could not traverse without being themselves seen. Midway to the top was a depression traced with moisture. There he dug down and found water that despite its gritty taste quenched his thirst.

Upon achieving the summit of the pyramid-tipped mountain the unicorn observed that the wind still blew hard through the places he had galloped. He began to feel safe. Even if wolves tomorrow found him, he could defend the platform of crumbled rocks at the top of this mountain. A rounded concavity chiseled by innumerable grains of sand blown through endless time, provided a protected place to rest. Naythorn imagined himself falling asleep in the hollow of a great stone hand.

The morning mist that shrouded the pyramid shaped crest permitted Naythorn to lick dry a rock basin where droplets of moisture had collected. The unicorn thought it a kind blessing that even an arid land could cloth-wet its face at the break of day. The still exhausted blackmane ambled back to the hollowed cleft and lay down to rest.

The unicorn decided that his present loneliness was not so unlike how he had been made to feel as a colt spurned by every other unicorn his age. With the exception of a grandsire shut in darkness, no one had taken interest in, or taken time for an odd-looking and unruly colt not socially smooth in play. At best, his mates had shown him indifference.

Lacking friends with whom to neigh conversation, he had never learned how to jest and brag like other colts. When surrounded by unicorns, he had before felt himself to be all alone. Naythorn was again alone. However, this time instead of being in the presence of aloof unicorn horses, he was beset by wolves that loathed him. He decided that his present situation alone in the middle of nowhere and running away from wolves, was still preferred to being shunned by the colts in his own herd of unicorns.

Because he could not, and would not let the sudden rupture with his past lead to brokenness irredeemable, the blackmane concluded that what really mattered was the friendship dwelling in the hearts of Buckmight, Taurington, and Mrs. Razorthwacker. The band's good will, kindness, and loving regard more than balanced out the hatred of the wolf soldiers hunting him. Thinking on the friendship of his band, he at last fell asleep. Before the blackmane straightened well-rested legs, a new sun had brought warmth to the mountain. As Naythorn walked the perimeter of the crumbling triangle crest he wondered who had so long ago carved and piled up the smooth-edged stones that now scattered down.

He became distracted by the flight of a black and white bird that reminded him of Rayalas. He missed the winged filly. But what exactly was it that he missed? Was it her innocence, her graceful gallop, her soft feathers? Since she had grown wings her eyes shone, well, more mature in age. Blackmane wondered if the word *regal* applied to Rayalas. If regal meant serious, graceful, dignified, and good then he was sure that word did to her apply. There was no doubt that the filly that had grown wings in every way fascinated him.

His neck arched high and his mind shoved back to reality. What he saw made his nostrils to flare. To the west raised what could only be another strange pyramid crested peak. The second triangular crest loomed higher than the one he now stood on. All alone in a high place he neighed, "The capstone to that mountain was as well piled up long ago. Why are there *two* unnatural pyramid crested peaks?"

Without pausing to think the unicorn began to

descend the mountain. By midafternoon sun he had drawn close to the second pyramid-topped peak. As the sun declined to bed, Naythorn zigzagged toward the peak's pyramid crown. Upon gaining the mountain crest, the stallion was astonished at what he next saw. Along a bent line in the direction of day's end raised a third pyramid crest.

The unicorn slept the next night on the third pyramid crowned mountain. At the end of the following day he was positioned on the triangular pinnacle of a fourth peak. One day later Naythorn found himself on the top of a fifth pyramid crested mountain. The placement of that pyramid crest was at a hard northward angle from the fourth peak. Once again, the unnatural look of the triangular crest was obvious.

Naythorn's mind flashed back. The placement of the pyramid crests hinted at the star pattern that was above the cave door that gave escape to the notch landing. It seemed logical that the next two pyramid crowns, should they exist, must then correspond to the ladle's in-line pointer stars.

In his heart Naythorn was convinced that two more pyramid crests did indeed exist, and that they had been built to point the way... *to something.* But why had so much effort been spent to raise triangular crowns made with cut stones? Just to think that this great work had long ago been accomplished made his blood to run fast. After clambering down the rocky side of the fifth pyramid mountain, the blackmane ran west. Standing later upon the sixth crested peak, found where he expected it to be, he glimpsed the distant crown of the second and last pointer peak.

That night the unicorn rested in a draw recessed into the heights of the sixth triangle topped mountain. The blackmaned unicorn galloped into a dream with stardust showering down on his flanks. In his dream he was a winged unicorn captivated by exhilarating flight. It was a dream unwanting of end, but when it did end he awoke with a question. Why did the cluster of pyramid crests not signal the direction pointed by the corresponding star cluster in the night sky? If the pyramid crests were built to commemorate the fixed star, why did they not point toward the cold north, but instead point southward? For the pyramid peaks not to point toward the celestial fixed star as they should be expected to do, could only mean that their placement signified a unique and extraordinary purpose. The two pointer pyramid peaks had to do with something that represented the fixed star of this land he traveled through. The same as with the previous six, the seventh pyramid crest drew him onward.

Naythorn came to the base of the mountain capped by the last pyramid crest. After the exertion of so much travel between, and up and down the triangle topped mountains, the blackmane decided he was due a long rest. His legs were spent, and his mind hurt from constant thought about the strange cluster of man-made crests. He slept, ate grass, and drank from a pool of sink water.

When on the following afternoon the unicorn reached the summit of the seventh pyramid peak, he was both astonished and disappointed. By a line connecting the two pointer crowns no visible mountain or monument was intersected. The two pointer peaks directed... at nothing!

A movement caught the unicorn's attention. Two wolves were busy scenting the ground at the base of the mountain he now commanded. When the wolves started to howl, Naythorn knew he had been found out. The unicorn was sure that from far away, carried through the gray light of settling day, came a howled response. More wolves would soon arrive to accompany the two scout wolves below. His time of rest and safety was to end. Once more the blackmane was to become *the hunted.*

Waking from a welcomed night of rest, the stallion stretched until his back cracked and his leg muscles pulsed and hardened. He picked his way down the south side of the seventh pyramid crested mountain. Traveling along the line projected by the two pointer peaks, Naythorn quickened his pace. He knew that he had again become the quarry on the run from vicious enemy wolves. But because he harbored the hope that he would soon discover the reason why seven pyramid crests had been so carefully constructed and placed, on this day he minded less being the prey. Until he solved the riddle that was leading him forward, he simply needed to stay ahead of pursuant wolves.

In a gulch he dug down and found trickles of water. Through the day, into the night, and then into new day he continued onward. The more he thought about the purpose of the pyramids, the more it took his mind off his growing thirst. Naythorn told himself that he was a stubborn stallion that, sooner or later, got done what he set his mind to do. And on this day the secret of the triangle crests should be deciphered *sooner,* and not *later.*

Again Wolves

At dusk Naythorn clambered up a little mesa with rocks streaked in jagged lines of multihued crystals. He noticed that toward the place he directed something, either the faint outline of a far mountain, a curious cloud, or both, loomed in the haze of evening. On top of the mesa the unicorn found a defensive position where puddled water graced the hollows of big rocks. Drawn close, the following wolves knew to not launch upward their bodies against powerful unicorn hooves and a sharp unicorn horn. As long as he kept the wolves below him, he would for them be a formidable adversary. Dozing in fits, Naythorn woke often to check for threatening movements of wolves. The unicorn imagined that sleeping wolves would that night dream of following him into a place from which he would not depart.

The unicorn wished that Rayalas would that night find and join him on his strange and outlandish quest for whatever place had been once marked by the fabrication of pyramid crests. But why should the winged filly come for him? It should have been Naythorn that had returned to her. When he broke away from trailing wolves he could have taken a circular route back towards where he had left her. Instead of exploring a pattern of pyramid crests, he should have found a new way to return to the valley of tall trees.

For his stubborn insistence on solving the riddle of seven pyramid peaks, he was now set to pay a high and perhaps ultimate price.

CHAPTER 22

THE TRENCH OF BROKEN STONES

Naythorn reclaimed the path signaled by the two inline pyramid pointer peaks. By midsun the pack of wolves trailing the unicorn had grown to number ten. The ominous threat of wolf attack would this day shadow every step taken by the blackmane's hooves.

Naythorn entered a trench of broken rocks that spread long in the direction to which he aspired. On his right and left he surveyed nothing but a dry expanse where stubby mesquite trees secured position amidst the cacti. The blackmane tried to think about what, at the place appointed by pyramid crests, awaited him. Would he there find another pavilion palace? Would it be a cave with underground pools of cool sweet water and a waterfall? When he imagined he was about to find the place to where the unicorns had gone, the horned horse grinned, albeit dryly. At the far end of the path of broken stones the shadow of a real mountain, and not a cloud, took form.

Three big wolves accelerated to flank the horned horse. Breaking rightward, leftward, and again rightward to all three Naythorn's hooves dealt mortal punishment. Of his own volition Naythorn would not depart from the direction proffered by the two inline pyramid peaks.

Neither would unrelenting wolves permit him to turn back. When soon after two more wolves charged at the blackmane, instead of hooves it was this time a unicorn horn that forbad wolf depredation.

As his legs carried him along the trench of broken stones, a sheer cliff face fronting many rock spires came into focus. The mountain obstructed and blocked the invisible line marked by the two pyramid pointer crests. Something about the mountain puzzled the unicorn.

Where Naythorn found one mountain thrust up, other mountains were found to be placed close by. While close mountains need not connect to each other to form a chain of peaks, they at least claimed a proximate relation to each other. The mountain ahead of him stood mightily unconnected to any other high place. Naythorn studied the needle-like spires carved into the upper half of the waiting mountain. They were more streaked with yellows, oranges, and reds than he had ever before seen. The look of the mountain called to Naythorn for exploration.

Compared to previous days, his pace had slowed. For that, wolves raced ahead to interpose themselves between the blackmane and the spired mountain, and so presented a defiant challenge to the unicorn's freedom of movement. The wolves were... *bullying him.* The stallion decided that if it was the last thing he ever did, he would climb the mountain that resolved upward at the end of the trench of broken stones. Naythorn mused that the wolves in front of him believed climbing one last mountain would be the last thing the unicorn ever attempted to do.

The unicorn wheeled to a stop, kicked apart a cacti plant, and sucked water from its fleshy parts. Rather than from thirst, he would die fighting. He would fight all the way to the mountain that would hopefully resolve the riddle of seven pyramid crests.

When Naythorn directed at the lupines disallowing his advance toward the spired mountain, he was engulfed by a mass of snarling wolves. Wolf claws scratched his hide, and wolf teeth grabbed at his legs. Whirling his body, Naythorn slashed back-and-forth his horn. Big hooves banged wolf bodies into each other, and onto the jagged edges of stones spread about the trench.

After fighting through the lupines, Naythorn emerged with painful wounds inflicted upon his neck, sides, and limbs. The battle between wolves and a young and powerful unicorn stallion would prove costly, and not just for the horned horse. Wolf blood would color red many broken stones.

After trotting another two thousand horse paces, Naythorn found a new blocking wall of wolves positioned before him. For a second time the blackmane scored headlong his body into wolves. Front hooves crashed down on lupine backs; rear hooves pummeled wolf faces and chests. His horn tore one way, another way, and then another. When the wall of wolves separated into two halves Naythorn stole through the enemy barrier.

After moving onward a thousand more horse paces, at the sight of a third wall of wolves Naythorn grew incensed. It was unfair of Albarochk to bring so many reserve phalanxes of wolves to do battle against one young stallion. Calming himself, Naythorn grudgingly gave credit to the new tactics of the wolf general that somehow knew the unicorn would not of his own volition turn back in an attempt to flee.

The unicorn crashed his head into the third blocking cohort of snarling wolves. His horn punctured tough hides and spilled wolf blood. Under his hard-as-rock hooves Naythorn felt the crunch of breaking wolf bones. Once more the power of the unicorn's hooves prevailed. Having fought through a third wall of wolves, the blackmane told himself that surely he would not face a fourth wall.

The sides of the trench of stones constricted, and a narrow pass opened before him. But something was wrong; his hooves did not move as before. Naythorn looked down to see the flesh of his right front leg torn open above the knee. Following wolves fixated on the gait of a crippled unicorn. Naythorn sensed the irony that both he, and the monster wolf he had before wounded, now ran on three legs.

The trench became a high-sided, narrow-necked passageway strewn thickly with what looked to be impossibly broken slabs of stone. More wolves darted past Naythorn. He knew they would set and form to stop his progress toward the spired mountain that called him onward.

The blackmane felt himself no longer to be a young unicorn, only a weary one. His trot slowed to a hobbling walk. Remembering the loyalty of Rayalas, Mrs. Pig, Timidthy, Featherspark, Buckmight, and Taurington the unicorn mustered his courage and exiled the reminders of hurt and pain from his mind. If only for the devotion of friends in his band, he could not give up. His fighting assets were the sharpness and durability of his horn, the strength of his muscled neck, and the velocity of now three instead of four crashing hooves.

The blackmane found his movement hemmed in by the confusion of rock pieces scattered everywhere in the constricted pass. Hobbling slowly ahead, he saw that eight wolves formed the final barrier to passage through the high place.

When a violent wave of claws and snapping teeth washed into and over the blackmane, the flesh of eight kicked and slammed wolves found the rock slabs to be sharply painful. Expending every portion of energy and strength still found in his exhausted frame, Naythorn fought on. In the space of one hundred horse breaths the unicorn dispatched four of the eight wolves from the fight, and gained entry into the highest part of the constricted pass. No matter how much his legs and sides hurt from their wounds, his defense could not slack or pause. If he fell to the rock strewn floor, he would not be permitted to again stand.

The blackmane vowed to close the final chapter in the lives of the four remaining wolves; each would pay a stiff price for blood lust. Naythorn again slashed his horn and kicked his hooves, but this time more slowly, and without resolution. His strength was departing his frame. The unicorn readied for the wolf attack that one way or another would be the last. When the four big and deeply scarred wolves hesitated to spring, a new realization struck the unicorn. Albarochk would be there, must be present, at his death.

Naythorn lowered his head and prepared to take his final breaths. Instead of thinking about his sire's strength, his grandsire's kindness, the beauty of Rayalas, the goodness of Buckmight, the sagacity of little Timidthy, or the laughter of Hamilton, only one thought passaged through Naythorn's mind... what powerful force had cleaved apart two rock shoulders to open the narrow pass where he was to die.

The blackmane could only wait.

CHAPTER 23

THE YOUNG PHOENICIAN WARRIOR

I n an empty part of a vast country Lucars stood on the topmost place. Since three days past the youth had observed curious wolf behavior. Never before had the apprentice blacksmith seen so many wolves travel seemingly toward one destination. Lucars reached a decision. He would know to where so many wolves were departed.

The small party of Phoenician soldiers in quest of the blue gold, of which Lucars formed exactly half, had reluctantly split apart so that singly they could scout through more country than if they traveled side by side. Sergeant Hammerclaw was big, strong... and slow afoot. Compared to the double weight of his older comrade, the slender Lucars could travel twice as fast alone.

For seven suns Lucars had by himself searched for the place of the blue gold. The past seven days had been as much a waste of his energy as had been the previous time of search teamed together with Hammerclaw. This final day of solitary exploration was to precede the appointed day for the two warrior blacksmiths to regain each other.

Much discouraged by day after day of unsuccess, they had agreed that if neither found Shining Canyon, they would reluctantly give up their quest and accept failure. For Lucars, not completing what he had set out to do was tantamount to defeat, and the youth hated the idea of defeat. That it would not be the first defeat suffered in the thousand year history of his land of Phoenicia, did not matter. Lucars still abhorred the idea of not fulfilling his orders to find the blue gold.

Knowing that time had run out and he should turn back toward the place of rendezvous with Hammerclaw, the youth muttered, "I am too stubborn for my own good."

The tall dark-haired lad with skin tanned deeply by the sun, had once before scouted this area. Lucars knew that neither the rocky trough, nor the spired mountain that it pathed toward, exhibited any signs of the magic gold. However, the southward movement of wolves led him to a second time enter the forsaken trench filled with impressively broken pieces of jagged stones.

Because the time allotted for a detour was limited, he broke into a run with his shield jostling loosely on his back. With each long stride his sheathed sword swayed to its own back-and-forth rhythm. As if it were an extension of his arm, the shaft of his spear was carried with a comfortable and effortless motion. In an army of a distant land he had been known as the most fleet runner. On this day Lucars ran hard and made good distance.

The youth came upon the crushed bodies of three dead wolves lying on the floor of the rocky trench. In Phoenicia his weapons had killed many wolves, but no sword or spear killed these three. Something powerful had thrown back so hard that it shattered ill-fated wolf ribs. Lucars decided the wolves had unfortuitously settled resentment upon a powerful bison bull. The youth followed onward the stony trench. Displaying deep gashes as if made by spear points, two more wolves were found that drew no more breath.

"So, it really is a battle between wolves and warriors," muttered Lucars. "Whoever killed these wolves is like my sergeant powerfully strong. But about this uninhabitable piece of wilderness, I have seen no native warriors. And surely my Hammerclaw cannot be anywhere close to this stone trench."

Lucars came next upon five struck down wolves, three of which still cried pitifully from their wounds. To something he was getting close. The youth was not sure if he should run faster, or move more slowly and quietly toward the terminus of the bloody trench. The humans fighting for their lives against marauding wolves, might be as well to him unwelcoming. He decided that he would not heighten his risk of exposure.

Ever since Lucars was a ten year old cub soldier he had been instructed to pursue the sensible solution in battle. The rule he had from his first days in the army been taught... was to stay alive to fight on. Wanting to comprehend a desperate fight not his, the young warrior moved forward more cautiously.

Lucars smiled as he recalled that in the Phoenician military respect was given to soldiers that exhibited intelligent fear. So long as the warrior displayed not cowardice in battle, and was not reckless, it was fully and completely acceptable to be afraid of the enemy.

Lucars knelt behind a protruding stone ledge. A few

hundred paces ahead of him an enormous gray hided wolf, three of four times larger than the biggest wolf Lucars had ever before seen, dropped front legs into the trench of stones. Behind the big wolf followed a small skinny wolf with a dirtied yellowish hide. With their focus entirely on what waited ahead in the arroyo of broken stones, neither wolf had paused to look back.

"Those wolves move their legs and heads like overconfident renegades bent on committing a robbery... or worse," muttered Lucars. "The crafty movements of their bodies rub me wrong. Hmph, they act like they are very close to their prey."

It appeared to the Phoenician youth that where the lesser wolves had failed, the giant wolf would succeed in the fight against warriors. Lucars noticed something more. The big wolf was limping. Notwithstanding his injury, the great wolf would be a devil to fight. Lucars wondered if he was soldier enough to take on the gargantuan wolf. A contest between himself and the giant wolf would be perilous, but also exciting. Touching the hilt of his blue gold sword, he reassured himself that he would indeed be up to that challenge.

The Phoenician youth decided it was likely that the warriors the wolves were closing on had dealt the blow that caused the great wolf to limp. If that was indeed the case, now looked to be the time to exact wolf revenge. To have killed that many wolves without falling themselves, the adversaries of the wolves had to number at least three men that were highly trained in military arts.

Without thinking through the consequences of

involvement, Lucars decided that he would use his sword to protect the human adversaries of these strange wolves. In this land so far away from Phoenicia, no one was there to object to a soldier volunteering to enter a fight that he knew little about.

Quickening his pace the youth quit trying to conceal himself. Every time the two wolves stopped to sniff a fallen wolf brother, the youth gained on them. From time to time the two wolves looked back at the youth. Lucars found it strange that the pursuit of a following warrior mattered not to the two determined wolves.

The Wolf General and his Lieutenant

As he marked the dead bodies of wolves lying along the rocky floor of the long arroyo, Albarochk's mood grew more sullen.

"The yellow wolf is not wrong," growled the big gray wolf. "This fight has become too costly. It is past time to finish off that foul unicorn." Words of wolf reassurance came next, "After all, I am the biggest wolf alive. I am the strongest. I am the craftiest..."

"But no longer the fastest," interjected the yellow wolf.

"I will break in two his horn!" barked Albarochk snapping teeth at the head of the smaller wolf.

"That would make a most fitting revenge on the horn that crippled your front leg," responded Yellowquist.

"When the blackmane bowed down to me, I *trusted* his word. I was sure that the unicorn recognized my superior might. Unicorns are not supposed to be deceitful. How was I to know that the traitorous and dishonorable horned horse would betray his promise to me?"

"Even as wise and crafty as you are, my enormous noble cousin, there is no way that you could have imagined that the unicorn would beat you at your own game of deception."

"You are *foolish* to vex me," growled Albarochk at the small and agile wolf. "With only a half blow from my remaining good paw, I could break your back."

"Given your towering strength, you could no doubt do that. Still, oversized cousin, I remind that if you broke my back you would also break the promise you made to your mother... your oath to protect me as if I were your brother wolf."

"*Yaarooowww...* I only made that vow because a runt like you needed protecting. My mother was blindly loyal to her sister wolf, your mother who sickened and died when you were but a newborn cub."

"The human person following us likely has no idea how to handle the sword at his side."

"Because my whole body is a weapon, I do not fear his sword."

"Well put, great cousin. But is not the size and shape of that warrior's sword similar to the unicorn horn that crippled you?" Gnashing teeth, Albarochk jumped at the yellow wolf that deftly dodged a bite from crunching jaws.

"Only an idiot wolf would dare to infuriate me with another reminder of the despicable unicorn treachery!"

"Cousin, you are today in a very foul mood. Speaking of *fowl*, do you remember when you used to jump high into the branches of a tree to grab a roosting turkey for our dinner? *Yipe! Yipe!* It is too bad that your three remaining good legs can no longer jump that high, for I would relish a big tasty drumstick for this night's supper." The yellow wolf swerved so that the blow aimed at his head cut empty air.

"When I destroy that horned horse I will drink his blood, gnaw his horn, and then I will be once more made whole... and bigger... and stronger... and one thing more. When that time comes, I will no longer have any reason to put up with your insolence.

"The taste of the blackmane's blood tripled my strength. All the unicorn blood did for you, runt cousin, was to splotch more yellow your coat. Are you as yellow on the inside as you are become on the outside? The name I gave you, *Yellowquist*, meaning *thin yellow twig*, fits you perfectly."

The yellow wolf decided that in spite of the fact that he could duck and dodge very fast, if he wanted to live to see this day's sun drop off the edge of the earth he had best end the provocation of his enormous cousin. The promise Albarochk had made to his fierce mother wolf, to protect his small-size cousin, was losing currency.

Yellowquist trotted onward hoping that his cousin's threats would never be fulfilled. Still, when the yellow wolf's mind proved no longer useful, Albarochk could send his diminutive cousin into exile. That unkind act would, at least on its face, not break the promise once made to the mother of the enormous wolf.

Albarochk, Lucars, and Naythorn

Lucars felt pity for the wolves he passed that

struggled forlornly to pull bodies up on limbs made useless. The youthful soldier could not comprehend why with fifteen wolves dead, and seven or eight more crippled on the floor of the rock trench, more wolves would continue their costly pursuit.

"For a reason I cannot fathom, this is become a prideful struggle to the very death."

The youth came to a place where the floor of the trench began to rise to reach a high point. Ahead of the two wolves that he followed loomed something big and bloody standing on four legs with its head slumped down. Noting a long solitary horn, Lucars gasped as he realized that a unicorn was beset by four menacing lupines.

The wolves surrounding the unicorn, each with coats deeply scarred from many vicious frays and fights, opened to entrance their general. Albarochk took some time to visually inspect the unicorn with sides everywhere bloodied.

"One grab of my teeth to your throat will end your wretched life," growled the wolf commander. "That will be the sweetest kill I ever made."

"Do not forget how it was that you lost the service of your leg," yipped Yellowquist to his leader. "What if the unicorn is only... feigning to be badly wounded and gasping for air? Perhaps he purposely bloodied his hide to make it appear that he is more wounded than he really is. Are you sure that after dispatching more than twenty wolves in this trench, that only these four wolf sergeants could really have beaten the unicorn?" Upon hearing that Albarochk took a step back, and put himself down on rear haunches. The big wolf's jowls opened in a macabre grin that grew to cover his whole face.

"I will take some time to observe my trophy, and so doubly or triply enjoy this kill. Why not study the unicorn so that I can always picture in my mind what my most memorable conquest truly felt, and looked like?"

"That, great cousin Albarochk, is very wise of you," agreed Yellowquist. "Let no one say that you let a unicorn twice over trick you."

"As I told you before, I am not only the biggest and fiercest wolf in the world, I am also the craftiest. I am the best at what I do, which is to kill unicorns. No one can damage my leg, lacerate my face, and expect to walk away unharmed. I always get my revenge..." Albarochk was interrupted by the approach of a fast-running warrior.

"Naythorn was the one left behind!" yelled Lucars. "This unicorn is my friend!" The youthful blacksmith apprentice remembered how strong and full of life the young blackmaned unicorn had looked at the side of his dying grandsire Cabalbard. Without explaining his actions to himself, the youth knew exactly what he would do. He would place himself between the wolves and the blackmaned unicorn.

As he surveyed the battle scene the youth's heart began to pound. There was precious little time to spare before six wolves fell irrevocably on the grievously wounded unicorn. Brandishing his sword and spear the warrior closed yelling, "Death to vicious wolves!"

The enormous wolf leaped and scratched his one functional front paw at Lucars. The running youth ducked low, revolved his body, and back-slashed with his sword the dangling left front leg of Albarochk. The giant grayback was astonished to find that his lame leg was, once again, cut and bleeding. That crippled leg was the one part of his body that should now be inviolate.

Lucars broke through the circle of wolves to gain the unicorn's side. Having glimpsed the sharp edges of the youth's blue gold weapons, four veteran wolf sergeants chose to exercise caution.

Amidst the snarls directed at him, Lucars heard the small yellow wolf say what he had recently said to himself, "This is not your battle! Depart from here while you still may!" The young Phoenician warrior was surprised to hear the wolf speak in the uniform animal language which he himself had used to talk with the old Cabalbard.

"Does the yellow wolf have a name?"

"I, the lieutenant of the enormous and ferocious General Albarochk who stands beside me, am called Yellowquist."

"As it so happens, Yellowquist, from this place my sword does not yet desire to depart. Can you believe that my magic blade has grown a mind of its own? That is more than I can say for you weak-minded wolves! Ha! I and my knife will linger right here with the unicorn." Lucars saw that the big grayback and his small yellow hided friend understood every word he had spoken.

"Here is something more for you to think about. If you or the other wolves move at me, the first thing my sword will do is sever the one good front leg of the big wolf brute. Then the grayback will have no front legs to walk on. At the same time the spear held in my other hand will penetrate the heart of Yellowquist. Unfortunately for you two, this is not a day for a wolf commander and his lieutenant to face a very quick Phoenician warrior, and expect luck to be on their side."

Eyes flaring, the slender but sturdy youth began to pace back-and-forth. It was hard for the wolves to know if the youth truly relished his face off with them, a confrontation to which he had not been invited, or if for the sake of dramatic effect he was posing as a half-crazed warrior.

"Now if luck this day truly absents from you, this very sharp knife will next hack off the big wolf's evil head." The youth flashed his spear at Yellowquist. "I am not worried enough to bother about the head of this harmless junior wolf. When I am done, the big wolf's headless body will join the many lifeless wolves that lie behind us on the rock strewn floor of this trench.

"Think on the cost of your *folly!* Today this unicorn has been extra busy doing bloody business with you wolves. And I now stand with the courageous blackmane!"

The four wolf sergeants that did not understand the uniform animal language were taken aback by the brash sounding tongue of the youth. Those four, plus their general and lieutenant, studied the youth's slender but strong arms. The tautly framed young warrior would not easily fall. Wolves noticed that his perfectly polished sword had an uncommon blue sheen. With the shining blade that looked to be sharp as any knife could be... he could do them much harm.

When the unicorn nudged his back, Lucars turned and saw that Naythorn's wounds had taken a very heavy toll on the stallion. Little time remained before the ground beneath the blackmane's hooves would be completely saturated by the spilling of magic unicorn blood. Lucars turned back to face the wolf commander and lieutenant.

"Here is what you insolent wolves are going to do. After defending himself courageously this day, only a few cups of blood still flow in the blackmane's veins. He has little magic left for you to drink. That being the case, from this trench of stones you are going to withdraw... *now!* I will remain here to close the unicorn's wounds and save his life. In a few days I will be settled on a long sea journey back to my own country. If in the next moon you can muster enough of your own courage, and can as well recruit another phalanx of dull wolf soldiers to help you do battle, at that time you can come back and have at this noble unicorn." The youth menaced his weapons as he added, "Depart now this stony trench or I swear that beginning with the big grayback, I will kill every wolf here!"

Wolf eyes glared hatred at the warrior youth that for no reason had interfered with their kill. With sword and spear raised and ready to do damage, Lucars stepped menacingly toward the big grayback wolf.

"*Grraaghhhrrowwouurrrr!*" Albarochk gave full voice to his resentment. "Because I this day did terrible damage to Naythorn, he will never fully recover from the wounds he now bears. In the next conflict my runty yellow haired cousin will not fail me with his strategy for defeating the blackmane. While the unicorn can never be made whole, by the next moon he will at least be able to walk. The taste of healthy unicorn flesh will be more appealing to me than the flesh of a magic horse that is right now... practically dead. And should you linger here, I will kill you as well!"

Followed close behind by his yellow hided cousin and four sergeant wolves, the huge grayback slunk away.

Naythorn sank to his knees and rolled onto his side. Lucars gathered the bloodied head of the unicorn in his lap. From his flask he dribbled water into the mouth of the blackmane. From ground saturated by spilt unicorn blood, the youth scraped wet clay. He mixed herbs from a waist pouch into the clay, applied the balm to Naythorn's hide, and caked the unicorn's wounds. Naythorn's blood no more spilled onto ground. With his cloak Lucars gingerly pillowed the unicorn's head. Stroking the black mane, with each thought the youth willed the unicorn to live on.

Past far mountains the sun declined into the place prepared for celestial slumber. Across an immense sky stars were one by one candle-lit to glow. Lucars convinced himself that the deep sleep of the unicorn would on the morrow help him to revive.

The youth began to walk a perimeter. Having not suffered wounds, nor exhausted his strength, he would stay alert. Over and over the warrior repeated, "I did what I could. Now the unicorn must decide to live on."

In middle night the youth rested a hand on the

unicorn's hard knit shoulder and said softly, "You this day survived horrific battle. While my part is to guard you from your enemies, your part is to rest and heal. Tomorrow we will hobble to the mountain and find a better place of defense.

"Having with my own eyes seen the grave damage your hooves and horn today inflicted on many wolves, my mind forms the idea that grown more in body, and as well strengthened in experience and judgment, you will in twelve moons become a magnificent war horse. Fighting alone, you were badly wounded. I would that there should come a future day when you and I together do battle."

Lucars imagined that every instant of the unicorn's profound sleep channeled healing into his body. Until the sun warmed the turn of the next day, deep unicorn sleep persisted unchallenged.

Wolf Commander and Lieutenant

Having traveled several leagues distant from the trench of broken stones, two wolves settled to rest the night.

"What a... *disaster,*" growled Albarochk breaking a heavy silence. "We lose too many wolves to the unicorn, the warrior clad in golden armor snatches the prize from out of my jaws, and for pure spite the young soldier cuts my already damaged leg."

"Master, twenty-five of our wolf cousins disobeyed your command... which was to only capture the blackmane. All by themselves they tried to make the kill. Ignoring your orders, the now destroyed wolves acted individually and selfishly. Had they not hastily and recklessly fallen before their time, your wolf company would be this day victorious."

"You are right. Only the four sergeant wolves waited for my arrival."

"Wounded as you are, it was not for you to alone defeat a warrior bearing a magic sword and spear. All that is now required is for you to heal, regain strength, and organize your wolf soldiers to fight together... as an..." the small wolf's voice trailed off as his mind began to wonder how the warrior youth came to join the battle at just the critical moment.

"Err, a thought occurs to me. Remember when I saw you kill the lion? The one wolf with you that day, I witnessed a magnificent display of the strength and cunning that made Albarochk the only wolf anywhere to single-handedly vanquish a full grown mountain lion. To help them better know what future miracles of battle to expect from your eminence, I shall use every opportunity to remind your wolf soldiers of your incomparable victory over the lion."

"On that day I was... *amazing*," replied a somewhat mollified Albarochk resting his head on his good paw. "But today the blackmaned unicorn was in my grasp. With one great leap I could have severed his throat. But, I had to think of what my wolf soldiers need most from me. They must be taught to blindly follow my orders. From now on my privates will be buffeted to enforce unquestioned obedience to my every command. I will see that my orders come to be by reflex obeyed." The wolf commander expelled a deep breath.

"And you alone will deliver the death blow to the

blackmane," soothed the small yellow wolf.

"Remember how so long ago my mother, your aunt wolf, would with her back warm us cubs? I feel the cold to enter into me. Even in the heat of middle day my body is strangely cold. Move over here; bring warmth to me."

Yellowquist shifted to put his belly against the back of Albarochk; almost immediately the giant wolf fell into a trance-like sleep. A wolf paw caressed the hide of a giant wolf that had changed so much since first confronting the blackmane, that the small wolf now scarcely recognized his cousin.

Wolfly Love

Troubled deeply by his relationship with his giant cousin, Yellowquist did not that night close his eyes. The thoughts of the yellow wolf turned to dwell on the dimensions and consequence of... *wolfly love*. He knew that it was the nature of wolves to be mean. But Albarochk was far more than mean; he had grown to become evil. The taste of unicorn blood had intensified the worst traits of his cousin wolf's character. In the same way that unicorn blood fed the outlandish growth of Albarochk's body, unicorn magic had also magnified his grayback cousin's thirst for power and his disdain for all life other than his own.

"How can I love a cousin changed to become a... *monster?*" muttered the yellow wolf to himself. "As a cub wolf I looked up to Albarochk as my protector; for long years he sheltered me. But does not my continued love require affection in return? Can my wolfly love, without condition, be ever and always given? Would not such an all-encompassing love for my cousin wolf, whose heart is deceitful above all things, be also *unnatural?*"

The lieutenant wolf whispered an unwelcome thought, "Can long continuance of a love unconditional lead to an outcome opposite that intended? Can my one-sided love actually bring harm to the great gray wolf by enabling him to commit more and greater monstrosities? How many more innocent wolves are to die because of Albarochk's desperate wickedness?

"I also tasted magical unicorn blood. For that my puny body is the one that should have grown larger. But strangely enough the taste of Naythorn's blood only made my hide to mark more yellow, and my mind to think larger thoughts. Could it be that the taste of unicorn blood made me to become a wolf... *more noble?*"

The wolf lieutenant addressed himself as if he were another animal person, "But Yellowquist knows that all wolves are supposed to be unnoble. His monstrous cousin growls that Naythorn's interference with wolf prey made the unicorn to become unnatural. So by the taste of unicorn blood was Yellowquist made to be a wolf... *unnaturally* good? How long will Albarochk tolerate a cousin's heart made delicate by goodness not becoming to a wolf?

"Yellowquist must guard and protect all the cruelty he still possesses inside. If he does not do so, he will by Albarochk be destroyed."

To himself Yellowquist admitted that in regard to the love he still held for his cousin, a love self-destructive and doomed, he was powerless. The yellow wolf felt tears moisten his eyes and roll down his jowls.

He decided that was the first time he had ever cried real tears. That he had cried tears that were real worried even more the yellow wolf.

CHAPTER 24

UNRIDDLED

"Wake up... wake up... *Naythorn*. We cannot longer tarry in this rocky trench. You and I must right away get to the mountain of spires." The unicorn opened his eyes, expelled a deep breath, and stirred himself. Even the slightest movement made him shudder with pain.

"From the look in your eyes I can tell that your whole body hurts," observed Lucars. "But please make to move your big frame, even if only a little."

Scraping the ground on which he lay, the unicorn's neck moved slowly back-and-forth. Naythorn next found he could move his tail. He managed to straighten and bend one leg, then another.

"Let me help you to roll onto your knees," said the youth. Naythorn at last stood upright.

The blackmane took one step. He took another. When compared to the unicorn's appalling and desperate condition the previous evening, his recovery to an ambulatory equine state was nothing short of miraculous.

"The poultice of my healing herbs combined well with the magic of unicorn blood," encouraged Lucars.

"The kind touch of a rough hand does much good," responded the blackmane. Lifting stiffly one leg after the other, Naythorn at last achieved entrance to the mountain.

"Excellent!" exclaimed Lucars. "Now I must find a place with water, grass, and cliffs of protection so that we are not ambushed from behind. Not for one moment do I trust the word of the wolf general." The youth was soon returned.

"I found a cave where a pool collects drip water. There you can drink deeply. Once you are settled in the cave, I will cut grass for you to eat." That evening Naythorn proved himself able to eat hay.

After Naythorn's small supper of mown grass, Lucars cautioned, "The water and grass in this place will not last you for more than a few suns. And, we have here no means of communication with my sergeant. He awaits me, and I am long overdue. Or, just maybe, Hammerclaw continues to search for the deposit of blue gold. If so, he will leave signs for me to follow and find him. We cannot, Naythorn, remain here long."

The response from the blackmane made to drop the youth's jaw. "Your blacksmith needs to come to us. In this lone mountain is found the canyon that shines of blue gold."

"That is not possible! You see, when Hammerclaw and I before traveled everywhere around and over this mountain, we found nothing."

"Your surprise is to be expected. Shining Canyon is a well-hidden place. Listen Lucars, I came toward this mountain following unmistakable signs that something is here to be found. The secret was finally revealed to me. Shining Canyon is the only wondrous thing that can be here hidden.

"Go ahead and shake your head, young warrior, but of my conclusion I am sure. You see, Lucars... *I feel its presence*. My horn connects to a magic place of blue gold found proximate to us.

"The only reason I traveled toward this mountain was to understand the signs I followed. I know now that the riddle of the seven pyramid crests has to do with the canyon of magic gold. Do you know what else, Lucars? When we find the place of the magic gold, my heart tells me we will also come to possess abundant water and precious safety." Lucars sat himself on the ground. From chin to forehead his face came to display a big open smile.

"What you say makes me proud of you... and also proud of myself. Thank goodness that when you were battling the wolves I recognized the right thing to do was to come to your rescue. But where exactly, Naythorn, raise the rock walls laced with veins of gold? When in the last moon I explored this side of the mountain, I came upon no entrance to a hidden canyon."

"The magic place lies in a part of the mountain not easily reached. If it were otherwise, Shining Canyon would not long keep its marvelous treasure well-hidden. We must tomorrow scout out places in this mountain that cannot be easily entered. The secret will be unlocked at a place of an impossible climb, where a far fall threatens, or where a whistled melody leads us to uncover a hidden door. Friend Lucars, tomorrow we will look for a place from where we can see well the singular features of this mountain."

Steadied by the young warrior, Naythorn the next day willed himself the strength to climb hooves until he finally gained a high ledge of prominence. A look exchanged between the two confirmed that they had both noted the same thing, at the same time. Behind the cliff containing the respite where Naythorn had slept, spires absented. For as far as they could see, only that one place lacked ascendant stone columns. On the other side of the welcoming cave was a depression, and that open area could cast down deep.

Still the problem they faced was not small. There was no evident way to find behind the cliff walls fronting them. Before exploring further, Lucars left Naythorn back at rest in the cave of respite. A lengthy amount of time elapsed before the youth returned.

"I double checked; the mouth of our cave presents the only break in this entire cliff face." That commented, Lucars proceeded to make himself comfortable.

"Hmph. Well, Naythorn, only one explanation makes sense to me. You feel close by the hidden presence of the blue gold that Phoenicians mined a thousand years ago. The fact that there is no evident way to penetrate into and behind these cliffs, suggests that the entrance into Shining Canyon was shuttered and closed off by the Phoenicians who long ago... hmph... but the pyramid crests that Hammer and I studied looked to have been made not by Phoenicians, but rather by Egyptians. Now that suggests that Egyptians also came here, raised the pyramid crests to mark the location of the magic ore, and then resealed the entrance to the canyon. Ahh...hah!

But since we know that where we now sit is the only place that directs into the mountain, we can conclude that within the furthest reaches of this cavern there is something more to learn."

"You know, Lucars, it would have taken many years to raise the pyramid crests that I followed. If as you suggest Egyptians came to this land a thousand years ago, and stayed behind to build pointed crests on the topmost parts of seven mountains, what happened to them? And what do Egyptians look like?"

"Rather than correspond to the bulky set and build of my blacksmith, Egyptians look a lot like me. And their dress is distinctive. Of one thing I am sure. In this land Hammer and I have come upon no Egyptians." The youth's face took on a puzzled look.

"I once read the saga of the Phoenician barges that carried unicorns to Wittanor Hold and returned laden with blue gold. That account made mention of a Lieutenant Abel and a Princess Maryeta. As I recall, no mention was made of Egypt. But it is almost impossible to imagine that the pyramid crests were not raised by Egyptian builders... and only unicorns could have shown Egyptians the way to Shining Canyon. Hunh, could Phoenician historians have deliberately failed to mention an Egyptian role in the establishment of Wittanor Hold, and the discovery of Shining Canyon?"

"Is Egypt not a friend of Phoenicia?"

"No, Naythorn. Only the magic of our blue gold swords has kept Phoenicia from being conquered by Egypt."

"Then, perhaps it was not convenient for your

historians to acknowledge Egyptian participation in the discovery of the magic blue gold. Anyway, when my grandsire neighed to you and Hammerclaw the clue about special rocks, it would have helped if he had remembered that they were piled to form pyramid crests. I hate to neigh this, Lucars, but so much thinking has made me tired. Our exploration shall continue tomorrow. I need to right now rest my mind, legs, and sides so that in the morning I can walk without trembling."

While the unicorn that night slept, Lucars was left to wonder why after having built the pyramid crests marking the magic ore of Shining Canyon, soldiers in Egypt did not possess blue gold swords.

"You look indeed better this morning." So encouraged by Lucars the unicorn got himself up, drank water, and ate cut grass.

"My horn will now light the way." The most promising cave passage ended without opening... to anything. The unicorn and youth backtracked and took an alternative, and more twisted passage littered with fallen rock. The second route extended deeper into the mountain. As the excitement of discovery rekindled energy inside of him, Naythorn's horn cast a bright and penetrating light.

In the innermost part of the second cave passage, the unicorn and the youth came upon a spacious room with rough walls. However, a place in the walls about the height and width of a big cattle's body and horns, stretched smooth. The more they studied the smooth part of the wall, the more out of place seemed its even finish. When with his sword the youth struck a hard descendent blow at the wall, clay plaster crumbled that could not have been formed by the mountain itself. The removal of more plaster revealed that a rock door seamed tightly into the wall. The youth's sword chipped to clean the seam between the jamb and the rock door. Lucars next began to use his sword as a lever. At last the rock slab moved ever so little inward toward the youth.

"Naythorn, it is as it should be. Because it is easier to push with one's shoulders than to pull with one's arms, the door from this side closes. Otherwise men could not leave the canyon, and from inside this cave push shut the door behind them." Prying and wriggling one side of the rock door, Lucars slowly coaxed the slab to open more.

"This is heavy work for two not huge arms, and one sword. And since the glow of your horn dims, we will tomorrow here continue. You know, Naythorn, I was worried my sword point would break. I can say that my blue gold sword has today proven its metal." As they made their way back to the cave opening both Naythorn and Lucars were certain they had found entrance to the canyon of legend.

On the next day the trueness of the blue gold sword was once more proven. Through a long morning of prying the point of the weapon did not break, and the blade ultimately prevailed.

"I feel a welcoming breeze from behind the rock. That means that I am almost through the cave wall." The youth rested his arms to enjoy the draft of fresh air.

"While you levered with your sword, for my part I

thought about the decisions I made that led me here. Wolves were already present when I stood on the last pyramid crest and gazed in the direction of this mountain... that was too far away for my eyes to see. Because in the midst of this desert-like plain wolves can outlast a lone unicorn, I knew that continuing forward would make me vulnerable to attack. Even knowing that, I chose to go forward to solve the riddle of the pyramid shaped crests. So, Lucars, I risked everything to answer a question that obsessed me. Had you not found me when you did, I would not have survived to see the puzzle solved. After so much wound and sacrifice, I would not have experienced triumph.

"In order to satisfy my curiosity about the pyramid crests, I stubbornly and recklessly abandoned my responsibilities to my animal platoon. Lucars, in my absence, I do not even know if my platoon has survived. The cattle, bison, razorbacks, waterfowl, dogs, and mountain sheep count on me. Upon coming to possess wings, Rayalas left behind her horse family to with me journey. So, just as I was always told, it seems that I remain a prideful unicorn in pursuit of my own selfish desires."

Lucars was taken aback by the negative self-assessment of the indomitable unicorn, that down to the roots of his black mane possessed undaunted courage.

"Let us both face the facts, Naythorn. You and I lack experience in these things. And just as you are stubborn, I am as well obstinate. I disobeyed a direct order from my sergeant when I chose to follow wolves into the trench of broken stones. Rather than return to the place of rendezvous, I willfully chose to chase after strangely possessed wolves.

"Now thinking more about what you just neighed, I can as well conclude that your detour to this mountain happened for an important purpose, which you do not yet comprehend. From what you told me, I think it was your destiny to find the canyon of blue gold. Although you suffered grave bodily injury, you survived, and you learned. You have come to better understand how much your life matters to others. When you consider well the fruits of persistent leadership that does not call it quits, you will find those achievements have more value than you before presumed. My friend, to yourself you are now known."

"But Lucars, for my stubbornness I came *this close* to dying. At the end of the fight in the trench of stones, my body was so beaten down that I wanted to simply give in to the ferocity of the wolves. I told myself I would never beat them, and it was useless to fight on. When you found me I was within a chin whisker of walking no more on the face of this earth."

"Let me, Naythorn, share something personal. On our voyage to the unicorn hold I once found myself helpless, and seemingly lost to eternity. During a fierce tempest a wave rolled over the barge and carried me headlong into the drink. I felt the power of the sea to overwhelm me. Swimming for my life, I fell further and further behind the barge. When all seemed lost, my spirit somehow stepped outside of my body. It was as if a part of me was floating in the air, looking down, and watching my arms and legs flail against the churning waves.

"Naythorn, in that visionary moment I realized I could not give up, not without fighting to my last breath. My spirit returned to my body, and I again fought on through the big waves. At last by the same fierce gusts of wind that tossed me into the sea, the barge became turned about, and I was seen. Naythorn, when I cheated death I learned two things. The first was to never underestimate the power of water and wind. The second was that Lucars will never give up his fight."

"I appreciate your words of encouragement, Lucars. Triumphing against terrible odds made me to learn things about myself that could in no other way be comprehended. On my own I took on a very large quest, and it turns out that the clues I followed gave me good reason to so do. The wolf general lost only the *Battle of the Stone Trench*. Not losing the war, he will attack again. In my next battle, I will count on past things learned to work to my benefit."

"After Hammerclaw and I complete our charge of duty in Shining Canyon, I may not happen further upon you. Even so, I will know that the blackmane is well-prepared for his next confrontation with wolves."

"You raise my spirits, Lucars. How would it be if we now rest and talk more at nightfall? The light of my horn dims. And in my present state I find that talking tires me more than moving my hooves. Tomorrow morning we will enter the forgotten canyon to see a treasure that for the past thousand years has remained unseen."

The man and the unicorn that now shared an

unalterable bond of friendship born of battle and rescue, walked side by side toward the cave entrance. Neither Lucars, nor Naythorn, would admit to the thought that their lives had been drawn to each other in order to share a destiny woven in magic. Neither dared recognize that side by side they would travel over many mountains, and across many lands. While their minds did not admit, and their words did not acknowledge that it was so, the secret hearts of the youth and the blackmaned unicorn already knew.

CHAPTER 25

THE RULER OF THE SEA

With slow methodic thrusts swam a leviathan. One great pull after another compelled the monster along an immense diagonal. It had been so long since the ruler of the sea had seen or felt the break of waves over its mantel, that the feel of air and the look of sky were unremembered.

The bulk of the sea beast was all and entire eight great arms and two gigantic tentacles that moved in a rhythm remindful of a sorrowful melody. The muscles pulsing throughout the massive arms were smooth, subtle, and myriad. Their great mass did not tire.

Called toward something irresistible, the sea monster moved upward toward a concept of destruction never before imagined. An overwhelming fascination stirred within the beast... the lust to crush in powerful arms *flesh-circumferenced magic.*

Fish that on any other day would be seized in enormous tentacles were ignored, as if invisible. Sensing that they did not matter in the course of what was about to unfold, and taken with curiosity at the movements of the greatest sea beast they had ever swum upon, fish lingered close to the leviathan.

Surface water churned as the monster's great bulk broke through waves and touched an invisible web of atmosphere, sun, and wind. The beast beheld what had provoked departure from a dark and cold abode in a deep canyon below a world of sea water. It was as the colossus had dreamed; upon open water floated five promontories. On the pieces of floating islands walked two-legged creatures clad with vestments that shined. With them stood the magic horned animals that the beast had been summoned to smash in its great arms and tentacles. The sea colossus sank down to continue onward unseen. Very soon the monster would know the satisfaction of battle and the savor of triumph over the magically horned creatures. The hostility of the sea colossus set fittingly upon the largest Phoenician barge.

The high escort had foretold that the attack would come to pass. The impending assault of a sea monster had also been sensed by the dolphin Quixsoar. Zoumar knew to believe both Aneilee and the dolphin. For that, unicorn foals and colts crowded tightly into the center holds of each barge, and sailors waited at the ready with weapons newly sharpened. The only question that remained was when the attack would come.

The barges were vulnerable to an enemy whose arrival was by deep water made invisible. The admiral knew that when the attack finally happened, for barges found in the middle of a vast sea escape was nowhere to be gained.

When the sea beast broke through watery surface, one moment became awaited destiny. The throw and velocity of the beast's extensions upon the deck of the flagship were like tree-size whips lashing down with the cracks of thunderous lightning bolts. Sword and spear thrusts could not counter the devastation brought by the great arms of the colossus. After wringing life from struggling lumps of flesh, the broken bodies of sailors and unicorns were tossed into the sea.

Zoumar picked himself up from where by a monster arm he had been swatted and thrown back. Beside him the racer-filly that he had so often reprimanded, crouched to spring at the colossus.

"That is suicide! Do not, Belaflor, throw your life away!"

"I will knock *back* the beast!" Seeing the determination of the filly, the admiral took a deep and acquiescent breath.

"Then we will together go at the beast. I and my men will with our swords attack the beast's great arms that pummel this side of our barge. Wait until the beast has seized us, and is tossing us overboard. When the monster's arms are lifted high with throat exposed, launch yourself with fleetness, like when you race against Alexzana and the dolphin. Stab at the base of the neck where run fibers that control the tremendous arms and tentacles. Cut the neck cords and paralyze the beast. Make ready."

Just as Zoumar had said would happen, when he and five men ran yelling at the beast, enormous arms and tentacles cracked down upon them. Six men were seized and whipped about like toys in the hands of a child throwing a tantrum. The beast's arms rose to snap the men out into the water. At that moment Belaflor's legs bought the fastest race of her life. She sped hooves so fast it was almost as if she flew at the sea beast. Belaflor hurdled over a great arm thrown at her. Before another enormous arm could broadside the filly, her horn closed on the neck of the colossus. The beast's tardy reaction failed to stop the unimaginably quick impulse of Belaflor's greatest leap ever.

The length of the filly's sharp horn planted into the flesh of the colossus. The deep penetration of the filly's horn struck into, and magically welded to the great nerve controlling the beast's appendages. As the powerful arms of the beast lost drive and power, an organic bond came to connect the filly to the darkness possessing the mind of the monster squid. Beset by the before unimagined experience of defeat, the anguish of the great sea colossus was unbearable, and in turn paralyzing for the neck-bonded filly.

Into the head of Belaflor flashed images of obscure ledges and escarpments from where the beast had terrorized every form of fish life. The sea monster that did not, and could not comprehend either the meaning of mercy or the concept of hope, lusted to swallow and utterly destroy innocence. The thoughts issuing from the innermost workings of the giant squid's mind terrified from head to hooves the unicorn filly.

A rush of strange recognition penetrated the colossus. The great sea beast perceived that the little horned horse had come to possess its most intimate thoughts. Belaflor, in turn, came to know that the ruler of the sea felt insufferable humiliation because of what the unicorn filly had done, propelling herself faster with movement more clever than the sea giant had presumed possible. The self-knowledge of loss, defeat, and overwhelming humiliation engulfed the mind of the sea monster.

As the thoughts of the leviathan begin to unravel and shake apart, the interconnection fusing two minds deepened, and a thing that was before inconceivable was revealed to Belaflor. The colossus of the sea came to know, for the first time, that its life was not an inexorable law unto itself. Along with the recognition of limit came a strange paradox of hope. There was a subtle comfort found in the certainty that even the ruler of ocean depths could not disobey the natural law that all things, someday, come to taste defeat and to death succumb. The revelation that the panorama of life is by circumscribed and encompassing purpose enlarged to include all things, carried fittingness.

Incapacitated by a new and inordinate concept of powerlessness, the body of the beast began to shake. With her horn still fixed to the monster's neck, Belaflor was pulled into the sea. As the body of the colossus began to slowly spiral downward, the force of the great beast's shuddering cracked and severed the horn of Belaflor. One half of a magic unicorn horn would ever after lodge in the neck of the leviathan. But the two pieces of magical horn remained invisibly connected, and in descent the thoughts of the colossus still passaged to Belaflor.

"Little filly, it was your turn on this day to conquer me. As you go on to live a life filled with more victories, know that no triumph on a future field of conflict will ever equal your feat of daring against the ruler of the sea." Made unparalyzed by a proffered gift of hope given to the unicorn filly, a prodigious tentacle grabbed hold of Belaflor and propelled her upward.

When the filly broke through the water's surface the Phoenician lad Mariano grabbed a rope, swam to the filly, and secured her chest. Belaflor was hoisted onto the deck and cradled in the firm grasp of men with sturdy arms. From the crossed horns of the matriarch and the high escort, magic sparks arced downward into the filly's half horn. After her coughs expelled prodigious amounts of water, Belaflor was revitalized.

"I was somewhere caught... as if in a terrible dream. When the monster's thoughts overlaid my own, I traveled far inside the beast's mind. The colossus lives in black hopelessness, and believes that only death can bring release from darkness and despair."

"When your hooves flew on the wind, your valor saved the white herd from destruction," neighed Elianor to sooth the valiant filly. "You have earned a much needed rest."

The horn of Aneilee sparked currented fire to unbreathing mariners and unicorns brought to the side of the admiral's barge. With a final caress of unicorn magic, the bodies of sailors and horned horses lost in the *Battle of the Sea Colossus,* turned to ash. Vapors burning magical with the memories of unicorn hearts, sparkled skyward.

After Battle

Pacing broken deck boards, the admiral would be alone with his thoughts. When the colossus exploded out of the water Zoumar had found it fitting that the most sturdy craft in his fleet, his flagship, bore the brunt force of the attack. Unfortunately, the great barge had barely survived the beast's crashing blows.

At the attack of the leviathan, the admiral had known awful fear. For that, his commands authored in distress had been woefully inadequate. He had led more battles than he could count, and yet in this battle he had been found completely wanting of strategy. The young bothersome unicorn, so often chided for racing about his crowded barge, had shown courage greater than he himself.

Zoumar decided that one is never too old, or become too proud, to accept a new measure of humility. He felt that as a war admiral he had now to enter an advanced phase of command training, in which he would need to not only learn new things, but as well unlearn old things. He wanted to become an admiral that listened three times more than he talked, and daily voiced kind words to lowly sailors. His resolve to be more humble would not be easy to accomplish, and would assuredly be many times tested. The proud man vowed to not scowl when he next heard the clatter of hooves in the forty-pace race.

On succeeding days the admiral began to relish the neighing and stomping of unicorn hooves, and the slapping and crashing of dolphin bodies. The sight of three scarlet feathered birds with luxuriant tails flying low over his barge brought warm welcome to his heart. The admiral became convinced that there existed purpose that he was each day led to encounter. Given his new resolve, Zoumar could not help but feel an unaccustomed lightness to his being, as if his life was like a circle that had suddenly doubled in circumference.

The admiral decided that before he refound Phoenicia, not only the destiny of the unicorn herd would become known, but his destiny would also be made clear. Having witnessed the heroism beyond belief of the unicorn filly, the admiral promised he would open his mind to embrace whatever strange new paths his feet were put upon.

Pacing back-and-forth a corrupted deck, the image of an innocent filly caught to the neck of the monster squid kept recurring to the high escort. Finding that compelling image to be discouraging, Aneilee made her mind to think instead on the playfulness of Belaflor.

In contrast to the innocence of the small filly, the gigantic ruler of the sea was all powerful in its dominion. The high escort of the unicorns paused to reflect on the pathos of a sea colossus possessing so much power and authority, undone by an innocent unicorn filly.

The hooves of Aneilee stomped as the sound of her neigh split the darkness, "Desolation is the final recompense for those by goodness untouched."

CHAPTER 26

CRIMSON TAILED PARROTS

She had been thrown about and bruised, and she had swallowed a barrel of salt water. Worst of all, the very essence of her unicorn being had been parted in two. Still, with Alexzana's constant nursing the broken horn, punished body, and spirit of Belaflor began to mend. On the second day of her recovery, the little unicorn filly raised her head. On the third day she rolled about on her belly. But on the fourth day of her recovery, the filly still could not make herself to stand.

That evening as was gathered about the sun a night dress made of purple-edged clouds fitted to soften the bed of solar slumber, hundreds of birds outlined against the western sky. The large birds with colorful tails as thick as a unicorn's, flew closer and closer to the admiral's barge. The sight of so many land birds flying so far out at sea was difficult to comprehend.

"Look at their beautiful red shoulders and tails!" exclaimed Alexzana motioning upward at the birds that had begun to circle above the admiral's barge. "And I just love their blue body feathers! But, what do they carry in their beaks?"

A long-tailed bird fluttered down and dropped a lavender colored flower upon Belaflor's neck. One by one every bird in the flock pursued the example of the first, until Belaflor's neck and sides were covered in delicate petals. Aneilee and Elianor delighted in the lavish spectacle of crimson and blue feathered birds, dropping rainbow petaled flowers upon the resting Belaflor.

"These beautiful birds, that I think are a new kind of parrot, have made you the best-dressed unicorn in the fleet," offered the admiral as he approached. After returning a knowing smile to Zoumar, the half-horned filly relaxed in the luxury of the bright colors, soft textures, and the subtle perfumes of myriad flowers.

"Have you ever seen such a display of bird affection, for a unicorn?" inquired the matriarch of Aneilee. She answered her own question, "I know that you have not. And for my part, I had no idea that birds paid any attention to unicorns."

"This very special moment for Belaflor, is also for me wonderful," responded the high escort. "How fitting that birds brought flowers to the brave unicorn whose very name means *beautiful flower*. Their flighted offering shows that nature entire extends thankfulness for the selfless bravery of our little filly."

"When your horn brought rescue to the flagship," neighed Aneilee, "you brought honor to our race of magical horses. And since your best friends are the native girl Alexzana, and the dolphin Quixsoar, you showed that a unicorn need not be separate and apart from other animal persons. For all that you have done, I now proclaim this day to be the half-horned filly's new birthday. You deserve not only flowers from visiting birds of lovely hue, you also merit our remembrance and praise for your bravery."

"But I only followed the example of Alexzana when she thrust a knife into a war canoe."

"Darling filly, about that you are right. I never thought I would see a girl come to be so brave as Alexzana. Now then, so that we will never forget what you did to save us from drowning in this great sea, from this ceremonial birthday onward you shall be called by the new name... Belfloralex. Your brand new name will ever remind us of a filly bathed in purple, yellow, orange, and blue petals. Your name shall also remind us of your very brave special friend. Having shared each other's courage, it is fitting that Belfloralex and Alexzana now apportion each other's names."

"It is *wonderful* that you now join to my name!" exclaimed Alexzana throwing her arms around the neck of the filly.

Closing her eyes, in the company of brilliantly feathered birds Belfloralex was in dreams escorted skyward. By unicorns and gold-clad warriors, the name Belfloralex was echoed throughout the fleet.

The Mesmerizing Isle

When a wide beach with black sand presented a hospitable mooring for the barges, Zoumar decided that both unicorns and sailors warranted a time of respite. Besides, following the battle against the sea colossus remaining repairs to the flagship barge could best be accomplished on the welcoming island.

A spring of fresh water became immediately popular. Unicorns found the grass to be delectable. Tree fruits and roots that could be tastefully fried, were plenteous.

On the morning following the landing, the admiral sent Captain Avalcar in the lead of a platoon to reconnoiter the interior of the island. Naythorn's sire, Cabalblade, provided liaison for the contingent of horned horses designated to be mounts for the sailors. Zoumar's instructions were to avoid contact with any inhabitants that should be encountered, to take no unnecessary risks, and to return to camp before the set of three suns.

The first day of exploration progressed perfectly. Camp was that evening made on the bank of a stream teeming with fish. On a night when the aroma of budding red and yellow tree flowers permeated the warm air, the sentries saw no movements nor heard any sounds hinting of danger.

The next morning the expedition followed a ridge that climbed ever higher. That afternoon the explorers were gifted a wide view of a coastline dotted with welcoming bays and inlets. The expeditionaries identified no human structures or camps, no trace of smoke from cooking fires, and no sounds however faint of voices, axes, or movement. The uninhabited island had rivers, mountains, forests, meadows, good mooring for barges, coastal waters that held the promise of plentiful fish, and a climate generous of sun and rain.

The expedition's camp the second night was by a waterfall. The swirling pool at the base of the falling torrent massaged the muscles of men and unicorns. Adventurous sailors climbed to the top of the falls and slid feet first in a swift torrent that carried them downward yelling and laughing. At sunset a little rainbow came to crown the waterfall, and so presented an auspicious sign of hospitality.

Avalcar allowed that he had never before seen such a paradise. His mount, Cabalblade, responded that living there would be even better than dwelling in the Hold of Wittanor before the mountain rained down destruction. Upon the platoon's return to the fleet, Admiral Zoumar was impressed with the broad smiles displayed by the members of Avalcar's expedition.

Favored by a fair wind blowing to the north, Zoumar the next morning ordered readiness to sail. His order was met with complaint. A gathering of sailors and horned horses formed to plead for further exploration of the entire island. Even barge captains and sage unicorns petitioned the admiral to belay the order to leave.

Remembering his vow to become a kinder man who listened better, Zoumar finally consented to delay. The next morning Zoumar awoke to a clear sky and an aromatic breeze. The island paradise with black beaches was proving difficult to depart.

CHAPTER 27

TO PRANCE IN BEAUTY

Upon consenting to delay his fleet's departure from the harmonious isle with black sand beaches, Admiral Zoumar focused upon additional provisioning and the tightening of decks and rigging. Quite understandably his sailors preferred to postpone return to the high sea where not only danger could and would present, but the tedious work of pulling long oars was a daily requirement.

Energetic colts had come to resent the constricted space offered by floating wooden platforms where they could scarcely kick out two legs at once. Nor did adult unicorns enjoy having their big frames compacted day after day on barge decks. Rather than resume sail to a destination unknown, and risk attacks from sea monsters or warring natives, the unicorn preference was to graze fresh grass, rest in the shade of palm trees, sleep at night on solid ground, and gallop on a beach that reminded them of Wittanor Hold.

For the delayed leave-taking from the island, Elianor began to worry. "I request, Admiral, an assembly to settle the issue of our departure. In that regard, the discipline of parade march will do us all good. I need you to require that everyone, with the exception of young colts, stand in formation. Your sergeants can show us how to form up a combined brigade of sailors and unicorns. Looking disciplined will help us to regain discipline."

"It shall be a mandatory military parade with strict adherence to protocols," agreed immediately Zoumar. "Dame Elianor, how long are unicorns to stand in formation?"

"Until the white herd agrees on the need to obey their destiny and depart this enticing island, or until the sun heats unbearably hot the backs of horned horses standing at attention."

Although unicorns had never before marched in a military formation, the idea of a dress parade where every unicorn was bathed, cleaned, and preened to look his or her best appealed especially to the mares and fillies. Because girl unicorns liked to prance with flair, and yearling colts and stallions liked to admire prancing fillies and mares, the idea of a parade was greeted enthusiastically.

The procession was delayed one day so that the unicorn horses could better learn to march not only with other unicorns, but also with the sailors they had come to respect. The procession was another day delayed so that the marching steps became more precisely timed and uniformly cadenced.

The one hundred unicorns and two hundred sailors from each barge wanted their battalion to be the one that most inspired the parade formation. For that, sailors took seriously the charge of combing manes, braiding tails, shining hooves, and offering their own insights on the finer points of military parade movement. Yearling fillies and colts, and shorter sailors, made up the first ranks. Stallions and taller men formed the closing ranks. The rear file of each military battalion was a drum corps.

Fillies became unmerciful in their criticism of those unicorns that could not cadence in time with the others, or stand at attention with manes arched to achieve the maximum effect. Because they formed side by side with magnificent unicorns, the parade also became a matter of pride for the mariners. When the day of the dress parade finally dawned, hooves and armor were shined to such a degree that it seemed a shame to dirty them marching across gritty black sand.

The Parade

Starting, from the admiral's perspective, at the right end of the beach each of the five battalions marched to the *tun... tun... tunning* rhythm of its own parade drums. Behind Zoumar and Elianor, who stood together at attention as they watched the battalions of sailors and unicorns march past them, unicorn foals frisked about comprising a very energetic audience for the parade.

Admiral Zoumar noted with satisfaction that at their fronts and sides the marching unicorns and sailors maintained a remarkably exact distance. Once the last battalion had passed the reviewing stand the parade formation executed a left-face march and then another left-face march to proceed back in the direction they had come. Upon regaining the reviewing stand parade right-faced, and then stepped forward to halt and stand at attention ten paces before the place of parade review. The admiral was pleased to see that his men formed the outer ranks of those facing him, and so symbolically protected the magical horses standing in the center of each battalion.

"Your idea, Elianor, was inspired," said Zoumar without turning his head. "I never would have imagined myself to live so long to see a parade formation of unicorns joined to sailors. I cannot believe how well the horned horses matched the timing of my mariners' steps."

"Look at how splendidly your men have polished their golden armor," replied Elianor. "Their metal plate shines brilliant in the sun."

"This has become more than a showy exercise. The parade has drawn together and unified my sailors and your unicorns."

Inspecting each file, the admiral began to walk between the battalions in the formation. He individually complimented the spotlessness of a sailor's armor, the cleanliness of a horse's hide, and the smartness of positions with back stiff and head held high. Zoumar resumed his place beside Elianor.

"I find, Admiral, that today you have fulfilled the desire you before mentioned, to be more solicitous to those under your command." For that comment Zoumar could not help but smile with satisfaction.

It was time to conduct a more profound business than the review of a military parade. Looking over the parade formation and the backdrop of the sea, the admiral began.

"The old saga of our people recounted the long ago unicorn voyage that set forth from Phoenicia, and returned bearing magic blue gold. Knowing that Phoenicia had for a thousand years benefited from the blessings brought by the blue gold magic that is component to horned horses, I readily agreed to my king's request to transport unicorns in their quest for a new hold. I and my sailors will not fail to escort the white herd to its new place of safety."

"Admiral!" neighed a big young unicorn guard stallion named Hoovefort. "This island of black sand beaches is a beautiful gift meant for the white herd to forever cherish!"

A veteran sailor stepped out and motioned with his arm for permission to speak.

"Permission granted."

"This island is also very much to the liking of us sailors. We could here begin a new Phoenician colony. Imagine the joy of awaking every morning in this paradise with food all about us, and a blue sky above us."

"To both unicorns and sailors," answered the admiral stepping forward, "I say that this island is a place to walk in beauty. But, we do not here walk in obedience. This wondrous island offers no natural defense. The flat shores of this island will not withstand an invasion from warlike tribes, one of which we have already dealt with on this voyage. Magic horses and sailors cannot here be well-defended. And, I am duty bound to return my barges to Phoenicia. Once I undertake the long voyage of return, to this island I can offer no more protection."

The unicorn matriarch stepped forward to share her most profound hope for the white herd.

"While my heart wants to rest on this island that is as pretty and fresh as the dreams of a new foal, my head tells me that cannot be. In order to fulfill unicorn destiny, we must face and overcome challenges that build our courage and grow our love. To promote creation's path toward goodness, the white herd must ever survive. We *must...* accompany our Phoenician benefactors to the land where they seek shining blue gold.

"After bidding farewell to the admiral and his sailors, we unicorns will seek a place of beauty that we ourselves can defend. Just as on this day you stand proud and resolute, let us stay the course set by Admiral Zoumar. We *must* continue on our journey to find a hold forever safe for our colts."

While Elianor had more admonitions for the unicorns, a thing happened that prematurely ended a discourse only half done. A small half-horned filly standing in the front file of her battalion strode out from the formation. Belfloralex bowed to Zoumar and Elianor. It was quickly understood that the five steps forward she had taken showed she would be obedient to the commands of the admiral and the matriarch. Marching in the first file beside the filly, Alexzana and Mariano moved to stand beside Belfloralex. Each rested an arm on the filly's mane.

The example of the young heroes that had fought valiantly against warrior canoes and the colossus of the sea, proved irresistible. With newly instilled pride, the entire battalion of Zoumar's flagship stepped ahead to stand with the three young friends. With Belfloralex,

Alexzana, and Mariano once again positioned in the first file, the barge's battalion of sailors and unicorns had reformed.

One parade battalion after another stepped forward to stand in a newly formed line before Zoumar and Elianor. With the exception of the one guard stallion, the horned horses had come to agree that the search for a far home would now be a journey of discipline in beauty.

"You must know that when the destiny you speak of is found," said Zoumar to Elianor, "it cannot meet the eye as pleasingly as this lush paradise surrounded by an emerald sea." Elianor was too absorbed in contemplation of the high spirits of the unicorns and sailors still standing at attention to initially notice what the admiral had said.

"Oh, sorry, I was distracted. My plan, Admiral, that the intense midday sun would force unicorns to recognize that the heat of this island is simply too hot to bear, did not work as I had hoped. Instead, young unicorns found that the pageantry of a military procession more than compensated for the discomfort of midday heat. So instead of being forced by wilting heat to accept and obey your authority and mine, unicorns and sailors themselves seized the opportunity to strengthen our harmony." Elianor breathed deeply. To her mind this beautiful island setting would ever be remembered as the *Field of Obedience*.

"You do know, Hoovefort, that unity becomes the white herd," neighed Aneilee later to the big unicorn stallion that had objected to the decision to leave the island. "I am disappointed that with your battalion you did not step forward."

"One day I will come to command the unicorn guards. Because the size of this island hold would require our guard unit to triple in size, here my authority would be enlarged. This island is perfect for me. And on this island there would never be a disruptive blackmane to sow dissent."

"So, Hoovefort has not forgotten that the blackmane humiliated him, Vor, and three of your followers in the game of bite-tag."

"I *loathe* the blackmane. You, Dame Aneilee, must know that the impure blackmane does not belong with the white herd. If Naythorn someday rejoins our herd, I can promise that as the future captain of the unicorn guards I will make the misfit's life... *miserable.*"

That night all was quiet until the admiral detected faint sounds of merriment. He would go and see about the laughter sounding at the end of the beach.

"Mariano, what are you three up to?"

"Alexzana asked me to teach her how sailors jig. Belfloralex is learning too."

"Hahah!" chortled the girl. "Mariano jigs as good as the grown sailors!"

"I see that Alexzana and Belfloralex also dance well," responded Zoumar rubbing his beard. The admiral moved to pat the back of the filly.

"Tell me, Belfloralex, how is it that a unicorn can jig steps like do mariners? As for your admiral, his feet are terrible at keeping rhythm. But mind you, with a sword in my hand my feet are quite nimble."

"Even for a unicorn... it just takes practice," neighed in answer the filly.

"And so, brave filly, I again today learned something brand new."

CHAPTER 28

SHINING CANYON

Working in tandem with a unicorn horn, a sword levered open a thick rock door.

"The grasp of your two hands fits onto one of the four handles carved into the stone door," neighed Naythorn to Lucars. "The handles were placed so that from the inside of the canyon, the door can by four strong men be pulled shut. That permits men to seal themselves in this canyon. But it will unfortunately take more than the strength of Lucars to close tonight this door, and so keep wolves away from us."

"After the drubbing you gave them," responded the youth, "no wolf would dare to enter tonight this canyon. Let me add that without possessing the unbreakable tips of blue gold swords, it would be next to impossible for men on the cave side to pry open this door."

Standing on the door's canyon side, Lucars rubbed away dust that had accumulated on the head jamb. Star shapes had been chipped into the stone. Looking closely the warrior observed, "The chipped marks represent the star cluster pointing to the fixed star."

"My friend, this matter of stars that brought me to the canyon of blue gold, will lead me on to refind the white herd now lost to me."

The fun of discovery began.

"This canyon is a treasure!" exclaimed the youth stretching wide his arms. "The veins of the magic gold, that transformed my people's first history, are here set as thick as my fingers! Finding this deposit signifies that the Phoenician army will continue to be protected by magic armor. Upon stepping into this canyon, Hammerclaw will find himself in a blacksmith's paradise. To this place he must come quickly.

"Just imagine, Naythorn, that here are found berries, edible roots, nut bearing trees, and grass. A waterfall adds beauty to this place, and fish leap up from the lake. In this hidden canyon you and I could dwell the rest of our lives... and know only plenty."

"Lucars, in all that you say you are not one word wrong. The beauty found here quits me of breath. To spill blood in this canyon created like none other, would be sacrilege. Had this place of treasure not been very great indeed, the pyramid path that I followed would not have been raised so bold."

"I just had the thought, Naythorn, that it requires much time and effort to truly measure the myriad subtleties and changing qualities of marvelous beauty."

That night under the light of a full moon, the walls of the valley shone not like gold, but like silver. For the hidden canyon they had found, the youth and the blackmaned unicorn remained in awe.

A Bold Plan

It was obvious that the closed canyon that shined in the moonlight presented a sound defensive position. The entrance was small enough so that a warrior and a unicorn could stop any number of wolves, even fifty or one hundred, from passing through the rock doorway into the canyon. From a strictly military standpoint, the blackmane and the apprentice blacksmith now had the advantage.

But while the two companions felt themselves to be safely hidden, Naythorn's animal band presumably remained isolated in a far away valley marked by tall trees. The blackmane hoped that at least for a while longer Rayalas, Buckmight, and Taurington could maintain and protect the band's integrity. The senior blacksmith was also somewhere distant from Shining Canyon. The unicorn and the young warrior knew that whether found close, or far away, they and their friends felt deeply the absence of union with each other.

That night as he watched sporting flames and their attendant playful shadows, the reclined horned horse leaned his side against a rock wall. Lucars stirred himself to separate three branches from the fire, and position them singly apart.

"My friend, like these branches, we and our friends comprise three groups. A sudden breeze passing over one of these separate branches will extinguish its fire." Lucars pushed the ends of the branches together, and added, "Placed in proximity, the three branches burn bright. In order to survive, our three separate parties need to soon reconnect to each other. We need to bring your platoon and my Hammerclaw here to us."

"But I do know where to look for my band," replied Naythorn. "Why must they come to us?"

"In this vale we find safety. Here we purchase time for you to heal and regain strength. Now since you do know where your animal platoon was left behind, you can describe their location to me so that I can bring them here. Tell me, is your band out looking to find you, or do they in a settled way wait for you to return?"

"Before I answer, Lucars, tell me where is the blacksmith? He has not given up on you, and so returned to his brigade of sailors?"

"With neither the gold nor myself in tow, Hammerclaw will not willingly retreat or return to the Phoenician vessels. It would be hard for him to explain how happened a strong warrior to abandon his apprentice. And my father, a ranking officer in the Phoenician army, would never forgive Hammerclaw for not bringing me back. Our warrior code requires that on a field of battle, no one be left behind.

"Your platoon and Hammer may be right now searching for us. I cannot imagine that Buckmight would not send out the winged members of your band to fly great circles, wider and wider, with the intent to find you."

"Not many suns past, Rayalas demonstrated that she can fly far distances. And mounted on wing her vision extends far... as if observing from the top of a mountain. But having given your question some thought, I truly cannot say if my band now searches for me. Friend Lucars, we accomplished great things today. Let us sleep on these questions. Tomorrow we will better decide how to find and reclaim our missing parts, the two scattered apart branches that still flame brightly in our hearts."

The requisite plan to act was the next day agreed upon. Lucars would venture out in search of both Hammerclaw and the band of Naythorn. Upon re-entering the cave Lucars would use his back, sword, and spear to push and lever shut the slab door. Positioned inside the canyon, the teeth and weight of the unicorn would at the same time help to pull shut the door. Carrying a torch in one hand and a leafy branch in the other, Lucars would swath away his tracks. The cave would again know darkness.

After three days travel northward, Lucars was to find himself on the seventh and last pyramid crested peak. On the top of that mountain he would set his shield to reflect sunrays towards the north and east, where Naythorn and Lucars felt sure their friends were still to be found.

Lucars was warned by Naythorn to be particularly watchful for wolves. For his part, Lucars instructed the unicorn horse to rest deeply and long, walk across the canyon three or four times daily, and drink very often from the little lake. Upon his return to Shining Canyon Lucars wanted to find the blackmane with the sparkle of renewed health glinting in his eyes.

The warrior and the unicorn knew that if things went badly, Lucars would not return to Shining Canyon. In that case if he could not by himself push open the heavy cave door Naythorn would remain trapped, albeit with plentiful grass and water, until found by one of his winged scouts.

Naythorn did not like that dangerous travel fell to Lucars alone. But he knew his horse body, that had suffered terribly from wolf teeth and claws, needed more time to heal. For now it must be Lucars that brought remedy to their isolated situation.

As he traveled the first day Lucars was sure that wolves were not in pursuit. The youth considered that

Albarochk and Yellowquist were occupied by the recruitment of more wolves to replace the many lupines lost in battles at the tall trees and the rock strewn trench. The second day of his journey went also according to plan.

As the youth trotted on the third day toward the pyramid crest that was his objective, he saw neither wolf nor human person. From the high height of the mountain top, Lucars that afternoon deployed his golden shield to reflect sunlight, and so signal his location.

Naythorn's Band

After Naythorn bolted into and through Albarochk, the remaining mostly smaller wolves were unable to prevail against the big beast triumvirate of Buckmight, Taurington, and Rayalas. When a new sun shone down on the bubbling pond, about Naythorn's exhausted platoon no wolf was to be found.

Roothyford complained that morning that she was not made to battle wolves, that she had had enough fighting to last two lifetimes, and that Rayalas needed to go and find a secure cave of respite. Practicia, Hamilton, and the Mama Sow immediately seconded Practicia's cave idea.

Buckmight instructed Rayalas to locate a cliff cave that provided a strong defensive position where wounds could heal in safety. Before the bison was able to also request that the cave be close to sources of water and grass... the filly had run away beating rapidly her long wings. It did not take Rayalas long to report back the location of a well-protected place. She then proceeded to lead the platoon to a grassy ledge backed by an ochre-streaked cliff. A sheet of water spilling out from between the limestone layers wrinkling the cliff's forehead, gated the entrance to a spacious cave.

Mrs. Razorthwacker was a natural worrier. But in the protected place found by Rayalas, about the safety of her offspring not even the sow bothered to concern herself. As one day succeeded another, much of the band's time was spent dozing under a warm sun. However, the morning that Taurington complained that from excessive rest and relaxation his leg muscles were too much softening, the bison knew that day after day of not doing anything had become too much of a good thing.

Buckmight, the animal person that band members reflexively turned to for counsel, brayed that a plan for future movement was required. So forewarned, on their own the rest of the band began to analyze options. Even while napping their minds subconsciously explored strategies for renewed travel.

Despite the calm and restfulness they had now for many suns experienced, the absence of their captain made their situation troubling. That is, except to the mind of Hamilton who groinked, "I vote that we do not worry ourselves about anything. What, after all, could go wrong in this place of plenty?"

"Come to think of it, I agree with Hamilton," qvackked Webstir fluttering his wings in an exaggerated manner.

"Harrumph," objected Taurington. "I can never tell if Master Hamilton is being serious, or is simply saying the opposite of what he thinks."

"When his stomach is full, Hamilton is *never* serious," clarified Practicia. "But of course everything for us could go wrong if we were to be here found by wolves."

"Well at that, Practicia, even I can admit that Taurington's stomach appears to have become over-full," rejoined Hamilton.

"There is truth to that," mrawed the cattle. "I am gotten huger and lazier. If we stay here doing nothing, my poor legs will soon not be able to carry about my swollen belly. If the touch of a unicorn horn made the bison to grow taller, why did the same magic make my belly... to too much fatten?"

"In that complaint Sir Cattle is not wrong," grunted the sow. "My belly is also getting too big. Wild animals are better off with activity and movement that keeps muscles hard, even if that movement sometimes involves running away from wolves."

"What does a smart boarling think about the vulnerability of our current situation?" inquired Rayalas turning to look at Timidthy.

"Since you asked me," responded Hamilton for his brother, "I am happy to expound on our situation... *grroinouuch!* That was mean, Practicia!"

"I bit you, because now is not the time for you to be hamming it up."

"My most humble apology, Rayalas," responded with feigned sadness Hamilton. "I was just unkindly informed that the smart pig you were referring to was not me... but was instead my littler brother."

"You are a bad influence, Hamilton," noted the

bison. "Even Naythorn has now learned to copy your mischievous smile."

"Some days ago," offered Timidthy, "I saw my reflection in the bubbling pool, and relative to the size of my body it looked as though my head was larger than it should be."

"*Grunkhaha!* We all know that your head is too big for your body!" groinked Hamilton who could not resist another jibe.

"Timidthy's head is not too large for his body, which at his young stage of life is every day stretching bigger," objected the mama wild boar.

"If you recall, I *did* ask about the vulnerability of our current situation," neighed Rayalas.

"After holding our position against the reduced number of wolfkind attacking us," responded Timidthy, "Rayalas brought us to this protective place to wait for our captain's return. Here we have recovered from the deep cuts authored by wolf teeth and claws. Duck and Goose have everyday flown circles above the camp to observe possible signs of either the unicorn's return, or of wolf scouts. On the face of it, we have complied with everything Naythorn instructed us to do. But just like the exaggerated reflection of an oversized boar head seen in the ripples of a pond, our state looks to be so much improved... that it is deceptive." Timidthy paused to let his words sink in.

"Things, here, are not what they seem. They cannot be, for we are unable to talk to or communicate with Captain Naythorn. The necessary thing to do is determine how we might, as quickly as possible, reunite ourselves with our leader." Timidthy began to walk back-and-forth before his friends.

"Of course, Albarochk knows that we are hereabouts to be found. But the wolf general considers us to be of little current consequence. For him, the value of the animal persons gathered in this assembly is like the paltry value he would place on a family of deer. The prize Albarochk seeks to capture is a magical horn. With Naythorn vanquished, we only signify some meals for wolves. However with Naythorn alive, because we are Naythorn's loyal soldiers we present a persistent difficulty for the wolf leader."

"So you are telling us that as long as Naythorn survives, we will be hunted by the wolves?"

"About that, Master Bison, you are right. In Albarochk's eyes, we are *the bait*. The grayback wolf knows that the horned horse wants to return to us. When he does, Albarochk pounces again upon Naythorn, and upon us."

"What happens, Timidthy, if the blackmane does not return to us?" inquired the cattle.

"Here is what I think. Without the presence of Naythorn in our midst, magic will unravel from our band. Knowledge of the uniform tongue will from our speech, fade away. We will eventually separate from each other, wander apart, and one by one become meals for wolves.

"Naythorn could be... in trouble. In some remote desert corner he could right now be surrounded by wolves. He could be gravely wounded, or dying of thirst. But if the unicorn were no longer alive, the gift of magic speech that he gave to us would already be diminishing, and it is not. So for now we know that the blackmane still possesses a heart that with magic blood runs full. Remind us again, Rayalas, what the unicorn told you before he dashed away."

"He told me, Timidthy, that some day we would meet again in Shining..."

"My boarling is right," interrupted the sow. "If we stay here, our magic will diminish until we someday become lost to one another, and to ourselves. If we find our captain, or find the canyon that shines of blue gold and there await him, we keep intact the magic Naythorn invested in us."

"That... settles it," brayed Buckmight with his customary gravity. "The promise each of us made to be loyal to Naythorn requires us to depart from this place of respite. As loyal soldiers we will do our utmost to refind our commander, or failing that, to find Shining Canyon. That we have scouts with wings gives us an enormous tactical advantage over the wolf army. Rayalas, Webstir, and Featherspark can guide us from one safe outpost to the next.

"Come to think of it, by moving out towards Naythorn we can present a factor of hindrance to our enemy. The movement of our band will force the wolves to take pressure off of the blackmane, and reapply that pressure to us. Perhaps the wolf army will be forced to split in two, with one battalion in pursuit of Naythorn while the other wolf battalion pursues us."

Buckmight's words were, with only one exception, met with agreement. Webstir nuisanced his wings in disapproval, and vigorously shook his tail at Timidthy, the instigator of the decision to leave their pleasant place of rest. Webstir gradually quit fussing, and instead began to reconcile himself with departure from a place that suited perfectly a duck.

CHAPTER 29

SUN SIGNALS

With no one in particular, for not even a coyote was near to hear him, the big-armed blacksmith began a conversation.

"I ask you... where *is* that reckless youth? I have waited too long at this river crossing for him. He was supposed to return here six days ago! I tell you that I am very distressed that Lucars keeps me waiting still. *Confound it!* I hate waiting for anyone! I do not even know what is most bothersome to me, having the blue gold still unfound, or having on my hands a youth lost. The truth is that both troubles vex me to no end. Of course the magic gold is vital to the defense of my people. The prophecy says that the Phoenician tongue will not perish so long as the armor of true-of-heart warriors is forged with magic blue gold."

"*Damnation!*" Hammerclaw uttered his worst swear word. "The youth comes from a family that was once princely. You know that if I return to my brigade without the youth, I will be charged with deserting my fellow soldier. If I return with neither the lad nor the gold for our armor plate, I will rot the rest of my days in jail. That I am twice his age makes the soldier lad even more my responsibility. *By thunder!* My pride will not let me return without the rash youth in tow! Sitting on a boulder, Hammerclaw slumped his shoulders.

"Because the crude map made at the instruction of the feeble old unicorn has proven useless, the canyon of the blue gold remains too well hid. And now the foolish lad is lost to me. No... I am not being honest with myself. Although the youth is sullen and prideful, when I push him hard Lucars takes it like a man. Losing that boy would hurt me as much as the loss of my own flesh.

"There, I have owned to it. The lad has much grown on me. I am known as the hammer that hits hard. Am I not also the claw that scraps and scrapes his way back from loss and defeat? From out of this land of endless jungles, deserts, and mountains I must find a way to claw Lucars back to me.

"You know I hate to give up on anything, let alone a quest as critical as the blue gold, but tomorrow I shall have to. I tell you that I simply do not know what else to do." Hammerclaw banged hard his maul hammer against the side of the rock he sat on, jerked both arms up in the air, and shouted, *"Where is my boy Lucars?"*

Shield Flashes

On his fourth morning away from Shining Canyon Lucars moved slowly right and left his shield so that the reflection might be seen from any point in a wide angle to his position on the seventh pyramid crested mountain. With no visible response, and with no signs of wolves about, he reconsidered his location. Perhaps he was too far west to be seen by Hammer or a winged scout of Naythorn. He would run toward the morning sun and climb the fourth pyramid crowned mountain, the last in the handle of the clustered formation.

The next afternoon Lucars signaled from the fourth pyramid crest. No shining reflection came back in return. He would not travel farther away from the canyon where Naythorn awaited his return. Instead, he would remain one more day on this pyramid crest to flash sun reflections in every direction.

The sun flashes that reflected the next morning from his shield were, once again, met by no answered response. Through the afternoon Lucars signaled more and watched more. It became too late to depart the mountain. After sending more sun reflections the following morning, the youth knew he could delay no longer his return to Shining Canyon. Albeit with reluctance, he began to descend the mountain.

Lucars froze. There was movement below him. On the mountain's flank that directed toward the location of Shining Canyon, a line of many wolves pushed upward.

"The last thing I need this day is to fight wolves," muttered the scowling youth. "And these wolves are about the cleverest lot anywhere. Blocking my return to Naythorn, I cannot permit so many lupines to catch me in the open. Their presence leaves me only one option."

Climbing again toward the pyramid crest to there do battle, Lucars surmised that after his rescue of the blackmaned unicorn, the enormous gray wolf had marked him as a bitter enemy. Had not Albarochk forewarned him about the dire consequences should he remain in this desert land? Having identified his location with the sun signals, the wolves had no intention of permitting him to escape. But if the wolves had seen his shield glancing out beams of sunlight, why had not Hammerclaw, Webstir, Featherspark, or Rayalas seen his signals?

As he waited the arrival of the wolves, the youth once again set about signaling with his shield.

"Huh? Was that a... I think someone, most likely Hammerclaw, signalled back." But no more light flashes came. The howling of wolves drew closer.

When the attack came in late afternoon the razor sharp edges of a warrior's spear became a fierce slashing lever. Swinging the sharp pointed staff with his left arm, Lucars batted two wolf bodies onto rocks below him. With his gold shield the youth saucered another wolf onto the rocks below. Jagged stone edges did not treat gently the bodies of flung wolves. Two more wolves were bloodied by the sword held in his right hand. Because neither Lucars nor the wolves would relent, the confrontation grew long.

The youth held his own until the fall of night. He was thankful that a full moon shed light on succeeding waves of attack. The warrior wondered which of the next five, six, or seven wolves to attack would tumble him down, and against his favor end forever the fight.

Hammerclaw on the Move

Something had flashed. Convinced that the signal was from none other than Lucars, in his excitement to regain his apprentice Hammerclaw had not taken the time to signal a second and third confirmation. With no delay he abandoned the agreed upon place of rendezvous. Knowing that his travel would last far into the night, he slowed his pace to a trot.

"Why is my apprentice so far west of where he should be? *Blast!* Something tells me to be worried for the youth." The blacksmith grew reflective, "Hmph. What strange reason could have compelled long ago men to retop mountain peaks with pyramid crests? Were not these mountains already tall enough?"

Air Scout

Soaring high in late afternoon flight, Rayalas jerked up her head. Out of the far distance had come several bright flashes of reflected light. Shaking brusquely her mane, the winged filly decided that a unicorn could not cause to happen sun reflections. But had Buckmight not been so insistent that she return before the fall of night, she would have flown on to investigate the flashes. She reluctantly wheeled wings in return flight.

Darkness was approaching when Rayalas informed bovines, waterfowl, pigs, dogs, and mountain sheep that she had seen a reflection of sunlight.

"That is strange," observed Timidthy. "The flashes that you saw could not have come from a unicorn, and certainly not from wolves. Were they very bright?"

"They were brilliant," answered the filly. "The sun reflections carried very far."

"Could the blackmane's magic have made the signal?" questioned Practicia.

"Perhaps the signal was sent by hostile natives that captured Naythorn," added Roothyford. "And what could native warriors think to do with a unicorn?"

"That question unsettles me," responded the bison shaking his head.

The consensus throughout the animal band was that

a signal of any kind merited investigation... but not in the coming darkness.

"Tomorrow morning all three of our winged scouts will together fly off to seek out the source of the sun reflection." Buckmight looked about and added, "Now, excepting for halfling wild boar sentries, everyone get some sleep."

But Rayalas could not sleep. She found herself troubled by Roothyford's question. Observant of the filly's restlessness, the mama razorback decided to lend a big floppy ear.

"I am not sure exactly why, Mrs. Sow, but I do not feel right staying here all night when the strange and unique signal might have had something to do with our captain. What if he was captured? I should right now be looking for him."

"It is probably nothing," soothed the sow. "I know that you worry a lot about Naythorn, but what if you get lost while flying in darkness?"

"My eyes are become like an owl's that see as well at night as during the day. And my wings are strong. I now fly fast and far before I tire and set down to rest. I remember exactly from which mountain top came the signal."

"Well my dear, if you think you should ascend now... then do it. In the morning I will tell Buckmight and the others that it was I who told you of a dream I had where Naythorn was fighting warriors, and needed your help to protect his chest and sides in the fight.

"Now do not worry. If you find nothing and your trip is fruitless, I will take the blame for something... that was in fact nothing. Anyway, if you three tomorrow flew together, the flight of two birds at the side of a flying horse would be a sight neither wolves nor warriors could ignore or forget. But for my sake do not let your wings become so spent that they spiral down to earth."

"I will fly more safely than I have ever before done. Shining stars will tonight light my way."

Making not the slightest sound Rayalas walked onto the grassy neck of ground before the cave entrance, and floated her sleek body starward.

CHAPTER 30

LUCARS AND YELLOWQUIST

Defending himself on the top of a crumbling pyramid crest, Lucars lost count of how many wolves he had killed and maimed. As he waited for the next wolves to attack, the youth wondered how a meal of his skinny legs could compensate for the loss of so many lupine soldiers. Lucars next asked himself if wolves could be possessed by an evil spirit. The youth decided that if that were possible, these wolves were surely possessed by something extraordinarily vile. Clearly the wolf leader had no regard for the lives of his wolf privates and corporals.

"What does it matter that young wolves do not know how to value their lives, and for that too soon die?" muttered Lucars. "Albarochk can always find more young wolves willing to obey his fiendish commands."

He knew that he could not last out until dawn. Still, the youth promised himself that before the blood from this battle stopped flowing, the chests of several more wolves would be dispossessed of beating hearts.

When snarling wolves all about crowded, the warrior youth's position became even more precarious. Without stepping downward, and thus weakening his fighting position, he could not proceed in any direction.

It was as if the sharp teeth of wolves snapped at a

thin thread from which dangled the youth's life. Lucars needed to somehow purchase time and delay the close of the final chapter of his fight on the pyramid crest, which despite all his bloody labor seemed destined to assuredly vanquish him.

"I call out the coward Albarochk!" yelled the youth as he waved wildly about his sword. "If any courage is remained in your wounded hide, show yourself! *Now!*"

As if in obedience to an unyelped command, wolves broke off their attack and parted way. Instead of Albarochk the small yellow wolf, whose heart the youth had previously threatened, stepped forward.

"Not you! I want the giant grayback wolf! An insignificant and puny yellow wolf *cannot* be the leader of all these marauders. Where is the big gray monster wolf that dangles a useless paw? I want him to tell me why, when I am no one for him to be concerned about, he has commanded my death!"

"*Arrrruuuuaaoo!*" growled the small wolf. "It is I, Yellowquist that is charged to destroy you. I find it fitting that with your own eyes you see who leads the fight that brings end to your obnoxious life. It was not many suns ago that you thwarted the plan of my master to drink the blood of the blackmaned unicorn. For that transgression you shall be forever unpardoned." The small wolf stood on hind limbs and waved a front paw. "But, before you die there is one small thing I want from you. Satisfy my curiosity for your name. I want to know who it is that I this night kill." The yellow wolf seated himself. "The information contained in a name... holds for me curious value."

"I am the Phoenician warrior Lucars."

"*Yipe! Yipe!* Well then, young Lucars, I commend your decision to fight this time on a high place rather than in a rock strewn trench. It was a smart strategy for you to meet us on this mountain top, rather than attempt to flee from my company of wolves.

"When to save a unicorn you before entered a fight not yours, I found you to be reckless. Having chosen to do battle on this high triangular crest, I now conclude that at least you are not slow of thought. You are also brave. Too bad you will not live long enough to rise to a military command of your own.

"I will have you to know, Lucars, that my big cousin's one weakness is that he cannot surmount his lofty pride. Any real, or for that matter perceived insult, incites his unquenchable lust for revenge. The unfortunate cut of your sword to his already wounded paw offended my master far more than your blade hurt him. For that insult you are this night condemned to pay with your life."

Lucars liked that the yellow wolf was a talker. The longer the wolf talked, the more rest was given to the young blacksmith's arms.

"More than once the unicorn with the black mane displayed the bad judgment to insult my cousin Albarochk. The last and most wretched offense was when he broke his promise to surrender, and instead stabbed my general's shoulder. After my master's left front leg became useless, his thirst for revenge became unquenchable. For someone like you that foolishly threw in his lot with Naythorn, my great cousin's need for revenge is a truly regrettable circumstance to bear." The yellow wolf pointed a paw at the young warrior.

"Now, had I been a youth lost in a strange land, I would have tried to make a deal with someone like Albarochk. You could have petitioned... to become his wolf-boy companion. I ask you, Lucars, why take the cause of a wounded and spent unicorn? For one or another task my master could put to use your strong arms, dexterous hands, and agile mind."

Lucars had listened intently so as to appear sincere in the parlay with the wolf lieutenant, but these words from an insolent half size wolf were too much for the youth to bear.

"I now say to the yellow haired wolf what I deeply feel. I would rather be *true* to a noble blackmaned unicorn, than *false* to myself." The youth sat down and relaxed his shoulders.

"I return the compliment you gave me. You, an extraordinarily intelligent yellow wolf, should reflect carefully on what I now say. Once healed, and another moon or two older, Naythorn will be stronger than before. From the day the blackmane learns of my death at your hands you, the raffish yellow wolf, will live in fear. You will become known as *Yellowquist the Fearful*. Other wolves will every day notice you looking back over your shoulders to see when and where the unicorn, his fearsome bovines, and the winged horse might be closing on you. That you now abstain, that you have your wolf lackeys to fight what should be your battle, shows that even now you are fearful. You think yourself cunning. But were you more intelligent, the moment you saw how easily I defied Albarochk you would have decided to join forces with the blackmane, and with me."

"Can you presume to think that with my superior intelligence, the plan I made was only about defeating a skinny warrior lad? Since you have no idea where at this moment walks the monster wolf, I will tell you. While I tracked your sun signals to this desolate place my master, and the greater number of our wolf army, are searching out the entrance to your hidden canyon. *Ruuffharrharr!* That place will soon witness the death of a half healed unicorn. Because he will himself experience an early demise, the blackmane will not be able to avenge your death."

"You thought of everything... except the logic of your plan has one flaw. At this moment there is a fierce and powerful animal platoon coming to fight with me. You cannot have forgotten the flashing hooves of the winged horse? Very soon I am to be formally introduced to her. To those with evil wolf hearts, her purity transfigures into winged death." In the game of minds Lucars had another card to play.

"And consider one thing else. If Albarochk were to kill the blackmane and drink his blood, what further use would the monster have for you? He would everyday find himself asking why he needs to maintain a servant like Yellowquist who is physically weak, and far less evil than has become Albarochk himself. Even I saw that the giant wolf disdains you.

"Why, thinking on it, I do not believe that you are *truly* evil. A perfectly vile wolf would not have taken the time to ask me for my name. Perhaps you are simply caught up in the circle of a wicked wolf general. You keep... *bad company.* Sooner or later Albarochk will doubtless destroy not just you, but every single wolf that reminds him of his former weak state before he was by unicorn blood transformed."

"Owing to me his great victory over the foul unicorn, I shall be made Albarochk's crown prince! One day I will succeed him to wolf leadership!"

"I can persuade the blackmane to touch your forehead with his magic horn. Once the heart of Yellowquist is transformed into nobleness, it is the blackmane that can help you to one day ascend to Albarochk's wolfly throne. Do not you see, Yellowquist, for you to survive the impending turn of Albarochk's character to pure evil you need for the blackmane... *to live on.*"

Reading the expression forming on the face of the yellow wolf, it appeared to Lucars that the lupine was seriously considering his tendered offer of alliance with Naythorn. At that moment many pairs of wolf eyes focused intently, not on Lucars, but on Yellowquist.

"*Yowrrr!* No... no... *never!* With your many words you bought time to delay your demise. But I know perfectly well that I, Yellowquist, am smart enough to handle Albarochk's future turns of behavior. I am the only wolf that was ever able to point out to Albarochk his weaknesses. In fact, I cannot stop myself from needling him. And... my giant cousin respects me for standing up to him. Actually, I would say that Albarochk even... *loves* me."

"If he still feels affection for you, that sentiment will cease," answered Lucars shaking his head. "Albarochk's heart will soon be barred shut to wolfly love. I only ask that you think long and hard on this matter. I can tell that inside the yellow wolf exists the worry that were Albarochk to achieve power over the blackmane, irritating weaklings like yourself would not long be kept about to trouble the big devil."

As he struggled to negate the argument made by Lucars, the yellow wolf's face furrowed and darkened. A thing snapped inside of him.

"*Aaghrragrowrrgh!* I can no longer brook your treasonous words! Death to the miserable and false Lucars!"

The change in the yellow wolf's tone of voice was the awaited signal. Rested and with strength renewed, wolves again sprang to singly attack the warrior. Soon after they came in pairs at Lucars, whose legs and arms were scarred anew by tearing claws.

The wolf attack evolved with a tactic that Lucars had not before seen. A line of wolves formed that from its center curved inward, with Yellowquist himself set in the middle. In unison ten wolves stepped slowly toward Lucars. Both Lucars and Yellowquist knew that if the entire line sprang at once, the fight would at last be concluded.

Lucars hesitated. Throwing himself headlong into the middle of the wolf line would end quickly his suffering. At this thought he reminded himself that Phoenician warriors never give up. They could lose a battle, but not surrender. He had once before learned a hard lesson of that kind when flailing against a storm-driven sea.

"Stop and think, Yellowquist! After he has destroyed the blackmane, you can never again place your trust in Albarochk! You kill me and the unicorn, *you kill yourself!*"

Seeing something in the night sky, wolves of a sudden stopped snarling and yowling. When Lucars turned to follow the gaze of the wolves he glimpsed a fleeting figure pass in front of a moon beam.

"It is a shadow of... *big wings*. It is... it has to be... the horse that grew wings!" The flying horse had found Lucars.

Feeling himself instantly refreshed by shadowy wings of hope, the youth turned back to the fight. As he flailed his sword right and left his footwork became that of a dancer. He played the advance of the crescent line of wolves as if he were moving his body to a musical melody. Lucars heard a neigh that sounded very close. He did not need to look up to know that his deliverance was at hand. Jumping back one step he pointed his sword for effect and exclaimed, "One day the yellow wolf will find my words of warning... rang true! I hope that day will not be his last!"

With flair Lucars sheathed his sword, turned, and from the highest part of the pyramid crest jumped with hands extended to grasp the mane of the winged filly. The youth swung himself onto the back of Rayalas.

Floating above Yellowquist's still intact wolf line, Lucars glimpsed wolf eyes focused skyward with hate. As the youth studied them, one thing more came to show in lupine faces. By the light of a full moon, more than one set of wolf eyes glared a look of pathetic helplessness.

"How did you find me, Rayalas? Yes, I know your name."

"And you must be the young blacksmith named Lucars that Naythorn has neighed about."

"Beset by a disciplined line of ten wolves, my fate was sealed. Can you dive back? I have a final message to give to the yellow wolf." The winged filly swooped down, and with her hooves scrambled left and right astonished wolves.

"There he is bounding down the mountain as fast as he can!"

"I see him."

"Yellowquist, do not forget the words I said to you!" warned Lucars as Rayalas gained the position of the scrambling wolf. "At the side of Albarochk you will never know rest! That said, for all the mischief you brought to this place, I owe you something!" Grasping mane in one hand, with the flat of his blade the warrior leaned out and slapped the wolf on the rump. The blow somersaulted Yellowquist forward. In a smooth and athletic motion the wolf rolled over himself, hopped back up, and shook dust from his hide.

"*Yipe!* For thinking you were untruthful about the flashing hooves of the flying horse, I suppose I deserved that spanking. You might rather have slashed... my throat. I am touched that you did not. So, Lucars, you won this night. We will see who wins the next round of a fight that... *grows long.*"

Hammerclaw Found

"I had before thought the landscape below us to be empty and harsh. But from up here under the delicate light of a full moon, the mountains and desert appear hauntingly beautiful." The warrior lad sank down and relaxed into wing feathers that he found to be as soft as a pillow. "Way over there to the east, do you see the movement?"

"Yes, it moves like a man." The filly turned her wings to the east.

"I hope that it is my Sergeant Hammerclaw. Oh! And I have to right away tell you that Naythorn awaits you in Shining Canyon." Upon hearing that Rayalas jerked up and down her head in excitement. Wrapped tightly around the girth of the filly, the legs of Lucars felt new vigor to flow through the sides of Rayalas.

The flying filly closed on the glint of movement that proved to be a heavily armed man trotting toward the mountain that Lucars had just quitted. Upon alighting, the man approached wearing a serious look.

"So... my wayward apprentice blacksmith *finally returns!* And who in tarnation is this horse that flies?"

"Sir, my name is Rayalas. I fly because a unicorn sacrificed his blood to grow me wings. Naythorn's gift of wings brought this night Lucars to Hammerclaw."

"I... apologize, Rayalas. Because of long frustration at the youth's absence I was too direct in asking so forthrightly the name of a magical horse. I am... delighted to meet you."

"This magical horse, Master Hammer, just rescued me from a pack of perverse and violent wolves bent on my destruction. Can you believe that a flying filly came to save me... just in the nick of time?"

"Dame Rayalas, for rescuing my apprentice blacksmith I am in your lasting debt. You also saw the golden flash made by the shield of Lucars?"

"Yes I did. Before nightfall I reported the glint of light to Buckmight," continued Rayalas. "In the absence of Naythorn, the bison is the leader of our animal platoon. In my heart I knew I had to quickly return and determine what it was that I had seen. I flew toward the location of the signal, but because I flew with promised caution, I almost arrived too late to rescue Lucars."

"Then, Rayalas, I am made doubly fortunate. You see, I am a better blacksmith than warrior. You as well saved me a bloody hard fight."

"We must be off," said Lucars.

"I am not strong enough or rested enough to carry you both at once. So, I will ferry you one at a time toward the place where Naythorn awaits. When I drop you off, proceed ahead on foot in our direction of travel. I will double back, collect the one that follows behind, and bring him forward past the man that walks ahead. In this way, like frogs leaping over each other, we will move quickly toward the canyon that shines of blue gold. I cannot wait to surprise Naythorn with the delivery of *both* Lucars and Hammerclaw."

"Can this be true? Is the blue gold... *really found?*"

"With my own eyes I have seen it!" exclaimed Lucars slapping the back of the big man.

"*Bull roar!*" responded excitedly Hammerclaw with his face relaxed into a big toothy smile. "Praise the heavens!"

"If you only knew, Rayalas, how long I have looked to find that magic place, and how distressed I have been at my interminable failure. At this moment I possess only the wish that I weighed no more than Lucars, instead of weighing twice as much as the lad. I will be a heavy burden for you to carry in flight."

"Sir, my joy in escorting you to Shining Canyon will overmatch yours. To me Naythorn means everything."

The leap-frogging travel became pleasurable. Like the rounds made plowing a field, that one pass after another mark steady progress toward completion, the back-and-forth ferried trips proved most satisfying to Rayalas. As she drew closer to Naythorn the winged filly seemed to grow stronger, and so carried one passenger longer and longer distances before turning back for the other.

There was no reason to disguise their trail. Yellowquist and Albarochk already knew that in the mountain of many spires Naythorn was to be found. In the pitch dark before the break of dawn, Rayalas quietly alighted at her final destination, and Lucars jumped off. Without neighing a word to a sound asleep unicorn stallion, the filly with wings was gone back into the night to collect Hammerclaw. She soon swooped the senior blacksmith down to the floor of the canyon seamed with magic blue gold.

Enveloped in impenetrable sleep, Naythorn rested on. Deep slumber was the most required medicine for his slashed and torn body. Rayalas reclined beside the unicorn she had come to love deeply, and carefully extended one wing to lay lightly over his back and warm him. She joined her mate in a flighted dream lit by silver shards of moonlight pathing toward a trembling sheen of curtained stars.

"Lad, thank goodness you were found safe and sound. Had I returned without you, I could not have faced Admiral Zoumar or the men in our brigade." The big man clamped a huge hand to a shoulder of his slender young apprentice and added, "I know this is not the way a loyal Phoenician warrior should think, but I had rather return without the precious gold, than without my apprentice.

"Finding at last Shining Canyon makes this a day I shall never forget. And to beat all, I was tonight privileged to meet and mount the only flying horse in the world, for that is what I will say until I find that Rayalas is not the only horse with wings. Why, she has lines more elegant... than the swords that I forge!"

"Master Hammer, seeing your teeth set in a smile lights up my night, as if it were day."

"Tell me, Lad, about the fight. I want to hear exactly what happened."

"Defending the highest point on a pyramid crested mountain gave me advantage. To buy myself some time, I provoked a long exchange with the wolf lieutenant Yellowquist. In a hollowed mountain he had taken part in an attack against Rayalas and Naythorn. From tasting in that fray the unicorn's blood, he received the gift of uniform animal speech. You do remember that this unicorn with the black mane is the grandcolt of the old unicorn that stayed behind in Wittanor Hold?"

"Of course I could not forget his black mane. On that

distant day Naythorn was in no mood to converse; his life was in turmoil. The herd of unicorns had sailed away and abandoned him. Had I been thinking, I would have insisted that Naythorn with us travel."

"Master Hammer, at the end of last night's fight the wolves formed together and fought as one disciplined line. The lieutenant wolf anchored the center of the wolf line. All together they advanced toward me one step at a time. I could not prevail against ten wolves at once. I was done for. The great wings of Rayalas rescued me from sure…"

"How came wolves to that way fight? And why on earth would an enormous pack of wolves risk great loss to insist on vanquishing a solitary warrior?"

"Some days back when the blackmane was beset by too many wolves, I stepped in to rescue him. Doing that made me an enemy of Albarochk, the vicious leader wolf. Hmm, Yellowquist said something that concerns me. When I told him that Naythorn would avenge my death, the wolf replied that Albarochk was leading an even larger number of wolves to attack the blackmane. Yellowquist said that Naythorn and I would on the same day fall, even though we were far apart from each other."

"So even as we speak we are beset by wolves." The master blacksmith shook his head as he added, "Normal wolves cannot do these things. In this new land the wolves are too clever. I cannot imagine that they developed the complex tactic of a precise line of infantry advance, and to top it off opened two parallel fronts at one and the same time."

Hammerclaw Content

When the darkness enveloping Shining Canyon changed hue to glow a soft purple, confident birdsongs coaxed an emergent sun to once more present its golden face. Embraced by the delicate strands of nascent morning light, the veins of blue gold began to glimmer and sparkle. Hammerclaw moved to examine a rock wall.

"Lucars, I thank the heavens that I lived long enough to see these veins of blue gold." Hammerclaw proceeded to give his apprentice a bear hug, and then began to jig until he jumped in such a way that he lost his balance and proceeded to land on hands and knees. Lucars could not help but laugh at the undignified fall of his master, whereupon Hammer joined to the laughter of his apprentice.

It was midday before the unicorn roused himself awake. As the blackmane scrambled to his hooves Rayalas fluttered wings excitedly, and impulsively rubbed her muzzle against Naythorn's. After touching long his neck to the neck of Rayalas, the blackmane addressed his guests.

"I am very pleased to see a second time Master Hammerclaw. It seems now so long ago that we met at the side of my dying grandsire. I am thankful to awake from my too lengthy slumber, and see all three of you looking so well. Because I find Rayalas here with me, I myself feel ten times better than I did yesterday."

Lucars recounted to Naythorn all that had happened since he had left the hidden canyon. At the news of the battle, rescue of the youth, and transport of the two men

Naythorn responded little. To the two men it became obvious that the unicorn wanted to spend time apart with Rayalas.

"Errm, Lucars," said Hammerclaw, "let us make our way to examine the quality of the gold ore on the other side of this canyon. We will after refresh our bodies with a well-deserved nap."

CHAPTER 31

THREE CIRCLES IN THE SAND

Naythorn, Rayalas, Lucars, and Hammerclaw attended an evening fire. Smiling wide at the other three, the youth offered, "Rayalas is now returned to Naythorn, and Hammerclaw is returned to me."

"Lucars tells me it was you, Naythorn that solved the riddle of Shining Canyon. For that this blacksmith will be ever in your debt." As he fingered nuggets of magic ore Hammerclaw could not conceal his feelings. "This has to be the richest deposit of gold ever seen by man. Since this canyon is half made of gold, it will only take a handful of days for Lucars and me to forge the gold plates I was charged to bring back to our barges."

"I am glad that my solving the riddle of the pyramid crests served a needful purpose," responded Naythorn. "Here I found peace to recover and mend, yet in this place I feel only half of myself heals. I remain apart from Buckmight, Taurington, Mrs. Razorthwacker and the other members of the band I promised to protect."

"From what you have told me, Naythorn," said Lucars fiddling with a stick in his hands, "and from all that I myself have been cruelly taught by wolf behavior in this land, when absent from their captain the members of your band are not safe. Since your wounds require more time to heal, and your body requires more time to strengthen, instead of you going to them your animal band must come here to you."

Turning her head toward Lucars, Rayalas *rrhhumrumbed* agreement to what the youth had said.

"Here is my idea for reuniting with the bison, the cattle, and Mama Pig," continued Lucars. The youth took the stick he had been rolling in his hands, and scratched three separated circles in the sand. "This mark represents Naythorn; right here the blackmane shall remain to guard Shining Canyon." Lucars scraped a line to connect the mark representing Naythorn, to the second circle. "This spot represents the fourth pyramid crested mountain that connects the handle of the formation to its cup, where Rayalas came to my rescue. Along this line travel Hammer and I on foot toward that mountain."

"What about wolves?" inquired the unicorn.

"After the drubbing I gave the wolves led by Yellowquist, I doubt the lupines will now risk bothering not just one, but two well-armed Phoenicians. Their primary target is Naythorn. The wolf general will not choose to lose twenty or more wolves in a fight with two foreign warriors, a battle from which he gains little."

"At that, it does appear that since we are now four, the wolves reconsidered their threat to here attack Naythorn," commented Hammer.

"This third circle represents the position of Naythorn's band members." That stated, the youth squiggled a line that curved from the first to the third circle. "And this wavy line represents the flight of Rayalas back to the band of Naythorn."

Lucars next scraped a line to connect the two topmost circles. "Along this line Rayalas will conduct her friends. In four days' time, Hammer, I, Rayalas, and the remainder of Naythorn's band will unite at the middle circle. Strengthened in numbers, we will then march together toward Shining Canyon to rejoin Naythorn. Upon our arrival here we will eat, rest, mine ore, forge blue gold, and plan our departure to find the unicorn herd and the Phoenician brigade."

"There can be no better plan than the one this youth drew in the sand," neighed Naythorn moving up and down his head. "I can no longer leave my band to linger in the valley of the tall trees. But since in the trench of broken stones I came too close to dying, my body does need to mend more. Lucars and Master Hammer will postpone the work of hammering and forging blue gold ore until our strength is made full. Just remember that the closer Buckmight, Taurington, Mama Pig and the others come to where we here sit and talk, the more likely it is that the wolves waiting somewhere beyond this canyon will present in battle. The swords of two blacksmiths will be needed to make safe my band's travel to this magic place."

"Now that we have found the blue gold, I am not about to risk losing my apprentice to wolves. Be assured, Naythorn, that along with your absent band members, Lucars and I will return to you. But there is one thing more. Without the protection of Naythorn and his band, Lucars and I may not enjoy safe travel back to the Phoenician sailors that will surely soon be in wait for us. With our backs heavily burdened with gold plate, defense against crazed wolves cannot be easily accomplished." Naythorn nodded his head in agreement with the smithy's voiced need for future protection.

As a hazel blushed horizon hinted the soon arrival of new daylight, the hooves of Rayalas climbed hundreds of invisible steps skyward. New sunlight lit the way of Hammer and Lucars into the trench of broken stones.

"Travel upon the path we now take cost Naythorn much bloodshed and hurt. In that regard, Hammerclaw, it is a good thing that Albarochk and Yellowquist do not now quarrel with our departure from Shining Canyon."

"You and I, Lucars, must never forget the sacrifice made by Naythorn. Had it not been for his quest to solve the riddle of the pyramid crests, neither of us would have entered the canyon of blue gold. On our return to Shining Canyon we must make sure that no blood is shed by any member of Naythorn's band."

The Absent Band Members

With untiring wings Rayalas flew, and then flew more. At midday she floated down to surprise a napping Taurington.

"Up and at 'em, Sir Cattle! Far travel awaits!" Taurington required more than a modicum of time to stand up and shake himself hard, with the latter motion making his belly to carom back-and-forth. There followed quacking, barking, grunting, baahing, mooing, oinking, jumping, butting, hopping, fluttering, wiggling, shaking, and stomping until everyone had satisfactorily welcomed and hugged Rayalas home to them.

"I found Naythorn! And the blackmane found the canyon that shines of blue gold!" For that welcome news she was interrupted by another round of loud animal sounds, and each and every joyous animal movement that band members could think to make.

"Please let me finish. Naythorn is recovering from deep wounds received in a fierce battle with wolves. Because wolf numbers grow, we are ordered to leave right now and rejoin our captain so fast as we are able.

"Our travel will be met by a Phoenician blacksmith named Hammerclaw, and his apprentice Lucars. Their swords and spears will strengthen our protection and defense. Against the wolves that pursue us, our only chance to long survive is to fight as one reunited platoon."

It was no sooner said by Rayalas, than done by animal persons big and small. Buckmight established himself in the lead. Taurington did not welcome marching last, but he rationalized that he actually ought to be quite proud of himself. Not every band member could perform adequate duty as rear guard.

The water birds flew opposing concentric routes of sky scouting. Featherspark flew at his normal speed. Flying a wider circle contrary to the flight of the goose, Webstir beat smaller wings faster. The two dogs scouted their own circles around the progress of band members.

For her part Rayalas flew a back-and-forth pattern. After one thousand wing beats forward, she would turn and fly another seven hundred or so wing beats back to where proceeded forward the band. Upon each return she would neigh words of encouragement. She would, on occasion, gently rest a wing on the broad backs of Taurington or Buckmight. On another return she would with a wing nudge Hamilton into Practicia, Roothyford, or Timidthy. So escorted and animated by the winged filly that they found to be lovely and special, the youngster wild boars kept up with the longer steps taken by Buckmight.

Through three days and nights the band marched, rested, and then marched on. Upon drawing close to the designated place of rendezvous, Rayalas began to breathe easier. During the march toward the fourth pyramid crest not one wolf had been sighted.

Meeting Place

"We have embarked on a good plan," offered Hammer upon reaching the base of the pyramid crested rendezvous point. "Soon, Lucars, we shall see the approach of Rayalas and the rest of Naythorn's band. Still I know to time and again ask myself... what can go wrong?"

"Because of my recent conversation with the yellow wolf, I have the nagging worry that something is not as we think it is."

"We both noticed that our departure from the mountain of spires was watched."

"Did the master smithy make much of the enormous lion spying on us from the cliffs above Shining Canyon?"

"Come to think of it, Lucars, that very large lion did not bother to be furtive."

"I had the sense, Hammer, that the lion was not pleased to be sharing with us the spired mountain. The big cat's attitude was strange. Hmph, could a mountain lion slip down into Shining Canyon?"

"Not be easy to do. And having accomplished that

arduous entrance, the lion would be unable to climb back out of the canyon. Lucars, that brings to mind something else that I have been thinking. If Albarochk were to convince the lions to throw in with the wolves, we would indeed have an abundance of trouble to deal with. So then, young man, if the need arises I will count on your agile mind to come up with a plan for us to battle both wolves and lions."

The heart of Lucars leaped when he saw the winged filly come into view. The youth was also the first to point out the flights of Featherspark and Webstir. The reunion on a low lying rib of the fourth pyramid crested mountain was so infectious that Hammer found himself hugging animal persons he had never before met.

Resting two nights later next to Buckmight, Rayalas noticed a cloud of worry behind her friend's eyes.

"What can trouble the bison when we are all of us soon to be once more gathered to our captain? The two warrior persons add strength to our numbers. And my wings have become stronger, so that I can also well-protect us."

"Now that you ask, the distant sounds of wolves and lions trouble me. But you are right. What can go wrong when the winged filly is found right beside me?"

"We have company!" hronkked Featherspark alighting the next morning on the back of Buckmight. "A lone lion sits on the sun-sleep side of us. He does not try to hide, nor does he move to hunt game animals. Since he is not eating or sleeping, the lion must be... *spying* on us."

"*Qvvaacck!*" Webstir dropped down to land next to

the goose. "In plain sight two wolves have come to rest on our sun-birth side! They are less than a league distant from us. That must mean something, right Buckmight?"

"About these matters we will talk with the two warriors."

The razorbacks and sheep quit their breakfasting and gathered around the men, bovines, dogs, waterfowl, and Rayalas. Buckmight informed that their march was being watched by a lion on one side, and two wolves on the other.

"Hmph!" responded Hammerclaw rubbing his broad forehead. "It is almost as if the lion and two wolves have placed themselves to be our escort. What do you suppose they can want, Lucars?" The youth placed his hands at his hips, exhaled a big breath, and took time to think.

"I imagine the lions were surprised to find that Naythorn survived the fight against so many wolves in the trench of broken stones that leads to the mountain of spires. No doubt the lions were again surprised that Naythorn and I found entrance to Shining Canyon. Perhaps the lions believe they have sole ownership of that magic canyon. One way or another, we must journey on and see what the wolf and lion escorts do next. If the escorts fade away and disappear, it is a sign that all is well. If, as we travel onward the escorts keep their position on our flanks, we can guess that a welcome party of wolves and lions awaits us at or before the entrance to Shining Canyon.

"This could, Buckmight, become a very difficult situation for us. Hammer and I are bound to return to the spired mountain to mine the magic gold required by the Phoenician army. If our way is blocked we cannot, for our sake only, ask Buckmight to endanger his friends."

"Because Phoenician barges saved the white herd from the flaming mountain," answered Buckmight, "the promise to recompense blue gold to your people is a vow that all of us in his platoon must help Naythorn to fulfill."

"Master Bison, your help signifies much to Hammer and to me. From this day forward count on two Phoenicians to be loyally joined to the platoon of the blackmane." The two men bowed low to Buckmight. His return bow accomplished, Buckmight walked over to the men and with his massive head playfully pushed one into the other.

"Our band welcomes you," brayed the bison. "But, just be forewarned by me that..."

"And by me!" interjected Taurington, who because of Buckmight's playful gesture knew right away that the comment in the offing would be humorous.

"As I was about to say... that our unicorn captain believes not only in a lot of discipline, but also in a lot of *marching guard duty.*"

Lucars played along with Buckmight's jest, "Even so, Master Bison, in that Naythorn cannot be a harder taskmaster than is my Master Hammerclaw."

Made newly cautious, Naythorn's band of animal and human friends resumed march toward Shining Canyon.

CHAPTER 32

BESET BY WOLVES AND LIONS

"The lion escort on our sun-sleep side has grown from one to two," qvackked the duck landing webbed feet on Buckmight's back.

"*Hronnkk!* Five wolves now escort us on our sun-birth side!" exclaimed Featherspark setting down beside Webstir.

"Rayalas, I have a request to make of you," brayed Buckmight. "Grab to your back Timidthy, and fly ahead to scout the entranceway to Shining Canyon. I want yours *and* a second set of eyes to scan the rocks and spires for evidence of an unwanted welcome party."

The boarling immediately jumped onto a rock and from there up onto the filly's back. Clutching paws tightly to not fall off, a half grown razorback found himself happily settled in flight. It was not long until the winged filly and her pigling cargo returned to the band.

"Our report, Master Bison, is troubling," groinked Timidthy after bouncing off the filly's back. "At least forty lions crouch on the sun-sleep side of the cave entrance to Shining Canyon. On the other side of the entrance, wolf numbers reach double that of the lions. It can only mean that a terrible time of battle awaits us."

"So then, at the entrance to Shining Canyon two armies of wolves and lions anticipate our arrival," brayed

Buckmight. "They will have the high ground from which to launch an attack on us. For our platoon, the battle will become too bloody. We cannot abandon Naythorn found trapped inside Shining Canyon. Nor can we remain here; against so many wolves and lions this trench of stones is not defensible."

"Then there is absolutely *nothing* that we can do!" exclaimed the always pessimistic Rambuncture.

"*Mrrawwnnngh!*" snorted Taurington. "Time and again cattle herds have learned that it is easy to walk into a trap, and costly to not know in advance a way to escape the trap. We need to find another pathway that gains entrance into the canyon of blue gold."

"But the cave offers the only way into the canyon," responded Lucars.

"If that is the case we are going to need reinforcements," groinked Practicia.

"Without the help of Captain Naythorn it will be *impossible* for us to secure allies," shared once more the ram his pessimism. "And without more reinforcements, we are done for."

"My dear ram, do not be so negative," admonished Ewelissas. "Although he stands not here with us, Naythorn's magic remains still on our side."

"Even with unicorn magic to strengthen us, there is obviously no time to gain reinforcements before we achieve Spire Mountain," responded Rambuncture.

"Since we cannot without a fight abandon our captain, who now finds himself sealed inside Shining Canyon," groinked Timidthy, "our only option is to put our heads together and think up a solution to our difficult situation." After looking inquisitively at each member in the band, the smart boarling groinked again, "Who do we know, who have we met, that can become our ally in this fight?"

"My fishing buddy, a strong bear, was once our loyal companion," qvackked Webstir.

"When brandished against adversaries, the hooves of my brother stallions are formidable," whinnied Rayalas.

"*Hmph...* if we detoured to the other side of the mountain we could delay perhaps another three days, the battle that is to overtake us," offered Lucars. "That would give us time to summon Tristanbear, and the valiant brothers of Rayalas, to there join us in battle."

"The big bear spoke of the wolves as the lowest of the low," grunted the sow. "I will wager a bite to my fanny that it will not be difficult for Tristanbear to bring along friends that just like our bear, entertain a powerful antipathy toward wolves."

"My brother stallions despise both wolves *and* lions," added Rayalas. "I know that if asked by no less than an emissary of the brave Naythorn, they would also come to our aid. They will do that for the blackmaned unicorn that they deeply admire and respect, *and* they will do that for me."

Rambuncture was once more *not* hopeful. "The impenetrable mountains and valleys that are everywhere about us make it almost impossible to search out Tristanbear and the herd of mountain horses, let alone bring them to us in... *only three days.*"

"Tristanbear departed our band a few suns before we came to Prow Mountain," grunted Mama Pig in reply.

"The bear may still be found close to where he left us."

"Compared to where we are now," offered Practicia, "the underside of Spire Mountain lies closer to Prow Mountain."

"As for my horse brothers," whinnied Rayalas, "they will likely be found on the back side of the mountain range that forms the western border of the valley before Prow Mountain."

"Our wolf and lion adversaries cannot anticipate our sending winged scouts to find bear and horse allies," brayed the bison. "While the winged scouts are in flight, the rest of us will embark on a new path toward the place of the morning sun. We will soon after circle south, and then continue toward our destination on the underside of Spire Mountain.

"We will defeat the gathered wolves and lions not at the entrance to Shining Canyon, but in a distant place of our own choosing. For our band there is no running away from the battle that looms. But we shall make this fight to be on our terms." Having finished what was for Buckmight a very long speech, he paused briefly before issuing new orders.

"Come here Webstir. I order you to take to heart the counsel of Mama Sow, and fly as fast as your wings can flap to where we last saw Tristanbear. Once you find him, tell him that his strength is needed to save our band. Instruct him to bring to Spire Mountain stouthearted bear friends. *Go find Tristan!*"

The bison next addressed Rayalas, "Fly with all speed to find your brother stallions. You know where to look for them. Bring your brothers to do battle with us on the south side of the mountain of spires."

"What about me?" complained the goose nervously crooking and straightening his black neck. "Since I am more responsible than Webstir, I should get to fly on an important mission!"

"*Qvackk!* I fly faster than the goose. And in spite of the fact that his big sharp teeth were scary, I had more fun fishing with Tristanbear than did Featherspark."

"As the rest of us circumvent Spire Mountain, I require Featherspark to fly scout for us," replied Buckmight.

Hammer removed from his wrist a protective gold brace, and from his waist a gold inlaid belt. That done he offered, "Made with magic ore, these reflect the sun better than any other metal that is known."

He clasped the brace around the neck of the duck, and the belt around the neck of Rayalas. With big hands skilled in touch delicate, Hammer squeezed the collar and belt closed, but not so tightly as to restrict motion or movement of duck and horse necks.

"Watch across the sky for sun reflections sent by these collars. The reflections will travel far, and when seen will let you know where flies your friend. If you find yourself in trouble, beat your wings rapidly about your neck to send out intermittent flashes of sunlight that signal you need help."

With no more words said by anyone, Webstir and Rayalas were aflight. For his part, the dour ram harbored the unspoken thought that for the next three days the sky would cloud over, rendering totally useless the gifts of the golden brace and belt.

"Do not sulk, Featherspark," cajoled Hammer. "I will make sure you come to sport something even better than the brace I placed around the neck of Webstir."

CHAPTER 33

SEARCH

B uckmight led into a deep ravine that presented on the band's sunbirth side. He soon enough brayed for Trackler and Blackler to join him.

"Am I correct, little fellows, that a wolf cannot catch you?" brayed the bison. "A lion cannot out-dodge you, right?"

"*Yelp! Yilp!* There is no wolf or lion alive that can match the dodge moves of me and Trackler. Maybe if they got lucky, three or four lions could corral me. But, my brother would jump in and distract them so that they could still not snare me."

"That, Blackler, is what I was hoping to hear you bark. You see, as our band circles the mountain of spires we have to find places of safety where we can at night rest our weary legs; places where lions and wolves cannot fall down upon us. Speed ahead and scout for a well-protected canyon or ravine with grass and water. Do not get caught. I need you back to me safe and sound."

For the dog brothers the only thing better than running and scouting, was to run and scout with the purpose of finding something important, like a perfectly defensible camp site. Without taking the time to bark anything more to Buckmight, the dogs sped away.

From out of the ravine Buckmight and Taurington emerged running fast. Surprised to see a blocky cattle turn hooves at them, five scout wolves spooked and sped away toward the spired mountain. Taurington shifted to place himself on the right flank of the band. Stationed there between the mountain of spires and his friends, his presence would be most protective. Rain began to fall, and as the platoon proceeded along a wettening gully the pace slackened.

"I think I know what is making you to smile," baahed Ewelissas catching up to the bison. "Because this rain looks to last long, water will come to wash through this gully. Our tracks and scents will be by wetness absorbed."

"Exactly my thinking, Ewelissas. Look, water already trickles beneath our hooves. This rain will make it hard for wolves and lions to track us to where we have disappeared." The female sheep made it two faces grinning broadly, hers and the bison's.

"It becomes your turn, madam sheep, to tell me what now brings such a big smile to grace your face."

"Since my mate has forgotten how to smile, I have to smile double, for him and for me."

"I could not forget... because I never *learned* how to smile," corrected the ram overtaking his mate.

"Actually, Buckmight," continued the ewe, "I was thinking that thanks to this fortuitous rain, the sparkling of Goose's feathers might this night serve to lead confused wolves and lions away from us."

"Why Ewelissas, *that* is a first-rate idea!"

Featherspark was by the bison soon given

instructions, "The washing of the rain that obscures our tracks provides us an opportunity to trick our enemies. As nightfall approaches you are to fly back to wherever wolves and lions are found behind us. After finding our foes, make your feathers to alert and sparkle while you circle above them. I assume that when you sight wolves, your feathers can still be made to glow."

"*Hronnkk!* Of course I can make them do that!"

"Very good! After the wolves spot you, wheel around as if you return to report to me the whereabouts of our adversaries. Trick them to follow your sparkling trail in the sky, but fly away from where the band actually travels. Lead our enemies far into the desert so that we may camp this night in peace, and so recover our strength and energy."

"Blackler, you did well," brayed later that evening the bison as Naythorn's platoon members together relaxed. "These steep cliffs make it impossible for wolves and lions to fall down upon us. If attacked head-on, we can from here leave by the back way, which is well-hidden."

"And thanks to my ewe's smart idea about Goose's sparkling feathers, the wolves will not tonight find us," added Rambuncture.

"Why Master Ram," responded Buckmight, "that is about the most positive thing I ever heard you to baah."

"We sheep will tonight stand guard," added an again smiling Ewelissas.

"At middle night me and Timidthy will spell the sheep at guard duty," volunteered Hamilton.

While later marching guard, Timidthy felt his mind to be unsettled. He finally grasped what it was that bothered him. The wolf general would have by now concluded that the only feasible route for Naythorn's band animals was to circle the mountain of spires. Timidthy also guessed that wolves and lions would *not* amicably travel together.

For that thinking Timidthy decided that if he were Albarochk, he would command that his force divide in two with the wolves, the great grayback's main force of fighters, following after Buckmight. The lesser in number lions would be sent the opposite direction to prevent Naythorn's platoon from successfully navigating all the way around Spire Mountain to reach Shining Canyon unimpeded. With the wolves taking one direction, and the lions traveling the other, the two enemy forces would reunite on the south side of the mountain of spires and there corner the band between them.

Webstir Looks for Tristanbear

Because Buckmight had given him a very important assignment, the duck felt special. For the members of Naythorn's platoon the success of his flighted reconnaissance could mean the difference between life and death.

Webstir promised himself that he would fly very fast. Calibrating each sprite of wind wafting over his soft feathers, the duck's wings soon left behind the spired mountain. It did not take long before he wove up one canyon, then the next, and eventually crossed the topmost ridge of a chain of low mountains. Late that afternoon, after crossing a chain of taller mountains, the duck sighted the part of the river where Tristanbear had separated himself from the band.

"Tristanbear likes nothing better than to fish a fast current," muttered the duck. "*Qvaacckk! Qvaarrkk!*" fussed Webstir at the river. "Bear! Tristan! Tristanbear!" No answer was returned. The duck followed further the winding river, but Tristanbear was simply not to be found.

Night darkness presented. Since the duck's only instructions were to return to the river place where Bear had departed Naythorn's band, Webstir circled slowly while he thought about what to do next.

The duck remembered Tristanbear as an animal person that did not like to climb hills, and liked even less to explore mountains. The bear was fond of river banks, and only river banks. Webstir finally decided that by staying too long in one place the big bear would have become bored.

"Tristanbear did not stay put where we left him," qvackked the duck to himself. "He decided to wander about. But where would our bear be most likely to go? *Qvackk!* Because he would come to miss Naythorn, and since he knew that Naythorn followed the fixed star, sooner or later the bear would decide to follow northward after the blackmane. Tristanbear would continue along the route of the river until he came to Prow Mountain. *Qvackk!* And I know exactly where to find the biggest fish in the Pavilion River!"

Webstir had remembered the big fish he had seen sporting about at the spot where he had gushed out the side of the notch landing to plop down into the river below. Although not exactly true, Webstir had said that at that spot a very big fish had injured his wing. At least the part about a big fish being close to where he had hurt his wing, was true enough.

After telling himself that Naythorn would be proud of him for coming up with an honest-to-goodness idea to solve a problem, the duck broke out of his circle pattern and headed north toward the mountain that held within a crumbling pavilion. He took his time so that he did not arrive at Prow Mountain until daylight once again peeked from behind feathery mists of receding darkness.

As the wings of Webstir gained the part of the Pavilion River adjacent to Prow Mountain, unmoving black forms became visible. Closer inspection of the gorge revealed bears sprawled along the rocky shoreline found beneath the notch landing, the exact place where Rayalas had first flown.

Making as much sound and spraying of water as a solitary duck could accomplish, Webstir splashed down. His head immediately dunked below the surface to make sure a big fish was not about to attack him.

"It serves big scary fishes exactly right to be eaten by bears!" qvackked Webstir.

When none of the bulky black forms acknowledged the arrival of a duck appointed to an important mission, he flapped wings excitedly and in loud duck voice issued an order, "Wake up you lazy bears!"

Tristanbear wobbled upward his head to discover what the commotion was about, and who exactly was responsible for interrupting his well-deserved sleep.

"*Qvackk!* Tristanbear! It is me, Webstir, your fishing

buddy! Naythorn needs you!"

The biggest bear the duck had ever seen shook twice his head back-and-forth, pulled upward his front legs, rubbed his face, and blinked his eyes before wuffing, "Is that really the green-head duck? What are you doing here?"

The duck flitted next to Tristanbear and with one wing and then the other, slapped him in the face.

"*Qvackk!* You big oaf! If you had looked for us and found us in the valley of tall trees, we could have won the battle against a hundred wolves, and then Naythorn would not have had to flee across the desert!

"An army of lions, and even more wolves, are readying to attack Naythorn's band. Grown even bigger than before, you are desperately needed by the blackmane that once counted you as a band member in good standing. The battle will happen on this side of the mountain of many spires. Against so many fierce enemies, Naythorn's band cannot long survive without your help, and the help of *all* your bear friends."

Tristanbear relayed to his now alert bear companions what Webstir had told him. Finding some of the bears to be uncomprehending, Tristanbear slowly repeated himself, "Yes, yes, it is as I just told you. Too many lions, and even more wolves, have surrounded the blackmaned unicorn and the rest of my old platoon, and that is... *not right!*"

Turning back to the duck, the enormous bear wuffed, "My friends and I tired of polite bear society. We became especially bored with the attitudes of the stodgy old uncle bears. So we went exploring and found this wondrous place. Actually, it was as though this place found us. It is not easy to arrive at this exact spot on this river. We have here caught a lot of big fish... maybe too many. You know what? I have the idea that every bear here would relish a truly big adventure."

Tristanbear stood up, stretched himself tall for effect, and participated in more bear conversation with his friends. Actually he growled rather harshly while his bear companions listened in silence. It was evident to Webstir that Tristanbear was the leader of the bears, and that the very big bear would soon have the matter settled in his favor.

"Webstir, since you tell me that we do not have much time, lead the way onward." Nine bears soon climbed out of the river gorge and began loping at a fast pace in the direction of Spire Mountain.

Flying above, the duck circled back from time to time to impart encouragement to Tristanbear, or alternatively to scold him for moving too slowly. Webstir never tired of reminding Tristanbear that the bears had a great distance to travel, that a terribly important battle awaited, *and* that his winged mission was very important.

Rayalas on a Mission

Upon being instructed to find her horse brothers Rayalas did what she most enjoyed doing; she began to course the wind. Her aerial path soon led close to Spire Mountain.

"Who can say?" she neighed. "As things now stand with a terrible battle looming, I might not ever again see the unicorn that shed his blood for me, and then made my wounds to heal." Rayalas banked wings for the place she had visited only a few suns past.

"I bring bad news, Naythorn. The way for Buckmight and your band to enter Shining Canyon is blocked by very many wolves and lions. For that, Buckmight is forced to take the band around the mountain to come to you by the back way, the long way. The bison says a battle against a large army, or rather two separate armies of wolves and lions, will unfold on the south side of Spire Mountain."

"How many wolves and lions will in battle be faced?"

"More than one hundred."

"That makes the odds in the looming battle... to be terrible. So, Rayalas, you must help me push open the stone door to this vale. Since I am now stronger, I must go to help my band. Should my band, and especially should you perish, I will have nothing more to live for."

"Because the eastern way is blocked by our enemy that follows after your band, you must take the western path around the mountain. But, promise me that you will delay one more day your departure. By tomorrow no wolves or lions will be found outside Shining Canyon."

"I shall wait until tomorrow. Pushing our shoulders hard against the door will make it to move inward into the cave." The unicorn and the filly timed their pushes to occur at the same instant. By only a small crack the door nudged a little, then a little more. The door at last opened wide enough for a horse body to squeeze through.

Naythorn watched as the winged filly mounted the winds and flew southward above high rock spires. Until the following morning, the unicorn could only wait.

Flying as fast as a wind gale, Rayalas left behind Spire Mountain. Upon gaining altitude she adjusted her eyesight to focus on far distances. Flying so high, she felt herself to resemble a great eagle.

At new light of day the entrance to the home valley of the herd of horses lay before her. No movement of horses was there to be seen. With suddenness a new thought struck her. If wolves were everywhere moving, the stallions would react by hiding the herd.

"Where would my sire hide so many horses? I do know that lead stallions feel most secure in high places with streams. Near this valley there are precious few places with access to both water and meadows, and only one such place has a lake. *Nyeeerrrrunungh!* It is in that place that I will find my horse herd."

Rayalas thought about her mare, sire, and brothers, and wondered if they missed her. She next wondered why she did not feel lonely for the company of her horse family. How could she not miss her sire? After all, he was a horse of great dignity and strength. His black coat was... wait... did he have a black coat or was it gray? Why could she not remember the exact color of her sire's coat? What was happening to her? Now that she thought about it, when she was flying she no longer felt to be a real horse. In flight, she felt herself *birdlike*.

A worrisome thought struck the filly. Perhaps one day she would even forget the faces of her sire and dam. The one animal person she could not, and would not ever permit herself to forget was the blackmaned unicorn that had gifted her wings.

When she realized that even her thoughts were being transformed from horse into bird thinking, and that she was losing the bonds that connected to her former self, her heart sank. Shaking her mane she tried to shrug off her worries, but the disturbing thoughts would not be left behind. Rayalas finally decided that the transformation from horse person to bird person did not have to become a big problem, not now anyway. If she was to become a horse bird, she would simply have to become a notable and distinguished horse eagle that remained ever loyal to the blackmane.

There it was! In a large depression formed between three peaks shone a large spot of blue. Splashing down, she found that her body floated high in the water. She wondered if her body felt lighter because her bones were losing density and weight. Gaining the shore she shook the water off her feathers and neighed, "*Yeeeherrrreeeppp! Nyeeeheherrrreeeppp!*"

She cleared her throat. What was that strange sound? Was she now chirping like a bird? At that ridiculous thought Rayalas had to smile. She heard hoof beats to pound the ground.

"*Nyeeaaaarrghh!* My lovely filly has wings that are grown full!" neighed the mare of Rayalas.

"Our filly has sprouted long, luxuriant, and deeply feathered wings that underneath are colored half black," neighed her eldest stallion brother.

"But where are the rest of my brothers?"

"It does not make me proud to tell you that... our hooves came to blows," responded the sire of Rayalas. "Your brothers did not want to wait any longer to have their own say about things. I refused to relinquish my authority as lead stallion. Only your oldest brother stayed with me. I miss your brother stallions... *terribly.* Now tell me, how does it feel to soar like a bird?"

Just like she used to do when she was a foal, Rayalas rubbed her head against her sire's stomach. She next did her best to neigh like a horse and not like a bird.

"Flying is just like running free, only running free across the sky. My hooves gallop the clouds! But sire, I need to ask my brothers for help. A terrible fight is to soon fall upon the band of Naythorn. More than one hundred wolves and lions are settled upon destroying the blackmaned unicorn. I need to find my brothers and request their help in the fight that soon comes to the mountain of spires. To where are they gone?"

"Naythorn is to fight at the same time wolves *and* lions?" responded the sire stomping his hooves. "That is unfair, especially for a unicorn that can count on only a few animal friends to fight with him. I grow tired of these new wolves that now also threaten my horse herd. If lions begin to copy the behavior of wolves grown arrogant, the mares and foals in my herd will come to never live without fear."

His decision was immediate. Resting his gaze on the remaining colt still with him, the big stallion neighed, "To you I leave leadership. You are strong. You are as well more patient than me. If anything, my colt is also smarter than am I. Take care of your mother mare. She is the meadow and lake of my life."

"I will miss you my darling," neighed the stallion as he nudged his head with affection against his mare.

"From the hard battle that waits I do not think to return."

The sire of Rayalas bowed low his head to his mate, to his stallion colt, and to the horses in the herd he had guided across many valleys. The leader stallion next reared hooves, neighed loud, and looked at Rayalas as if to say *follow me*. The sire and his filly were off running.

"I shall not... forget... my mother mare and brother stallion!" whinnied Rayalas looking back while she ran. Into trees disappeared Rayalas and her sire. They ran higher and higher until they came to the crest of a mountain.

"To get away from me, my colts went this way," informed the sire. "They will be found somewhere along the base of these mountains." The stallion and his filly began picking their way down the mountain slope toward the big valley to the east.

"Sire, looking down from the sky I will spot them sure." Rayalas jumped upward with wings extended full. However, the brother colts were nowhere to be seen. While Rayalas circled and wondered whether to look more closely south, east, or north, she noticed... light flashes. Upon seeing the reflection of sunrays Rayalas knew that Webstir wanted her to come. She glided back to her sire.

"I must go into the desert to see why I am by sun reflections called. Until I return, follow the foothills in the direction of the mountain of many spires. My sire, I will soon catch up with you."

Webstir hovered vertically with his wings fanning out the signal that said, *here I am!* He had amazingly not only found bears, he had managed to spot horses hidden in the middle of a sandy place. The found horses were resting on the very oasis where Blackler and Trackler had joined the band of Naythorn. But, those stubborn stallions found it inconvenient to listen to a bothersome duck that was only the size of two horse hooves put together.

Upon receiving a returned signal, Webstir knew it was Rayalas fanning answer to him. When the flights of Rayalas and Webstir joined together, the duck explained that he had come upon her horse brothers. The problem was that the stallions pretended not to understand his qvackking. In a very bad mood about something, the recalcitrant stallions did not want to hear a small duck explain anything of consequence to them.

"Just take me to them!"

"Wait! I almost forgot the other thing! I found Tristanbear! He and his bear friends are right now headed toward Spire Mountain." At the second report of good news Rayalas whinnied hearty horsebird approval.

Side by side the winged filly and duck flew toward the oasis. When Rayalas united with the rest of her brothers the oasis broke out in all manner of jumping, kicking, and horse play. As she cavorted, she was thankful that she could still remember each stallion sibling.

When the panting stallions calmed, their sister told how she had come to acquire wings in the cavern below the crumbling pavilion. Rayalas next recounted how Naythorn had made a promise to the human persons that had saved the magical white herd, and that until his promise was fulfilled he could not run away and abandon the canyon of blue gold found in the spired mountain. She lastly informed her brothers of the perilous situation in which Naythorn and his band of friends found themselves, with wolves and lions readying to attack them.

"My brother stallions, will you help the blackmaned unicorn who on all sides is threatened? I need you! Will you with me fight?"

"Count... me... in," neighed her second oldest brother stepping forward. One stallion after another stepped forward in agreement to join their filly's fight.

"Nyeerrheherreepp! Nyeerryaaarpp!" She neighed with whinnies that sounded half horse and half bird, "In this battle Sir Cattle, Master Bison, Blackmane, and I will now fight with other big animal persons at our sides! Brother stallions, I must now return to accompany our sire to the battle that comes upon us. He had a premonition that he will die fighting wolves and lions. Follow fast after the wings of Webstir. You cannot get there too soon. Know that the unicorn will be much heartened that you bring him aid." The wings of Rayalas remounted in flight.

With Webstir now *officially* commissioned as their winged guide, the brother colts galloped fast toward a majestic spired mountain that stood solitary and alone.

CHAPTER 34

THE BATTLE OF SPIRE MOUNTAIN

Rayelas settled hooves to earth to run beside her sire. When the following day the clearly defined features of Spire Mountain came into view, the sun sat directly above them. Possessing the keen eyesight of a bird of prey, Rayalas identified movement.

"Sire, the battle started without us! The lions are for now held back as a reserve enemy battalion. And Naythorn has rejoined his band. I must get quickly to the blackmane." After the filly took to wing her sire began a race against only himself.

With their backs against high cliffs, Naythorn and his band fought from a tight triangle formation. The blackmane was positioned at the apex, the two bovines at one back corner, and the two men at the opposite corner. While the five razorbacks arrayed between Naythorn and the two Phoenicians, the sturdy mountain sheep and the scrappy dogs connected Naythorn to the bovines.

Drawing close the winged filly heard the air to fill with the sounds of wolves snarling in rage and Naythorn's band members grunting, neighing, and mrawing. The winged filly was proud to see the members of the blackmane's platoon defend themselves so valiantly.

Wings batted wolves, and her hooves sent them tumbling. After swathing through a phalanx of wolves, Rayalas alighted at the side of Naythorn.

"My sire comes to fight for you. And Webstir found both Tristanbear and my horse brothers. While the bears travel apart, the duck leads the stallions here. They will all surely join us soon." At this news, Naythorn's gratitude was so great that he choked with emotion, and could not neigh answer to Rayalas. The deepening color in the unicorn's eyes said everything that mattered to the winged filly.

The grand entrance of Rayalas to the battlefield had not been anticipated by the enemy commander. Her absence at the start of the battle had given Albarochk an excuse to deploy only his wolves. It seemed that in battle against the unicorn he never had enough reserves, and the wolf general wanted not to share with the surly and irascible lion captain his great triumph over the unicorn. The monster wolf began to second guess himself. Perhaps it had been unwise to hold the lions back. The wolf general needed time to rethink his battle plan. For that the fighting ceased.

"My dear filly... thank goodness... you finally arrived," grunted the sow gasping for breath. "It does not seem to matter that we stop the advance of many wolves, we could not have held out much longer. Had the lions joined in the fight, I fear it would have been over for us."

Through the ranks of wolves opened a path. With his wolf body looming even bigger than in the last battle at the place of the tall trees, Albarochk limped toward Naythorn's line of defenders. In the wake of his big lupine cousin weaved the nimble paws of Yellowquist.

"This is not the blackmane's day! The battle fares badly for my traitorous, lying, and despicable foe. I will this day drink your blood and supper on your flesh! How does that strike your unnatural and malignant heart?"

Stepping out from the defensive line of his band, Naythorn walked to within five paces of the wolf general. The self-confident unicorn surprised the huge grayback wolf by sitting hind haunches in a relaxed attitude. Instead of answering the monster wolf, Naythorn shook his head back-and-forth and yawned. Seeing that, Albarochk inwardly raged at the insolence demonstrated by the deliberate nonchalance of the blackmane.

"Are you this time going to offer me a deal that will save your miserable friends? Be forewarned that I have learned not to trust your lying neighs."

"I have no deal to offer you, at least no deal that you would like. Although thinking on that, I will generously extend to you the opportunity to flee my magic power. I remind that with a broken limb you cannot travel fast. For that, I advise the wolf general to get a head-start by right now running away. *Nyeerrr...* there now occurs to me a question. How uncomfortable is it to flee on only three paws with your tail tucked between hind legs?"

Albarochk turned to growl menacingly at Yellowquist, who had been so ill-advised as to chuckle at the mental image of the monster wolf limping away in retreat with his tail tucked in the fashion of a cowardly dog. The wolf general settled down on his belly.

"I will tomorrow, when you are no more, actually

miss your feeble attempts at wit. For someone of limited horse intelligence your perverse way with words is amusing." Since it came unnaturally to his malignant wolf face, Albarochk only half succeeded in his attempt to form a wide smile. "You cannot like, that as well as wolves I now command lions. Along with the size of my frame, you see that my power each day grows. Because I before experienced your deceit in battle, and because I wanted this victory to belong to wolves alone, I held back my lions as a reserve. But now that you are reinforced by the freak horse with wings, I will summon the lions to join my fight." Albarochk smirked with his tongue hanging out the side of his teeth.

"But I can still be a little generous. The bones of the cattle, bison, two abandoned men, wild boars, waterfowl, dogs, and goats matter not to me. If you and the magic horse with wings lie down and stretch your throats to convenience my thirst, I will pardon your friends. It is magic blood that I crave."

"They are *not* goats, Albarochk, but horned mountain sheep. My answer will not be to your liking. I say nay... *NaaayyyTHORN!* I and my loyal friends fight on. And I here and now guarantee that this battle will not end to your liking. My magical intuition tells me that my destiny is not to this day fall in battle. Not even lion soldiers will have an answer for my horn, or for the wings of Rayalas. While I know that my old enemy will not listen to my counsel, I tell you straight-out that this day's battle belongs not to you."

"Really, Blackmane? I am about to bring fifty lions against you. Neither you, nor the winged horse, can halt the attack of so many lions."

"Your lieutenant, this Yellowquist, knows better than you what is to be the outcome of this day. Is not that right, yellow wolf?"

Most times the yellow-hide cousin to Albarochk could not control his sardonic wit, but for once he guarded his tongue and said nothing. The lieutenant wolf knew better than to, on this day of harsh battle, interject mocking and satirical remarks that would hold up his gigantic cousin to ridicule.

"You should, Albarochk, take the counsel of your yellow haired lieutenant and withdraw and regroup to fight some other day. Since your unorganized wolves fight as individual soldiers disconnected from each other, they cannot penetrate the disciplined line of my platoon." Naythorn rose to stand, stretched tall his neck, and walked back to his position in the defensive formation of his band.

Stunned at the unwarranted confidence of his enemy, Albarochk reassured himself that the entry of fifty lions into the battle could not be so easily dismissed by the blackmane. The monster wolf became more upset when he thought about Naythorn turning his back and walking away, without being dismissed. After all, the great Albarochk had called for the meeting to begin, and the meeting with the blackmane was the wolf general's to end.

Upon being summoned, the yellow wolf knew to be especially attentive when the huge grayback wolf was in a nasty mood.

"*Yarrgkkarrhk!* As it will take me some time to

introduce the lions to the battle, my wolf soldiers can take some breaths of rest. I am going to place the lions on the desert side, against the center of Naythorn's Band."

"The lions would more agreeably fight on the side of the battle that lies against their mountain," yipped Yellowquist in a voice made to sound purposefully small.

"I need them on the desert side to block the unicorn from making a running attempt to escape me. Just like at the *Battle of Tall Trees* he will try again, but this time the blackmane will not flee far into the desert sand. A lion running at full speed is a most formidable enemy to suffer. Two fleet lions can corral a running stallion, sink claws into his sides, and bring him down. The lions will have the members of Naythorn's band for their supper, except of course for the unicorn and the winged horse. Bring the lions around to the desert side of the battle, and tell them to there wait for my signal to launch the final attack. Now be gone with you, runt!"

"I do always as your ominous and true self requires," barked with deference the yellow wolf saluting stiffly. As he trotted toward the boulders where reclined the lions, Yellowquist found himself troubled. The small wolf slowed his pace and did what he usually did to clear his mind... he began to think out loud.

"Because the blackmane is not naturally haughty, his arrogance concerns me. The unicorn must know... something. But what can he know that I do not? Against so many wolves, and now lions also, the blackmane's tactical position is indefensible. Hmph! *I have it!* It must be that Naythorn waited not only for the winged horse and the old stallion to join him, but that he anticipates the addition of more fighters. But... who can he await?

"If as I think the blackmane expects more allies to join him, we should right now be on the attack with wolves pushing Naythorn's platoon toward lions positioned on the cliff sides of the fight. Lions fight best when from rocks and boulders they launch down on their prey. *Yripe, yruff,* it will not surprise me if the clever Naythorn once again somehow outsmarts my general, and even worse, outsmarts me. Do not forget, Yellowquist, that your silence is the best policy in the presence of the numskull Albarochk.

"No wolf, not even your great cousin, is born stupid. But your monster cousin would be better served if his too prideful cunning were replaced by common sense wolf thought. For my part I accept that I am a runt wolf. Still, because I suffer no illusion of false pride, I find myself emotionally and intellectually superior to my enormous cousin." The wheels churning in the mind of the yellow wolf would not stop moving.

"This fight is going to become interesting. Come what may I will be... my own yellow wolf. I will stay true to my character, which includes sowing a few harmless seeds of disunity. It is a good thing that for tasting the blackmane's blood, I can growl something of lion-speak." The yellow wolf decided that even at rest, the hard sinews weaving through the lion captain's hide were impressive to see up close.

"I bring orders from General Albarochk. Since he commands you to now enter battle from the desert side, it is well that your big muscles bulge strong today." With arrogance of tone intended to provoke the ire of the proud lion chieftain, Yellowquist added, "If General Albarochk's orders are not in every aspect obeyed," the yellow wolf grinned, "there will be terrible trouble for you."

"The grayback has no right to show me disrespect. While unicorn magic made your master to quadruple in size, never you forget that my hide is as hard as the rock my belly now rests on. *And,* I do not forget that it took only the horn of one unicorn to cripple a limb of Albarochk. The monster wolf must recall that I joined this fight only to dislodge the blackmane from the magic canyon, which is the birthright of my lions. I cannot permit the band of the unicorn to there trespass."

"Be that as it may, this battle is the only thing that now concerns my master. After you march your lion battalion around the enemy, and from the middle attack the unicorn's band, you are to prevent the unicorn from escaping into the sand. Your reward for obedience is that you can do what you will with all the captives, except for the unicorn and the winged horse. Those two kills belong to my master. The magic of their blood will feed not you, but the great wolf general alone. That will make my master's magic to become even more singular. Unicorn blood will make Albarochk's leg to heal as good as new, and make dominant his power over all animal persons, even to include... *lions.*"

At this remark the big lion scratched huge front paws at Yellowquist, who jumped quickly back to avoid being sliced by sharp-nailed lion fingers.

The order to abandon a side of the mountain that they claimed as their own was not to the liking of any lion. For that, much time was lost amid feline growling and contentiousness. At last the lion captain marshaled his force to depart rock ledges and file toward the battlefield. The members of Naythorn's band watched lions, in a noticeably bad mood, saunter to the center of the enemy formation.

"*Qvvaaacckk!* The sulking of a battalion of lions almost matches the sulking of a flock of geese!"

"But ducks are much better at pouting than geese are at sulking," responded Featherspark extending up and down his black neck.

"Thank goodness my sire arrived to help us against so many lions," neighed Rayalas paying no mind to the banter of the two waterfowl. "But where are my brother horses? And, why are Tristanbear and his friends not yet here? We right now *need* them!"

"They will surely come soon," reassured Naythorn. "We just have to last out the fight until they arrive."

"So this is how it will be," brayed Buckmight, "with lions against our center, wolves against our flanks, and our backs against a cliff that permits no escape."

More Battle

Against the center of Naythorn's line advanced the lions. Arrayed on each side of the big cats, wolf companies joined the assault. In order to gain entrance to the fight, wolves climbed over wolves, and lions bounded over other lions.

Naythorn and the sire of Rayalas fought in tandem with the four hooves of one slashing in coordination with the four hooves of the other. Against their part of the attacking lions, the two stallions held their ground. Nonetheless at both ends where fought Hammer, Lucars, Taurington, and Buckmight the defense began to bend inward, and then inexorably more inward. Without Rayalas, who showed herself to be a lethal winged weapon, for Naythorn's platoon the fight would have gone disastrously.

The filly had become as quick and agile as a falcon in flight. Aided by the force of great wings that hardened when by battle required, her hooves kicked down bloody hurt upon lions not used to countering attacks that directed at their heads. Rayalas would steal precious moments away from protecting the more vulnerable pigs, sheep, and dogs to swath through the lions engulfing Naythorn and her sire. Fierce felines came to fear the approach of her shadow.

Naythorn's platoon withstood the first, second, and third charges of the jointed wolf and lion armies. For that Albarochk grew furious. The angrier became the wolf general, the larger and more threatening loomed his enormous body.

Halting the fight, Albarochk moved through his ranks threatening and haranguing wolves and lions to make the next assault the last. The cowering of wolf privates revealed more fear of their general's wrath, than of the slashing hooves of two bovines or the flashing swords of two warriors. Were the battle not to end in victory over the unicorn, no wolf wanted to experience the resultant rage of the savage monster general.

Stealing moments of rest, Naythorn observed that

the captain of the lion battalion was the only feline not manifesting fear of Albarochk.

"I find, Buckmight, that I am drawn to admire the lion captain against whom we fight. Of both his will and his strength, he is confident and sure. How can we get the captain of the lions to change sides? Should I try to approach him and parlay with him?"

"Not now, Blackmane. The situation is presently too well-controlled by the enormous grayback wolf."

Rayalas took advantage of the lull in the battle to push up on wings in order to survey the desert horizon. What she saw made her heart to jump. Two black dusty splotches were from the south moving fast toward the site of the battle. Rayalas dived back toward her captain and neighed, "I saw them out in the desert! Black bears and black horses come to fight with us!"

"We must hold!" neighed Naythorn upon receiving the good news from Rayalas. "Reinforcement and rescue are soon at hand!"

"Each of us will now fight *twice* as hard as before!" responded the bison speaking for all in the band.

A new attack, more ferocious than the last, commenced. Excepting Albarochk, not a single wolf or lion was held in reserve. In no corner of the battlefield could the members of Naythorn's platoon gain relief from slashing claws and gnashing incisors. Naythorn's defensive formation was pushed back and made to compress even more inward.

"If I this day am to die, I will do so fighting at the side of the noble unicorn!" grunted the sow upon seeing Naythorn's eyes show unmistakable fear. With four halfling wild boars trailing close behind her, Mrs. Razorthwacker charged to plant her dangerous tusks before the unicorn she had grown to love. The sharpness and length of her upper whetter tusks, and especially her lower cutter tusks, did gruesome damage to the bellies and sides of lions. The strength of the mother sow's steadfast heart quickened the spirit of the blackmaned unicorn.

Buckmight and Taurington bore the worst of the punishment given by wolf soldiers that fought possessed by anger, rage, and as well fear of Albarochk.

"I order that Master Bison not fall until ten more wolves are trod beneath our hooves," mrawed the cattle.

"Not ten, but through eleven more wolves will Taurington and Buckmight remain standing!" answered the bison.

Sand was everywhere kicked up. The dust became so thick that band members grew fearful they would blindly cut down a companion fighting at close quarters. Besieged by a pride of four particularly intrepid lions, Naythorn's eyes became clouded by dust and his breath became constricted. The unicorn was caught in a precarious balance between life and death.

Upon seeing the mortal threat to the blackmane, the sire of the winged filly vowed the unicorn would not die... *before he did*. The sire threw hooves and head at the fierce pride of lions. Knowing at that moment no fear, the big stallion bought time for Naythorn to recover his sight and lungs. Caught in the teeth and claws of four fierce lions, the old stallion whinnied loud, *"For my filly!"*

Upon hearing her sire's desperate neigh, horse wings exploded in anger. The hooves of Rayalas made certain that four felines paid doubly-hard for exacting the life of her sire. Lucars and Hammer fought their way clear to take the place of the fallen horse stallion. In wolf and lion blood the sand before the two warrior's feet stained crimson.

"For the sake of the brave sire horse, we will now revenge ourselves on eight more lions and wolves!" brayed Buckmight to Taurington.

"We will make it revenge upon your eight *plus* one more of the enemy!" answered the cattle.

On all sides the battle exploded. Naythorn's densely packed platoon came to be completely surrounded by wolves and lions. Too late Naythorn saw Albarochk jump at him. With nowhere for the unicorn to retreat, the teeth of the monster wolf tore at Naythorn's mane and neck. What next happened was almost impossible for Naythorn to comprehend. Instead of prolonging his attack, the wolf general turned about and was gone. The blackmane came to realize that it was new desperation that had made the lame Albarochk decide to join the fray, and launch a last gasp attack. The monster wolf had glimpsed a tight *V* column of stallions begin to trample into his army.

When all appeared to be lost, the brothers of Rayalas had joined the battle. When they came upon their sire's deeply cut body, the rage of the brother stallions was impossible to restrain. They fought with unflinching tenacity that only the deep conviction of love and duty, compounded by grief, could summon.

Naythorn glimpsed the strong arms of bears punching their way through the other side of enemy wolves and lions. The unicorn knew that Tristan would be in their lead.

Around Naythorn and his band the new allies formed an outer wall of defense that was not to be pierced through. Knowing what remained to be done, the jointed wall of stallions and bears fought outward. By the ranks of spent wolves and lions, the ferocity of Tristan's bears and the brother stallions was not to be countered.

With pain, fear, and pleading in their eyes the still-standing wolves stole glances at their aloof commander. The monster's resolve did not sustain. Made to swallow his pride, the wolf general howled the command for retreat. Wolves with bodies intact fled into the desert. With limbs dragging, wounded wolves came after. Lions that had entered the fight with insolence, with sullenness gave off the fight. Retreating lions roared their vexation at the spired mountain, their birth home that came to welcome them anew.

A fresh breeze began to eddy and swirl; the dust of battle settled. Naythorn looked up to see the sun once again seek permission to enter into the realm of far western mountains. Because he remained standing at the close of a day of hard-won victory, the unicorn exhaled a deep breath of profound thankfulness. Bovines, wild boars, dogs, sheep, waterfowl, and two Phoenicians collapsed onto backs and sides so that every muscle of every band member began to relax in the sweet exhaustion of battlefield triumph. Joined to their winged filly, the horse brothers honored in silence the body of their fallen sire. Tristanbear and his friends lounged apart. Even in shared victory the bears were disinclined to fraternity with other animal persons.

CHAPTER 35

THE NAME OF THE LION CAPTAIN

The arms of a declining sun grabbed downward.
While there remained softening light, Naythorn
needed to move muscles and clear his head of the
terrible life-and-death scenes that played unrelentingly
through his mind.

After shaking long his mane in the hope of not
dwelling more on the death of the sire of Rayalas, the
blackmaned unicorn walked into the desert. Seeing the
unicorn on the move, Timidthy trotted out to take the
lead in front of his captain. When their eyes met,
Naythorn knew that whether he liked it or not, on this
walk he was going to be guarded by a very observant
razorback boarling.

Timidthy slowed his trot. Without feeling the need
to speak, the unicorn and boarling began to walk side by
side. Naythorn noted that the boarling's steps numbered
exactly twice as many as his own. Upon climbing
upward, the two found themselves on a knoll sprinkled
about with clump grass. There they paused to absorb a
panoramic view of sand drifts, grasslands, and far away
mountains. More than three times taller than a not full
grown wild boar, Naythorn was the first to see the pair
approaching.

"Timidthy, we are about to have company."

After nodding solemnly at the lion captain, Naythorn turned to the wolf lieutenant and neighed, "Your earlier silence, Yellowquist, had me worried. Not many scratches from the fight? I do see that like mine, the hide of the lion captain wears far worse this evening. By the way, Timidthy is the name of the sharp-toothed young razorback found at my side."

The boarling sat rear legs down. Following the example of his small friend, the unicorn propped himself on his rump with front legs extended. The two were confident that if attacked by a big lion and a small wolf, they could quickly scramble to give back worse than they received.

"It is now your turn to talk," neighed Naythorn focusing his gaze on the pair that had intruded on his walk.

"We are here sent by General Albarochk," answered the yellow mottled wolf stretching his neck and scratching his belly with a paw. "You will find that his gracious and generous proposal is to your advantage."

Motioning his left front leg in the direction of Naythorn, the captain of the lions rumbled a growl that was louder than it was threatening. Something in the tone of the growl caught Naythorn's attention.

"Hmph! I must devote a few moments to the friend of Yellowquist." That neighed, Naythorn looked over at Timidthy and saw from his expression that the extra smart boarling grasped what he had in mind. The unicorn pulled himself up on all fours, and with measured pace walked slowly toward the lion. Naythorn stretched downward his head so that the tip of his softly glowing horn hovered close to the lion. As he moved a paw to firmly grasp the tip of Naythorn's horn, the lion's growl transformed into a purr that was deep and throaty. When magical sparks coursed from horn to paw, the lion slackened his frame. Sizzles of blue gold sparks wormed along a front limb to the head of the lion. At that, the lion several times nodded up and down his head.

"I suppose that Albarochk and Yellowquist ventured to talk your language as best they could," addressed Naythorn the lion. "You and I will now interpret perfectly each other's words."

Naythorn turned to involve Timidthy in the conversation, "What, at this moment, is my stalwart boarling thinking?"

"The next first thing that should happen is for the lion captain to acquire his very own name. And real names have to be... by someone given."

"That is *not* a bad idea. This will be the first time that Timidthy, not his mother sow, will be the name giver."

"Sir Lion, it is for me an honor to bestow upon you your name," groinked the boarling as he approached and bent his knees in a slight bow. "Looking at you, I say that you are a lion that is hard as an anvil." Timidthy stretched as high as his short legs permitted, and then lowered the tone of his voice to sound more official. "From this day onward your name shall be *Lianvil*, a lion that to his enemies is anvil hard."

"The conversation of this reserved lion is also *dull* as an anvil," jested Yellowquist. "He could alternatively be named *Anvildull*."

"And to his enemies this lion is a fearful *Lianvillain*," quipped Timidthy.

"Ahem... this lion will never by anyone be called *Lyingvil*," continued Yellowquist. "I might someday for him tell a lie. But he will not himself tell falsehoods, because that is not something he understands to do."

Lianvil rested his head on his paws. While he could now say anything he wanted to, the big lion chose instead to listen.

"Before pitch dark is upon us I will convey the message that Lianvil and I bring," barked the yellow wolf. "General Albarochk offers a truce during the passage of one moon. Without fear of attack from wolves or lions, you can for thirty suns dig the magic gold you seek. After the lapse of all the phases of one moon you will depart Shining Canyon, and the entirety of the mountain of many spires will be returned to the rule of Lianvil."

"What do you think, Timidthy? Is this proposal for us advantageous?"

"*Grungharmphkk.* What Albarochk offers to Naythorn is no bargain at all. The wolf leader offers us nothing that is not already within our power to take. Thanks to the timely presentation of our horse and bear reinforcements, the wolf general today lost badly. With his force of wolves and lions decimated and in disarray, the monster grayback finds himself powerless to stop our progress toward Shining Canyon.

"If Albarochk holds to this agreement, and I do not trust his word to so do, it will benefit him more than us. After suffering on this day exorbitant losses, the wolf general requires a lengthy and untroubled time to rebuild his defeated legion. While he rebuilds his army, Albarochk wants to be able to move freely without suffering depredations authored by the band of a blackmaned unicorn, stallions, bears, or two Phoenician warriors."

"Little boar, you are right about Albarochk's motives," answered the blackmane. "He does not want that tomorrow our band, and especially our horse and bear allies should pursue him.

"I do *not* accept the promise of the wolf general. But... I will accept the promise of Lianvil. Sir Lion, do you agree to freedom of movement without harm or threat to my band or to my bear, men, and horse allies, to persist all the days of the following moon? Do you give your oath that during the passage of thirty suns neither lions, nor for that matter wolves, will do us bodily damage while we linger in and about Shining Canyon? If you agree to my terms, then I make a solemn promise that I and my allies will thereafter depart Spire Mountain."

"The truce agreement is with Albarochk," yipped Yellowquist. "It is *not* for Lianvil to accept a deal made with Naythorn."

"Naythorn and I are agreed," growled Lianvil shaking off the yellow wolf's warning, and for the first time uttering words in the uniform tongue. "For the space of the next moon I will guarantee the blackmane and his company the freedom to enter and depart Shining Canyon. After the passage of thirty suns, Spire Mountain will be by me alone commanded."

The yellow wolf saw that this parlay had come to overshadow and transcend him. For that it became Yellowquist's turn to relax on a sprawled belly.

"I will report to Albarochk that Naythorn accepted the offer of truce. One minor detail will by the yellow wolf be overlooked. I will fail to mention to my big wolf cousin that this agreement was actually made between the blackmaned unicorn and Lianvil. To know more about this pact, than what is convenient, could provoke my great wolf cousin to distrust his alliance with the lions. You see, I find that for my great cousin some things are better left untold.

"I give you credit, Naythorn, for being smarter than I thought you were. I must also admit that your boarling thinks a lot like me. But, I am not sure that what I just said will be taken by Timidthy as a compliment. *Yapp... yrraypp...* no matter." After bowing to each of the other three animal persons present, the yellow wolf turned head and paws toward a darkening patch of desert.

With not another word grrrd, Lianvil departed toward the spired mountain.

"Yes, Timidthy, Lianvil liked the name you gave him."

"You know what, Naythorn? I would wager a fanny-bite that you are completely right about that. You know what else? In this meeting of captains you designated to me, a lowly private, the kindness of making me to feel important."

That comment from the boarling brought a smile to current Naythorn's long face.

Sharing the conviction that business with their

adversaries had gone well, a blackmaned unicorn and a wild boarling made their way back to where had ended the *Battle of Spire Mountain.*

CHAPTER 36

UNITY IN SHINING CANYON

Two days after the desperate struggle against wolf and lion armies in the *Battle of Spire Mountain* the reunited band of Naythorn, and its allies, entered Shining Canyon.

Hammerclaw right away went to work with the thing he trusted most to grasp in his big hands, a maul hammer with bottom rounded and head formed into a chisel claw. He banged, scraped, chipped, and scrutinized pieces of rock until he was satisfied he had found the most pure sources of the ore he needed. The blacksmith then proceeded to crumble blue gold from the selected veins. His buoyant exclamations made it clear that when hammering the rich veins of ore found in Shining Canyon, he was in his glory. It did not take very long for Hammer and Lucars to build a waist high mound of magic gold that glinted yellow and blue. The senior blacksmith next declared his need for a very hot fire.

Lucars set off through the cave tunnel carrying his cloak, and as well the cloak of Hammer. Bison's curiosity was piqued. Lucars soon noticed that following him was a band member that could become a particularly useful beast of burden. Lucars sat down and waited for the stroll of Buckmight to catch up with him.

"Master Bison, the other day I noticed some deposits of black rock the softness of which I am bound to believe will burn hot. Do you accompany me on my errand?"

"While I had thought to take a stroll, I just changed my mind. We will together explore the spires of this mountain."

The youth led the bison into a ravine which funneled long. Before day's end, Buckmight twice freighted two cloaks made heavy with soft black rock back to Shining Canyon. The next day Buckmight freighted dead branches fallen from hardwood trees.

After a pit was dug, a process of closed heat converted wood to charcoal. Hammer, meanwhile, had prepared an above ground oven built of stones and fired clay where in various stages the heat from coal and charcoal served to melt blue gold.

Pliable gold ore was hammered and formed into a first sheet. The blue gold ore was surprisingly light of weight and malleable. Because each vein of the magic gold claimed its own subtle composition, dependent upon the qualities of the ore the characteristics of the forged sheets varied. Some were as thin as the stem of a wild flower, and very flexible.

Hamilton and Timidthy sat, stood, and sat again, all the while transfixed by the process of forging blue gold into metal sheets. The two boarlings were scarcely able to believe that human persons knew how to transform pieces of rock, into what they called sheets of golden birch bark.

Hammerclaw would have been at home in a

classroom. The smithy liked to pause and explain why he did things the way he did, how he heated until a certain color was reached, and then hammered to texture the burned and crusted ore in a certain way until he had achieved exactly the kind of golden birch bark he required.

The razorback sow was proud to observe Hammerclaw take a liking to her boarlings that had the perspicacity to ask insightful questions. The sow observed that when thoughtful questions were asked, much was learned from the answers given. Her halflings understood that good conversation is all about asking questions that elicit interesting responses, and so deepen shared understanding. The fascination of Hamilton and Timidthy with the process of forging gold elevated Hammerclaw into a purveyor of wondrous technology.

After spending much time during past years with a blacksmith that had every day worn a furrowed brow, Lucars could not believe that by exposing veins of blue gold ore the blacksmith had uncovered in himself a vein of good humor.

"Hammerclaw, did you know that when you stop scowling, your brow actually changes to wear a lighter color? Ha! I much prefer your brow this way instead of the wrinkled and heavy way it was customarily worn before."

"Lucars, these are the days that I was born for. The privilege to forge blue gold makes the ten years I spent as an apprentice smithy, mind you pledged to other humorless hammerers just like me, worth all the furnace heat, sweat, and even tears."

Horses and Bears

It seemed that no new tradition of friendship could be established between bears and stallions. Practicing innate diplomacy, the bear and horse allies of Naythorn chose alternate days to visit and revisit Shining Canyon.

With affectionate touches to shoulders and necks, Naythorn and Rayalas greeted the horse brothers that had in battle come to their aid. The stallions would commence to rear, buck, and kick all about as they began a time of tag and playful romping.

Upon each visit Naythorn told the young stallions that their entrance to the battle had turned sure wolf and lion victory, into sure wolf and lion defeat. The stallions would vigorously shake heads back-and-forth, break away, and deliberately not pay attention to Naythorn's commendations. The horse brothers wanted the battle to be about the bravery of the unicorn, his platoon, and their sire rather than about stallions that arrived at the very end of the conflict.

The loss of their sire in battle meant the brother stallions could freely return to their herd. Still, it was not at all clear to Rayalas that her brothers would abandon their self-imposed exile and return to the horse herd now commanded by their eldest brother stallion.

"It seems to me that your horse brothers relish the opportunity to explore new mountain meadows," grunted Mama Pig,

"About that we shall see," answered the winged filly.

While the stallions were immediately playful upon their entrance into Shining Canyon, on the other hand the bear squadron waited until their departure from the canyon to commence to wuff loudly, tumble about, and box each other in scary games of bear tag. Given the tumult of bear departure, the sow would gather her four offspring close to make sure that they did not accidentally get in the way of wrestling and tumbling bears.

"I did not before believe that a huge bear could be anything more than... *barely* humorous, but that one is really funny." remarked Timidthy gesturing toward a bear with a particularly comical form of play.

"His humor is almost... *unbearably* comical," responded Roothyford.

"I disagree. His... *bear-bones* humor is too sparse to be really funny," offered Practicia.

"Just... *bear in mind* that the biggest boarling, that being me, is far funnier," interjected Hamilton.

"You have no idea how many times I needed your strength in battle," reflected Naythorn relaxing one afternoon with Tristanbear.

"But you do recall that the only reason I left you was to preserve peace between your band and a clan of distant and unpredictable bear relatives that took unkindly to intruders happening upon their river kitchen."

"I do not for a moment believe that excuse," gruffed the mama sow overhearing the conversation. "You simply wanted to impress your bear uncles with how big your limbs had grown. And, of course you know it was the magic Naythorn sparked into your head that compelled your frame to grow extra large."

"Well, Mrs. Sow, there could be some truth to what you say. And among bears near and far my uncles did pridefully publicize that their visiting nephew had become the biggest bear to be anywhere found."

A day came when the stallion brothers and the troop of bears returned no more to Shining Canyon.

"When our horse and bear friends left for good, why did they not say their goodbyes to Naythorn?" inquired Roothyford.

"It is because the bears and horses plan to one day rejoin us," responded Practicia. "Their attitude upon departing the blackmane was... *farewell for now.*"

Naythorn could not help but notice that at the departure of her horse brothers, Rayalas shed no tears. The blackmane told himself that the feelings of the winged filly ran not behind her eyes, but coursed deep within her heart.

"I will never forget that your wings brought us rescue," offered Naythorn turning to Rayalas and the duck perched on her back. "You two brought back the allies I needed, and their timely arrival reassured me that nothing right need be forever lost. So long as the brothers of Rayalas and Tristan's bears remain our steadfast friends, I know that even on my darkest day rescue will somehow present."

No one complained that twenty five suns had come and gone without anyone having to march guard or fly scout duty. Nor could anyone believe the undiminished energy of Hammerclaw as he day after day fashioned more sheets of golden bark. But it *was* obvious that the smithy was as well busy at something other than stretching out sheets of gold.

"Hammer has no right to exclude you and me from our duty of forge observation," complained Hamilton to his boarling brother. "What do you think he and Lucars are making over there? Do not tell me it is only golden bark board."

"I have the idea that we shall soon find out what new things the smithies are fashioning from blue gold," replied Timidthy. Just as predicted by the smallest boarling, on the next day the special project of the blacksmiths was put on display.

"The renowned blacksmith Hammerclaw here and now requests the entire band to join him!" Once the band assembled the smithy stretched himself important, and requested Buckmight to approach. The blacksmith turned about and momentarily busied himself with something. When he turned back, his hands held a delicately hammered gold harness made of interlocking plates. After clasping the beautifully crafted piece of armor on the neck and shoulders of the bison, the smithy held up a gold sheet as a mirror so that the bison could see how he looked in his new vestment.

"I cannot believe that something made of metal weighs... next to nothing. Because the flexible discs hinge so fluidly together, this attire will not slow one step my run. This piece of armor will surely protect my neck and back from bites authored by long wolf incisors. Wolf teeth that try to puncture this armor will instead... *be broken.* This is the very best thing anyone has ever given to me, err except for the splendid name of Buckmight bestowed by Mama Pig."

"That armor is the only *real* thing you have been given, ever!" qvackked Webstir. "But that is understandable, for why would anyone want to give a nice present to a bossy bison?"

"Sporting gold on my shoulders," responded the bison shrugging off the duck's attempt at humor, "I will have to start acting *important!*"

"Continuing with Sir Cattle, I will fit the rest of you with your golden armor. If the fit is not perfect, I will make it so. I will even rework the collar of Webstir to be more delicate." Noticing Featherspark fuss wings and crook his long neck up and down, the smithy added, "I will have no more commotion by the goose. His brand new collar will be every bit as special as the one worn by the green-head duck."

"Even though fitting thin bird necks with a collar is a tricky process, Featherspark and I want to wear gold that looks... stylish!" insisted Webstir.

As they traveled into far lands the followers of Naythorn would wear matching gold armor that would mark for all to see, their unity. Their new shining look would make band members both more proud, and more respectful of military discipline. Addressing a concern raised by the bovines, the gleam of the golden vestments would in the dust of thick battle help band members to immediately identify each other. More than once on the recent dusty field of conflict, Buckmight and Taurington had by mistake almost bowled over mountain sheep and wild boars.

Upon donning their gold attire the members of Naythorn's band would also be indelibly marked in the eyes of their enemies. The blue gold armor would seal a destiny from which the blackmane's band of friends could not rescind their loyalty to one another.

Mrs. Razorthwacker Takes Notes

The mama sow was a noticer. Mrs. Razorthwacker observed that more than anything else the younger of the two blacksmiths liked to stroke the mane and sides of Rayalas. The two had formed a deep friendship. The sow also observed that Buckmight and Taurington played more than before, as if they had grown younger in age. Time and again the bovines raced from one end of Shining Canyon to the other, often with Blackler and Trackler nipping at their heels.

The sow noted that the two dogs had begun to fill out and grow taller. Become more confident *and* less cowardly, Trackler and Blackler counted themselves to be band members in full and good standing. The sow perceived that the two mountain sheep treasured apartness.

"I finally enjoy the vacation I always wanted," confided Ewelissas one day to the sow. "Every day Rambuncture and I eat, nap, and frolic amidst lush grass. Whenever we so desire, we bathe in the stream. My perfect honeymoon... came at last."

The sow was sure that upon the band's departure, Webstir and Featherspark would most miss Shining Canyon. They were constantly paddling back-and-forth from the base of the waterfall to where the brook disappeared into the base of a cliff.

The mama sow could not help but nod approvingly at the sight of Timidthy and Hamilton petitioning

Hammerclaw for more exact explanations about the fashioning of gold sheets and armor. The big smithy joked that he was glad the paws of the razorback brothers did not curve to grab and hold hammer handles, or Timidthy and Hamilton would take over his job leaving the veteran blacksmith unemployed.

When the sow heard her two daughters make a mental list of all the memorable things they had seen and heard traveling with Naythorn, the sow felt her heart to become young again.

As for the blackmane, it seemed that he slept through most of each day. For that the big sow had no explanation, except that after all the physical suffering he had endured their captain certainly deserved long rest.

The sow observed that Rayalas and Naythorn enjoyed sleeping back to back, and that they frequently napped with necks intertwined. The razorback sow was certain that the bond between the unicorn and the winged filly had become deep and intimate.

CHAPTER 37

WATCHERS AND DEATH WHALES

Admiral Zoumar steered his fleet toward where set the sun. On an early morning when a gray sheen covered the waves, land came to be seen on the starboard side. The dolphin escort led the little armada closer and closer to the shoreline, and then into a channel with favorable currents. Where left off an island on one side, an island on the other side of the channel came into view.

Clear skies, fair winds, and an open waterway gave the admiral the sense that sailing conditions could not be improved upon. The fleet took advantage of streams with plentiful fresh water, and stream banks verdant with grass to sustain the unicorns. The tree covered hills on the islands about the channel gradually rose higher, and the beaches presented more evidence of habitation by human persons.

Canoes manned by native warriors began to follow the fleet, but at a distance. Drums began to pound. Two mornings following the sighting of canoes, the admiral found that almost the entire dolphin escort had disappeared during the night. On the next day canoes with warriors were glimpsed not only behind, but also in front of the Phoenician fleet. That night the drums talked to each other in an unusual staccato of loud rapid sticks and disparate pauses. Natives on the shore were monitoring closely the progress of the barges.

Zoumar began to worry. That the unicorns had grown increasingly restless and irritable heightened his unease. The admiral wanted that the matriarch's magical instincts should decipher whether his fleet was in danger of attack from native warriors.

"Having never before seen an expedition like yours, the watchers on these islands are distrustful of animals so large as we unicorns, and apprehensive of the weapons carried by your sailors. The drum talk tells me that island dwellers do not bear us friendship."

"Do your fears impel us to leave these waters?"

"The advantages of these becalmed waters are by unicorns prized. I can only warn, admiral, that a thing builds against our purpose."

"As for me, Elianor, my inclination is to continue to take advantage of these favorable winds and currents. We once before well-defended ourselves against war canoes. If need be, we will do so again."

A New Danger

"Astern! Two large breaching fish!" sounded the call of the lookout.

Although Zoumar had not before seen fish like these, he immediately knew they were what sailors called *death whales*. The ferocity of these black and white beasts was legendary. When through the entire afternoon the huge whales continued to maintain position behind the last barge in the fleet, superstitious sailors took on worried looks. That death whales had taken an interest in the progress of Phoenician barges, was a portent malevolent.

At half night the sailor stationed in the nest at the top of the flagship's main sail, hallooed to the deck that fires shone ahead on the starboard side. The fires were with regularity spaced.

"Admiral Zoumar, those many fires are not lit for warmth or to cook food," observed Captain Avalcar. "Why are signal fires lit?"

"Their purpose is to frighten us to leave off these waters."

"Admiral, where our barges now sail is found no opening to depart this strait."

"That is so, Captain."

The next day was uneventful, and thankfully so. When the fleet stopped to replenish barrels of fresh water, the admiral set a double guard around the perimeter of grazing unicorns. Since Zoumar knew that the fire builders were hidden in the dense forest backing the beach, he did not long tarry on land. Unfortunately, the two death whales returned to provide a rear escort to barges put once again under sail.

Signal fires were again that night seen, but this time the fires burned on both sides of the channel. Captain Avalcar remarked to the admiral that the larger fires were now accompanied by drums that pounded more ominously.

"Sir, the sage stallions are convinced that the fires and drums foretell evil to be inflicted upon us," neighed Elianor upon finding the admiral. "Should fighting come to be our destiny tomorrow, what must we unicorns do to prepare for battle?"

"The fires and drums, Elianor, have become too many. I am forced to agree that native warriors have been summoned for battle. My sailors are now on full alert. We must be prepared to fight, perhaps hundreds of war canoes. The danger presented by this channel that here has no outlet to the open sea, is that from all sides we can at the same time face attack.

"Elianor, the presence of a magical unicorn mist would be most helpful to shield us from arrows and thrown spears. I will also count on the horns and hooves of your stallions to rupture and capsize canoes. Look for the attack to happen when the channel narrows. And what, Elianor, of the two big fish that trail our barges?"

"Sir, the sage stallions feel that in this dangerous business at hand, the death whales that block our retreat have a treacherous role to play."

A fearful thought coursed back-and-forth across the matriarch's mind. By gripping a stallion, and then diving under water so that the equine could not breathe, the jaws of death whales could quickly extinguish a unicorn's life blood. A somber matriarch informed both sages and guard stallions that they would be called upon to be valiant in battle.

The first light of new morning revealed that the enormous whales had moved to swim one on each side of the flagship. It seemed that their intention was to destroy the largest barge and its cargo of magical horses.

Death Whales

She was as long as seven men placed end to end, and weighed as much as seventy men. The dorsal fin projecting up from her back was taller than a man. Huge pectoral flippers guided a body that was beautifully tapered from her head to her powerful fluke. The white of her belly and the white patches behind her eyes and dorsal fin offset the blackness coloring her back and sides. If anything, the white markings on her hide heightened her look of ferocity.

The larger male whale was supremely confident that he was the most fearsome creature to do battle in the seas. The male whale knew that he could, at will, shred life from the largest warm blooded creature carried on the floating tree platforms.

A strong unknowable attraction had brought the two whales to follow the strange vessels. An even stronger urge compelled their hunger for the flesh of the freighted four-legged creatures. With their hatred provoked by the purity of horned magic, to the death whales the unicorns were anathema.

The two whales were confident that they would soon feast on the flesh of the horned creatures. They had only to wait for a distraction that was sure to come. Once the conflict was set into motion, with unimaginable speed and ferocity the two enormous whales would destroy and devour. After a colossal victory they would contentedly return to the colder waters they relished.

Rounding a hook of land, Zoumar found that the width of the strait had narrowed to only three stone throws wide. At that moment, an astonishing number of canoes came to be launched.

Sparks emanating from the horns of the circle of sage unicorns brought an orb of blue flame to suspend in the air. Out of the orb a cloud-like mist umbrellaed downward to camouflage the barges. Canoes filled with warriors sending arrows skyward, and yelling fearsome threats of destruction, receded into the magic mist.

"Admiral Zoumar, I just realized that we remain vulnerable," neighed Elianor. "Approaching below the surface of the water, the death whales will not be detained by the protective unicorn shield."

"*Damn!* You are right!" responded the admiral. "I had not thought of that!"

A sudden premonition of terrible disaster overwhelmed one and all the unicorn sages. When from fear the magic of the sage unicorns weakened, the magic mist began to dissipate. Arrow points struck sails, planks, or as bad luck permitted sailor and unicorn flesh. For mares and foals gathered in the open holds, the hail of whirring arrows was terrifying.

The flagship shook, as if the bottom of the hull had scraped a stone wall hidden under the waves. With their rocking of the lead barge, the attack of the death whales had begun. The whales breached and together cracked their backs downward against one side of the flagship. As the barge tipped and rolled, mariners and unicorns including the matriarch, were thrown into roiled waters.

Elianor's rear quarters became clamped in the jaws of the giant male whale. The matriarch kicked and swung her horn to prick the leviathan, and did what damage she might. When the horns of two unicorn stallions speared the beast behind a pectoral flipper, the whale spewed the matriarch out of his mouth, and slammed his fluke to wallop hard the sides of Cabalblade and the guard lieutenant Hoovefort. The whales withdrew, but Elianor knew they would return.

Avalcar's sailors threw spears at the warriors whose canoes had drawn alongside their barges. Flattened on bellies, the mares did their best to shield colts and themselves from harm.

With astonishing alacrity the jumps and twists of Belfloralex avoided every sharp incoming point as she raced across the barge and launched herself as high as she could at a closing war canoe. Her hooves tore apart its bottom, and the impact of her speed and weight upended the canoe. Finding herself in the frothing sea, her half horn delivered a spear wound of her own to a painted warrior floundering in the water.

The filly felt her half horn to throb with unbearable pain, as if it had a second time been torn asunder. An image of the colossus with giant tentacles pulsed through her head.

Strong arms pulled Belfloralex onto the barge. From spear points she had escaped hurt, but the fearful image of the beast that had broken her horn caused the brave unicorn filly to black out.

CHAPTER 38

THE COLOSSUS DRAWN BACK

Paralyzed by a neck-lodged piece of unicorn horn, the leviathan had for many days drifted in a painless and timeless state. Only its two long tentacles, twice the length of its other arms, had maintained any semblance of purposeful motion.

When a new destiny took control of the beast, two things happened simultaneously. From the giant squid's arms and mantle the paralysis lifted, and the painless respite ended. The throbbing in the great trunk of the beast's neck again pounded harsh and unrelenting. As the beast was drawn back to the five floating islands and their magical occupants that walked on four legs, overwhelming mental pain came to accompany compelled watery movement.

With powerful and unflagging thrusts the sea colossus entered the destined channel. Revenge, once and for all time, would be exacted upon the horned animal that once before had had the unimaginable audacity to attack the ruler of the deep. As the giant squid drew closer and closer to the magic equines, the beast knew that final revenge would soon resolve the hurt and desolation before inflicted by unfathomable defeat.

Upon sighting the sea vessels, the colossus sensed

that fear had come to possess the being of the despised half-horned unicorn. Drawing closer, the marine giant saw that the four-legged creatures were again caught in a desperate conflict. It was the premonition of this new battle that had ended the beast's throated paralysis, and provoked the return to a sea of destruction.

"Am I not the ruler of the deep?" seethed the colossus. "Does not the magic horn lodged within my throat entitle me all revenge?" The half-horned creature was to be a feast for the tentacled monster's *own* revenge.

Muscles of the giant mantle forced water through a tubular siphon to propel the beast with marvelous velocity. As its powerful tentacles readied to bring down unparalleled destruction, a sudden realization presented to the colossus. Death whales were present! When young, only death whales had before dared to attack the ruler of the sea. Only death whales had feasted on the offspring of the colossus.

Belfloralex Bound to the Colossus

Coughing water, the half-horned filly regained consciousness. While her bones ached from the jolted landing upon the war canoe, the pain that now washed through her mind had only to do with the frightening image of the sea giant that not long past had nearly ended her life.

"The colossus comes to join the fight of the death whales! Elianor, the enormous eyes of the beast *haunt* me. Because I wounded him badly, his hatred for me is overpowering. How can our barges survive a battle against death whales *and* the colossus?"

"Dear filly," answered the matriarch, "the herd of unicorns has not so far sailed to only perish at sea. Some way will be found to thwart our adversaries. After all, we did not provoke the death whales or the sea colossus. For no reason they seek to destroy us, at least for no reason that has an element of good in it."

"The colossus is a... *she!*" exclaimed Belfloralex with eyes opening wide in astonishment. "I thought because of its great size that it must be a giant male squid. It was just revealed to me that the females of her species grow largest. She thinks she is the greatest sea beast that ever lived."

"I go to advise the admiral that the sea colossus approaches," replied Elianor resolved to not show panic. "Perhaps we can still make for land." The news of the tentacled monster's return brought a look of anguish to the face of Zoumar.

"No Elianor, we cannot beach and abandon our barges. Only on these vessels can we contend with the war canoes. The strict confines of the barges serve to keep us together, and at least the barge rails provide some protection that we would sorely miss on land where we would have our backs to either the sea or the jungle." The admiral touched a hand to the neck of the matriarch and added, "Out here on the water we retain at least *some* maneuverability."

"For now your barges are withstanding the attack of war canoes and death whales," continued Elianor, "but allied together, the whales and the giant sea colossus can overwhelm us. I truly fear the great size of the monster's arms and tentacles."

"Please bring new unicorn magic to thwart the monsters," pleaded Zoumar. "We need to destroy the confidence they have in their brute strength, and somehow put them off balance." That said, the admiral was off to plan for what was next to come.

Elianor was left to contemplate what could be done to stop a three-pronged attack by great sea monsters. The paralyzing force of the half horn, now buried deep within the monster, was the only thing that had before saved them from annihilation by the dread colossus of the sea. But the giant squid was no longer paralyzed, and having learned from experience, the tentacled beast would be better able to anticipate and defend herself against the deep prick of another unicorn horn.

The images of the she-monster that had just presented to the mind of Belfloralex meant that the filly's horn fragment yet remained lodged in the neck of the colossus. By some unknowable unicorn magic the filly's remaining half horn had become intimately communicant with the fragment of unicorn horn lodged in the beast. For that, Elianor decided that gaining control of the monster's mind could help to withstand the colossus.

Belfloralex felt her body to weaken. Her half horn was fast losing its magical strength. It was as if the possessed part of her horn was being propelled through sea water to reconnect with the other half of her horn still embedded in the neck of the fast approaching leviathan.

Belfloralex found that she, not the great tentacled giant, was now the one seized by paralysis of body and mind. The unicorn filly became no longer aware if sailors were maintaining their defense, or were instead losing military advantage to the war canoes and the death whales.

Finding the filly lapsed into a semiconscious state, Elianor grasped that the magic of Belfloralex had been *reversed.* Their minds made inseparable, the sea colossus now governed and controlled Belfloralex. Upon finding that the goodness and generosity of the unicorn filly had succumbed to the monster's heartless cruelty, an idea presented to the matriarch. Elianor would make use of the strange solidarity affixed between *Good* and *Evil.*

"She, for the colossus is a *she,* will soon be upon us," neighed Elianor to Aneilee and the sage stallions. "The tentacled colossus uses the filly's own horn fragment to poison the mind of Belfloralex. In order to unseat and turn away the beast's anger and rage, we must gain control over the filly's mind."

Unicorn horns arrayed over the head of Belfloralex. When from the throats of unicorn sages low-pitched neighs sounded a disconnected rhythm, healing power directed into the filly's mind. Possessing the purest and most beautiful heart of any unicorn, Aneilee's confidence inspired the sages.

"I feel her!" exclaimed Aneilee. "She is now connected to the great monster that hates her. But, there is more. The beast also hates her great enemies the death whales. We must make the colossus to know that she can never fight side by side with loathsome death whales."

"Use the mind of Belfloralex to tell the colossus that

we are not her enemy," neighed Elianor to the high escort. "The filly must inform the giant squid that our only desire is to leave these waters far behind us."

As they interposed magic into the invisible connection between Belfloralex and the colossus, Aneilee and the sages became lost to the world. The grunted neighs of the sage stallions came more quickly, and pitched higher.

By the colossus, Belfloralex came to be fully known. The filly that had lodged a fragment of horn deep within her neck was the most pure in heart creature that the ruler of the sea had ever come upon. She did not anywhere in her heart possess an empty room that could be made to fill with hatred. The filly even comprehended the desolation of endless queenly predation in a deep and dark realm.

The colossus came to know a thing extraordinary. The filly felt love for her, a love based on comprehension of the natural reason for unbounded rapacity at the bottom of the sea. For the half-horned filly, the beast was a marvelous and sublime fact of creation made for a purpose in the plan of all life. One more revelation penetrated the mind of the colossus; the half-horned equine had no mother to call her own. Like the great tentacled beast, the filly was a creature alone.

Admiral Zoumar was growing desperate. From the prior devastation wrought by the two whales, his barge's deck planks were everywhere broken and thrust up. For the attacks of warriors and whales upon all five of his barges, many sailors had perished. How many men had he lost from his barge alone, thirty? And the battle had only started. The thought that the colossus would erupt from the sea to provide a third monstrous enemy to contend with, horrified the admiral.

Close to the flagship the sea began to boil. Two long tentacles thrashed through the surface of the water.

"Not now!" exclaimed Zoumar at the sight of the closing sea monster. The colossus with the great eyes and huge mantle was about to pounce upon the flagship. As he was forced to consider the unthinkable, the admiral's heart sank. If by warriors and three sea monsters his vessels were destroyed, with survivors cornered on a beach facing hordes of superb native warriors, it would be next to impossible for his sailors to defend either themselves or the unicorns.

The Battle of Three Sea Monsters

When the colossus glimpsed the flukes of two enormous death whales, her feelings became terribly conflicted. For a few instants she hesitated. But, her priority was fixed. The matter of death whales now attacking the barge closest to the flagship, could wait. She had been summoned to wreak revenge on the magic horse that had once before stung and humiliated her. The colossus reminded herself that while each day she ruled over a world of death, the filly and her unicorn kind represented hope, and everything else that the colossus despised.

She would crash down her long and powerful tentacles to break apart the barge that carried the half-horned filly. That act of war would be a great feat that only she could accomplish. Carrying with it the insatiable appeal of ultimate revenge, the devastation of the biggest barge played back-and-forth through her mind. Weighed down by thoughts of destruction, the sea colossus sank below the waves.

"If my flagship is sunk," muttered the admiral to himself, "the battle for us is as good as…"

"Admiral," interrupted Elianor the commander's worries, "the colossus is now to attack us. We pled with her to challenge her natural adversaries the death whales, but she does not consent. The magic of unicorn sages utterly failed to change the mind of the colossus."

"Blast! My fleet does not hunt the colossus! We do not want to cause her harm! Tell that to…"

Propelling herself out of the sea, the tentacles of the colossus whipped about to grasp hold of the flagship's deck. Sighting the filly that had remained her half horn inside her neck, the giant squid grabbed and pulled Belfloralex toward herself.

Less impressed by fear than loyalty, one dolphin had stayed with the fleet. With her teeth Quixsoar grabbed an arm of the giant squid… *and was crushed.* The dolphin that had befriended and raced Belfloralex and Alexzana would no more swim with her friends, or surf the waves lapping the hull of the flagship barge.

Intent upon stabbing with her horn, Elianor charged at one of the monster's arms. With another enormous arm the beast slapped back the matriarch. Then it happened so quickly that no one understood what had changed, how one moment turned irrevocably the fortunes of the sailors and unicorns onboard the flagship barge.

Against the starboard side of the biggest barge the

assassin whales, like two giant torpedoes, crashed down their combined weight. Consequent to that tremendous blow, the port side of the flagship jerked hard upward. It was the soft part of the giant squid's neck and mantle that was exposed to the blow. From a strangling grip, Belfloralex was released to fall limply back to the heaving deck of the barge.

Enraged, the colossus threw her two great tentacles across the barge. Other long arms grasped rails, planks, and mast posts. Jerking hard her arms, she propelled her mantle up and over the barge.

The monstrous arms of the giant squid fell full upon the whales, and enveloped them. The heart of the colossus leaped at the thought that with one fierce embrace she would rip and squeeze life from two enormous death whales. Never before had she been given the opportunity to attack two whales at once. Nor had she known that she could finely orchestrate the sinews of her brawny arms in a simultaneous attack against two massive sharp-toothed sea monsters.

A previous thought still raced through the monster's head, "The filly is... mine and only mine to break asunder. As she is torn apart the broken-horned creature will feel my revenge."

When their focus shifted back to the destruction of the biggest barge, the assassin whales had not noticed the simultaneous arrival of the giant squid. Too late they acknowledged the force of the tentacled calamity that now strangled them. Manacled in a vice of impossible strength, the attack at one and the same time upon both whales proved constrictive to the practiced movement and tactics of death whales in battle. The giant squid's tentacles rasped through whale skin. About the flagship whale blood spilled to color deep red the sea.

Having been thrown hard against the deck, Admiral Zoumar shook himself to clear his head of the leaden pain pulsing through him. As the rocking of the barge gradually subsided he unsteadily rose to his feet, and heard sounds that were hard to register and impossible for the commander to understand. He slapped his head in an attempt to restore his senses.

"What in blazes are the men shouting?" yelled Zoumar to no one in particular.

"Commander!" an excited Avalcar grabbed Zoumar's limp arms. "Look! The war canoes retreat! Native warriors have abandoned their attack. Our men are shouting the impossible news... *of victory!*"

"The warriors believe that we summoned the colossal beast to defeat the whales," neighed the matriarch upon joining the two officers. "The natives will no more challenge the fabulous magic they now perceive that is ours. And, perhaps they are right to think that. Although not wanting so to do, it was Belfloralex that summoned the colossus to our barge."

"What happens, Admiral, if after the colossus defeats the whales she returns to hunt us?" inquired Captain Avalcar observing closely the churning water.

"All I know, my friend, is that we could not fight at once the whales, the war canoes, and the sea colossus. Providence today showed herself merciful. The beast, or beasts that triumph in the fight now taking place beneath us, will in victory be gravely weakened. If, just as you think, the colossus ultimately vanquishes the assassin whales she will find herself exhausted from the greatest fight of her life.

"Captain Avalcar, today we owe Belfloralex, Elianor, Aneilee, and the sage unicorns a great debt. It was their communication with the colossus of the sea that cemented her attention upon the death whales and re-awakened her hatred of them."

The matriarch rubbed gently her mane against Zoumar's bruised side and neighed, "Admiral, I have once more seen unicorns and mariners together secure a triumph of *hope.*"

The Colossus in Victory

By the teeth of two death whales her tentacles and mantle flesh had been horribly cut. But for one reason, and one reason only, the hurt that pulsed everywhere through her body did not matter. Her unrelenting mental anguish was no more.

Upon vanquishing two assassin whales she had won the greatest battle in the history of her kind. After feeding long on her kill, she abandoned the carcasses to the hordes of sharks attracted by a great feast of free whale meat.

Toward the object of her odyssey of hatred and revenge, her thoughts softened. After all, compared to the vast bulk of the two assassin whales upon which she had sated her enormous starved appetite, the filly was but a small morsel of flesh.

In a before time the filly had not only been brave to attack, but intelligent enough to have found a way to deeply wound the tentacled beast. The colossus decided the small filly was even more valiant than the assassin whales.

After being compelled to travel far through deep waters, that the object of her revenge had changed from a filly to great death whales did not now matter. Victory over two death whales fit harmoniously with her destiny of utter destruction. In that regard, the small magic horse was no more than a mere traveler passing through foreign waters.

With her mind still melded to the thoughts of the little unicorn filly with half a horn, a memory flashed of Belfloralex racing a girl upon the deck of a barge. For that, a new thought came to penetrate the monster's mind. She decided that not even a colossus of the sea was born to vanquish perfect innocence.

A strange and surprising question presented to the monster. Could so great and impossible a victory over two assassin whales have been in some way purchased by the magic of the unicorn horn fragment lodged in her neck? After all, it was her neck that controlled her enormous arms and tentacles, and on this day her tentacles had whipped about stronger than ever before... more quickly than she had ever thought to be possible. Perhaps she owed a debt to the filly with a broken horn.

Once more the filly's memory of a time at play channeled across the leviathan's mind. The giant of the deep decided the playful, brave, and motherless unicorn possessing only half a horn... *should live on.*

CHAPTER 39

DANCE

The *Battle of Three Sea Monsters* had in every way been costly. Every Phoenician barge had been heavily damaged. The flesh and bones of too many survivors had been cut and broken. Even worse, many sailors and unicorns had been lost to the sea. The fight against war canoes, death whales, and the colossus of the sea had taken as well a heavy spiritual toll on sailors and unicorns.

Admiral Zoumar brought his barges to a broad beach cut on each end by a stream of fresh water. After several days of barge repair and reconstruction came an afternoon of much needed rest, and as well a time of quiet and sad farewells given to the memories of the fallen in battle. Upon an otherwise somber beachscape, only Belfloralex and her energetic friends Alexzana and Mariano never seemed to stop dashing about.

Zoumar noticed young unicorns swarming about cohorts of their elders, apparently leading them in some form of activity. To no one in particular the admiral offered a comment, "That is... strange. It is as if... young unicorns are teaching older ones... *to prance.*"

Upon the approach of evening a cool and resilient breeze wafted a perfect excuse for still recovering sailors to laze together beneath palm trees shading a high part of the beach. Relaxing with his men, the admiral noticed that healthy and recovered unicorns had made their way to the far end of the beach. It was from that side of the encampment where commenced the sound of two drums.

Turning heads to the left, sailors asked each other... *why the drumming?* After suffering many losses in a bloody conflict against war canoes and sea monsters, airy drum playing seemed completely out of place. When virtually all the mariners found themselves to be still hurting from the physical and psychological wounds of tumult and battle, and moreover depressed at the thought of sailing farther into the dangerous unknown, what good could come from noisy camp drums? The intent of the drumming soon became clear.

At the far corner of the beach Alexzana and Mariano stepped in a stationary cadence while smartly tun tunning. Their noise-making evidently had to do with unicorns formed in ranks behind the drummers. Interest in this strange behavior motivated sailors to take to their feet and stare. Head held high, on a raised part of the beach Elianor came to stand *facing* the curious sailors. Led by the two youthful drummers, a parade of unicorn horses began to move along the water's edge.

The smiles on sailors' faces showed they were impressed with the ability of unicorn horses to stay in step with drum beats, and also with each other. In the previous parade the sailors had marched at the sides of unicorns. Sailors noted that the acknowledged experts at parade march were this time made to be the audience. On this lovely evening the mariners were not forced to participate in a military parade undertaken for the purpose of officer review.

In cadenced step five battalions of unicorns marched past the gathered sailors. When ahead remained no more beach, the beat of the drums signaled a change. The unicorn parade formation right-faced, right-faced again, and marched in return. Upon achieving the place where stood the sailors, the formation of unicorns left-faced and halted at parade rest. Fifteen steps behind Elianor, the files of the unicorn formation stood at attention. Zoumar wondered why the five unicorn battalions were distanced unusually far apart from each other.

For some time the drums pattered softly as if to heighten the suspense of what this military parade was really about, and to hint at what was still to unfold. The drum beats stopped.

"Admiral Zoumar, barge captains, and brave mariners of Phoenicia," neighed Elianor, "we salute today your loyalty to the unicorn herd. You have many times risked everything to protect us. As you stand before us we feel your sense of loss and sacrifice, and we honor your courage and steadfastness. Unicorn horses will now show how deeply our hearts beat in thanks to the gallant sailors of Phoenicia!" The unicorn matriarch bent one knee in a very stately bow, turned about to face the unicorn formation, and resumed a rigid stance at attention.

Belfloralex, two drummers, and the front rank of young unicorn fillies stepped ahead, and then turned about to face the five battalions of unicorns. Made clearly visible for standing high upon the beach, it was obvious that the unicorn fillies were to be the choreographers of what was to come. Zoumar smiled at the idea that whatever movement the fillies displayed would be mimicked by the horned horses in the formation.

The drums grew in crescendo until all could feel an energy that made the very air to suspend with anticipation. In response to a pop of the drums the line of fillies reared, pawed the air with front hooves, and whinnied. The unicorns in the parade formation copied the movement of the fillies by rearing up on back legs, waving front legs at the sailors, and whinnying with fervor while shaking about their heads. The hooves of the fillies and the unicorn horses fell back to ground.

As the drums marked a new crescendo, with the blue sea and sky providing a glorious background, the unicorns reared a second time in salute. After saluting a third time, the drums stopped. The silence that lasted for ten breaths was broken by a new qrrrrrrr, qrrrrrrr, qrrrrrrr of drum beats. At the signal of the drums something marvelous happened. Unicorn horses for sailors... *danced.*

With tails and heads arched high, in a slow staccato of pauses unicorns pranced in place with hoof raised, foreleg made horizontal, hoof lowered. And then the sequence was repeated with the other front hoof. Hundreds of unicorns pranced in unison the exact same steps.

As the drum beats quickened the fillies choreographed a faster pace of prancing. When the drum beats slowed, the pace of prancing correspondingly slowed. When drum beats marked a sharper and more marked rhythm, the sequence of prancing shifted to become right front hoof, left rear hoof, left front hoof, right rear hoof. When the drums signaled a new beat, the entire formation of unicorns stomped left hooves with their heads turned right, and then right hooves with heads turned left.

When a newly changed rhythm sounded, each of the choreographer fillies began to prance her own individual steps. In like fashion, the unicorns in formation began the moves of his or her own unique dance. The prancing cadence of one unicorn would move slowly, double in speed, and again move slowly... all the while maintaining rhythm with the drum beats. If a unicorn felt to double stomp two front hooves followed by two rear hooves, that is what was done. Another unicorn would prance, flash out front hooves, and prance again.

When the fillies leading the dance melted back into the formation, the dance became even more motivated by the music embedded in each unicorn heart. Stallions moved to dance in layers of inner rings. Mares pranced in circles outside and around the stallions. Colts and fillies pranced in an outer circle around their elders. Unicorns moving in a circle whirled, reared, and pranced.

One unicorn copying the steps of the next unicorn evolved into a line of unicorns repeating the same steps. At other times the unicorn dance would turn completely spontaneous, with each unicorn moving in a solitarily unique manner.

The elegance and passion of the unicorn dance was something never before seen by Phoenician sailors, nor ever observed by other human persons that knew next to nothing about the existence of magic horses.

Comprehending the beauty displayed by the race of pure white unicorns, and the significance of the honor bestowed upon those for whom the dance was made, tears came to wet the eyes of the hardest and roughest-cut seamen.

The drumbeats softened. Dance steps grew smaller and more subtle. When the drumbeats halted, unicorns reformed into their respective battalions. Heavily breathing unicorns quietly drew a last time to attention. Elianor, whose hooves had remained firmly planted, turned about to bow to each part of the assembly of Phoenician sailors. She lastly bent her head and knee to Admiral Zoumar.

For the beauty of the unicorn dance the half-horned filly could not restrain the joy gushing through her heart. Belfloralex ran to where stood the matriarch and began to jump jubilantly about her. Alexzana the island girl, and Mariano the youngest Phoenician sailor, set down their drums and ran to Belfloralex to give her neck a hug. With arm signals the two youths turned and motioned for sailors to come and do likewise. Unicorn horses, every one, were lavished with hearty hugs bestowed by their Phoenician protectors. The unicorns rubbed their noses against the cheeks of the men, and with their heads and necks nudged playfully the chests and sides of the mariners.

The inspiration of Belfloralex, that unicorns should

dance for sailors, transformed the atmosphere of the camp from sadness and loss to friendship celebrated.

"Sailors hate to drill for a military parade," remarked Avalcar to Zoumar. "Unicorns feel differently; they love to prance steps in unison. In their innermost parts magic horses feel the rhythm of the parade procession."

"The deepening spirit of unity we this day observe between our men and the unicorns," offered the admiral, "will ensure the final success of our long journey of escort."

That evening the men did spontaneous jigs and sang old and merry songs. Sailors slapped each other on the back, laughed about the strange things that had happened during previous moons, and remarked on all the beautiful things they had seen during the long sea passage.

Seated together by a fire, the admiral and his barge commanders spoke of their longings for wives, children, parents, friends, food, festivals, even their very own goats, pigs, cows, and vineyards. On an island so far distant from their homes and loved ones, it no longer hurt inside sailors' chests to talk openly about the things held most dear.

From a knoll above the beach Elianor looked over the camp and gladdened at the interaction of men and unicorns. The matriarch marveled at how the fear she had felt when she first boarded a barge had come to be replaced by full hope. Her thoughts drew back to the three young friends that had invented a wonderful and unique way to thank sailors for their sacrifices made. Elianor knew that Belfloralex, Alexzana, and Mariano would continue to do astonishing future things to make safe the unicorns.

"Tell Mariano to come to me." Of a sudden an idea had occurred to Elianor. The Phoenician lad soon stood before the matriarch, of course with Belfloralex and Alexzana at his side.

"Few warriors, Mariano, no matter how experienced are more courageous or capable than you. I foresee that your manhood will be walked in greatness. You do know that it is my right to mark distinguished behavior. To be given the gift of a new name by no less than the matriarch of the white herd... is not a small blessing. Aneilee before made the name Belafloralex constituent to Alexzana. As for you, Mariano, from this day forward you shall be known as *Marsand*. Your new name signifies the blessing of the sea joined to the sand that unicorn horses this day danced upon."

Marsand threw himself down on the beach, and proceeded to laugh and roll about until his skin was completely covered by moist sand now component to his new name.

Three exultant young friends walked that night together on the beach. Pointing her half horn at the waves, Belfloralex neighed to Alexzana and Marsand, "I summoned her and she came. She still lingers close to us. I am so glad that the colossus of the sea beheld the dance of the unicorns. Can you imagine how much good it does her heart... *to know joy.*"

CHAPTER 40

ENCOURAGEMENT IN SHINING CANYON

The razorback sow could every time sense when someone in Naythorn's band was hurting.

"These last days in Shining Canyon should for the winged filly be an occasion of much happiness. Like the rest of us, you are now clad in beautiful blue gold armor. Does Rayalas find herself sad because the agreed upon thirty suns of our stay in Shining Canyon are soon to end? If so, perhaps the king of the lions will permit Naythorn's band to here remain longer."

"Our soon departure from Shining Canyon, Mrs. Sow, is not the cause of my worries. It is rather that I no longer feel myself to be... a *real horse.*"

"Do share your troubles with an old mother pig." The two directed toward the little lake and its waterfall.

"Mrs. Razorthwacker, when I turn back my neck I see that my body has become too sleek and too compact. Compared to Naythorn's muscled shoulders and legs, mine are grown too delicate. I am become so light on my hooves that when I gallop, rather than stride in the elongated horse way, I now *glide.*"

"Your body, Rayalas, is renewing and transforming itself into a lighter form. *Groinkhaha!* I wish I could say the same for my belly!

"You are prettier than ever. My sweet filly combines the beauty of a horse whose forehead gleams with an elongated white star, the wings of a great pelican, and the elegant grace of a swan. And when required in battle, magic transforms your wings to be as hard as iron. I only wish that you smiled and laughed the way you did before we left the secret pavilion."

"Mama Pig, I feel my heart to beat twice as fast as before. My blood runs so fast that it makes my mind race through too many thoughts at once. Sometimes my voice chirps more like a bird than neighs like a horse.

"When my sire neighed that he was to die in battle, that he had foreseen his own demise, I could neigh nothing back to him. Then when I saw to die in battle my sire, I did not shed tears. It was as though he was no longer my father stallion.

"I do not feel things like I should. In the battle against wolves and lions my wings were torn and cut deeply. I would before have cried many tears for my hurts. But not even painful cuts now make me to cry. What is worse, I no longer know how to cry *tears of joy*.

"I think I am turning from a horse to be... *only a bird*. A bird cannot know and remember the things that a horse does. Can you believe I have forgotten what my own mare looks like? Something is wrong with me, and I fear that this time it cannot by unicorn magic be made right."

"There now, my precious filly," soothed the. Razorback sow. "You have suffered through too much. When in the secret pavilion you were attacked by wolves, we almost lost you forever. But you survived. I shall be ever grateful that your new wings carried the day in the *Battle of Notch Landing,* and now as well in the *Battle of Spire Mountain.*

"Dear Rayalas, more than anyone you know that the touch of unicorn magic brings change to an animal person. Our captain's horn made Timidthy to be very smart, and Featherspark's feathers to glow. I can also conclude that Naythorn's horn has made Webstir to dart faster on wings than any other duck, made Trackler's nose more sensitive to smells than any other dog, and made Blackler to dodge faster in a fight than even the eye can follow."

"His magic also made the bison to grow very tall," added Rayalas, "and the cattle to grow more square."

"Since you received the gift of wings you have been on constant duty scouting and fighting. Just as your body needs more time to rest, your mind needs more time to become accustomed to your marvelous wings."

"The filly that used to romp and play horse tag has somehow come to be concealed under the feathers of my wings."

"You do know, Rayalas, that some thinnish animals are less prone to frolic. My pudgy Hamilton does more funning than does my skinny Timidthy. So, maybe to frolic more you need to eat more. Or perhaps because your very life is a miracle, your serious demeanor has to be for a very special reason, an absolutely unique future purpose that remains for now a mystery."

After snuffling a grunt filled with emotion, the sow added, "I am proud to call you my friend. I have never had a truer friend than an innocent filly with beautiful wings."

Bending down her head Rayalas glimpsed pig tears. "See, Mrs. Sow, I should at this moment cry with you, but my emotions are too wrapped up in dry feathers for me to cry."

"If pigs grew wings, I would fly always at your side. I would ever make sure that you were kept safe." The sow's tone of voice changed, "That reminds me, I was going to ask Naythorn that my magic gift, whenever it comes to me, should also be wings. It must be wonderful to mount the wind like you do." The kindhearted sow sat her rump down; hog eyes and jowls took on a very serious demeanor.

"Rayalas, because you are the only half horse half bird in the whole world, there is no one to help you learn how to develop trueness as a winged filly. I do not want to lose who you were before, the filly that everyone in the band came at once to love.

"I know that you cherish our blackmaned captain. Spend time walking beside Naythorn. Each neck hug you give him will to you be returned, and I dare say with even more affection. Time spent with the blackmane will soothe your heart and mind. In the same way it has done since his healing blood first entered your body, the magic of Naythorn will continue to preserve you."

"Naythorn is a very noble unicorn. I promise you, Mama Pig, that connected by my love for him and by his love for me, I will not lose myself to become... *only a bird.*"

The matron hog jumped paws to a shoulder of the filly and grunted, "Even when compared to the sagacity of Buckmight, my counsel is worth at least a little. Without your wings we would not have survived the last battle. Absent your wings, our band will not well survive the next great battle against Albarochk. Naythorn needs you. I need you. Everyone in our band needs you. Of all the fillies in the whole wide world, you are *the most lovely.*"

CHAPTER 41

EPILOGUE

B ecause the blackmane had suffered much in two successive battles, with not enough between-time to adequately heal, Mrs. Razorthwacker insisted that Naythorn trot, gallop, and sprint back-and-forth along the course of Shining Canyon's small lake and stream. During daily exercise the unicorn began to notice that as he approached the lake, the mist from the water cascade would at times thicken. To himself Naythorn remarked that the thickening mist had to it *strangeness,* and that before leaving the canyon of blue gold he and Rayalas should attempt a second session of water magic to see where moved the wolf soldiers.

As Naythorn napped close by the waterfall on the afternoon before the band was to leave Shining Canyon, Blackler and Trackler began noisily barking to awaken the unicorn. When the entire band went to see what the fuss was about, they found that waterfall mist had whirled into the outlines of five unicorns that cavorted in play before the falling water.

"Oh my!" exclaimed Roothyford. "They are delicately beautiful!"

"Wait! Something is happening to them!" exclaimed Practicia. "The mist unicorns have changed to walk on hind legs only!"

"That is incredible!" brayed Buckmight. "But what does their walking on hind legs mean? For it must signify something. Wait, they are again changing! I cannot believe what my eyes see. Their right side forelegs grew... swords!"

"Now, just like Hammer and Lucars do, they thrust swords... at adversaries," added Timidthy.

"Invisible adversaries!" corrected Practicia.

The apparition melted into the cascade of falling water, and so disappeared. It was not long, until one mist unicorn reappeared before the waterfall. With its head held strangely down, the magical form began to walk over the surface of the water until it neared where stood the band members. When the delicate figure reared upward, both forehooves suddenly were seen to each hold a sword. The mist unicorn began to thrust both forelegs... at nothing. It was not long before the figure melted into the lake.

"What can the ghost unicorns be telling us?" neighed Naythorn. "The strangest part was to see five unicorns stand and step only on hind legs... something I have never before seen an equine to do."

"No four-legged animal likes to walk on two legs," observed Buckmight. "It is one thing to rear upward and paw the air, or even to rear up and jump into a fight, but it is out of the question for me to walk more than four paces on hind legs."

"Master Bison is right," agreed Rayalas. "Unlike birds, horses cannot walk naturally on only two legs. When my wings and Naythorn's horn once conjured a mist vision of wolves, we learned that they were coming after us to do us harm. As for me, I find that the portent of this vision is also disconcerting."

"Ermm, just like the misty unicorns, Hammerclaw and I walk on two legs," observed Lucars. "Do you suppose that the presentation of the five unicorns was meant to tell us that human persons are coming to Shining Canyon? If so, I cannot imagine it could be our Phoenician sailors. They must still be far away floating on sea barges."

"Dear Rayalas," instructed the blackmane, "take with you this evening our two water bird companions and search the surrounding country for movement, especially movement by human persons. If warriors are found close to us, do not let them to see you. And be mindful that warriors shoot deadly darts into the sky. Since it is time to fulfill my agreement with Lianvil, upon tomorrow's departure from Shining Canyon I wish no trouble with warriors."

When Timidthy tilted his head and began to look very focused, Naythorn knew the boarling had something to say. "Timidthy, please tell us that the visions in the mist portend good news for my platoon."

"I think the first vision informs that we shall, to our benefit, encounter more warrior allies like the two blacksmiths. Hammer forged our protective blue gold armor, and in the trench of broken stones Lucars saved the life of our captain. Clearly the Phoenician warriors that walk perfectly on two legs have much strengthened our platoon, and we have gained much from their friendship. Still, I am puzzled as to why the second presentation of the lone mist unicorn first walked stiffly on four legs, and then changed to walk on two legs. It is as if a four-legged animal person was somehow... *transformed.*"

"The mist-unicorn was sent for one reason only," snuffled Hamilton. "The purpose of the apparition was to instruct Webstir that he should not be so mean to the two human persons here present with us. Our duck has the very bad habit of nipping them when they are relaxed. So, Webstir should be nicer. And, in particular the duck should be... *nicer to me!*"

"Look, Naythorn! I can walk on my back legs!" yelped Blackler as he half walked and half hopped. "Your magic touch can transform my paws to grasp swords!"

"I can walk as well as you!" exclaimed Hamilton. "And like the misty figure, I can also punch!" That said, standing on only two legs the boarling took a swing at Blackler. Dodging the punch, the dog adeptly delivered a pawed undercut to land against Hamilton's jaw, which made the boarling to lose his balance and fall backwards.

"I am undone!" complained the biggest boarling. "From that nasty blow I will *never* recover."

"As for me, I am going to be a positive pig," groinked Roothyford shaking her head reprovingly at Hamilton. "Just like Timidthy, I think the unicorn vision was meant to tell us that in a time of future danger, human persons will come to rescue our band."

"I want to know what my other daughter thinks," grunted the mama wild boar.

"Perhaps Roothyford and Timidthy are both right," answered Practicia. "Hammer and Lucars have convinced me to like human persons. I agree that someday soon we will be joined by other valiant warriors, that just like the two now found beside us are destined to become our fast friends. But... the unicorns looked to be fighting with swords against other sword bearers. That tells me that we will also come to do battle against enemy warriors."

"Perhaps a courageous company of human persons will swear to protect Naythorn's band, and so take the place of a departed Master Hammer and myself. Whether we like it or not, to the army of Phoenicia we both swore oaths of loyalty."

"The two presentations of the mist vision... may have two separate meanings," offered Practicia.

"That is a very interesting thought," groinked Timidthy. "It may be that human warriors befriend us, and also that one animal person is transformed to walk and fight on two legs only."

"That interpretation... sounds like a stretch to me," baahed Rambuncture. "We cannot read that much into a misty apparition."

"And... I cannot imagine that the horn magic of a young blackmaned stallion is strong enough to transform a four-legged animal person into a two-legged one," reflected Naythorn.

After all that had been said, the true significance of the two visions in the mist remained mysterious.

Readied to Depart Shining Canyon

The day came for Naythorn's journey to renew toward the fixed star.

On a morning that found the canyon of blue gold bathed in softed sunlight, band members wearing brand new gold plate armor formed in a line. Before them stood Naythorn, a stack of blue gold sheets destined for Phoenicia, and two newly forged blue gold swords. The blades had been prepared by Hammerclaw in the event that the second misty unicorn apparition, the one that hinted at a four-legged animal person becoming transformed to fight with front paws or hooves, came true.

With his large armor piece brightly reflecting sunrays, the tall bison stood at the far left of the line of sixteen band members standing at attention before Naythorn. Standing next in line, the cattle's armor stretched across a wider back than the bison's, and for that shone even more. With a look made more delicate, the neck armor of the filly ended where the roots of her long wings planted upon withers.

The armor of the big-horned sheep, wild hogs, and black dogs ran the entire length of their backs. The new gold collars adorning the necks of the duck and goose cast down onto bird breasts. With their well-worn Phoenician armor shining bright, positioned last in line were the two blacksmiths. Hammer and Lucars smiled proudly at Naythorn whose neck and chest armor shone brightest of all.

To salute in the way of bovines, forelegs raised a cloven hoof shoulder high. A hoof of Rayalas, Ewelissas, and Rambuncture copied the salutes of Buckmight and Taurington. The raised paws of Mrs. Razorthwacker, Hamilton, Practicia, Roothyford, and Practicia almost touched in salute a razorback ear. The four wings of Webstir and Featherspark set in impressive double salutes. Paws of Blackler and Trackler copied the traditional hand-to-forehead salutes of Hammer and Lucars. With salutes held in place, smiles spread wide across faces of many different sizes and shapes, and hope filled the eyes of all assembled.

Observing with pride the sharp military formation of his friends, Naythorn could not help but feel confident that his quest to refind the white herd would in the end prove successful. In return salute the blackmaned unicorn reared high, boxed out his forelegs, and neighed with full-throated vigor.

Clad in shining armor, the seventeen smiling companions looked to be the intrinsic and complementary parts of a magical military platoon that every day in a long ago time showed to one another loyalty, kindness, *and love.*

THE END

ABOUT THE AUTHOR

G. D. Hanson taught at Auburn and Penn State Universities. He has academic degrees from Dartmouth College and the University of Minnesota. Married, he and Isabel reside in South Dakota and Costa Rica.